"I don't want to date just anyone. The only one I'd love to take out is you. From the moment you came here, it's all I've wanted."

She wanted to give in to the joy of hearing those words, but her reality wouldn't allow it.

"I don't know who you think I am, but I'm telling you that if you just got to know me a little more, you would see that you wouldn't want a woman like me."

"I know you, whether you want to admit it or not."

She gave a sardonic chuckle. "Just because we've been passing each other on the ranch since I got here doesn't mean you know me. You have merely seen me. We have fundamental differences. Number one—you have more dates than a fruitcake. I don't want a man whose attention I have to struggle to keep."

"Unless we go out, how do you know if we have fundamental differences?" He leaned against the chair closest to him. "And, wait…does fruitcake even have dates in it?"

MR TAKEN

BY
DANICA WINTERS

Llyfrgelloedd Caerdydd
www.caerdydd.gov.uk/llyfrgelloedd
Cardiff Libraries
www.cardiff.gov.uk/libraries

First Published in Great Britain 2017
By Mills & Boon, an imprint of HarperCollins*Publishers*
1 London Bridge Street, London, SE1 9GF

© 2017 Danica Winters

ISBN: 978-0-263-92932-4

46-1117

Our policy is to use papers that are natural, renewable and recyclable products and made from wood grown in sustainable forests. The logging and manufacturing processes conform to the legal environmental regulations of the country of origin.

Printed and bound in Spain
by CPI, Barcelona

Danica Winters is a multiple award-winning, bestselling author who writes books that grip readers with their ability to drive emotion through suspense and occasionally a touch of magic. When she's not working, she can be found in the wilds of Montana, testing her patience while she tries to hone her skills at various crafts—quilting, pottery and painting are not her areas of expertise. She believes the cup is neither half-full nor half-empty, but it better be filled with wine. Visit her website at www.danicawinters.net.

To Mac,
From sea to shining sea,
it will always and forever be you and me.

Thanks for making life such an amazing adventure.

Acknowledgments

This series wouldn't have been possible without a great
team of people, including my editors at Harlequin—
thank you for all your hard work.

Also, thank you to Suzanne Miller and the crew at
Dunrovin Ranch in Lolo, Montana. Suzanne is the
inspiration behind one of my favorite characters in this
series, the fantastic Eloise Fitzgerald. Just like Eloise, she
always greets you with a warm smile and an open heart.

Chapter One

No matter how hard Whitney Barstow tried, there was one memory that never seemed to fade or be twisted by time—it was the moment she had nearly died. The smoke had filled her lungs, stealing her oxygen and making her head ache. The acrid smoke was like hands covering her mouth and nose, and however hard she tried to breathe, they only clenched harder. She had torn at the invisible hands, leaving faint scars on her face—a personal reminder of her desperation to survive.

Every time she closed her eyes, she was back in the barn. The door was closed, and when the spark had hit the hay, it was like a bomb that had gone off. She could still hear the *whoomp* as the dry tinder erupted into flames. And the heat. Oh, the heat. Some nights she would wake up in a cold sweat, her body's reflexes kicking in at the mere thought of being trapped in the inferno once again.

A tear slipped down her cheek as she stared out at the barn that sat at the heart of Dunrovin Ranch, and her thoughts turned to the lives she'd lost. There would be no replacing Runs Like the Wind, her black Thoroughbred. She could still smell the scent of hay on the horse's breath and feel her smooth gait from high in the saddle. Nothing would ever be the same. There was no going back and stopping evil from entering her life. There was no undoing what had been done.

There was only one thing she could do to keep the memories at bay—she could never ride again.

Even now, almost ten years later, she could barely step foot in a barn. If she was forced, it was only if the door was kept open and the breeze drifted through like a promise of freedom. She couldn't be trapped again. Not by a person, and never by fire. Never.

"Whit, are you okay, sweetheart?" Mrs. Eloise Fitzgerald called out from the main office.

Whitney angrily wiped away the tear that had escaped. She didn't have room in her life for weakness—or vulnerability. It was emotional weakness that always got her into trouble. If she just stayed tough and shut the world out—even Mrs. Fitzgerald, the kindly matriarch of the Fitzgerald family—she would never have to worry about getting hurt again.

"I'm fine," she called back to her boss. "Just wanted a bit of fresh air before the guests started arriving for the weekend."

Mrs. Fitzgerald walked out onto the porch and wrapped her arms around her body, shielding herself from the bitter December air. "Brr… You are going to catch your death of cold out here if you don't get your skinny buns inside, little thing."

Whitney snorted a laugh. It would be ironic, dying by hypothermia after nearly dying by fire. "I don't mind the cold," she said with a smile she hoped would calm Eloise's nerves.

Eloise waved her inside, not letting her get away with such disregard for her well-being. "You know what I always say… *You don't have anything if you don't have your health.*"

Her health was just fine, thank you very much… It was the rest of Whitney that could really have used some work. She hadn't been on a date in two years, and her best friend was the ranch dog, Milo, that no one else seemed to notice. Some days, when the phones were not ringing and she found herself looking for work to do, it was almost as if she and the dog were really nothing more than apparitions.

She walked over to the fence and ran her finger over one of the red Christmas lights that were looped between the posts. Maybe she was just like the Ghost of Christmas Past, an enigma sent to warn others that if they were like her, and continued living set in their ways, only bad things were bound to happen.

Or maybe she was just spending entirely too much time alone, wrapped up in her head and the things that needed to be done around the place. Ever since the murders, everything had slowed down—guests weren't filing in and out as they once did, and even their annual Yule Night celebration was barely getting off the ground. It was almost as if the deaths of the women in and around the ranch were only a precursor of what was to come—like some dire warning that nothing could be warm and fuzzy, not even during the holidays.

Maybe she really needed to talk, to lay bare her feelings. Maybe she wasn't alone in her fears. And as much as she dreaded opening up, if she was going to communicate with anyone, Eloise would have been a good choice. The woman had seen it all and experienced even more. She'd raised handfuls of kids from all kinds of backgrounds, been through famine and hardship, and yet always seemed to have a smile on her face and soup on the stove. She was the epitome of perfection—always put together and selfless when it came to those she cared for. And of late, all her energies had been focused on looking after the ranch and handling the uproar it had been facing. Yet, even with all this, she had been making time to come and see Whitney and ensure that she was settling into her new role on the ranch.

"You need to come on in," Eloise called again, her teeth chattering slightly as she spoke.

For the woman's benefit, she made her way over to the door and stepped into her cramped office, and Eloise followed. The place was overflowing with books, and papers littered the desk in no discernible order. She grimaced as she looked over at Eloise, who was staring at the mess as though it was the first time she had taken notice.

"Sweetheart," Eloise started, "do you think it's possible that we could get a few of these things filed away?"

"Not a problem, ma'am." She set about shuffling the papers that sat on the farthest corner of the desk and shoving them in the already burgeoning bottom drawer of the desk. She tried to push it closed, but the drawer burped the extra copies of the ranch's tri-fold brochures and a notepad filled with scrawled notes.

She laughed as she turned around and tried to hide the mess behind her.

Eloise smiled, ever elegant and kind even in the face of inadequacy. "Do you want me to show you how I would organize all this?"

Whitney loved how the woman didn't try to force her through guilt, but rather the gentle and practiced hand of patience; yet she wasn't the kind to accept acts of pity. "I think I can—"

Thankfully, there was the harsh ding of the bell at the front desk and it saved Whitney from having to ask for help. She could handle the responsibilities of the front office. In truth, the mess had diminished in size since last week, but she was sure Eloise wasn't ready to hear that though her office was a disaster, it was cleaner than it had been in nearly a month.

As she walked out the door toward the parlor where they received guests, she was stopped when she ran into a man. Well, not any man, but Colter. The well-muscled, ridiculously handsome Fitzgerald brother who was nearly as reclusive as she. "Oh, hey, sorry. I didn't mean to—" She took a step back from him as she realized she was so close to him that she could smell the traces of smoke on his skin even though it was masked by the heady aroma of his cologne.

It struck her that no matter how many showers a person could take or how much perfume he used to cover up the smell of a fire, it wasn't something that could be fully erased—just like her memory, it had a way of nearly permeating into a person all the way to the soul. Or maybe it was just the fact that she knew what he did for a living, the risks he took and the panic he had to face each and every day, which brought the scent back to the front of her mind. It was almost like one of Pavlov's dogs except firefighter equaled smoke, and smoke equaled…fear.

She took another step back. Though he was one sexy hunk of man, with his dark black cowboy hat and whiskey-colored eyes, he was the living embodiment of danger.

"You're fine," he said, a giant, almost comically large grin on his face. "But you know if you wanted to touch my body, all you had to do was ask."

"Ugh. You really are full of yourself. Aren't you, Colter?" She couldn't help the heat that rose in her cheeks as he teased her. It wasn't that she hadn't imagined running her fingers over the lines of the muscles that adorned his chest. Every staff member at the ranch had a fantasy about at least one of the Fitzgerald brothers—who, of late, had been getting scooped up by women prettier and far more accomplished than her.

"I've been called full of something, but it ain't usually myself," he said, his Montana drawl kicking into an even higher gear than his smile.

"Well, if no one has had the guts to call you on it, then I'm more than happy to step up to the plate. You, Mr. Colter Fitzgerald, aren't God's gift to women. In fact, in case you didn't know, you are the last man I would ever think about dating. I'd rather date…" She paused as she tried to come up with a man in place of him, but none came to mind. As the seconds ticked by, her heart rate climbed. He couldn't see her like this. She had to be cool, calm, collected and, above all, witty—and she had nothing.

"You'd rather date whom?" he asked, with that all-too-cute grin and a wiggle of the eyebrow.

"Dang it, you know what I mean… I would rather date anyone than you."

"As long as it's no one else in particular, I think I like my odds." He laughed, the sound as rich and full of depth as his eyes.

She groaned, but the sound didn't take on the edge of real annoyance like she had wanted it to; in fact, to her ears it almost sounded like the awful noise a woman made when she was trying not to fall for a man. And she was definitely, absolutely, categorically never going to fall for the infamous jokester Colter Fitzgerald. Nope. Not gonna happen. She would never let him win her over as long as she stayed in her right mind. Not that she had a left mind, but...well... She sighed.

No.

The bell tinged to life again from the parlor, reminding her of the guests who were undoubtedly growing more impatient by the second with her absence.

"Excuse me—I have work to do. Unlike some of us," she said under her breath as she pushed past him, careful not to touch him again.

His laughter followed her into the parlor until she shut the door to drown him out. The last thing she needed to do was spend a moment thinking about that man.

Standing at the front desk was a man and a woman. They looked to be in their midthirties, and based on the woman's coiffed hair, to-the-sky black stilettos, and brown Louis Vuitton purse, they were definitely among their elite clientele. They had probably come here to spend their trust-fund money on some idealistic and romantic getaway that involved a horse-drawn sleigh and a bearskin rug in front of the crackling fireplace.

The woman was carrying what looked to be a slightly oversize fur ball, or maybe it was just one of those New York rats everyone talked about. Yet, as Whitney drew closer walking to the desk, the rat-looking creature picked up its ears and growled. Dog. Definitely a dog. It probably had one of those stupid names like Fifi or Fredrico. It was funny, but most of their elite guests had a dog just like that one, an accessory to their out-fit—but most were cuter than the one this particular woman held.

"How may I help you folks?" Whitney said, using her practiced service-industry charm.

"It took you long enough," the woman said, nearly spitting the words.

"Dear, I'm sure she was busy," the man said, patting the woman lightly on the hand and drawing Whitney's attention to the massive diamond that adorned the woman's ring finger.

For a moment she wondered if they had drawn her attention to it on purpose, some well-practiced motion that drew even more attention to their status and wealth. Whitney forced herself to smile just a little bit brighter, but the truth in Montana was simple—no one really cared about how much money anyone had or the number of things a person owned. Respect and honor were only given to those whose character merited such accolades. It was one of the reasons she had picked this state as her home instead of staying in Kentucky.

"I don't care if she was busy or not. We have flown halfway around the country to be here. The least she could do is be present when we arrive," the woman said, continuing her rampage.

Whitney bit her tongue instead of telling the woman that Dunrovin Ranch was a beautiful and majestic place, but it was a long way from the Four Seasons. If the woman had wanted to be catered to hand and foot, she should have picked a resort that would have done that—and not come to a guest ranch.

"If you like," Whitney said, forcing herself to behave, "and are interested in relaxing, there is a spa about ten miles back down the road. I can set up an appointment for you."

"Ten miles? Where are we, on the back side of Hell?" The woman glared at her husband, who must have been the one to book their trip.

The man smiled at Whitney, clearly embarrassed by his wife's atrocious behavior. "Is there any way we could have the masseuse come here?"

"I'll see what I can do," Whitney said, though she was fully aware the local masseuse, Jess Lewis, would throw a holy hissy fit at the request. Yet if they gave her a few extra bucks she would quiet down in no time.

She took down the couple's names and got them the keys to their room—the nicest private cabin at the ranch, a two-story, nearly three-thousand-square-foot log home with marble and leather everywhere. "Let me know if there's anything further I can assist you with," Whitney said, the forced niceties like sand on her tongue.

"Actually," the woman said, handing over the rat creature, "I don't want Francesca to be a bother to me this weekend. I need you to handle her."

Whitney balked at the woman as she stuffed the dog into her hands.

Handle her? The last thing on her long list of duties was dog handler or kennel master. Whitney had work to do. She slowly lowered the dog to the floor behind the desk. "I… Uh…" she stammered.

"That's great. Perfect," the woman continued, clearly not used to her requests being denied no matter how asinine they might have been.

The man opened the door and waited as his wife pranced out, her stilettos clicking on the floor like the shrill impatient cadence of fingers. Whitney just stared at the computer screen for a moment as she reminded herself these kinds of people played a big part in why she had left her home state, and she took some level of comfort in the fact that they were outsiders and going to leave just as quickly as they came.

A cold wind kicked up and spilled through the door, whipping dry fragile snowflakes onto the guest book that sat at the side of the desk. She walked over and touched the door. As she looked outside, running toward the entrance of the roundabout driveway was the little rat creature. Its dark fur sat stark against the snow as it sprinted toward freedom. She stood still for a moment, letting it get away. With an owner like hers, the dog deserved to have one go at escaping.

On the other hand, Whitney would have to answer to said owners, and she could only imagine their response if the dog was actually lost. No matter how soft-hearted Eloise was, Whitney would probably lose her job, and therefore her room at the ranch. She would have to start all over.

This dog's freedom wasn't worth it.

What was the dog's name again? "Fifi!" she called, but the dog didn't slow down. "Fredrico!" Again, the dog simply kept running. She ran out the door, her cowboy boots thumping on the wooden porch as she made her way to the driveway. "Lassie, come home!" she cried again.

There was the boom of laughter from behind her. She turned to see Colter watching her. "Did Timmy fall in the well again?"

"Really?" she scoffed. "If you're not going to go after the dog, at least you can be quiet."

His laughter lightened, but he didn't stop chuckling. "All right, all right. I'll come to little Lassie's rescue. Where did she go?"

She turned back and looked out at the driveway. A '90s blue Dodge truck was rumbling down the road toward them.

"No. Stop!" she screamed at the truck, almost as though the driver could hear her through the closed windows and the crunch of gravel under the tires. The man driving didn't even seem to see her.

He barreled down the road. Just as he was about to cross over the steel cattle guard, the little rat creature ran out. It wove in front of the truck, stopping as it stared up at the blue beast careening toward it.

"No!" Whitney yelled.

The dog took off running toward the truck. Just as they were about to collide, the dog slipped between the bars of the cattle guard that stretched across the end of the driveway, and disappeared. It wasn't Timmy or the well, but it looked like they would have to pull off their own version of a rescue.

Chapter Two

He'd been at the save-a-life game for a long time now, but this was the first time Colter Fitzgerald had to save a dog from the jaws of a cattle guard. He waved at the guy driving the truck, motioning for him to go ahead. The guy had dark, oily hair that sparkled in the winter sun. Sitting on the man's dashboard was a wooden bat, and the sight made chills ripple down Colter's spine.

In a split second, everything could have really gone downhill. The driver's grim face and demeanor were far from friendly. So much so, Colter was thankful he had not climbed down to confront them about the dog that had appeared from nowhere in front of his vehicle. He watched in relief as the trucker drove past them with a curt wave and the taillights vanished in the distance. The last thing he needed, especially in his quest to impress Whitney, was a run-in with a hard-edged stranger.

Whitney Barstow hadn't been his mother's employee for very long. From his recollection, it had been exactly three months since she set foot on his mother's porch and asked for any job that didn't involve the care and maintenance of horses. At the time, he had thought it was odd anyone would want to come to a ranch and not work with the animals, but he had let it go—everyone had their quirks. Besides, every time he caught a glimpse of her gray eyes, they made him nearly forget his name, not to mention any of her faults. To him, she was perfect, even the way she seemed to be constantly annoyed by him.

He glanced over at her as she stared into the grates of the cattle guard. "It's okay, sweet puppy. We're going to get you out. Don't worry," she cooed, her voice taking on the same soft edge she must have used with small children.

Colter smiled as she looked up at him and the sunlight caught in her hair and made it shine like each strand was spun out of gold. "What are we going to do?" she asked, motioning toward the grate.

The steel bars had been bent, apparently just enough for a small pooch to fall between. Yet instead of staying where they could simply pull it, the dog had wedged itself deep into the corner of the trough beneath. The pup shook as it stood on the collection of cracked ice and looked up at them, its eyes rimmed with white. It had to have been cold down there, and the poor creature was ill-prepared, with its short hair and low body fat, to withstand frigid temperatures for long. They'd have to act fast.

He stood up and rushed toward the barn. "I'll grab the tractor," he called over his shoulder.

She nodded but turned back to the dog. "Come here, baby."

He didn't know a great deal about the little animal that looked like a Chihuahua, but he did know that no amount of calling was going to get that dog to come to her. A dog like that was notorious for being a one-person animal. According to one guest he'd talked to, who had owned a similar dog, that was the allure—to have an animal that fawned over only its owner. It was like owning the cat of the dog world.

The barn doors gave a loud grind of metal on metal as he slid them open. He took in a deep breath. He loved the smell of animals almost as much as he loved the animals themselves. Most people might have found the scent of feed, sweat and grime too much, but for a firefighter like him, it was the perfume of life—and it reminded him how lucky he was to have the opportunity to live it. It wasn't like the smell of ash. He'd read poem after poem that likened the scent of ash to renewal, but it never drew images of a phoenix to his mind; rather, it only reminded him of the feeling of what it was to lose and be destroyed from the inside out.

He grabbed a steel chain and the keys that hung on the wall just inside the door, and made his way back outside to the tractor parked just under the overhang.

The tractor started with a chug and a sputter. The old beast fought hard to start, thanks to the cold, but it had been through a lot. He pressed it forward and moved it out of its parking spot by the barn. The vehicle made groans and grumbles that sounded like promises of many more years of service. His parents had done a good job with the place, always setting everything up to last not just their lifetime, but for generations to come. It was hard to imagine that his parents used to have a life before—lives that didn't revolve around the comings and goings of the ranch, its guests and the foster kids who had passed in and out of their doors.

They had spent their lives giving everything they had to this place. He could have said the same things about his intention as a firefighter; he undoubtedly would give everything he had to his job, and the lives he would affect, but it wasn't the same. His job and lifestyle were finite. As soon as his body gave out and he was no longer physically able to do the job, someone new, younger would come in and take his place. In fact, as soon as he walked out of the station's doors, it would be like he had never really been there at all—likely only the people whose lives he'd touched would have any lasting thoughts of him.

He blew a warm breath of air onto his chilling fingers as he drove the tractor around the corner and onto the driveway. Maybe he was wrong in thinking that he had nothing in common with the phoenix. Maybe he had simply already risen from the ashes of a firefighter who had served before him, and when he aged out, another would take his place to renew their battalion.

The thought didn't upset him—it was an unspoken reality of their lifestyle—but when compared to his parents' lifestyle he couldn't help wondering if he had made the wrong choice. In all reality, he had only ever pulled one person out of a burning building, and it had been the town drunk after he had passed out with a cigarette listing from his lips. Most of his calls were accidents on the highway, grass fires and medical emergencies. If he had stayed on the ranch, he could have helped build the place up and worked on creating a legacy for his family for generations to come. As it was, none of his brothers had ever spoken of what would come.

What would come. Even with the roar of the tractor's engine, the words echoed within him. If things continued going as they had been doing over the last few months, there wouldn't be anything left to worry about. Reservations for the upcoming month had been tapering off rapidly. If they didn't turn things around, by next summer they would be unable to support the overhead it took to keep the ranch up and running.

He hated being the pessimistic type, so he tried to push aside his concerns. Things were never as bad as they appeared. For him, it always seemed like things had a way of working out. Hopefully the same could be said for the ranch. At least this month they had Yule Night.

Maybe if Yule Night went especially well, it could lighten some of his parents' burden. The last thing they needed after the murders was money troubles. It wasn't his job, but he would do everything in his power to make sure that the ranch would stay afloat—especially if that meant he could save puppies and look every part of a hero to the one woman he wanted to like him.

Whitney stood up and waved him to bring the tractor closer. She really was incredibly beautiful. She stretched, moving her shoulders back as she pressed her hands against her hips. As he looked at where her hands touched her round curves, he wished those hands could be his. It would be incredible to feel the touch of her skin, to run his fingers down the round arch of her hips and over the strong muscles that adorned her thighs.

She was so strong. Not just physically, but emotionally, as well. In fact, she had always made a point of being so strong that he barely knew anything about her past. She kept things so close to her chest that he longed to know more, to get her to trust him enough that she would open up. As it was, all he knew about her was that she had originally been from Kentucky—but that was only thanks to the fact that he had managed to catch a quick glimpse of her application on his mother's desk before she was hired.

Why was she so closed off? For a moment he wondered if she was hiding from something or someone, or if it was more that she was hiding something from them. No one came to nowhere, Montana, and hid on a ranch unless there was something in their lives, or in their past, that they were running away from.

Maybe one day, if he was lucky, she would open up to him. Though, just because everything seemed to work out in the end for him, he'd never call himself lucky—and that would be exactly what it would take to make Whitney think of him as anything more than just another source of annoyance.

"What took you so long?" she asked as he climbed down from the tractor and laid the chains over his shoulder.

He didn't know what was worse: the heaviness of the chains that dug into his skin or the disgust that tore through him from her gaze. He hadn't been gone more than a couple of minutes, yet he understood more than anyone that when there was an emergency, time seemed to slow down. Minutes turned into millennia, and those were the kinds of minutes which had a way of driving a person to madness.

He smiled, hoping some of the contempt she must have been feeling for him would dissipate. "I guess I could have put the tractor in third gear, but the way I see it, that dog ain't going nowhere."

She shook her head and turned away from him. Yeah, she hated him. She looked back and reached out. "Hand me the chain. We need to get the dog out of here before it gets hypothermic."

"Here," he said, handing her one end of the chain. "Hook this to the tractor's bucket. I'll get the guard."

She took the chain and did as he instructed while he made his way over to the cattle guard and peered in at the little dog. It looked up at him and whimpered. The sound made his gut ache and he wrapped the chain around the steel so that when he raised the bucket on the machine, it would lift the gate straight up and away from the dog. He'd have to be careful to avoid hurting the animal. Something like this could get a little hairy. One little slip, one weak link in the chain, and everything could go to hell in a handbasket in just a few seconds.

He secured the chain and made his way back to the tractor. In one smooth, slow motion he raised the tractor's bucket. The chain clinked and pulled taut, and he motioned to Whitney. "Ready?"

She gave him a thumbs-up.

He lifted the bucket higher, and the tractor shifted slightly as it fought to bring up the heavy grate that was frozen to the ground. With a pop of ice and the metallic twang, the grate pried loose from the concrete and the tractor hoisted it into the air. He rolled the machine back a few feet, just to be safe in case the chain broke. No one would get hurt, not on his watch.

He ran over to the dog and lifted it up from its den of ice. The pup was shivering and panting with fear. He ran his fingers down the animal, trying to reassure the terrified creature.

Whitney stood beside him and looked at him for a moment and smiled. There was an unexpected warmth in her eyes as she looked at him and then down at the dog. As he sent her a soft smile, she looked away—almost too quickly, as though she was avoiding his gaze. She reached down and opened up the buttons of her Western-style red shirt. "Here, let me have her," she said, motioning for the animal.

"You're a good dog," he said, handing her over to Whitney.

Ever so carefully, as though she were handling a fragile Fabergé egg, she moved the dog against her skin; but not before he caught a glimpse of her red bra, a red that perfectly matched the color of her plaid shirt. His mind instinctively moved to thoughts of what rested beneath her jeans. She was probably the kind of woman who always wore matching underwear. He closed his eyes as the image of her standing in front of him in only her lingerie flashed through his mind. His body coursed to life.

It was just lust. That was all this was. Or maybe it was just that she seemed so far out of his league that he couldn't help wanting her.

"Hey," she said, pulling him from his thoughts.

"Hmm?" he asked, trying to look at anything but the little spot of exposed flesh of her stomach just above the dog where, if she moved just right, he was sure he could have seen more of her forbidden bra.

"Want a beer?" She pointed to something resting in the snow not far from the other side of the cattle guard.

He jumped over the gaping trench and leaned down to take a closer look. There, sitting in the fresh snow, was a green glass Heineken bottle. Jammed into the opening was a cloth, and inside was liquid. Picking it up, he pulled the cloth out and took a quick sniff. The pungent, chemical-laced aroma of gas cut through his senses like a knife.

He stuffed the rag back into the bottle and stared at the thing in his hand for a moment as Whitney came over to stand by his side.

He shouldn't have touched it. He never should have picked the dang thing up. Now his fingerprints were all over it.

"What is it?" she asked.

He glanced over at her and contemplated telling her the truth, but he didn't want to get her upset over something that may turn out to be nothing. Yet he couldn't keep the truth from her forever. It couldn't be helped.

"Unfortunately, it ain't beer," he said, lifting it a bit higher. "What it *is* is what we call a Molotov cocktail."

Her jaw dropped and she moved to grab it, but he pulled it away. If he was right, her fingerprints didn't need to be anywhere near this thing.

"You can't be serious. Why…? Who?" She stared at the bottle, but let her hands drop to her sides.

His thoughts moved to the guy in the blue truck. He hadn't seen the man drop anything out of the window, but that bottle hadn't been there long. Or maybe Colter was wrong and someone else had come, chickened out and left the flammable grenade as a warning.

Either way, it looked as though someone had planned to act against the ranch. More, someone had wanted to hurt the place and the ones he loved.

Chapter Three

Whitney wasn't the kind who got scared easily, but seeing that bottle in Colter's hand had made every hair on her body stand on end. There were any number of people, thanks to the news of the deaths and the kidnapping, who had a bone to pick with Dunrovin; yet it just didn't make sense to her that someone would come here with the intention of making things worse. Why throw a bomb? Why harm those who worked here? None of the people who currently worked or lived on the ranch were guilty of any wrongdoing.

Well, at least any wrongdoing when it came to the ranch. She couldn't think about her past, not when it came to this. She bit the inside of her cheek as she mindlessly petted the dog that was safely tucked into her shirt.

"Do you think we should call the police?" she asked, tilting her chin in the direction of the dangerous object.

Colter sighed. "We probably should, but I'm not sure that having any more police out to the ranch is a great idea right now. Maybe this is nothing. Maybe it was just something someone had in the back of their pickup and it just bounced out as they drove over the cattle guard. Maybe it's just spare gas or something, you know."

His feeble attempt to make her feel better didn't work. She could hear the lie in his voice. They both knew all too well this wasn't just some innocuous thing. This was someone's failed effort to cause damage.

Yet to a certain degree she agreed with him. The last thing the place needed was more negative press. Even though his brother Wyatt was a deputy for the local sheriff's office, it didn't mean they would be able to keep this thing under wraps. If they called 911, everyone in the county would hear about the latest development in the melodrama that the ranch was becoming. But if they didn't inform the police, there wouldn't be a record of it, and if something else happened…

She swallowed back the bile that rose in her throat.

Nothing else would happen. They had gotten the person responsible for the murders. They might have had a bad track record, and a bit of a target on their backs, but that didn't mean the entire world wanted to take them down. Maybe it *was* just someone's spare gas.

"Is there oil in it?" she asked, motioning to the green Heineken bottle.

He glanced down at the bottle and swirled it around, the green glass looking darker, almost as if the liquid inside had a slight red hue. "Yeah, I think so. Why?"

She smiled and some of her fears dissipated. "You know… Maybe someone was just passing through. Maybe you were right. I mean, if it's a mixed gas—"

"It could be for a chain saw. Maybe they were going out onto the federal lands behind the ranch looking for a Christmas tree or something," Colter said, finishing her sentence. "You are freaking amazing, you know that?"

She smiled and tried not to notice the way her heart sped up when he looked at her like that. She tried to reaffirm that her self-esteem wasn't dependent on his approval, but no matter how hard she tried to convince herself, she couldn't fully accept it as truth. He was so darn cute, and when he smiled, it made some of the sharp edges of her dislike soften. He wasn't as bad as she had assumed. If anything, he had a way of making people relax; and that was just the kind of person she needed in her life. Though he couldn't know that. Nothing could happen between them. Not now, not ever. She needed to stay independent, indifferent.

"I'm not amazing." Even to her, she sounded coy. The last thing she wanted him to think was that she was playing some kind of demure game to get him to fall in love. She wasn't and would never be that kind of woman—a woman who belonged more on the debutante circuit, the kind who could turn on the Southern charm with the simple wave of a hand.

He slipped his hand into hers and she stared at it in shock for a moment before letting go of him and turning away. He couldn't like her. She couldn't like him. If he knew the truth, he would want nothing to do with her.

"Wait. I'm sorry, Whit," he called after her, but she didn't slow down as she made her way back to the office.

She couldn't let herself turn around. She couldn't let him see the look in her eyes that she was sure was there—a look which begged for him to touch her; more, to love her with every part of his soul. She desperately wanted a love like that, but just because she wanted something, that didn't mean that she should have it. Not when she might or might not have been done running.

The dog scrambled out of her shirt and jumped to the floor as soon as she closed the door to her office.

The poor thing was covered in dirt and muck, and a piece of what looked like chewed gum was stuck to its ribs. The little thing rushed over to Milo's bed and snuggled into the pile of blankets. She was never going to be able to explain what had happened to the owners if they found out.

If they found out.

She couldn't tell them. No. She chuckled as she thought about all the *Nos* that were suddenly entering her life. Everywhere she turned, every choice she had to make came to that stark end. No.

Things really hadn't changed that much from Kentucky.

When she was home in Louisville, it had been the same. She had told her parents she was leaving, that she was never coming back, that she was following her gut—and every word had been met with the same "No." But they hadn't understood. They had thought it was only out of some selfish need to spread her wings after everything that had happened with Frank. They hadn't known the whole truth, a truth that haunted her every move and threatened to rear its ugly head and re-enter her life as long as she stayed there.

And maybe part of it had been the fact that she wanted so much more. She wanted to be around horses again—not close enough to touch, but close. Once you had a love for the animals, there was no turning your back to it, no matter what kind of pain had come from them in the past.

She pressed her back against the office door and closed her eyes. No. She couldn't dig up the past. No.

There was a knock on the door, and it sent vibrations

down her spine. She turned around to see Colter standing there, looking at her through the glass.

Why couldn't he get the message that she just wanted him to leave her alone?

Instead of opening the door, she pulled down the shade so he couldn't see her. She couldn't deal with him right now. And seeing him look at her like that, like there was something more than friendship budding between them, it tore at her heart. If something happened…she'd have to run. She'd have to leave this place. She couldn't reveal her past to him or to anyone. She couldn't allow her feelings to make her vulnerable.

"I get it—I have chapped hands," he said with a laugh, and what she assumed was his best attempt at relieving the tension between them, but he was wrong if he thought it would be that easy.

"Or maybe it's not my hands, but you just don't want to talk to me," he continued. "That's fine. I just wanted you to know that everything is back in place and the cattle guard is down. If you need anything just let me know. I'm going to stick around and help my dad." He stood still, almost as if he was waiting for her to answer, but she said nothing.

After a few long seconds, she heard the sounds of his heavy footfalls as he made his way off the porch. She was tempted to peek out from behind the curtain to see where he was going, if he'd finally gotten the message that she wasn't interested, but she stopped herself. She had to be strong.

The phone rang, and she had never been more grateful for the obnoxious sound.

"Dunrovin Ranch Guest Services. This is—"

"We need more towels," a woman said in a shrill voice, cutting her off.

She glanced down at the room number that lit up the phone's screen. Of course it was Ms. Fancy Pants. She bit the side of her cheek as she thought of all the comebacks she would have liked to say.

"Absolutely, ma'am. I'll have one of our staff bring them to you. Is there anything else you will be needing?"

There was the rumble of a truck and the squeak of brakes from the parking area.

"Where is the nearest club? We wanted to go dancing. You know…honky-tonking, or whatever you rednecks call it."

She swallowed back her anger, only letting a sardonic chuckle slip past. "Ma'am, the only club we have out here is a sandwich. But if you are looking for a bar, we have several. There's the Dog House, which is about five miles from here. It's mostly locals, but on the weekends they usually have a few people dancing." But it was a far cry from the country-style bar that always seemed to fill the movie screens in which everyone was dancing and there was a mechanical bull in the corner. The Dog House was one step away from being somebody's garage. In fact, it would have made sense if that was what the place had once been.

Ms. Fancy Pants sighed so loudly that Whitney wondered if the woman had put her mouth directly on the mouthpiece. "I guess it will have to do. And I won't even bother asking about restaurants. I'd rather go hungry than eat anything this town has to offer."

Whitney's dislike for the woman mounted with each of the woman's passing syllables.

"We'll be right over." She hung up the phone, unable to listen to the woman's prattling for another second.

There wasn't a snowflake's chance in July that she was going to face the woman who'd just called. She dialed the number for the housekeeper, but the phone rang and rang, and she left the girl who was supposed to be working a message about the towels.

She set down the phone and stared at it for a moment. On second thought, maybe she could ask Colter to help. He didn't work for the ranch, but if he was as interested in her as he seemed to be, he might jump at the chance to come to her aid; and it might get him out of her hair for a bit and give her the time she needed to get back to center about him and her feelings.

She sighed, content with her plan, as she opened the door. There was a black Chevy truck parked in the lot, and a tall, thin blonde had her arms draped around Colter's neck. As Whitney watched, the woman threw her head back with a laugh so high and perfect that it bounced around the courtyard until it was finally, thankfully swallowed up by the dark barn.

It was stupid to stand there and watch as the woman flipped her hair and then ran her fingers over the edges of Colter's jacket collar, but she couldn't make sense of what was happening. Sure, the woman was coming on to him. Whitney could understand a woman's attraction to the trim firefighter with a gift when it came to making people at ease, but she couldn't understand the swell of jealousy and unease that filled her as she watched.

He had held her hand, yet now his hands were on the blonde's hips. Was Mr. Eligible Bachelor really Mr. Taken?

Had he been playing her? He had to have been. Heck,

he was probably thanking his lucky stars right at that very moment that she had turned him down in time for Ms. Blonde in Tight Jeans to come and wrap her model-ish body around him like a thin blanket.

She gritted her teeth, making them squeak so loudly that it was a wonder he hadn't heard them even at a distance.

The mysterious woman moved to her tiptoes and gave Colter a kiss on the cheek.

It was the last straw.

Whitney turned around and went back inside, slam-ming the door in her wake. That was fine. If Colter wanted to be with every one of the town's available women, that was fine. He could be with all of them except her. She had better things to do with her time.

On the wall, just beside the door, was a picture of Colter in his bunker gear, a smile on his face. It was ironic. Here was a man who was sent into the flames to save people's lives, but the best thing he had done for her was to save her from falling in love.

Chapter Four

Colter squirmed out of Sarah's grip. At one point he wouldn't have minded having her hands all over him, but not now—not with everything that had happened between them. That attempt at a relationship had crashed harder than the housing market. She cared about only two things: her catering business and how she could make herself happy—no matter the cost to others. Sure, the blonde chef was cute, but beauty was a depreciating asset; being genuine, kind and selfless was far more important than any outward attributes.

He glanced back over his shoulder toward the office where Whitney was working. He could have sworn he'd heard a door slam, yet thankfully, she was nowhere in sight. He would have hated for her to get the wrong idea.

"Colter, when are you going to take me out again?" Sarah asked, running her finger down the buttons on the front of his shirt.

He took hold of her hand and lowered it gently as he gave her a firm but unwavering smile. "It was fun, but—"

"But what?" she asked, fluttering her eyelashes up at him.

He hated this kind of confrontation. The last thing

he wanted to do was hurt her or lead her on, but she was making it difficult.

"But we just don't *fit*. You know what I mean?" he said, trying to take the path of least resistance.

"I bet we could fit together if we just tried, Colter," she said, her voice soft and airy. "I just... You know when we went out, I had just broken up with Kent. I wasn't at my best. I'd like another shot."

"It's not you—"

"It's *me*." She stepped back from him. "Get a new line. Or at least just learn how to tell the woman the truth. If you're not into me, that's fine..." Sarah flipped her hair back off her neck and straightened her jacket like she could simply brush off his rejection.

"Sarah, it really isn't you. I'm just not looking for anything right now." He glanced back to the ranch office as the weight of the lie rolled off his tongue and fell hard. Sarah was right; he wasn't into her. He didn't know why he was bothering to lie other than to save her feelings. The woman he really wanted was Whitney, and she wanted absolutely nothing to do with him.

"When you are looking... I'll be waiting," she said, her playful smile returning as though she thought there was still room to hope.

He gave a resigned sigh. "Why are you here?"

"I need to finalize the catering details with your mom. Is she around?"

He motioned to the house. "I think she's inside."

"Are you coming to the party?" Sarah asked.

There was no right answer. If he said no, she would see him there and be upset, but he knew if he admitted he was going to be there, she would pressure him for something. He didn't feel like dancing around another come-on.

His father walked out of the house and made a bee-line for the barn. "Actually, I need to run along and help my father set things up."

Her face fell with another rejection, but before she could say anything he jogged toward his father.

"I'll see you at the party, then?" she called after him, but he didn't bother to turn around; instead he slipped into the safety of the barn.

Throughout his life this kind of thing seemed to be a recurring theme—the women he didn't want were desperate for him to commit to them, but the women he really wanted to date wouldn't give him the time of day. He dated a lot, but it seemed like things never went too far. With the last woman, he'd gone on one date and she'd spent the entire time talking about her job. They had hit it off all right, they had been able to talk, but, like all the other women he'd gone out with, the woman wasn't what he was looking for. The way things were going, he was never going to have another serious relationship.

Maybe he was just destined to be on his own. To some degree, he liked it that way. His fridge carried only the staples—meat log, cheese and mayonnaise. It was just like the rest of life—simple, uncluttered and what some people might have considered a bit habitual. If he did end up finding himself in a relationship, he'd have to give his routine up—women were never simple. None being more complicated than the curiosity that was Whitney Barstow.

He chuckled as he imagined her walking into his

house. She'd probably turn around and walk right out if she saw how bare the place was.

It was just easier this way, deep in his world of habit and minimalism—even if it was a bit lonesome at times. He could deal with lonesome. At least it meant that he wouldn't have to deal with heartbreak.

As the word sank in, the thoughts of his biological father moved to the front of his mind. He had only one memory of the man. Colter was two years old, and his father was leaving him and his brother Waylon on the fire department's doorstep. He had just woken up and his eyes were still grainy from the residue of sleep. Yet he could still see his father's eyes, the color of rye whiskey and their edges reddened with years of what he knew now was hard living. More than his eyes, he could remember the raspy smoke-riddled words he'd last said to them: "Boys," he'd whispered, making sure he didn't give himself away to the firemen just behind the doors. "You all don't go into the flames. When life burns at ya…*run*."

Opening himself up for a relationship was just running into the flames.

"I see Sarah's at it again," his adoptive father, Merle, said as he wrapped a bit of baling twine around his arm.

Colter grabbed a handful of pellets and let the mare at the end of the stalls nibble it out of his hand.

"She's still… Sarah…" He said her name like a verb, and it was met with his father's chuckle.

"Well, at least you can't say that she's a quitter. One of these days she'll get ya tied down. Come hell or high water."

"If she does, I'll be in hell all right." He rubbed the

old girl's neck, running his fingers down her silken coat. "What can I help you with?"

"If you're really that afraid of going back out and facing your ex, I could use some help getting down the decorations for the party," his father said, motioning toward the hayloft. "We need the lights and the rest of the wreaths. Your mother is making a fuss about everything being just perfect."

Colter didn't need his father to tell him why or how much was riding on their success.

"Did we sell any more tickets?" he asked as he made his way over to the ladder that led up to the hayloft and stepped up on the bottom rung.

"We're up to about fifty. Some donations are coming in, but as of right now we are thinking that we're only going to just about break even on the thing. We're going to need to sell at least a hundred more tickets."

"Who knows what will happen?" Colter said, making his way up the ladder so his father wouldn't see the concern that undoubtedly filled his features. "Last year we had a lot of people show up at the door, right?"

"That's what we're banking on."

Colter could hear the concern in his father's voice.

"I'd hate to have to start letting people go, but if things don't turn around..."

Whitney hadn't been on the ranch that long. If his parents decided to start laying off staff, he had no doubt that they would do it as fairly and equitably as possible—which meant it would be based on time at the ranch, and Whitney would be among the first to be let go. He couldn't let that happen.

Colter stepped off the ladder as he reached the top and made his way over to the corner where his parents kept the Christmas supplies for the barn. There were green and red tubs, each carefully marked with WREATHS, LIGHTS and TREE DECORATIONS. He loved how meticulous they kept everything. It made life so much easier—when there were labels to everything and instructions on how to keep things from going out of control.

The floor was covered in a thick layer of dust and scattered bits of broken hay. It was warm from the bodies of the horses below and it carried the sweet scent of grass. He remembered coming up here as a kid, hiding in the boxes and making forts with the horses' blankets. He and Rainier, being the two youngest brothers, had spent most of their time up here, close to the horses and the things they loved the most.

He sucked in a long breath as he thought of the careening path to disaster that Rainier's life had taken. If only his parents had made a label, or a set of instructions, for his brother, maybe his life would have gone down a different path.

Colter pulled the top bucket off the stack and moved toward the ladder. "I'll hand this down and grab another."

The floor creaked loudly, and as he took another step, the board beneath his foot shifted. The box in his hands blocked his view, and as he twisted to check his footing, there was a loud crack. The board gave out, and before he could move away, he was falling.

The jagged edges of the wood tore at his legs as he fell through the floor. The pain was raw and surreal, almost as though it was happening to someone else.

He'd always had this fear, but in his mind's eye, he'd always thought that something like this would happen only at his job, when a floor was burning out from underneath him—not in the safety and security of his parents' barn. His world, the one he'd created in his mind where everything was controlled and safe, was betraying him. It was almost the same feeling he'd had as a child… And he couldn't believe he was back here again—feeling powerless as his world collapsed around him.

He threw the bucket and a strange, strangled sound escaped him—the guttural noise as instinct took over. The box clattered onto the floor, the lid flying open and a garland spilling out. Holding out his hands, he scratched at the floor around him. He had to stop. He had to catch himself before he hit the ground below.

His father made a thick sound, somewhere between a gasp and a call to help, just as his fingers connected with the needlelike points of the broken floor. The wood pierced his hands, but he gripped tight. Holding on in an effort to slow his fall.

Though he was strong, his elbows strained with his weight as he jerked to a stop. His feet dangled in the air, just above the bucket of pellets.

There was the grind of metal of the door and the sound of Whitney gasping behind him.

"Colter!" she called, a sharp edge of fear in her voice.

There was the warmth of blood as it slipped down his leg and spilled into the top of his boot. He let go of the wood and fell into the galvanized bucket. It tipped with his weight as it broke his fall, spilling the horses' treats onto the dirt floor.

He threw his arms out, catching himself as he fell, but all it did was slow his descent into the dirt, muck and bits of the broken flooring. For a moment he lay there, taking mental stock of his body. He'd jarred his ankle and he was cut up, but he was going to be fine.

"Colter, are you all right?" Whitney asked, rushing to his side. She touched his shoulder gently, almost as though she would hurt him even more if she pressed too hard.

"Yeah, yeah… I'm fine," he said, trying just as much to convince himself as her. He pushed himself up to sitting. His jeans were torn and there was a deep gash on the side of his leg. The blood was flowing from it, dotted with bits of sawdust and dirt from the ground.

"What in the hell happened?" his father asked.

Colter looked up at the floor. Where he had fallen through, the plywood was jagged on one end, but suspiciously straight on three other sides. He picked up a bit of the flooring that had landed on the ground beside him.

There, on the bit of wood, were the distinctive marks of a saw blade. He lifted the piece for his father and Whitney to see. "Everyone at the ranch knew we would be going up there for the decorations for Yule Night."

His father took the piece of broken lumber and turned it around in his hands, inspecting the marks. "No, Colter… It had to be just some kind of accident. Maybe one of the volunteers just cut through the floor on accident. These things happen."

Colter could hear the lie in his father's voice.

No one would cut almost a perfect rectangle in the floor by accident. Anyone in their right mind would know the likelihood of someone getting hurt if they stepped on the spot—a spot he'd had to step on in order to get to the boxes. Someone had intended to set a trap—albeit a poor one, one that would hurt anyone who went up there and not someone specific.

He thought of the bottle of oil and gas they had found. While he had tried to convince himself the device wasn't a threat, and was just some random discarded item, now he couldn't be so sure. The odds of two things like this happening on the same day had to be slim to none.

Yet the bottle hadn't been in a place where it would do much damage. In fact, if they hadn't come across it by accident, it could simply have been covered by more snow in the coming days. Unless someone had dropped it there in an attempt to not be seen carrying it. It didn't make sense.

If anything, this all seemed like the ill-conceived plan of a teenager, or else this was someone who wanted to simply send a message—a warning that Dunrovin was coming under attack.

Chapter Five

She could understand acting tough, but Whitney couldn't understand Colter's need to pretend his body wasn't racked by pain. He walked with a limp that he couldn't disguise as they made their way to the ranch house.

"Let me clean you up," she said, motioning to his torn pants and the blood that stained the cloth.

"Don't worry—I'll be fine. It's just a little flesh wound," he said, but the darkness in his eyes and the deep, controlled baritone of his voice gave his pain away.

"Don't be so stubborn. Flesh wound or not, it needs to be cleaned up. And that's to say nothing about maybe going to the emergency room."

Colter shook his head. "There's no way I'm going to the doctor." He lifted the injured leg like it was stiff as he made his way up the stairs and into the house.

She followed him inside and pointed to the oversize leather chair that sat beside the fireplace in the living room. "Sit down. I'll be right back."

His mouth opened as though he considered protesting for a moment, but as he looked at her, he clammed up and hobbled over to the chair and thumped down.

She made her way to the bathroom and got the first-aid kit out of the closet. She was still angry with him. Hurt or not, he'd had his hands all over the blonde in the driveway.

Though she shouldn't have been jealous, she couldn't help it from swelling in her like a fattening tick. She had no claim on Colter Fitzgerald. In fact, no one ever seemed to have a solitary claim on the man. He dated too much and too often for her to let herself even think about him. Yet she couldn't help her thoughts as they drifted to the way he had looked holding the puppy.

No. She couldn't let the thought of how cute he was alter the fact that he usually drove her crazy. They couldn't be a thing. She wasn't looking for a relationship—especially not with a man like him.

She walked down the hallway. As she turned the corner, the blonde and Eloise were standing beside Colter. Before they could see her, she ducked into the tiny little room that was Merle and Eloise's private office. She felt out of place and unwelcome in the room that was neatly organized, its bookshelves color-coordinated with three-ring binders and business books. She stood there listening as the blonde fawned over the hurt Colter.

Whitney stared around the room. She shouldn't be in here, but there was no way she was going to walk out in the living room and fake nice with the woman who was clearly head over heels for Colter—and, if truth be told, probably more up his alley than Whitney was.

The lump of jealousy inside her swelled further, threatening to burst.

She stepped back, bumping against the desk as she tried to make physical distance work in the place of the emotional distance she needed. A piece of paper slipped to the floor, landing with a rustle at Whitney's foot.

Leaning down, she picked up the page. It was a bill from Cattleman's Bank to the tune of more than five thousand dollars. Printed on the top, with large red letters, was the word *Overdue*. Though it wasn't her bill, a feeling of sickness passed over her as she stared at the number at the bottom. There was no worse feeling than looking at a bill that you knew couldn't be paid.

She had seen those kinds of things over and over as a child when her parents were going through their divorce. The red letters were like shining beacons from a time in her life that she never wanted to remember, yet was forced to face as she looked at the paper in her hands.

No wonder everyone on the ranch had seemed on edge. She had known things were tight with her employers, but she had no clue that things were this bad.

Laying the paper back on the stack of bills in the inbox, she stepped away from the desk and the memories it wrought.

Maybe they weren't as bad off as she was assuming. Maybe it was just one bill that had slipped through the cracks. She was tempted to flip through the other bills that were there, but she stopped herself. It wasn't her business. And even if she knew, there was nothing she could do to change the outcome.

On the other hand, it was her future at stake. If they couldn't pay their regular bills, then there was no possible way that they could continue to carry a staff. She had been lucky to get the job, and it was only when she'd told Eloise about her life in Kentucky that the woman had told her to come to Montana.

The woman had been so kind to her, even offering to pay for her flight here, which now, seeing what she had, Whitney knew the woman and the ranch couldn't afford.

And now she would just have to turn around and go home. She wouldn't be able to find another job in the tiny community that was Mystery, Montana. There was little in the way of anything here, and no one would want to hire a girl like her—one with a past spattered throughout the media.

Whitney stared at the papers. Once again, her future was at the mercy of the world around her, and there was nothing she could do to control her destiny.

She rushed out of the office, unable to stand the indelible red ink at the top of the bill a second longer. The blonde was still standing with Colter, but before Whitney could turn and rush back down the hall, Eloise noticed her.

"There she is," Eloise said, waving her over. "Whitney, have you met Sarah?"

She felt like a dead man walking as she made her way to the living room. Sarah was smiling, her radiant white teeth just as straight and perfect as the rest of her.

"So nice to meet you, Whitney," she said, reaching out to shake her hand.

"Likewise." Whitney played along, but broke away from the handshake as quickly as she could. She didn't want to meet Colter's girlfriend, or friend with benefits, or whatever it was that this girl was to him.

"Sarah is catering the party," Eloise added, almost as though she could sense the tension between the two women.

Whitney forced herself to smile in an attempt to comfort Eloise. Her friend didn't need to worry about some drama that was happening between her and Sarah. Based on the paper she had just seen, there were already enough things going on in Eloise's life.

"That's great. I'm sure it's going to be marvelous," Whitney said, her voice dripping with sugary sweetness put there only for Eloise.

Colter looked up at her and frowned. "Are you okay?" he asked.

"Sure. Just fine," she said, but she looked away out of the knowledge that if he looked at her face he would see just how bad she was at lying. She grabbed the first-aid kit out from under her arm. "Here," she said, handing it to him.

He took the box but looked up at her like he wanted to ask her to help him.

She glanced over at Sarah.

Eloise took Sarah by the arm. "Why don't we run along and finish up going over the menu? You were saying something about the shrimp?"

Sarah opened her mouth to protest being pulled away from the man she was clearly moving in on, but before she could speak Eloise was herding her toward the kitchen.

Whitney walked toward the front door, uncomfortable with being so close and alone with Colter. There were pictures on the wall of the staff over the years, and for a moment she stared up at them.

There was a man in one of the pictures from the early '90s. His hair was slightly longer than everyone else's and his eyes looked dark, almost brooding. As she stared at his features, something about him felt familiar—perhaps it was the look on his face, or the way that he seemed alone when he was surrounded by others, but she couldn't quite put her finger on it.

Colter grumbled and cringed as he limped his way over to her side and looked up at the pictures. "This place has seen a lot of things."

"And a lot of people come and go," she said, instinctively glancing toward the office and then toward the kitchen, where she could hear the garbled sound of Eloise and Sarah talking.

He glanced toward the kitchen.

"What is going on between you two?" she asked, motioning toward the closed kitchen door.

His eyes widened and his mouth gaped like he was waiting for the right answers to simply start falling out.

"I saw you guys in the parking lot." She turned away from him, unable to look him in the face as she talked. "I know it's not any of my business. But I know... I know you date a lot. And I don't want her to think..."

"She can think whatever she wants," he said, finally finding his voice.

"So you're not dating?"

He shifted his weight, but jerked as though the movement caused him pain. "I... She and I, we were a thing once. It wasn't anything serious."

"But she's your ex."

He looked over at her, catching her gaze. "I would hardly call what she and I had a relationship, so I wouldn't really call her an ex."

"I would," she said, feeling the acidic tone of her words straight to her bones.

He stared at her for a moment before looking away, and her heart sank. She shouldn't have come at him like that. They all had a past, and if he looked too deeply into hers, she had no doubt that he would find things that he didn't like, as well. Her thoughts moved to the fire and the man who had caused it.

Colter turned to walk away, but she stopped him as she grabbed his wrist.

"I'm sorry," she said as he turned to look at her. "I'm just upset. You didn't do anything wrong. And I have no reason to be jealous. You can date whoever you want."

It wasn't as if Colter liked her anyway. If he got to know her, everything would fall apart and whatever crush he had on her would rapidly diminish.

"I don't want to date just anyone. The only one I'd love to take out is you," he said, pulling her hand off his wrist and wrapping her fingers between his. "From the moment you came here, it's all I wanted."

She wanted to give in to the joy of hearing those words, but her reality wouldn't allow it. She was so close to losing her job, her place here, and that was to say nothing about the odd things that were starting to happen around the place.

She pulled her hand from his. "I don't know who you think I am, but I'm telling you that I'm not perfect. I'm not the kind of woman who most men want to date. If you just got to know me a little more, you would see that you wouldn't want a woman like me."

"I know you, whether you want to admit it or not."

She gave a sardonic chuckle. "Just because we've been passing each other on the ranch since I got here, that doesn't mean you know me. You have merely seen me. There are things in my past that a man like you would never accept. We have fundamental differences. Number one—that you have more dates than a fruit-

cake. I don't want a man whose attention I have to struggle to keep."

"Unless we go out, how do you know if we have
fundamental differences?" He leaned against the chair
closest to him. "And wait... Does fruitcake even have
dates in it?"

She groaned as she tried not to smile. He might have
been right, she didn't know if there were dates in fruitcake, but she was never going to admit it. He never
ceased to irritate her. He couldn't take anything seriously—but then again, it was one of the things she
couldn't help being attracted to.

"Just sit down," she said, pointing to the chair he
leaned on. "I will fix your leg. As long as you promise
not to ask me out again."

"Today or ever?" he said, giving her a cheeky grin.

She sighed, not wanting to give him the answer she
should have. She equally loved and hated the feelings
he created within her. It was so much easier to not give
in to her attraction, to keep out of the reach of any
man's attentions. As soon as men entered her life, only
bad things seemed to follow in their wake—drama, intrigue and danger.

Love was just too risky—especially with a man like
Colter, the most eligible bachelor in the county.

He plopped down into the chair and she went to get
the first-aid kit. He pulled up his shredded pants leg, un-
veiling his bloodied and badly cut leg. Slivers of wood
were embedded in his skin.

"Maybe you should go into the emergency room?"
she asked, sitting down on the floor at his feet.

He waved her off. "It's fine as long as we get it
cleaned out."

It struck her how strong he was. He had to be hurting, yet he still fought through it to make jokes with her. She didn't want to admit it, but he really was an incredible man. Not that she was in the market for a man—no matter how incredible.

"You didn't give me an answer about asking you out again," he said as she set about cleaning the wound on his leg.

She patted at the cut with the gauze soaked in hydrogen peroxide as she tried to come up with the right answer. "It's not you... You're great. It's just that right now..." She glanced toward the office.

His face dropped and she watched as the hope faded from his eyes. It was almost as if part of his soul had seeped from him, and she hated herself for making something like that happen. Yet she couldn't change her mind. She had to stick to her guns.

"Besides," she continued, "you need to focus on where you're walking. If you think about me all the time— I mean, look at what happened this time." She motioned to his leg. "You fell through a floor. I'm a risk to your health." As the words escaped her, she couldn't help thinking about how many times that had been true for the people she had gotten close to, throughout her life.

No matter where she went, or what she did, she only brought danger, sadness and loss to the ones she loved. To protect him, and the people of the ranch, she could never love again.

Chapter Six

Overnight the sky had opened and fresh glittering snow-flakes adorned Colter's front yard. The weatherman was calling for another six inches of snow today and possibly another six tomorrow. Yet in rural Montana, six inches could turn out to be two inches, or it could be two feet—it all depended on the way the wind decided to blow and the fickle whims of the winter storm.

He loved this time of year. Some hated the cold and the constant grayness that came with living in the valley, but he'd always thought of the world around him like a blanket. The mountains were his borders and the clouds were his cover, as though he were protected from the brutal world thanks to the bosom of the world itself.

He pulled on a red sweater his mother had given him last Christmas. He needed to get back to the ranch. His parents would need his help plowing and getting ready. There were only two more days until the party. He'd need to fix the floor of the barn. Not to mention being on hand to greet the visitors who would be starting to arrive for the ranch's holiday festivities.

If truth be told, though his parents would appreciate his help, he knew they could do it on their own—what and who he really wanted to help was Whitney and the poor little dog they had saved. Or, if she asked, that would be a convenient excuse for finding his way to the ranch's main office.

The snow crunched under his boots as he walked out to his pickup. He started it, letting the engine warm up and stave off the bitter cold. His breath was a white cloud even in the cab of the truck. According to the dashboard temperature gauge, it was ten below. This kind of weather only lent itself to three things—breakdowns, house fires and frostbite.

He wouldn't be surprised if he got called into work. It would be an overtime shift, but the last thing he wanted to do right now was find himself there. His hand and leg were sore from yesterday's fall. He'd be all right, but it would be an annoyance that he would have to ignore in order to do his job—and anytime something like this happened, he always had a sinking fear that it could hinder his attempt to save someone's life. He hated the thought of letting someone else down thanks to his own weakness.

As he drove toward the ranch, his mind wandered to his other weakness—Whitney. He couldn't get her out of his thoughts. She didn't want to be with him; she had made that clear. Yet, when he was around her, there was just some…a spark. Something seemed to buzz between them, and from the look in her eyes, she couldn't ignore the feeling, either.

He just had to be around her, even if it wasn't as anything more than a friend. He was simply drawn to her. Maybe it would turn into something more than it was, and maybe it wouldn't, but at the very least he could have her in his life.

Whitney really was one of the most confusing

women he'd ever met. One minute she seemed open to the world and a future, and the next it was like a curtain fell over her and she slipped back into the shadows of her thoughts and closed him out. Colter understood it. He had seen the look a thousand times with his brother Waylon. It was the look that came with loss and pain.

She had never really talked about her life, but she didn't need to tell him in order for him to understand that she had some baggage. Everyone had a past. Though he tried hard to hide from his, enveloping it with humor and lightheartedness, it didn't hurt any less when he pressed too hard against it. If she would only talk to him, maybe they could work through it together.

He hoped.

Or maybe her secrets were darker than he could ever imagine. Maybe she'd killed a man. Left someone on the side of a road. He laughed at his ridiculous thought. She wasn't the kind. She was a tad rough around the edges, but was soft in all the ways that were important. Yet, as much as he was attracted to her, he couldn't help feeling like he was in the dark. She was hiding something from him, something she feared sharing with anyone, something that he desperately wanted to know.

Maybe that was what he was most attracted to her for—her mysteriousness. She challenged him in a way no other woman had. She was like a quest, and it made him want her that much more.

As he neared the ranch, there was a line of cars in the middle of the road. One of the drivers was standing beside his car, holding up his cell phone as though he was searching for a signal.

Colter stopped next to the man and rolled down his window. "What's going on?"

"The road's blocked. And of course there isn't a cell phone signal to be had," the man said, his voice flecked with a Northeastern accent, as he pushed his phone deep into his pocket. "And I don't even know if we're in the right place." He motioned to his car.

It was a white rental, the kind that most picked up when they arrived at their little airport. It had regular tires that made a day like this, one in which everything was slick and treacherous, that much more dangerous.

"You heading to Dunrovin?" Colter asked.

The man nodded. "We heard that it was magical, but so far all we're finding is crappy roads and poor technology. Even your airport was like walking into a living room from the seventies."

Colter couldn't help the laugh that escaped him. If he had to explain to someone what the place looked like, he wouldn't have come up with something as perfect as the man's description. The airport was all orange and brown, and its walls were accented with the dark cherrywood that harked back to the day it had been built.

"No offense," the man added, his breath clouding the air.

"None taken. Admittedly there are times when even I have to agree we are a little bit behind the rest of the country."

"But that's all part of its charm," the man said. "Except when you need to make a call." He laughed.

"Don't worry about it. I got a phone that works. Why don't you just go and get warmed up? I'll make sure you get to the ranch."

The man gave him an appreciative nod and, tucking his face into the collar of his jacket, jogged back to his car.

Colter got out of his truck and made his way to the front of the line. There, in the world of white, was a fallen pine. Its dark green boughs and its buckskin trunk were partly masked in newly fallen snow. Yet, as he neared the tree that lay across the road, he could see the fresh cut marks of a chain saw at the tree's base.

Tacked to the center of the tree, between some branches, was a red envelope. It was flecked with snow and he blew it off, his breath warming some of the flakes enough to make fat wet blobs on the paper that looked almost like tears.

He grabbed it and opened the seal. The cold winter chill bit at his fingers as he pulled the card from the envelope. The card had a picture of his family and the staff in front of the ranch's sign. He recognized it as the family's yearly newsletter. They sent it out to everyone in the community and former guests. Thousands had to have gone out. Yet this one was different. Each of the people's faces had been x-ed out with a black marker. He flipped over the card. On the back it read:

Mess with my family. I'll mess with yours.
This is WAR.

Chills rippled down his spine as he looked at the jagged handwriting.

The bomb, the floor…it all made sense. Someone had been trying to send them a message. Someone was coming after them.

He stared at the letter. Whose family had they been messing with?

His thoughts moved to William Poe and his wife's death. William had threatened them, as he had sworn that their family was to blame for his wife's demise, but he wouldn't do something so treacherous. He was the kind who would pull political strings, not obstruct roads to deter guests from making it to the ranch, or send makeshift Molotov cocktails as a warning.

His wife's killer's only relatives had been Christina and her young daughter, Winnie, who were both in Fort Bragg with Waylon until they came back in a few weeks to celebrate Christmas. Truth be told, Colter had a feeling that part of the reason Christina had been so willing to go with Waylon was that it was so hard to face the community after everything that had happened with her sister.

If only his answers were so easy. Right now all he had was a threatening note, the remnants of a bomb and a series of scrapes and bruises.

He glanced back at the note, trying his best to see something about it that would help him get an idea, yet he found himself concentrating on the dark ink of the letters.

Maybe there was something going on, something deeper in the past that he didn't know about. His parents didn't share everything.

He walked back to the guy in the car and tapped on his window as he stuffed the envelope into his pocket.

"Is there anything you can do?" the guy asked.

Colter barely heard the man as he ran his fingers over the edge of the envelope in his pocket. "Huh?"

"The tree," the guy said, frowning. "Is there something you can do?"

"Oh, yeah. No worries. I have a chain saw in the back of my truck."

"You carry a saw around with you?" the guy asked, giving him a look of disbelief.

In Montana, there was a culture of live and let live, and with that came a certain amount of self-reliance. If you needed something fixed, or to get yourself out of a jam, it was up to you and your ingenuity. In his world, he had to be like a Boy Scout and always be prepared.

"This is hardly my first tree across a road. It ain't nothing," he said, forcing a smile. "I'll get it out of the way in a sec."

It took a few minutes thanks to the pain in his calf, but before long he'd cut the tree into manageable pieces and loaded it all into the back of his truck for next year's firewood. He waved the cars on, but all he could think about as he worked was the fact that someone had done all this to send them a message.

If he hadn't come along, the guests would have been stuck out there for hours until someone found out about the tree. It would have been an even worse start to what, for many of their guests, was meant to be a restful vacation away from these kinds of headaches.

The ranch was bustling as he arrived. The man he'd talked to had a key in his hand and was making his way to his room as Colter parked. Luckily, the guy had a smile on his face. He must have been talking to Whitney. She always had a way of making people happy. It was why she was so good at her job, and no doubt why his mother had hired her—even though it had to be hard on the ranch's finances.

Another couple walked out of the office. They were carrying hot chocolates, complete with big white marshmallows and cups that looked like snowmen.

He waited a moment for the guests to make it to

the ranch's assortment of houses and to their appointed rooms. It felt good as he watched the movement of the comings and goings of the place. It reminded him of the many good years that they'd had, years when there were so many guests that they would be booked six months to a year in advance.

They would get there again. He knew it.

He reached into his back pocket, took the envelope out and glanced at the card. Someone wanted this all to end just as much as he wanted it all to continue. The perpetrator was right—the place was at war. He'd have to give this place everything he could to bring it back to life—and a bright future—even if that meant giving up his own dreams.

He put the envelope on his dashboard and sat back for a moment. What were his dreams?

It had been a while since he'd really given any thought to his own life and where he wanted to go. As it was, his job was the kind that had a certain cap. He'd never get rich doing what he was doing. He'd probably never become the fire marshal or the captain, no matter how many years he put into the place—the odds were stacked against him for that kind of job. However, none of that really mattered to him.

If he had to put words to his true feelings and desires, what he wanted most was a family of his own. He thought about Waylon and his daughter, Winnie. He loved that girl, and it made his heart heavy to think of her all the way across the country. She had brought such joy and lightheartedness to the ranch.

He was ready to have a life that revolved around the smile and cheers of a kid like her. In fact, it would be great to have children about the same ages as his brothers'. It would bring them all back together again, all back to this wondrous place and to share his world with.

More than that, he wanted a woman in his life, a wife whom he could share it all with—the joy of having a family, spending nights around a warm fire and taking the horses out for a ride on the weekends. He wanted a wife who would light up when she saw him come home. He wanted a wife to help him make a home, a wife who could be his partner in everything life brought.

Until now, he hadn't realized how lonely he was. Sure, he had his parents and brothers, but it wasn't the same as being in a loving and committed relationship— a connection that was true and deep. He longed for the kind of bond in which they could finish each other's sentences, become their better selves.

He wanted to be completed.

Whitney walked out of the office and, not seeing him, made her way toward the end of the house. She picked up from the ground an orange plastic box that held his father's chain saw and made her way to the woodshed. He reached down and was about to open the truck's door, but stopped. Why would she have had his father's chain saw? It didn't make sense.

He sat back and watched her as she disappeared into the woodshed. A few minutes later she came out and tucked her hair behind her ear and locked the door.

She reached down and picked a bit of sawdust from her jacket and flicked it into the snow and glanced around like she was checking to make sure no one had seen her. Was it possible that she had been putting the saw away after she had used it to fell the tree in the road?

He shook the thought from his head. Just because he

didn't know who had sent the threatening note didn't mean everyone around him was guilty. And the last person he could see being responsible for the fallen tree was her. She had no reason to disrupt the flow of guests. Her future was just as dependent on the success or failure of the ranch as the rest of them. It would have been counterintuitive.

Yet whoever was behind the sabotage that was occurring had to know a bit about the comings and goings of the ranch.

He moved slightly and Whitney caught sight of him and waved. He smiled and returned her wave before getting out of his truck.

"What are you doing out here?" she asked, approaching him and stopping by the front steps of the porch leading to the office.

He couldn't ignore the way she quickly glanced back over her shoulder toward the shed.

Her eyes were bright and her face was red from the cold, but she stood there and waited until he walked to her side. "I thought I'd come out and give you all a hand after the storm. Thought you'd need a little plowing to be done or something."

"That was thoughtful of you," she said. "How's your leg doing?"

He lifted it up high for her, wiggling it about. "It's still attached. I'm sure it will be fine. Just a few scrapes and bruises."

"If you want, I can take another look at it for you."

Though it was bitterly cold, a warmth rose to his cheeks as he thought about her hands traveling all over his leg once again. It had been a long time since he'd let a woman touch him. Sure, she hadn't meant it like that, but there had been something about it. And she hadn't made it a secret that she had hated him being around Sarah.

She had seemed so upset, jealous almost, at the thought of him having once been with Sarah. And as badly as he wanted to ask her if she was okay now, the last thing he wanted to bring up was her feelings from last night. Especially when she had made him promise not to ask her out again.

He'd never been the desperate kind. He had enough self-respect to know when a woman didn't want him in her life, but he couldn't ignore the spark between them and how he still felt the same charge now that she was near. Sure, she had rebuffed his advance and he wasn't about to make another pass at her, but that didn't mean he didn't hope she would come around.

She started to walk toward the office, and as he stepped after her, he looked back at his truck. There, glaring in the windshield, was the red envelope.

He'd have to call Wyatt and let him know about the letter. But if he was even a tiny bit right that Whitney was involved with this…she would be in trouble. Wyatt could be intense when it came to defending his family. He would make sure, regardless of Colter's feelings toward Whitney, that she—or anyone else responsible—would be sent a message that the Fitzgeralds and Dunrovin weren't to be messed with.

Colter was positive that he had it all wrong. He had just seen something out of context, but until he knew for sure, he couldn't take the risk.

Chapter Seven

Colter was staring at her so intently that it made the hair on the back of her neck rise. He didn't look upset or sad. Instead he was looking at her like she had done some unspeakable thing.

Was this about last night?

She had spent all night tossing and turning as she had gone over every word that she had said to him. By 3:00 a.m. she had finally convinced herself that she had said what needed to be said, albeit she could have been more eloquent. Yet now, standing here with him looking at her like that, she was back to square one in thinking she had gotten things between them all wrong.

"I… I'm sorry about last night," she said, finally breaking the awkward silence between them.

He blinked for a moment, almost as if he were pulling himself back to reality, and his familiar grin returned. The simple action and change made some of the tightness in her chest loosen.

"You're fine. I mean…" He ran his hand over the fine layer of stubble on the side of his jaw. "I hear you. I don't want you to think that…you know… I won't respect your boundaries. If you don't want to go out with me, I get that. You have nothing to be sorry about."

She had plenty to be sorry about—number one, that he'd actually believed her. She wished she could tell him that it wasn't about him. But there was no going back and fixing what she had broken between them. She could see it in his eyes—he didn't trust her anymore.

Two people couldn't have anything if they didn't have trust.

She wasn't sure what to say that would make the look in his eyes disappear. "Thanks."

"What were you doing?" he asked, glancing toward the woodshed.

"Huh?"

"I saw you with the chain saw. Did you become a lumberjack overnight?" he asked with a chuckle, but the sound was forced and high.

"One of the guests mentioned that it was sitting out when they checked in," she said.

He nodded, but as hard as she tried, she couldn't catch his gaze. "Did they say who put it there?"

In truth, she hadn't even given the saw a real thought. The man in the white car, David Hellman, had just told her about it when he checked in. He'd also told her about a downed tree.

"You don't think I had anything to do with the thing out in the road, do you?" she asked, taken aback at the sudden realization of what he must have been thinking of her. "I would never do anything to jeopardize this place. Dunrovin is my home. And, if I have my way, I plan to stay here for years to come," she said, not waiting for him to answer her question.

"Years to come?" he asked, his grin widened and some of the seriousness melted away from his gaze.

"I know we don't know each other well," she said,

trying to control her temper as she thought about how affronted she was that he would think her low enough to do something to upset the ranch. "But you should know that I'm not the kind of person who would hurt those that I care—"

"About?" he asked, but from his tone she knew what he was really asking was if she cared about him.

Yet all she could think about was that day in the barn, the day of the fire. What she was trying to convince him of was entirely true. She had been the reason her horse had been hurt. She had tried to save him, but if only she'd tried a little harder. And now here she was, with a firefighter again.

"I just mean—" She was cut off by the ranch office's door swinging open.

The little rat dog came loping out, yipping loudly as Eloise followed at its heels. "Where you going?" Whitney asked, motioning toward the little dog.

Milo plodded out of the office. The old ranch dog was a mutt but looked a bit like a Labrador retriever with a shaggy coat. Next to the well-kept Chihuahua, who was complete with a set of red nail polish, he looked even more derelict than he ever had before.

Whitney smiled as Milo stopped beside the little dog and gave it a wet, sloppy kiss on the top of its head, promptly putting a stop to the menace's barking.

"Don't you think she's a little bit out of your league, buddy?" Colter reached down and patted Milo on the head.

The dog looked over at her with his big brown eyes, and she swore that she saw him smile. It was almost as if the dog thought the same thing about her and Colter and was trying to send her some kind of message. She stuck her tongue out at the dog. She didn't need anyone or anything, especially not her closest buddy, trying to remind her of who she was.

Eloise chuckled and turned back to her. "If you wouldn't mind, when you're running into town, I have a note for Sarah about the menu. Would you drop it off? I can't seem to reach her on her cell phone. It's going straight to voice mail and I don't want her to miss a chance to get to the grocery store before they close for the night." Not waiting for an answer, Eloise handed her the note.

She looked down at it and saw Sarah's name printed across it.

Thankfully, Colter reached over and took the note from her hand. "Did you try to text her, Mom?"

Eloise put her hands on her hips and gave her son a matronly glare. "Do you think that I'm really that behind the times?"

Colter shrugged, his smile shining bright. "Okay..."

"Thank you. And when you get the food for...the little dog," she said, like she couldn't remember the dog's name, either, "her owners wanted to remind you that she only eats organic and GMO-free dog food."

Whitney smirked. It hadn't been an hour since she had seen the dog go out with Milo into the pasture. Whatever it ate out there couldn't have been the prized dog food that the owners had requested, but she would make sure to keep that out of her report when and if they called to check on their dog over the next few days.

"No problem. Did they want the filet mignon or the prime rib flavor?" she added with a sarcastic laugh. "But hey, I get it...wanting to give your animals the best." Whitney glanced toward the barn and the stables where a few of the horses had stuck their heads over the gates to watch.

She knew all too well how much she had been willing to sacrifice for the animals she loved.

"If you're running into town, do you mind if I ride along?" Colter asked. "Actually, why don't we take the truck? I need to get some lumber to fix the hole in the hayloft's floor. Unless Dad already did it?" he asked, looking to Eloise.

She shook her head. "Your father's been running around like a chicken with his head cut off all morning. He's out feeding the animals, but I know he was talking about getting the rest of the barn cleaned up before the dance."

"If you see him, tell him not to worry about the floor. I'll take care of it," Colter said, motioning in the direction of the barn. "And when we get back, I'll help him with the rest of it."

Eloise looked over at her and gave her a knowing smile. It was so warm and full of implied meaning that Whitney forced herself to look away, unsure of how to respond. She wished she could just tell Eloise everything, but there were so many things…things she would never understand, and even on the off chance that she did, she could probably never look at Whitney the same way again.

It was just easier this way, keeping an emotional distance from everyone around her. Yet no one at the ranch seemed to understand.

THEY DROVE DOWN Main Street and toward the hardware store. The antiques shop that had once belonged to William Poe's wife was boarded up, but the front windows were still filled with the knickknacks that she had put up for sale before her death. In most places, life had a way of moving on after someone's death, but here in Mystery, it was as if even one person's death was reason for the entire town to go into mourning.

Even though it was getting near Christmas, business was slow in the downtown stores. A few people were carrying shopping bags as they walked out from the drugstore, and one woman had rolls of wrapping paper tucked under her arm.

Colter pulled into a parking spot and turned off the engine. The ride to town had been quiet, almost too quiet. Yet all he could think about was the glaring red envelope on his dashboard and all the things it could mean.

He believed Whitney was innocent—she couldn't have had anything to do with the felled tree—but she hadn't seemed surprised at all when he brought it up. She'd appeared upset only when he broached the subject of her somehow being involved.

From his police buddies he'd learned that when someone was truly innocent they got angry when accused of a crime, and those who were guilty typically gave reasons they wouldn't have done such a thing. She had done both.

He stepped out of the truck and walked around to her side and opened her door. She turned and looked up at him. Her eyes were full of pity and something else that he couldn't put his finger on.

He was making something out of nothing. Being cynical wasn't his strength. He had always left that to Waylon—and now, pressed to be that way, he didn't like it. He liked living in a world where people were innocent until they were proved guilty.

As she stepped out of the truck, he yearned to take her by the hand and help her.

She walked to the sidewalk and turned to face him. "Colter, do you ever think that some things are too big to let go? That no matter how hard you try they will mess up your life forever?"

The question made him stop in his tracks. "Where did that come from?"

She shook her head. "I don't know. I guess I was just thinking about…everything."

He wasn't sure exactly what she meant by that, and if she was talking about them or not, but he wasn't sure he wanted to ask. She was finally opening up to him, and this was one gift that he didn't want to screw up.

"I think everyone has things that happen in their life that they're not proud of. No one is a saint. Life can be messy, but that doesn't mean that we wall ourselves off and stop living."

"Protecting yourself from getting hurt again isn't stopping from living. It's being smart."

To a certain degree he could agree with her. It was so much easier to just not put himself out there—even with her. Rejection could be so hard to deal with. It made people jaded if they let it go too deep.

"I don't want to grow older and be one of those bitter people you see… You know what I mean?" he asked, the question as non-accusatory as possible.

"Are you saying I'm bitter?"

"No… Not at all." He tried to mentally backpedal. "I just mean that I don't want to be unhappy when I get older. When I find the woman I want to marry, I want to be with her forever. I want a life where there is nothing but great happiness—no matter what it takes."

"Life isn't all sunshine and daisies. It's pain and reflection. It's making ends meet when there isn't enough. It's about struggle and hardship. And marriage would be just as hard."

"If you love someone with all your heart, you can get through anything—especially the hard times."

She smiled, but there was a deep pain in her eyes that the smile couldn't camouflage. "Two people can't love each other like that."

He couldn't disagree with her more, and it hurt him to imagine what she had been through in life that could have made her this skeptical and dismissive of what was one of life's greatest pleasures.

"If you don't think so, then you've never really been in love," he said.

Her eyes widened with surprise and she opened her mouth to speak, but held back.

"If you really, truly love someone and they love you back, you can take on the world and whatever it has to throw at you."

"How many times have you been in love?" she asked.

There was nothing quite like walking into an unwinnable situation like that. There was no right answer. "How many times have you?"

She held her hands tightly in front of her and stared down at her fingers. "Just once. And that was enough to show me that maybe love isn't right for me."

"When did it end?"

She sucked in a long breath. "The moment he struck the match."

Chapter Eight

The old adage of still waters running deep crossed his mind, but even that didn't seem to quite fit the woman he wanted to pull into his arms. She was deeper and far more full of secrets than he ever could have guessed, and she was finally deciding to let him into her life and her past. He was honored but at the same time absolutely terrified with the pressure that he could let her down.

"Was he trying to kill you?" he asked. His voice was thick and he tried to swallow back the bile that rose in his throat as he thought about someone coming to hurt her.

"My death wasn't enough for him. He wanted to take away all the things I loved first. He wanted to break me."

"What happened?" He leaned back against the front grille of the truck, relaxing his body in hopes that she would see that he wanted and was ready to listen to whatever she wanted to tell him.

She bit at the skin of her bottom lip. "I don't want to talk about it."

He stood back up, convinced his attempt at subconsciously swaying her to open up thanks to his body language hadn't worked. As he stood, she moved closer to him, so close that he could smell the floral bouquet scent wafting up from her hair. She smelled so good, like freshly washed hair and dryer sheets.

She balled her fists and then opened up her fingers and slipped them into his. "Thanks for just listening. I just needed... I guess I *need* a friend."

"I'm here," he said, lacing his fingers between hers, "for whatever you need."

He hated the dreaded friend-zone, but he would take what he could get from this incredible woman. She had so much to offer the world, if only she would come out of her shell a little bit more—and if he could be the catalyst she needed to feel safe, wanted, and loved again, he'd be more than happy to help.

She squeezed his hand in hers and smiled up at him. "You don't know how much that means to me. I haven't... I haven't talked about what happened ever since I left Kentucky."

"Does my mother know?"

Whitney shook her head. "Only the basics. She knows there was a fire, and I couldn't stay there."

"My mom has always had a big heart. She's probably the only reason that me and my brothers are doing as well as we are."

Whitney went rigid as he ran his thumb over the back of her hand, but as he stroked she started to soften under his touch, just like a horse.

"You know, you and your mom are a lot alike," she said. "You both try to make everyone else around you happy. You're so giving."

It made him happier than she could possibly know that she thought that much of him. Most women only complimented him on his looks or his jeans or some other superficial thing… Not that he minded that they thought him sexy—it was just nice to be recognized as something more.

He lifted her hand, wanting to kiss her skin, but he stopped himself. She only wanted a friend, albeit friends who apparently held hands, but it was up to her to decide the speed of whatever was going on between them. "Thanks," he said, lowering their hands back down. "But really, I'm just as flawed as any other man. I have my quirks."

She smiled and the darkness that had always seemed to fill the space around her lightened. "And those quirks would be…? You know, for research and friendship purposes only."

The way she spoke made a dash of hope move through him. Maybe she did want something more, or maybe he was just a fool for hoping.

"Are you the kind who moves too fast?" she continued, not waiting for him to answer. "Wait…are you a mouth breather?"

"What?" He laughed. "Definitely not a mouth breather. Would that be a deal breaker for you?"

Her smile widened. "I wouldn't date a man who was unkind to his mother. I think that, with some exceptions, a man can be judged by his relationship with his mom."

"Do I pass that test?"

Her eyebrow quirked. "What if I said no?"

The way she teased made the little bit of hope inside him grow.

"If you said no, then I suppose that I would have to hang out with you some more—I would show you what kind of man I really am."

"Hmm… I was going to say that your relationship with your mother was good, but now I'm rethinking it. So much so that we may need to spend a little more time together."

He laughed. "Before I commit to something so extreme, are there any more quirks that I need to know about? You know, major turnoffs?"

She started to lead him toward the hardware store. She looked back at him with a smile, but had started to nibble her bottom lip. He'd noticed the little tic before, and he loved the way it made her lips grow redder—it was almost the same color as if she had just been kissed. And a kiss, just one single kiss, was the only thing in the world he wanted right now.

"Let's see…" she said as they walked into the store. The place smelled like old popcorn and motor oil. "I don't like when a man thinks he can boss me around. And I need someone who's patient."

He had patience in spades and he'd learned not to try to tell a woman what to do a long time ago. He couldn't understand the women who let their lives be controlled by the men they said they loved, and on the flip side, he didn't want or expect to be controlled, either. "The only relationships that I have found to work in my life are when we work in tandem, side by side, and raise each other up. By telling those who we care about what to do… Well, I think it's kind of patronizing. You know what I mean?"

"Yeah, it's almost like you can't think for yourself." She let go of his hand and motioned toward the lumber department. "If you wanted to run and get what you need, I'll get us some popcorn. Sound good?"

She was running from their talk, but he couldn't

blame her. As much as he loved talking to her and learning about what made her tick, it was always uncomfortable and challenging to open up and reveal yourself to another person. She might not have realized it, but he held the same fears. It came with who he was, a part of him that was as deeply ingrained as his will to breathe.

He grabbed a cart for the board and moved through the aisle, making quick work of getting the plywood. He pushed the monstrous, wobbling cart through to the front of the store as Whitney came walking toward him. She smiled and lifted up the popcorn like a peace offering. Yet, as she looked at him, she mustn't have noticed the display of Christmas ornaments that were in the middle of the aisle and her foot connected with the corner of the boxes, sending the popcorn in her hands flying. The kernels flew through the air, and as she moved to instinctively correct herself, she fell forward, landing on the floor in a sea of yellow corn.

She glanced up, her mouth opened in shock, and looked toward him to see if he had been watching. He let go of his cart and rushed to her side. She put her forehead down on the concrete floor as he neared.

"Are you hurt?" he asked, kneeling down beside her. "That was a hard fall."

"Ugh," she said, the noise coming from somewhere deep within her. "I can't believe I just did that…and you saw." She started to giggle and she pushed herself up to her knees. "I swear I'm not the klutzy type—I'm no Bella Swan. Really."

"Bella Swan?" he asked, totally confused.

"You know… The girl from *Twilight.*"

He laughed. "So you're a fan of vampire novels?" He took her by the arm and helped her to stand. He brushed the front of her jacket off, careful to avoid the gentle curves where her breasts pressed against the firm cloth of her coat.

"I always love a good story," she said, but he noticed that her already red cheeks grew a shade darker.

"Taking out a thousand ornaments at a hardware store is a good one…" He laughed, motioning to the boxes of ornaments that had tumbled on the far side of the stack.

She ran her hands over her face.

He walked around to the other side and started to pick up the boxes and set them up on the remaining stack.

"Are any of them broken?" she asked, moving to his side and picking up a box, flipping it around in her hand.

He looked at the boxes in his hands. "None so far. But hey, if the first ornament that we have to buy together is a broken one, I'll take it."

She stopped moving and stared at him for a moment, making him wish that he hadn't pressed her about anything involving what might or might not have been his hopes of a relationship.

Glancing away, she set the box in her hand on the top of the stack. "If, and only if, we had a relationship, I would hope we would start it without broken things."

The hope inside him grew one size larger, making him think of the Grinch and the little box exploding as his heart grew three sizes. "If we started dating… What would be your ideal first date?"

She kept moving, but he could see her chewing at her lip. "I don't know. What about you?"

He shrugged, picking up another box. "I guess I

would want to go horseback riding. It's something I always did as a kid. It always calmed me down when I was having a hard day."

"If someone didn't ride, would that be a deal breaker for you?"

He nodded. "It would be hard. It's a big part of my life. I grew up around horses, you know. They are like other members of the family to me. You know what I mean?"

Her shoulders fell and she turned her back to him. She stopped moving and he could see her shoulders start to quiver. Reaching over, he touched her shoulder and turned her around. A tear slipped down her cheek.

"Are you okay? Did you hurt something when you fell?" he asked, trying to make sense of her spontaneous crying.

"I... I don't ride anymore. I can't." She wiped the tear from her face, the motion so hard that it left a red mark behind. "We...can't... There are so many reasons."

The last thing he had wanted to do was upset her. The hope in him receded. He couldn't fix her. He couldn't make her feel something that she didn't want, or wasn't ready, to feel.

"You don't need to worry about that," he said, but the disappointment rattled through him. "Did you ever ride?"

He scooped the popcorn into a pile and left it beside the stack of ornaments. He was so attracted to her, and all of her perfect imperfections, but she had rejected him.

He had been stupid to hope for anything more than being her friend. He gave a resigned sigh. He needed to be happy with that, and he would just have to keep reminding himself that it was better to have her as that than nothing at all. At least this way, he could keep her in his life.

She picked up the last ornament. "I used to have the best horse. He was from the Secretariat bloodline. He was worth so much money and I had plans to start using him to stud. His papered name was Runs Like the Wind, but I just called him Rudy."

"What happened?" As soon as he asked, he chastised himself for asking her something so personal. When would he learn that she would balk if he pressed too hard?

Sucking in a long breath, she slowly made her way over to his cart.

The look in her eyes reminded him of a skittish horse—one that had been hurt in the past so badly that it would take a long time for it to be able to trust again. "You don't have to tell me if you don't want to," he continued, trying to make her feel at ease.

"He was… He died in the fire."

"The fire your ex set?"

She glanced around the store, but he couldn't tell if she was looking for her ex or an exit. "He… I tried to save him."

She pushed the cart toward the checkout stand and they stood in silence as the cashier rang them up. He wanted to talk to her to ask which *he* she meant—her ex or the horse—but as they pushed the cart through the parking lot, it clanged and jingled so loudly on the asphalt that he would have had to yell to be heard over the sound.

He slid the board into the back of the truck and looked back at Whitney as he pushed the cart to the front of the store. There was something she wasn't telling him. Something she feared, or was it something that she feared admitting to?

She was texting something on her phone as he got back into his truck. Before he could see what she was doing, she stuffed the phone into her pocket and out of his sight.

He got into the truck, sliding into the seat next to her. He started to open his mouth to speak, but thought better of it. If she wanted to talk, she could do so on her own time.

He knew better than most that some secrets were better left alone.

Chapter Nine

Whitney couldn't decide what she was more embarrassed about—falling all over the Christmas display, or falling all over her words and opening up to the one man she wanted to share her secrets with, but knew she couldn't. If she told him everything, he would be just as much in danger as she was. She couldn't protect everyone in her world; she couldn't even protect herself. And if Frank found her… This time she doubted that she would make it out of his grasp alive. She had only been lucky last time.

Her phone buzzed in her hand as her mother texted her. It was another one of her invitations to come home for Christmas, but they both knew that it wasn't an option. She kept asking where Whitney was and asking if she was safe, but the conversation only frustrated Whitney more. She couldn't tell her mother anything, and the loneliness and secrets were starting to get to her. She'd never been one to keep everything hidden, so she hated living this kind of life.

Colter was humming with the radio as he drove and she longed to reach over and take his hand back in hers again. It felt good to be touched again, and he clearly liked her. Yet she thought of the thousands of articles that she'd read in magazines and on the internet that talked about starting a relationship and dealing with stalkers. If Colter posted a picture of her online or said anything on Facebook, Twitter or any social-media site—it would only be a matter of time before Frank would track her down. She would have to run again.

She was so tired of running. So tired of hiding and the constant fear that came with it. And if she wasn't done running, no matter how badly she wanted a man like Colter in her life, she had to do what was best for both of them. And this time—it was just to let things go. He could find a woman who didn't have such a ridiculous amount of drama in her life. He could have a woman who wanted to get on a horse again. Or he could have a woman who was ready to simply start living again, who wasn't afraid of having her picture taken out of fear that the ghosts of her past would come back to haunt her. He could have a woman who was *safe*.

They parked in front of Pretties and Pastries, Sarah Rizzo's little café. Ever since her little accident at the hardware store, Whitney had nearly forgotten their other errand. Her stomach balled with nerves as she looked up at the pink-striped awning that sat over the front window of the café. The glass had a painting of Santa's workshop, complete with three little elves as they worked on parts of a train.

Everything about the caterer was too perfect for words. She owned a business. She could cook. Her hair was the perfect shade of blond. And unlike Whitney, she didn't have two little love handles around her waist when she sat down. Moreover, she didn't have drama.

Whitney swallowed back her insecurities, or at least

she tried to, but they crept up from the depths of her belly like tiny mites climbing up the leaves of a rose.

Sarah was the woman Colter should have been with. He had sworn that he didn't feel anything for the woman, and that she wasn't the one for him, but on paper even Whitney could see all the reasons he was wrong. Sarah had everything that a man like him, a man who was stable, could want.

"Do you want to wait in the truck?" Colter asked, motioning toward the oh-so-cute shop.

What she wanted was to be back in the confines of her office, safe and secure and not overwhelmed by the confusing mess of emotions she was feeling, but since that wasn't an option and she was forced to face reality… Well, she had to make the best of it. That started with her facing the fact that there were other women in the world who wanted to be with Colter. As his friend, she couldn't be jealous or possessive of him. She needed to point him in the right direction, even if that meant pointing him toward Sarah Rizzo.

He needed to realize that maybe the pretty chef really was the best fit for him, but he would never do that if he thought there was something between Whitney and him.

In the fight between her head and her heart, she needed to let her head win this one—even if it went against everything that she felt and wanted to continue to feel.

"No, I'll go in with you. I should pop in and say hello to her at the very least," she said, forcing herself to smile.

He frowned as he looked over at her, but no matter how long he looked, she was sure that he would never start to understand exactly what she was thinking. Men were smart, but they were never going to understand women.

"Okay." He drew the word out as if it had more than two syllables. "We don't have to stay long." He grabbed the note his mother had sent for Sarah. Next to it on the dashboard was a red envelope, and as his finger brushed against it, he jerked back as though it had seared his skin.

For a second, she thought about staying behind and looking at whatever it was that had made him recoil from the letter, but she shook off the thought. Just like her, he was allowed to have aspects of his life that she knew nothing about.

He helped her out of the truck, their hands brushing against each other, but he didn't move to take her hand. She appreciated him not moving closer. It would make what she had to do that much easier if she didn't feel the heat of his skin against hers.

The door of the café opened with a jingle, and he stood holding it open for her to walk in. She took a long breath and stepped inside. The place smelled wonderful, like fresh bread and butter. It was warm and there were antique teapots and cups on shelves throughout the room. The place made her imagine a little English tea shop. It even had a kind of matronly air that was in direct contrast to the slim blonde who made her way out of the kitchen.

Sarah was wiping her hands on her apron. When she saw Colter she beamed, but as her gaze moved to Whitney, some of the brilliance in her smile faded. It was okay—Whitney could understand her disappointment. She had felt the same way when she saw Sarah with her arms wrapped around the man—it was a competition to her, a competition that no doubt she thought she was losing.

"Heya, guys," Sarah said. "How can I help you?"

Colter smiled. "My mother said she's been trying to reach you all day but couldn't get ahold of you. So she sent us here with a note about the menu." He handed her the piece of paper.

Sarah opened it, mouthing the words as she read. "Tell her that this shouldn't be a problem. I hadn't started to wrap the shrimp yet. I can make the change." She stuffed the note in her pocket. "Do you guys want to come in and take a peek at everything?"

"No, we better get—" Colter started, but Whitney cut him off.

"Actually, that would be great," Whitney said, trying to sound far more excited than she was feeling.

"Okay." Sarah looked surprised and glanced over at Colter like she was trying to make sense of what was happening by reading his face.

She turned away and led them to the kitchen. Inside the doors there was a team of three young women. One was rolling dough, and the other two were making what looked like some kind of chocolate confections in the shape of horseshoes and Christmas trees.

"I was hoping to get as much done ahead of time as possible. That way I only have the final touches to do and put things in the ovens before heading out to the ranch." Sarah waved around the kitchen. There was a small table in the back. "Why don't you guys sit down?" She pointed toward the table.

Colter motioned for Whitney to lead the way, but

from the way his body stiffened, she could tell he was deeply uncomfortable.

If he was that upset with her and Sarah being civil toward each other, and in the same room, then he had to feel more toward the woman than he was admitting to. The thought made a new tendril of jealousy grow through her. Even though Whitney had told herself this was what she had wanted, standing here in Sarah's den, it was harder than she had imagined. It almost felt like she was the other woman, infringing on Sarah's territory.

Maybe Colter had been right and she should never have come in, yet there was no turning back now. She had to simply be strong and face her fears, even if it meant watching Colter being attracted to another woman.

Whitney sat down in the chair at the table with as much grace as she could muster.

"Let me grab us some plates," Sarah said. As she rushed around the kitchen, the other women looked over at her like she had lost her mind. "Oh, by the way, these are my cousins," she said, almost as if she had completely forgotten they were there until now.

"Nice to meet you," Whitney said, forcing herself to sound much happier than she was feeling.

Colter dipped his head in acknowledgment.

The cousins working on the chocolate whispered something to each other and they both started laughing as they glanced over toward her. Uncomfortable, she ran her hands over her hair, even though she was sure that what they were laughing at had nothing to do with what she looked like, but more to do with the man and the situation that she was in.

Sarah grabbed three plates and went to the stove and spooned meatballs out from the pot while Colter took a seat at the table. Opening the stove, she took out three twice-baked potatoes and plated them. She laid them on the table in front of them like they were in her home instead of in her shop and she was playing a welcoming host.

"I'm making these for the party. What do you think?" Sarah asked, clenching her hands together in front of her nervously.

Whitney followed Colter in taking a bite. She bit into the warm meatball, and its salty juices filled her mouth. It was delicious, and she popped another into her mouth. Sarah was a lot of things, and a good cook was at the top of the list. If the situation was different, Whitney would have loved to have her as a friend, a friend who could teach her the art of cooking.

"These are great," Colter said, motioning toward his missing bite of potato.

"Well done, Sarah. I'm totally impressed," Whitney said, wiping her mouth on a napkin.

"That's kind of you, Whit." Sarah lit up. "I feel like we got off on the wrong foot. I'm glad to see that I was wrong."

Whitney wasn't about to correct her and admit that whatever tension the woman had felt was real. This was her chance to fix things and be the bigger person, and who knew—maybe they really could end up becoming friends. Heaven knew she was a few short of a full quiver when it came to friends lately. And sometimes the unexpected friends were the ones who came to matter the most.

"Mom is going to love these," Colter said, filling

the tense silence between her and Sarah as she tried to come up with the right thing to say.

Sarah nodded. "I hope so. I'd love to keep catering your family's events."

"I can't think of a reason that wouldn't happen," Colter said, but he glanced over at Whitney like he was trying not to step on her toes.

"Do you all have big plans for your guests, Whitney?" Sarah asked. "I've heard good things about you from the people staying at the ranch."

"Well, bless your heart, Sarah. That's sweet of you to say," Whitney said with her best smile. "In the morning, we're gonna be taking the high-cotton guests out for a sleigh ride."

"High-cotton guests?" Sarah raised an eyebrow. "I've never heard that one before."

"You know… The ones who're living high on the hog."

"Oh, I get it," Sarah said, as she flipped back her hair. She took a bite of the meatball and swallowed it down. "Colter, I heard that there may even be a wedding or two coming up soon?"

Colter shifted in his chair and glanced toward her, before nodding. "Waylon and Wyatt are lucky men."

Whitney prayed that the woman wouldn't push the wedding talk any further. It made her want to sink into her chair, even though she didn't quite know why.

"Do you know when they are thinking about tying the knots?"

Colter shrugged. "There was some talk that they would do it over Christmas. You know, when all the family is home."

"Is Rainier getting out soon?" Sarah asked.

"Who's Rainier?" Whitney asked, feeling as though she was an outsider in their conversation.

Sarah laughed, but checked it just as quickly.

"Rainier is my youngest brother," Colter said, with a look of disbelief. "I thought everyone knew about him. My family always has a bit of drama, it seems."

"Especially lately, but I hardly think any of it is you guys' faults," Sarah added.

"Thanks," Colter said. "But I'm sure there are people in town who think otherwise."

"Well, I know just as well as you do that no one should be judged by the actions of their relatives," Sarah said, laughing as she motioned toward her cousins, who were obviously listening to the conversation but still pouring chocolate and working with the foods.

"Hey, now…" the woman closest to Sarah said with a laugh. "You ain't no saint, either."

Sarah nodded, looking over at Colter. "You're right… There are things that I am not proud of. But I'm sure we could all say the same, couldn't we?"

The statement made Whitney wonder exactly what they were talking about when it came to the perfect Sarah. Was there a side of her that she didn't know anything about? Were there as many skeletons in this woman's closet as there were in her own?

She doubted it.

Colter stood up, putting his napkin beside his empty plate. "I'll let my mother know about everything. And hey, thanks for the snack." His face was filled with an edge of panic at the reference to Sarah's past.

There had to have been more between him and Sarah than what he had told her. Whitney stood up, and picking up their dishes, she took them to the industrial sinks.

"Yes, thank you," she said, relieved that the time had come for them to leave.

Sarah walked them to the front door as a couple made their way in. "If you guys need any other changes, it might be tough, but I'll try my best to make them happen. In the meantime, stay safe."

There was something ominous about the way the woman spoke, but Whitney tried to ignore the way it made the hair on her arms rise. She was seeing something that wasn't visible on the surface when it came to Sarah.

"Oh, and hey, Colter," Sarah called after them. "Don't forget to save me a dance!"

The door closed behind them. Whitney tried to stop from grinding her teeth at the woman's invitation. Now she had to be doing it to rub her friendship with Colter in her face. The woman should have known better—she had already won; she didn't need to keep coming after him.

"I'm sorry about that. You know you didn't have to come in with me," Colter said, the words rushing from him.

She smiled. "That was fine. Sarah is nice."

"You think so?" he asked, watching her as if trying to gauge her reaction.

She couldn't give away anything that would make him see the jealousy and insecurity she was feeling. When it came to this, she had to stick to her guns—and what she knew was right, regardless of what she wanted. And the only thing that was right was for Colter to be with a woman who would fit in his life, not a woman he would have to help conceal from the hands of a madman.

Chapter Ten

Why did Sarah have to make everything awkward for him? After what felt like months of trying, Whitney was starting to open up and really talk to him, and then he found himself in the middle of some weird game he didn't understand. Whitney was staring out the window as they made their way toward the ranch.

The last place he wanted to be was back at the ranch. No doubt as soon as they hit the parking lot, Whitney would disappear and any progress they had made today would disappear right along with her.

"Do you want to go get some dinner or something before we get back?" He motioned toward the clock on the dashboard. "By now they've all eaten dinner. We're going to be on our own."

Whitney looked at him with a soft, placating smile on her lips. "We just ate at Sarah's."

"Right," he said, chastising himself for such a stupid idea. "But that wasn't a lot of food. You have to still be hungry."

She gave a resigned shrug, and the motion was so full of sadness that it made a pit open up inside him.

"There really isn't anything between Sarah and me, I promise," he said, trying to bring back the girl he had seen not an hour before—the bright, vibrant version of her that he loved so much.

"There should be something going on between you two—you're perfect for each other. You both have your lives together. My life…" Whitney threw her hands up in the air. "There's nothing about me that you should be attracted to. I have nothing to offer you. Nothing like Sarah does. She's smart, funny, ambitious, and she clearly is into you."

"Don't compare yourself to her. You are nothing like her," he argued.

"That's exactly my point, Colter."

"I meant that as a compliment. I mean that you're your own person. I don't know exactly what happened… you know, in Kentucky, but from what you told me, you are already stronger in my eyes than most women."

"How is running away strong?"

Was that what she had done—run away from home, from the man who'd tried to kill her?

"Is the guy still on the loose—your ex?"

Whitney looked over at him and he could tell by the set of her jaw that she was trying to decide whether or not she should tell him what she was really thinking.

"He got off with a slap on the wrist and credit for time served. In the end, even though he had burned down my family's barn and killed three prize horses, and nearly me—which is what he was after—he ended up only serving three months. You can read all about it on the internet. The jury decided that it wasn't premeditated—it was just some accident."

"But it wasn't?"

She shook her head and tears filled her eyes, but she wouldn't allow them to fall. "He wanted to kill me. He

told me that he was going to. He locked the doors…"
She took a deep breath. "I can still smell the smoke."

He knew the smell, that deep tarry scent of the world
around him erupting into flames. He had dreams sometimes in which he was standing in the middle of a burning house without an exit—forced to face the flames
and knowing that he would die. Yet he always woke up
from the terror of his dreams. It was another thing to
be standing there, in the middle of the flames, with nowhere to go and nowhere to hide.

"I knew that if I got out of the barn…he would be
there waiting for me. Yet I had to try. I broke through
the side of the wall near where the fire had started."
She pulled back her sleeves. There, on the backs of her
arms, were the telltale marks of third-degree burns. "I
covered my face, but a piece of siding fell on me when
I was running."

"Holy…" He reached over and ran his finger down
the rough edges of her scar. She jerked at his gentle
touch but didn't pull her arms away. "I'm so sorry,
Whitney. I had no idea how bad…" He stared at the
puckered pink scars on her arm.

"When I got back up, I could hear the sounds of
Rudy in the barn. He was so scared. I ran to go back
inside, but just as I got to the barn another piece fell—
it knocked me out. And I… I let the thing I cared most
about in the world die." Her voice was thick with her
checked tears, and though they brimmed in her eyes,
she wouldn't let them come.

"That fire. Rudy. None of it was your fault," he said,
pulling the truck over to the side of the road so he could
just talk to her. "Even if you could have gotten to your
horse, the chances are that you would have been killed

trying to get him out. You never go back into a burning building."

"But that's exactly what you do. Why is it so different for me to try and save something I loved?"

He moved closer to her and pulled her into his arms. She didn't resist; instead she put her head on his chest and let him hold her.

"Baby, what I do and what you did are two different things. I have gear. I'm trained to know how to read a fire's behavior. I know when and how it's safest to go about these things. And if the firefighters made it to your barn and didn't go in for the horses…then you have to know that you shouldn't have gone back in, either."

Her breathing was deep and he relished the feeling of her body against him. "I should never have left without him in the first place. I opened his stall, and the other horses', but he wouldn't come to me, and I went to open the barn door and found it locked. If I had just grabbed him and made him come with me… But I was… I was so scared. All I could do was just stare at the door, praying that it would fly open and we could all be free."

He didn't know what to say that could make her feel better. He couldn't imagine all the things she was feeling right now, but it was no wonder she had gone just about as far away from Kentucky as she could get.

"And Frank…" she continued. "I had a restraining order filed against him, but just one week out of jail he came back and came after me. Paperwork doesn't stop hate. In fact, I think it only made it worse."

"Did he threaten you? What happened?" He tried to stop the anger from filling his voice with hatred, but even he could hear its hard edge.

She pushed her hair behind her ear and didn't say

anything. Instead she pressed her head harder against his chest. "I can hear your heartbeat," she said.

"Answer me. Do you think he is going to keep coming after you? Do you think he could know that you're here, in Montana?"

She nibbled her lip. "I haven't told anyone where I am, but you know as well as I do that if someone is desperate enough—they will find you. I just want to stay hidden as long as possible. Maybe he'll come to his senses and fall in love with someone else. Maybe he will realize that what he did is wrong."

"People like him don't change. He won't stop. Sure, he may leave you alone, but you know he's just going to refocus his attentions to someone else."

"Or something else—like Dunrovin," she whispered.

"Do you think he's the one behind the floor—the bomb?" he asked, anger filling him with a fire of his own.

She shook her head. "If he wanted to come after me, he isn't coy. He drinks. That's what always starts it. He gets drunk and thinks he can take on the world. The next day, when he sobers up and realizes what he did, he comes around and apologizes. Then he feels bad and gets drunk again. It's a vicious cycle."

He ran his hand over his face as he thought about Frank coming after his family. He reached up and grabbed the red envelope off the dashboard. No one at the ranch, besides Whitney, knew the man. He flipped it over and, reaching around her, pulled the picture out. "Do you think he would have done something like this?"

She took the picture and stared at the faces before flipping it over. "'Mess with my family. I'll mess with yours,'" she said, reading the note on the back aloud. Her face looked paler in the thin moonlight that streamed through the front window of the truck.

Sitting up, she slipped the card back into the envelope and gingerly laid it back on the dashboard. After a moment she turned to face him. "I... I don't think he would do something like that. He wouldn't come after all of you—only me." She ran her hands over the knees of her jeans. "He never went after my parents. He is terrifying, but I don't think he wants to kill everyone who's ever been around me. I mean..." She motioned to the space between them. "You and I... We haven't even kissed. He couldn't know—"

So she was finally admitting that she felt it, too—the spark that always seemed to fill the air when they were near each other. He was glad he wasn't alone.

"That you're attracted to me?" he asked, with a teasing lilt to his voice.

She smiled. "I've said this a few times over the last few days, Colter Fitzgerald, but please let me remind you again—you are not God's gift to women. No matter what you think."

His laughter rang through the cab of the truck, and with its arrival some of the tension seemed to disappear and he was able to relax again.

"You say that, but your smile says something else," he joked.

She stuck out her tongue at him.

"My mother always used to tell me that if you stuck your tongue out, a bird would come along and poop on it," he said with a laugh.

"That's ridiculous. Plus, it's the middle of winter, at night, in a truck, and we're in the dark."

He lifted his hands in surrender. "Hey, it's just something my mom always said."

She laughed. "My mother always told me not to go to bed on an empty stomach," she said with a lift of her brow. "If you're still up for it, we could go somewhere… Get ice cream or something."

"Ice cream. In the middle of December?"

She shrugged. "We all have our vices—mine just happens to be ice cream and chocolate. Preferably, I like to have them together, but concessions can be made."

He laughed. "I always like a woman who knows her own mind but is willing to compromise when push comes to shove."

"Oh, and you know I would shove someone to get to Rocky Road."

It felt good just to laugh.

He turned the truck around and headed the couple of miles back to town. It had started to snow again, the tiny glittering flakes reminding him of a snow globe and how, even though his world had been shaken, it could still be beautiful in all its swirling chaos.

The town's other café, the Dew Drop, was closed, and the only Open signs on as they drove through town were in the steamy window of the bar and at the gas station just down the street.

"Do you ever feel like it's just not your day?" he asked with a laugh.

"What does that say, since you are hanging out with me?" She gave him a playful little shove.

"Trust me when I say that you are the best part of my day," he said, reaching over and resting his hand on the seat between them, waiting for her to slip her hand in his. "To tell you the truth, I didn't have to come to the ranch today. I knew my parents could handle whatever was thrown their way."

"So why did you come?" she asked, her voice playful and soft. She tiptoed her fingers across the seat to him and rested just the tips of her fingers in his open hand.

"Do I need to say it out loud?"

She smiled. "Well, I'd hate to assume something that I might have all wrong."

"What is it that you're assuming?"

She ran her fingers over the line of his palm as he pulled the truck into the gas station and parked. "I wasn't assuming anything," she said, her face catching the reds and blues of the neon lights that adorned the twenty-four-hour convenience store. "I guess I was just hoping that you had come to see me. I know it's a long drive from your house. And I'm sure you have better things to do."

He unclasped his seat belt, and leaning over their hands, he reached up and cupped her face. "When it comes to you, no distance is too much. I would travel across the world to be near you."

She leaned into his hands and closed her eyes. Her cheek was cool in his palm, and her skin was as soft as silk as he ran his thumb over the roundness of her cheek. He stared at her with her eyes closed, taking in the way her breathing slowed as she touched him, and the gentle curve of the tip of her nose. She was so beautiful. She had been the woman who had always come to him in his dreams, and he'd never known it until now.

He wanted to kiss her, but he simply watched her breathe, living in this moment as long as he could. As she gently opened her eyes and batted her eyelashes, she gave him a tiny smile.

"I don't know why, or how you feel the way you do… but I'm the luckiest girl in the world." She bridged the gap between them on the seat and climbed onto his lap.

He was taken aback by her as she straddled her legs around him. Leaning in, she took his face in her hands and looked him in the eye. "Whatever happens tonight, we're going to stay just friends. Okay?"

That was the last thing he wanted, but he knew if he didn't agree she would move away. He couldn't make that sacrifice. He had waited so long to have her like this…this willing and open.

"You agree?" she pressed.

He opened his mouth to say something teasing and noncommittal, but he couldn't find any words, so he finally just nodded.

She moved over him, rocking her hips. "No talk of relationships…and definitely not love. Love only makes things that much harder."

As the last word rolled off her lips, she leaned in and brushed her lips against his, making his body stir with the warmth of her breath and the unmasked lust of her words. He reached up and took hold of her hips, drawing her down onto him to let her feel what she was doing to him. If she wanted things harder, she needn't look any further.

She sucked in a breath, making the warmth of her kiss on his lips disappear. The loss was unacceptable and he took her mouth with his, flicking his tongue against her lower lip. He wanted to taste her…all of her. Yet she was in the driver's seat.

He chuckled at the thought.

She leaned back. "What?" she said, eyeing him with suspicion.

"Nothing," he said, his voice hoarse with want. "I just was thinking that maybe we shouldn't be doing this in front of the convenience store. You know, they have cameras." He pointed toward the tan camera that was pointed directly toward them. "In fact, I bet there's someone inside watching us right now."

She gave him an impish smile. "You want to give them a real show?"

Just when he thought he couldn't get any harder, she reached up and slowly unzipped her jacket.

"What do you think, Colter?" She let the coat slip from her shoulders, revealing her white sweater underneath. As she said his name, it was almost like it was coated with honey, sticky and sweet and full of the lifeblood of summer—a promise of life in the dead of winter.

"Anything you want, Whit… I'm yours," he said, reaching up and pushing a wayward piece of hair behind her ear.

He doubted the camera was in use anyway. In a place like this, half the time the cameras were only for show. And in this moment, it was a risk he was willing to take.

Whitney slipped the coat from her and threw it onto the seat next to him. She turned and adjusted the volume on the radio and found a country station. "Tennessee Whiskey" was playing and her body moved with each heady beat. He'd always loved that song, but now…now it would be unforgettable.

She put her mouth against his earlobe and sucked as she reached down and unbuttoned his pants. Her hand was cool as she slipped it inside his jeans, and he gasped when she ran her fingers down his length. He tried to throw his head back with ecstasy, but her teeth grazed the skin of his earlobe, reminding him of who was really in control. Not that he needed a reminder. She could have as much control as she wanted…and he'd love every second of it.

He reached up under her sweater and felt the rough edges of lace as he skimmed over her bra. It made him ache for her even more. She stopped stroking him and pulled her sweater up and over her head and dropped it on top of her coat.

Seeing was even better than feeling. The lace was pink and it made him wonder if it was the same shade as her nipples. She shifted on him, and he moaned as his body shook with life. He ran his hands over her soft cream skin, taking in the lines of her waist and running his fingers under the waistline of her jeans. He slipped the button open.

Flipping back the edges of her pants, he found that the underwear matched. Either she was meticulous and the kind that planned out her outfit down to every little detail, or she had planned ahead. He liked the thought of her thinking about them like this, skating over the fine line between friends and into the realm of lovers.

He ran his hands up her sides. She was covered in goose bumps, but he wasn't sure if it was the chill of the winter that managed to penetrate the cab of the truck, or his touch, so he reached over and turned up the heat. To him, it already felt like a sauna, but he was sure that it had nothing to do with the temperature of the air around him, but rather everything to do with the heat of her touch.

He unclasped the hooks of her bra. She slowly let the straps drift down her arms, the pink lace bra teasing him as it trembled when she took the cups into her hands. Holding the bra in place, she slipped her arms out of the straps.

He longed to see her, to feel her naked body against him. To take her nipples into his mouth and taste her. He wanted it all, everything she had to offer.

He took her lips in his, letting her feel the need in his kiss and how badly he wanted this. Her. Now.

There was a rap on the driver's-side window.

"Oh, my God," Whitney said as she jumped off him, grabbed her sweater and pulled it over her head. "No. No. No."

Colter turned and wiped away the bit of condensation that had accumulated over the window. Standing beside the truck, in his full deputy uniform, was his brother Wyatt.

As he looked in, he smiled.

Behind him, sitting in an old beat-up blue Ford, was a man. His windows were frosted, but Colter could make out his greasy, long dark hair, bordering on black, and his weathered hands on the steering wheel. On the man's dashboard was a wooden bat.

Colter forced himself to look away from the man as he rolled down the window. The cold wind stole the warmth that his and Whitney's bodies had created. He cleared his throat and ran his hand over his hair, more out of instinct than the need to make sure everything was in place. "Yeah?" he asked, trying to sound far more innocent than he was feeling.

Wyatt leaned down and smiled at Whitney, who was slipping her jacket back on like nothing had happened. "You two having fun?" he asked, with a chuckle.

"We were until you showed up," Colter said, but he wasn't sure if he should admit anything or play dumb for Whitney's honor. He had never been the kind to kiss and tell, but he could hardly deny what they had been doing—and what more he had hoped for.

"I'm glad you were, but you do realize that you are being filmed." He pointed at the camera. "And even here, in Mystery, we have public indecency and exposure laws. And I was made to understand that the clerk, while he loves a good show, wasn't impressed."

"I doubt that," Colter said. "I'd bet my bottom dollar that the guy was just jealous."

"Be that as it may…" Wyatt said, smiling.

Colter raised his hands in surrender. "Won't happen again." As the words escaped him, he heard the mistaken finality, and as he glanced over at Whitney, she nodded. The smile she had been wearing disappeared, and with it, his hope for more.

Chapter Eleven

She could not have been more embarrassed. Her mother would have tanned her hide if she had found out what Whitney had just done and then given her a lecture on the merits of class and acting like a lady. Yet she was tired of being a lady all the time. She was tired of living within the strict confines that fear and heartbreak had placed around her—for once, she had stepped outside her comfort zone. Of course it had ended with her deeply shamed.

She felt more than stupid. If only she had gone with her original plan of just getting a little ice cream and she hadn't followed her heart instead.

Now she couldn't even look over at Colter without blushing. Though she was in her early twenties, it was like she was back in high school and heading home after a date. Yet this hadn't been and wasn't supposed to be a date…until she had pushed it there. If only she hadn't taken his hand, none of this would have happened.

There was no going back and undoing what had been done, and there was no getting past the fact that not just one, but two of the Fitzgerald brothers, a cashier and possibly an innocent bystander had seen her in her underwear.

She groaned as she ran her hands over her face, like the simple action could scrub her mind of the thoughts running through it. There had been a million reasons she shouldn't have acted the way she did, yet she hadn't listened to any of them.

It was like she was back in Kentucky, dating Frank and not listening to the little voice in her head that had always told her to run—and yet she had stayed, up until the fire. It was only when her life had been in danger that she had finally found the strength she needed in order for her to follow the direction that her heart had been leading her toward.

She glanced over at Colter. He was gripping the steering wheel with both hands, squinting as he tried to see through the whitewash of snow in the headlights.

It was odd that her heart had led her to this place, this moment in time, and straight to him.

No. She had to be logical. Emotions be damned. She couldn't fall into the trap of the feelings. Desire and lust were fickle beasts.

Yet as she stared at him, she couldn't deny the fact that there was no being fickle when it came to Colter. And the way he had touched her... It had felt so good. He was a real man. The kind who took what he wanted, when he wanted it—and didn't wait to ask for permission. On the other hand, he wasn't forceful or bullish; being with him was like dancing. Each of their movements had been a complement of the other's, as if every motion were choreographed and perfected.

She could only imagine what he would be like if they ever ended up in bed together. She blushed at the thought.

"It's okay, Whit," Colter said, but he didn't take his

eyes off the blinding snow as he drove. "Wyatt won't say anything."

She hadn't even thought of that. Wyatt seemed like a stand-up guy, but that didn't guarantee that the entire family and staff at Dunrovin wouldn't find out about their little escapade.

"Are you sure? And what if he saw something...?"

Colter smiled and shot her a naughty look, one that made her flush again—making her wonder if every time he looked at her she would have the same reaction. If she did, it would make work that much more challenging—which was the last thing she needed.

"We Fitz boys were raised to be gentlemen. If he did see something, which I doubt, no one will ever know it." He reached over and put his hand down between them again, but this time she vowed that she wouldn't take it, even though every part of her wanted to.

He wiggled his fingers, baiting her to take his hand, but she stood her ground and crossed her arms over her chest and forced herself to look out the window and into the night. There was something magical on nights like this, when the blizzard engulfed them, reflecting the snowflakes in their headlights like bits of confetti. Though the world might have been telling her to celebrate, she couldn't join in.

"Are you mad at me?" He took hold of the wheel, giving up on her.

She glanced over at him and shook her head. "Not with you."

"Then with who?" He tried to win her over with his trademark grin, and though she melted with it, she didn't return his smile. "You know," he continued, "that cashier was probably just upset that you were with me.

You are a beautiful woman. And if you think you're mad at him, trust me when I say that you can't be half as mad as me."

A giggle sneaked past her resolve. "I'm not mad at the cashier…no matter how jealous you think he is. Which, by the way, I think you are mistaken about."

"Then why are you upset?" he asked. "You aren't mad that you decided to kiss me, are you? I don't want you to regret that…ever."

"It's not you. It's just that I shouldn't have let things go there. It was a—"

Colter slammed on the brakes and she grabbed the dashboard to stop herself from slamming against it. The tires skidded on the icy road, twisting the truck in slow motion. He moved the steering wheel in a smooth circle the opposite direction of their slide, correcting the movement but sending the truck fishtailing in the other direction.

He threw his arm out, protectively holding her in place as he tried to control the truck.

Her stomach ached as they thudded to a stop against the snowbank the plows had left behind. This time of year they were so frozen that she wondered how much damage they'd done to the side of the truck.

"Are you okay?" he asked as he dropped his arm from her chest.

She nodded, but her body was numb thanks to the shock of the accident. "What about you?"

He ran his hands over his face, but nodded. "Did you see the horse?" he asked, motioning into the dark.

She hadn't been paying attention to anything except the swirling vortex of her thoughts.

"It ran out in front of us. I don't think I hit it, but we were close."

"What is a horse doing out in a snowstorm in the middle of the night?" she asked.

"I have no idea, but it looked like Clark."

"A ranch horse?" In the storm, she hadn't realized how close they were to the ranch. Though she had been driving up and down the roads leading to the place for months, in the darkness and snow she might well have been driving on the back side of the moon.

"Doesn't your mother check on the horses every night before she goes to bed?"

He nodded. "And she would have had them in the stables on a night like this. It's too cold."

"Are you sure it was one of ours? Your mother would never have left them out."

Colter's face pinched. "She wouldn't have, not unless something was very wrong."

He put the truck in gear and pressed on the gas, but the tires couldn't get the traction they needed to pull away from the snowbank and just spun in place. He tried to rock the truck back and forth, no doubt hoping it would afford him more traction, but the truck wouldn't budge.

He cussed under his breath, but she could tell he was trying not to show her that he was starting to panic. It snowed in Kentucky, some places averaging around two feet a year, so this was hardly the first time she had been stuck in a snowbank. Yet there was something about the night that suddenly felt ominous. Her thoughts moved to the bomb and the threatening note.

"You don't think someone did something to your

mother, do you?" she asked, the pain in her stomach intensifying and bile rising into the back of her throat.

The lines around his eyes tightened and he set his jaw, making her wish she hadn't said anything. He had to have been thinking the same thing without her saying it.

"I'm sure she's okay," she said, trying to rectify her mistake. "Maybe the horses just got out or something."

"I hope so," he said, reaching into the pocket of his jacket and pulling out his phone. He scrolled through the numbers until she saw his mother's cell phone number pop up and he hit Call. He left it on speakerphone, and it rang until it finally gave up and went to voice mail.

"Don't worry," she said, trying to ignore the burn in her throat as she lied. "I'm sure she's just sleeping. It's the middle of the night, that's all."

"My mother always sleeps with her phone right next to her—just in case of emergencies like this."

As each second ticked by, she had to admit he was right—this was becoming more and more of an emergency.

"We're going to have to try and push the truck out," Colter said. "You slide over here and steer while I go around front and see if we can get her moving." He jumped out as she slid over into his seat.

She watched for him to give her the signal and she gunned it, revving the engine. The tires whirred against the ice and snow, and she could feel the truck rock as Colter pressed his weight against it, but they didn't move.

He pressed again and again, but each time the tires just slipped on the ice and their right tire dug deeper and deeper into the snow on the side of the road. Finally, he came around and got back in. His cheeks were red and there was a layer of sweat on his forehead as he took off his hat.

"Dang it," he said, half-breathless. "I was hoping that would work."

"How far are we from the ranch?"

Colter peered out into the night as though he were searching for some lights in the distance, but everything was under the veil of snow. "I'm guessing that we can't be more than a half mile. I mean, the horses…if they were in the barn…they couldn't have gotten too far. Right?" He asked the question like he was trying to comfort himself instead of looking for an answer, but that didn't stop her.

"Right," she said, trying to sound hopeful, but her attempt came out tinny and fake even to her own ears. "And who knows? Maybe they just walked over the fence thanks to a drift or something. You Montana boys get a lot of snow."

He tried for a smile, but it was just as forced and out of place as her attempt to comfort. "Let's go see if we can find the horses and round them up. If so, maybe we can ride them back to the ranch. You can ride, can't you?"

She had been riding her entire life, until recently, yet there was no way she could get back up on a horse—no matter how cold it was outside or how far they were from the ranch. She had no doubt in her ability to hike back, but horses… She couldn't risk being around them again. Just like men, they broke her heart—and all she did was let them down.

"I can't, Colter," she said, shaking her head. "But

I can help you find them. Then you can ride back or something."

He looked at her like she had lost her mind. "It's not far, but that wind is cold and it's easy to get lost."

"But if we don't do something, who knows where the horses will be by morning? Is there any shelter out here, a wind block or something they can use to get out of the cold?"

Colter peered out into the night. "It's all pasture-land."

She nibbled at her lip. "As long as they aren't shivering, I think the horses will be fine. They should all have winter coats by now."

"Yeah, but my mother has been putting them in the barn every night. I don't know if they'd be up for this kind of cold. Plus, if we find them, we can get a ride home."

"First we have to catch them," she said, motioning outside to the flurrying snow.

He got out of his seat and reached behind the bench, grabbing a flashlight and handing it over to her. "Let's just stay together. The last thing we want is one of us getting lost in the dark. On a night like tonight, the cold has a way of sneaking up on you."

She took the flashlight from him and clicked it on as she stepped out of the warmth of the truck. "Don't they say that you should always stay with your car in cases like these—just to avoid hypothermia, Mr. Fireman?" she asked, only half teasing.

He chuckled. "In most cases, they would be right, but I think we have a couple of extenuating circumstances. Plus—don't forget—I'm a professional."

"Is that kind of like, *Hold my beer and watch this*?" she said with a laugh.

Colter nodded. "Exactly like that, except I have no intention of this ending in disaster."

She didn't want to mention the old adage that the road to hell was paved with the best of intentions. Besides, she'd already seen hell and it made this icy world look like a dream.

Chapter Twelve

They walked down the road, the world around them illuminated by the headlights behind them as Whitney called for the horse. The fresh layer of snow was littered with several sets of horses' tracks, making it look like there were at least five horses out.

"Clark couldn't have gotten far," Colter said. "And the others have to be close. They would stick together."

She nodded, sinking deeper into the warmth of her scarf as the cold night bit at her skin.

If there was more than one out, it didn't automatically mean foul play—horses always wanted to stay with their herd—but it was unlikely that one had just randomly gotten over or through a fence. Something else had to be at work, either a broken fence and an open barn, or someone had intentionally put them out. But why? Why would anyone let the horses loose?

By this time of night, everyone at the ranch had to be in bed and sleeping. If it hadn't been for them staying out late, no one would have known about the horses until the early morning feeding. Maybe, if someone was behind the horses being out, they had hoped the horses would go for a few miles and be harder to find.

But why would they do something that was mostly just a nuisance?

On the other hand, they had scheduled rides with the guests in the morning. It was possible someone would know about their plans and would want to make them look bad in the eyes of their elite guests, but it seemed far-fetched.

Or maybe it was all set up to be some kind of distraction.

The world grew darker as they moved farther and farther away from the truck and its headlights, which were becoming two pinpricks in the night. The air around them grew colder, and as they walked, their boots squeaked on the snow.

"Mom would never put the horses out on a night like tonight—at least not without a blanket," Colter said, concern in his voice.

She had worked at the ranch for only a few months, but Eloise had always made sure that the horses were pampered. Colter was right that she wouldn't have put them out, but Whitney didn't want to make him even more worried than he already seemed to be.

"I just can't make heads or tails of this," he continued. "I mean, why would anyone go after the ranch's horses?"

They had told Sarah about their morning plans. After they left, she would have had plenty of time to come out to the ranch and let out the horses without anyone seeing her. She had been somewhat catty, but it wouldn't have been in her self-interest to make a move against the ranch.

Then again, the move wasn't really against the ranch—maybe in Sarah's mind, this had been more of a move against Whitney. Maybe she was trying to make her look incompetent to the guests. She had to have known that she was the one who would have to deal with the clientele when things went haywire with their reservations and social events.

She thought back to the moment they had left the café—Sarah *had* seemed to threaten them. Maybe it hadn't been as idle as Whitney had assumed.

"Do you think Sarah—"

"Sarah what?" Colter asked, cutting her off.

The way he said her name made her back down. She had no proof, only a nagging feeling in her gut that she was missing something that was hiding in plain sight, something that tied all these mysterious events together.

"Do you know Sarah's family?" she asked, thinking about the ominous note.

"Not really. She and her family moved into town just a few years ago. One of her cousins married a Carter boy. I think they were from somewhere around Idaho."

He didn't have a relationship with her family, which seemingly put her out of the running—at least when it came to the note. Yet that didn't mean she still didn't have a hand in the horses being let out.

As they walked, the scent of wood smoke grew stronger. It carried the sweet smell of cottonwood and pine, and the smell reminded her of her winters in Kentucky. The aroma elicited thoughts of her family sitting around the Christmas tree, watching as the fire roared in the fireplace. Until now, she hadn't missed home.

She had loved waking up on Christmas morning to her mother's cooking. It had always been the same breakfast casserole—sausage, eggs, hash browns—all melded in the Crock-Pot overnight. And her mother's coffee… It had been so strong and dark that her father had made jokes about it having the power to melt the spoon.

Her mouth watered.

It was funny how one little smell could pull her back so far in time. Just like that, she was a child again, waiting impatiently for Santa to come and to make sure that she really had made it onto the good girls' list.

This year she was more unsure of her status on Santa's list than ever before. She had made so many mistakes. When she looked at herself and the woman she had been forced to become, it was almost as though she didn't even recognize herself. The things she had loved were merely memories now. Her home was no longer her home.

When Frank set that fire, he hadn't just made her lose the things she had loved—he had also made her lose herself. And that was just as impossible to bring back. She'd never be the same girl she had once been. She'd never be carefree again. She had seen the underbelly of humankind, the dark sickening world of those who, simply put, just weren't right in the head.

Almost as if he could read her mind, Colter slipped his gloved hand in hers. "You warm enough?"

She moved her fingers between his. Though she was wearing thick wool gloves, the tips of her fingers had started to go numb and she basked in the warmth of his touch. "I will be." She smiled. "I was just wishing that maybe we had gotten that ice cream."

He stopped. "I hope you don't regret anything. You know…"

She didn't regret getting into trouble with him, not entirely anyway. It had been a long time since she had felt that nibble in her belly and the need to be touched the way he had touched her. "Nothing like that," she said, squeezing his fingers. "I'm just hungry." As if on cue, her stomach growled.

"Are you saying you wish you would've gone for the ice cream instead?" he teased.

"Never, but I am starting to pretend that the snow is marshmallow fluff. Don't worry about me if I dive in headfirst here in a minute or two."

He laughed as they started to walk again. Her flashlight bobbed around, lighting the way in front of them, and occasionally she flashed it around in the darkness. As she moved it to the right, she caught the shining reflection of a large set of eyes.

"Clark, baby," she cooed, squeezing Colter's fingers and motioning toward the horse in the distance. "Do you have anything, a halter or a lead or something?"

Colter shook his head. "I'll just climb up. You can ride with me."

Just the mention of her riding made her blood pressure rise and her heartbeat begin to thunder in her ears. There was no way...no way she could get on the back of the horse. Yet she didn't want to let him down.

She stepped off the road, carefully picking through the deep drifts of snow as she worked her way slowly to the horse. A part of her wanted the horse to spook and for them not to be able to catch him, but if they didn't get him and he tore off into the night, they would lose track of him—or spend all night trudging around in the open fields in the freezing cold.

Clark threw his head and pawed at the snow as they neared him. He was shivering, and the whites of his eyes were visible as she grew nearer. He must have still been scared after his close run-in with the truck.

"Don't move too fast," Colter said, stepping beside her. "If he runs off, we're going to have a long walk back to the ranch."

If they didn't get their hands on the horse, the cold was going to make the midnight trek nearly unbearable. As it was, even though she had been prepared for the cold, her toes were starting to ache. She was tough, but there was no amount of toughness that could prepare someone for below-zero temps made colder by the harsh chill of the wind.

The wind… She turned around. Her tracks were already beginning to get filled in thanks to the drifting snow. If they didn't get to the horse and start back, their footprints would soon be nearly indistinguishable from the natural dips and valleys in the dark.

She hadn't been really scared about their safety… until now, with the full reality of the whipping snow blasting against her face. In an instant, this could become a fight for their life.

Maybe this was what someone had planned on all along—maybe they'd known full well that she and Colter would find the horses and be forced to go out into the night to wrangle them. And maybe they hoped that they would get lost and be found as ice cubes in a snowbank somewhere the next day.

She brushed off the thoughts. She was being absurd. No one could have expected anything. Horses were horses. They were always just a bit mischievous. No doubt Clark was probably the ringleader in the escape. Maybe they had been spooked by the storm. Maybe someone forgot to close the barn and they had simply walked over the fence.

Not everything bad that happened was meant to threaten them or the ranch. Sometimes bad things just happened. And nearly everyone who had ever owned a horse had had them break loose at least once. It was in their nature to want to be free.

She stuck her hand out, hoping to entice the horse to come to her. Clark took a few tentative steps, but threw his head again as he caught her scent.

"You try," she said to Colter, hoping that the horse would pick up his scent and it would make him feel safer.

This horse, this beautiful black gelding who looked so much like Rudy, wasn't her beloved boy. To this horse, she was nothing more than a stranger who wasn't to be trusted. Yet, if the horse was like her, he would have realized that it wasn't the ones whom you didn't know that did you the most harm.

Colter moved slowly toward the gelding, his head down. "Hey, handsome boy," he said, his voice comforting but strong. "How'd you get out, baby?"

The horse shivered, drawing in a long breath and huffing a greeting to him.

"Good boy," Colter said, coming close and lifting his hand.

Clark took a hesitant step toward Colter's hand and let him slip his fingers under his mane. Colter smiled as he stroked the horse. "That's a man," he said, walking around the horse's body. He leaned against the horse and, in one fluid motion, lifted himself up and onto Clark. The horse looked back, giving the man a side-eye and taking a step forward.

"Hey, now, Clark," Colter said, "I didn't tell you to get moving. We have to pick up our rider, man."

Clark stopped, shifting his weight.

"He's voicing his complaint," she said with a giggle.

"He isn't one who likes to be bossed around—not that I know anyone else who is like that or anything," he teased.

"Hey, I'm a fine employee. I have no idea where you got that idea," she joked.

"I wasn't saying anything about you as an employee. My mother loves you. I just happen to know that you aren't the kind that is ever going to let someone push you around against your will."

Her thoughts instantly went to Frank, and her heart sank. She had let him push her around, not physically, but emotionally, for too long. She had been all too acquiescing when it came to him and what he had wanted. Yet, since she had come here, she had changed. Maybe Colter was seeing her as she wanted the world to see her—strong, uncompromising and brave.

Was that who she had truly become or was it nothing more than a show?

If she ever had to face Frank or a man like him again…she doubted that she could keep up this strength or bravery. She would probably fall to her knees and beg for mercy. She could never go back to being the girl in the barn—the girl who had hoped to survive. In fact, she couldn't help wondering if in her survival she had already used up all her lucky stars. Next time, if there were ever a next time, she doubted that she would have the strength or good fortune to survive.

Colter stuck out his hand, motioning for her to take it so she could climb up behind him.

She took a step back. "I'll just walk. It'll be fine."

"It's going to be at least a mile. If you sit up here with me, you can snuggle close and I can keep you warm," he said, his playful grin taking over his face.

She knew it didn't make any sense, her fear of riding. And really, it wasn't the act of getting back on the horse that bothered her. It was just, for her, that the act of riding was a way of bonding with an animal—it was the smooth motion of her thighs against its back as they worked in tandem. It was a promise the rider made the moment she got on to take care and treat the horse with kindness and do nothing that was against the horse's best interest, and more than anything, it was just the feeling of being up there that she feared the most. If she got up, it would be like being on Rudy again.

It would bring up far too many memories…and even more disappointments.

If she got up on Clark, there was a good chance it would open her heart to things that it just wasn't ready for. It was just too risky.

Being with Colter had already made her more vulnerable than she had intended to be when she came here. Only time would tell if her opening up to him would be a mistake. She couldn't give any more of herself when she couldn't be sure that she hadn't made the wrong choice.

"Colter, I'm not ready."

He closed his hand and laid it on his thigh, nodding. "Okay. If that's the way you feel, I understand."

She wanted to think that he meant what he said, and he really understood the way she was feeling, but a part of her doubted it. He couldn't understand what it was like to experience what she had been through. He couldn't understand the way her chest constricted at the mere thought of riding again, and the way the scent of the fire would spring to the front of her mind when she had gone near horses. He couldn't understand the trauma. No one could—she herself barely did.

She turned away from Colter, afraid that he would be able to see the pain in her face if he looked at her. He needed to see her as emotionally strong and nothing else.

Colter rode up beside her and she walked next to the horse and rider until they made it back to the road and started heading east in the direction of the ranch. As they started down the road, there was the crunch and nicker of the other horses as they caught up. Looking behind them, she saw the line of four other horses nose-to-tail as they walked in the trail Clark and Colter had broken in the snow. She was moving at a slower pace than the horses, but Colter kept them in step with her.

The horses looked tired and the palomino was shivering as the wind whipped against her. They needed to get the horses back. Though they would likely have been okay in the cold, it made her cringe watching them combat the elements.

Pellets of snow pelted against her face as the snow started to fall harder with each footstep. Though she was dressed for the weather, her fingers had grown so cold that she couldn't feel her fingertips and she bumbled as she moved to wipe her nose, bumping her fingers against her cheek.

She could feel Colter's gaze as she moved, and even more, she could feel his concern. He pulled Clark to a stop and got down. He took off his scarf and wrapped it around Clark's neck, using it as a lead rope.

"You can ride. I'm doing fine," she said. She motioned toward the bit of Christmas lights that were glowing in the distance. "We're almost there."

He took her hand, and his warmth burned through her gloves like he was on fire. He frowned as he must have felt the chill. "No, you're not," he said, lifting her hand to blow on her fingers.

They ached as the heat of his breath moved over her nearly frozen skin, but it wasn't her hands that came alive with his touch and his kindness; rather, it was her heart.

Chapter Thirteen

Everything last night had gone wrong. Until they had gotten back to the ranch and found his mother and father warmly tucked in their bed. He hadn't bothered to wake them up when he found out that they were safe and sound.

He hadn't been that scared of losing his parents in a long time. That fear of what could possibly have happened to them had brought up so many memories of when he'd been young and his biological parents had left him alone. He'd always thought they were never coming back, that something bad had happened—until the last night he had spent with them, and his father had left him on the fire department's doorstep. As a child he had often wondered if all that worry had caused all the bad that had come of them—almost as though he had wished it upon his parents.

He had given up the thoughts of a boy. He had finally found some reprieve thanks to his new life and the realization that he wasn't in control of anyone else's destiny but his own. He hadn't caused his parents to leave him, he hadn't caused their addiction or neglect, and he couldn't cause his parents to be hurt just because he had secretly wanted them to disappear.

Yet, last night, that fear had returned—as though perhaps his curse had returned and because he had even voiced the possibility that his mother had been hurt. He had half expected to find her on the floor, and the illogical thought made goose bumps rise on his arms.

Colter shook his head as he went out to the barn and looked in on the horses. Two of the escapees were poking their heads over the doors of their stalls and they nickered as he grabbed a handful of pellets and made his way over to them.

"You rebel," he said, feeding the mare, Jingles, a pellet. As she nibbled at his hand, looking for another, he scratched her forehead. "At least one of us got a little sleep, I hope."

The horse stopped nibbling and looked up at him, and he could have sworn that she was laughing at him.

When they'd gotten back to the barn, they found the door open and the stalls unlocked. Though they had questioned everyone at the morning meeting, no one had come forward and admitted to any wrongdoing— not that he had expected anyone to, especially with his mother in the state she had been in.

There was only one other time he had ever seen her so mad, and it was the day that Rainier had been arrested.

The barn door opened behind him with the familiar sound of grinding metal.

A dark-haired man about sixty, his hair slightly too long and pulled back into a tight man bun, poked his head inside.

"Can I help you?" Colter asked, not recognizing the man as an employee but he had seen him somewhere before.

"I was just looking for Sarah. Is she around?" the man asked, his voice the throaty rasp of a smoker's.

"Sarah… Sarah Rizzo?" he asked. "The caterer?"

The man nodded. "She asked me to meet her here today about a job."

"Why would she want to meet you here?"

The man shrugged. "Look, buddy, I was just doing as I was told."

"What's your name?"

"If Sarah isn't in here…" The man ducked out of the door without bothering to answer Colter's question.

He rushed after the stranger. "Wait up!"

The man was halfway across the parking lot, on his way to the ranch office, before Colter caught back up with him. "Stop, man. What's your name?"

The man stopped and turned to face him. "The name's Daryl."

"Daryl what?" Colter pressed.

The man looked toward the office almost as though he wished he had walked a little bit faster so he wouldn't have had to answer any of his questions. "It's Daryl Bucket."

The name rang a bell. "Do I know you?" Colter stared at the man and the way his mouth puckered at his question, making the fine smoker's lines around his lips deepen.

Daryl shrugged. "Who am I to go on and say who you know and who ya don't?"

Was this the kind of guy who was really coming to Sarah in hopes of getting a job? What did he plan on doing—pissing people off?

"I don't think Sarah's here. I haven't seen her to—"

"In that case, I'll just go on into the office and wait for her." The guy motioned to Whitney's office.

The last thing Colter was going to do was leave this guy alone with her. Not on his life. "Why don't you just move along? I'll tell Sarah that you stopped by."

The guy smiled. There was something dangerous about the way his lip quivered over his stained yellow teeth. "I don't know who you think you are, man, but I need a job. I've been a trucker all my life and things dried up. It's the holidays. I got bills rolling in that need to be paid. I ain't gonna screw this chance up."

The dude could play at his heartstrings all he wanted, but with things like this, Colter always trusted his gut, and it was warning him that there was more to the guy than what he was telling him.

The door to the office opened up, and his father, Merle, and Whitney walked outside. As his father saw the man, his face lit up. "Daryl, is that you, old man?"

Daryl smiled, the motion losing its dangerous edges as he looked over at Colter's father.

"What are you doing here?" his father asked as he and Whitney made their way over to them.

"I was hoping to get a job with your party's caterer. She wanted to meet me here when I told her about you and I." The man looked over at Colter. "Your man here was giving me a hard time."

Colter's dad looked over at him and gave him a wink. "Oh, he can be a tough one when it comes to strangers. We tried to train it out of him, but, well…you can see how well that worked out."

Daryl gave him the side-eye.

"Mr. Fitz, this poor gentleman is going to think you're serious," Whitney said, coming to Colter's rescue.

He gave her a smile, but as he looked at her, he couldn't quite catch her gaze. He couldn't be sure if she was intentionally avoiding his eye or not, but he hoped for the latter. They had moved quickly last night, but he didn't want her to regret it. For him, their time together was something special, and something he wanted to repeat, but if he had another chance he'd love to see it to completion.

"Just joshing you, Daryl," Merle said, slapping the man on the shoulder. "This is my son Colter—the fireman."

Daryl's eyes widened with surprise and he stared at him, not speaking for a minute.

"Nice to meet you, officially," Colter said, attempting to mend the broken fences between them for his father's benefit.

"Yeah, likewise," Daryl said, but he looked Colter up and down like he was trying to figure him out.

"Daryl used to work at the ranch when we were first starting up. It's been a long time. Hasn't it?" Merle asked.

Daryl nodded but didn't really say anything, nor did he look too happy.

"Daryl did a great job teaching me how to use the heavy equipment and getting the ranch up and running."

"I always had a connection to this place," Daryl said.

"As you can see," Merle said, motioning to the world around them, "we made things work. Couldn't have done it without you."

Colter's father might have liked the guy, but that didn't mean he had to.

Thankfully, Sarah drove up in her black this-year's-model Chevy truck and got out. She waved as she walked over. Everyone stared at her, the seconds ticking by as slow as cold oil dripping out of its jug. He tried to ignore the dread that crept through him with each of her nearing steps.

"Heard you all had a little bit of a rodeo when you all got home last night," Sarah said with a laugh.

"Nothing we couldn't handle." Whitney's face pinched, but she forced a smile. "How'd you hear about it all so fast?"

Sarah waved her off. "Oh, you know nothing that exciting can go too long without hitting the phone tree. Your mom had business this morning with Ms. Babinski, who called her sister, who called Mrs. Long, who called me."

It was a wonder anything ever stayed private in their little town with an information dissemination system as active and on-it as the women of Mystery.

"What happened last night?" Daryl asked, making Colter feel at least a little bit better in the knowledge that not everyone in the town knew every one of their movements.

"They near ran into one of our horses who, along with his comrades, managed to escape. Got run off the road," Merle said. "They're damn lucky that they made it home before they froze their buns off. Weatherman said with the wind chill it was nearly forty below last night."

"Were the horses okay?" Daryl asked, looking toward the barn.

For the first time since he'd met the guy, Colter actually found something to like about him.

"Yeah, they are all fine. Luckily, they had pretty

good coats going, but they were all a little out of sorts this morning, so we gave them a little extra hay."

Daryl nodded his approval.

"What are you doing here, Sarah?" Whitney asked.

Colter was sure that she hadn't intended to sound suspicious, but her tone was less than cordial. After their taste testing at the shop, he had thought things between the two women had started to get better, but on their walk back, Whitney had asked about the woman's family—making him wonder if she suspected that Sarah was in some way involved in the horses' escape.

He looked over at her and Sarah sent him her best dazzling smile and a lift of the brow as though she had heard the implication in Whitney's tone, as well. Sarah was conventionally pretty, skinny and blonde, what most guys would call stacked thanks to her ample upper assets, but she wasn't his type. However, no matter how much he tried to convince Whitney, the more she seemed to dig her heels in when it came to believing him. He could hardly wait for Yule Night to be over so he wouldn't keep running into the woman, but without the coming festivities it also meant he had less of a reason to keep popping in at the ranch—and seeing Whitney.

"I have a few interviews this morning," Sarah said, her tone almost questioning. "I just thought your boss, Mrs. Fitzgerald, would want to weigh in on my selection." She turned to the man standing next to Merle. "I assume you are Daryl?" She stuck out her hand and Daryl gave it a tight and swift shake. "Why don't we head to Mrs. Fitz's office? I know she's going to be waiting for us."

Merle glanced down at his watch. "If you don't mind,

Colter, I'm going to talk with Daryl. I'll take a hand to go and get your truck in a bit."

Whitney looked as though she was literally biting her tongue as Sarah, Merle and Daryl made their way toward the house.

"Sarah, wait!" Whitney called after her. She gave Colter an apologetic tip of the head, but turned and walked toward the woman.

Sarah stopped, motioning for the men to go ahead. "Can I help you?" She put her hand on her hip as she turned to face them.

Colter followed Whitney, and the dread he had been feeling intensified. Whatever Whitney was planning on doing with Sarah, it wasn't going to play out well. He could feel it in his toes. There was just too much tension between the two women for any progress to be made. He wished he could just make them both stop. There was enough going on at the ranch without him having to stand between the two women.

Whitney stopped just out of the woman's reach. "What did you do after we left your shop last night?"

"What? Why?" Sarah asked, looking to Colter as if asking him to help her decipher Whitney's sudden line of questioning.

In all truth, Whitney's suspicion had gotten him thinking, and after he kissed her good-night he'd gone back to his place and had tossed and turned all night as he tried to come up with a list of possible suspects. Sarah didn't seem to entirely fit the bill, but no one he had thought of really did, either.

He knew it was naive, but the only thought that had finally allowed him to get some sleep was the hope that all these little incidents would simply come to a stop.

Perhaps whoever had left him the threatening picture would come to realize that this wasn't a fight worth having.

"Colter, are you really going to let your little secretary treat me like this? I've been nothing but good to your family. I can't imagine what she is trying to get at," Sarah said, motioning toward Whitney.

He was pretty sure he could almost see the steam rising from Whitney as her face pinched into a tight scowl at the woman's questions. "Look, Sarah. You're right. You've been great to work with so far. We've just been running into a few *things* that are a bit strange and worrying. If you'd just tell her where you were last night after we left, then we'll be along. No big deal. We just want to make sure that we cross all the innocent people off our list."

"How big is your list?" Sarah asked. "Only me?"

He scuffed his boot against the grit they had put down on top of the ice in the parking lot. "Where were you, Sarah?"

She huffed. "I was working on getting the appetizers together last night. My cousins and I were there until about ten and then we went home."

"Did you go home alone?" Whitney pressed.

"What is that supposed to mean?" Sarah asked, affronted. "Do you think I'm going home with random men? What do you know about your little friend here, Colter? Has she told you who she really is? About her past?"

He looked over at Whitney. Her jaw was clenched tight and her face was red, but he doubted that it was because of the cold. "This isn't about Whitney and her past. This is about you and where you were and who you were with. Don't try to deflect, Sarah."

"This is crazy, Colter. And if you don't see that, then you deserve to be with a woman like her—one with a closet full of skeletons…and not just the figurative kind." Sarah pointed toward her. "I don't know what she has you thinking about me, but all I care about is my business and my family."

Whitney gave a derisive snort. "How did I know you would say something about your family? You say you're innocent…but it's strange how everything we know about the suspect points straight toward you."

"What's in this for you, Whitney?" Sarah asked, turning toward her so their faces were only a few inches apart. "Do you think you can come here and stir up trouble in hopes that it will make people forget about who you really are? What you did? I know all about you—and how you falsely accused your boyfriend of starting a fire in your barn… All so you could get the insurance money. You should be in prison."

"You don't know what you're talking about," Whitney said, the color draining from her face. She looked toward him. "Don't listen to her. I promise it's not like she said. I had nothing to do with that fire."

"From what I heard, she staged the whole thing," Sarah said, looking to him with self-righteous indignation. "If you were smart, you would have her hit the road before a mysterious fire breaks out here. Dunrovin doesn't need any more trouble—especially her kind."

Chapter Fourteen

Whitney stormed off, bumping against Sarah as she made her way to her office, and slammed the door. He thought about going after her, but he'd learned long ago that sometimes the best thing he could do when it came to dealing with an angry woman was to give her a few minutes to collect her thoughts. And he still had Sarah to deal with.

"That was cruel, Sarah," he said, though he could think of several more colorful words he could have used instead of *cruel*.

She looked at him, her eyes brimming with angry tears. She looked like a broken woman. "You don't think I *wanted* to call her out like that, do you?" she asked, motioning after Whitney. "She just made me so angry. I wouldn't do anything to hurt this ranch or stand in the way of its success. Your success means my success. Just like everything else in this community, we are all interconnected. A rising tide raises all boats, you know?"

He believed there was some validity to what she had to say, but the way she was fighting so hard and throwing such low blows made him wonder if there weren't some things she was hiding as well—things that Whitney had brushed against, and had caused the woman to lash out.

"Did you go home alone last night?" he asked, his voice as soft and understanding as he could make it.

She sucked in a breath. "The only person I want to go home with is you, Colter." She reached out and took his hand.

Her touch felt foreign, cold and unwelcome even though she was wearing thick black gloves. She squeezed his fingers, but instead of returning her affection, he pulled out of her grasp. "That's not a good idea, Sarah." He couldn't look her in the face. He hated this moment, when people weren't at the same emotional place. It always made things so awkward. "You are a great gal, but I'm—"

"Dating her?" Sarah interrupted, finishing his thought.

He nodded. "She's pretty amazing, regardless of what you seem to think about her."

"You are being stupid, Colter. You are passing on someone, me…a woman who has her life together, all so you can play house with her. She is nothing but trouble." She looked up at him, anger filling her eyes. "You're going to regret this."

The hairs rose on his arms at the threat in her tone. "What do you mean by that, Sarah?"

"Really?" She sneered. "I can't believe you." She turned around and stormed off, but turned back and pointed at him. "You are going to call me and apologize when everything between you and her goes to hell. And I'm going to tell you that I told you so. Mark my words."

She stomped into the house, slamming the door behind her.

There seemed to be a lot of that kind of thing happening in his life right now. He hadn't said anything to start this, yet here he was, dealing with a potentially dangerous suspect, who was coming after his family, and two women who wanted to have him chase after them.

Luckily, the repairing of the loft's flooring waited.

He walked back to the barn, making sure to close the door to keep some of the residual warmth from the animals from getting lost to the cold. Clark looked over at him, smacking his lips as though asking for a pellet.

"Keep wishing, you little rebel," he said, but the horse made some of the tension in his shoulders dissipate.

The horse threw his head, nickering a response that he didn't have to guess too hard to know was a rude comeback.

"That kind of talk isn't gonna get you what you want, old boy," he said, with a slight laugh.

He walked over to the bench. Hanging on the wall above it was a collection of farrier tools, scissors, hoof picks and the like. His stress was nothing a little hammering wouldn't help bring back under control. He grabbed the supplies he'd need and the board and made his way up to the loft. One of the horses huffed and stomped, and there was the shuffle of hooves and heavy bodies as he carefully stepped around the hole in the floor.

He put down his supplies and ran his finger along the rough, saw-cut edge of the floor. It still didn't make any sense to him why someone would have done this. Merle had been the one who intended to come up here to get the decorations. Which meant that someone must have been coming after him, but Colter's father was one of the most likable people he knew. Sure, he was quiet and a bit stoic with people he didn't know, but if anyone needed anything he would be the first person there to lend a hand.

His mother was the same way.

This all must have had something to do with the threat—they really were targeting members of his family, yet none of his brothers or their significant others had mentioned anything suspicious or off-putting to him. Then again, he hadn't mentioned any of this to them, or their parents, either. Maybe they were trying just as hard as he was to make sure everything kept running smoothly.

He wouldn't have put it past them, to try their best to keep a secret of that magnitude. They had all been through enough over the years that when push came to shove they would all do whatever it took to make sure the people they loved were safe. It was the one thing they all had in common—aside from their love of animals.

Picking up the box of wood screws, he let it slip from his cold fingers and crash to the floor, spilling its contents all over. Several of them rolled off the edge of the rough-cut hole in the floor.

"Son of a nutcracker," he said with a grunt as he caught more from falling into the hole.

He didn't need them getting into the pellets bin below. If one of the horses got a screw, he'd never get over the guilt.

He scooped the screws into the box and, getting up, made his way over to the boxes where several had rolled. On top of the box closest to him was a green cap with a red star on it. It was the kind that could be found on a beer bottle. He picked it up, flipping it over in his fingers.

When he looked up, something green caught his eye from in the shadows behind the box. He moved the box. Behind it were three empty green beer bottles. The same kind of bottles as the one he had found near the cattle guard.

Beside the bottles was an old, grease-smattered towel. Several pieces of it were gone, and a piece had been ripped free and was sitting near one of the bottles.

He moved another box, bumping it against something. He stepped carefully over the green bottles, not touching them as he moved. There, sitting in the darkness, tucked behind another box, was a plastic gas can.

He took out his phone and dialed. Wyatt answered on the first ring.

"Hey, brother. How's it going?" Wyatt said, sounding glad to hear from him.

He hated to ruin someone else's day as well, but he needed to bring him in on this—he couldn't let something else happen if he could stop it. "I need you at the ranch. Are you close?"

"I was just leaving my house. What's going on?" Wyatt asked, the excitement leaching from his voice.

It didn't take Colter long to tell him about his findings and the events over the last few days—including the picture.

Ten minutes later, there was the screech of metal as Wyatt entered the barn, phone still in hand. "I'm up here," Colter said, with a nod.

"Why didn't you tell me about all this before?" Wyatt asked, stuffing the phone into his pocket. "I can't believe you, of all people, would allow this kind of thing to go on for this long without getting me involved. It was stupid, Colter. Stupid as hell. Who knows what this person is capable of."

Colter sighed. He should have known this would be how Wyatt would react. He had always been a little bit of a pessimist when it came to human nature, while Colter had always been more of an optimist. Up until now and the recent events at the ranch, Colter had thought his brother was wrong—that living a life focused on the evils that another could do was unhealthy. Yet now he had to admit that maybe that kind of thinking was better for a person. At least you could be prepared when the worst happened.

"You know, Colter, someone could have gotten hurt."

Someone had already gotten hurt and her name was Whitney, but he wasn't ready to tell his brother about their relationship and all the things he'd come to learn about her and her past. His brother would immediately want to ask him questions—questions he wasn't sure he was ready to answer, at least not without talking to her again. Especially after Sarah's accusations.

They had shaken him. He was sure Whitney had told him the truth about her past and all the things that had happened in Kentucky, but from the way Sarah had spoken, there was more to it than what Whitney had told him.

He pushed the thoughts from his mind. Whitney wouldn't have lied to him. No. She wasn't the kind. And who knew where Sarah had come across the information? Probably from Facebook or something equally as unreliable.

"Why can't you take anything seriously, Colter?" Wyatt asked, coming down on him full force.

"This has nothing to do with me not taking things seriously. I'm taking this as seriously as a heart attack. I just thought I could handle it," he said, trying to make his brother understand.

"You thought you could single-handedly take on a potential killer? What were you thinking?" Wyatt took out his camera and started snapping pictures of the bottles and the scene. "Something like this could go federal… Did you ever think about that? Can you imagine if the FBI found out that there was someone potentially making bombs at the ranch?"

"I'm not stupid, Wyatt," Colter said, picking up his saw and cutting the hole square so he could fit the board into place and taking a minute to cool off before he said something he regretted.

Wyatt was just upset. He had every right to feel the way he did about Colter concealing the truth. He would have been pissed if his brother had done the same thing, but Wyatt had to understand that there was more to all this than just a secret.

Colter set down the saw as he finished his cut. "I was fully aware of all the things that could happen, Wyatt. That's why I wanted to handle this myself. I didn't want anyone else getting involved. The more people who are involved, the higher the chances of everything going haywire."

"That's ridiculous, Colter."

"No, it's not. The last thing this ranch needs is more drama. Mom and Dad are already struggling to make ends meet. Don't you realize that everything is at stake?" He slid the board into place as Wyatt moved toward him.

Wyatt squatted down and held the board in place. "Are they really that bad off?"

Colter nodded. "If this stuff gets out, it'll only get worse. I didn't want to risk it." He screwed the board into place. "As long as we work together, you and I— and this place—we got a chance. United we stand…"

"Divided we fall," Wyatt said, finishing his sentence.

There was the sound of the barn door opening, and they fell silent. Colter looked over the edge of the loft. Standing just inside the door, looking as though she wanted to be anywhere else but there, was Whitney. She looked up at him, her hand still on the barn's door.

Wyatt looked over the edge and forced a smile. "Heya, Whitney. How's it going?"

"Hey," she said, with a little wave. "I saw your car outside. What's going on?" She frowned up at him.

She must have been upset still, rightly, but Colter didn't want to talk about it in front of his brother. Knowing Wyatt, he would point fingers at her as a suspect— right now he'd be looking at everyone with that cynical scrutiny of his. Whitney didn't deserve that kind of thing. She'd already been through so much, and in his gut Colter just knew that, regardless of what Sarah had accused her of, she wasn't capable of that kind of evil.

Wyatt leaned over. "Does she know everything?" he whispered.

Colter nodded. "We found more, Whit. Someone has been up in the loft and making more of the Molotov cocktails."

"Is that why you called your brother here? You think I have something to do with it?" Whitney asked, wringing her hands nervously.

"What?" Colter asked, confused.

"You know, after what Sarah told you. You don't think I'd really do something like that, do you?" Her voice was strained, making her sound as though she was on the verge of tears. "I promise… I don't know where she heard something so stupid, but I loved Rudy. I loved… I loved it all… I love that world. I miss it so much." She covered her face, masking her tears as they fell.

Colter climbed down the ladder and walked over to her, taking her into his arms. Wyatt and his opinions be damned. "You're okay. I know you. I know you wouldn't do something that heinous. She's just jealous and upset."

She shook in his arms as she sobbed. "I thought that coming here… Everything would get easier. That I wouldn't have to face it every day… That I could start fresh."

"Shh… You don't need to cry. You are starting fresh. We're starting fresh. And more than anything, I want you to know that I trust you." He ran his hand over her hair, trying to soothe her. "You're okay."

Wyatt made his way down from the loft, and as he hung the hammer and saw on the wall behind the bench, he gave Colter a questioning look, but Colter wasn't sure if it was because of their relationship or the things that she was saying. Either way, he would have to answer a slew of questions when he and Wyatt were alone.

Whitney stepped out of his arms and moved backward toward the open barn door as though she suddenly had realized where she was standing. "I'm sorry, guys. I didn't mean to interrupt. It was just—"

"No worries," Wyatt said, waving her off. "I know how it can be. Gwen and I have been through a lot, too.

Sometimes you just have to communicate. At least that's what she tells me," he said with a chuckle.

Whitney smiled, dabbing at her cheeks. "I'm not a crier, I promise."

"I know you're tough stuff. My mother wouldn't have just anybody working for her," Wyatt said, clearly trying to make her feel better.

He and Colter both knew only too well that their mother and father didn't always have the best judgment when it came to the hiring they did for the place. They always had a soft spot for sob stories and hard-up cases, but Colter appreciated his brother's gesture to make her feel better.

Whitney looked over at him, and he could see that she was thinking the same thing.

"Thinking about Mom and Dad," Wyatt continued, "do you think that we should tell them anything?"

Colter shook his head. "I think we could tell Dad, but he'd tell Mom. Let's just wait until Yule Night is over. In the meantime, is there anything you can pull from the bottles? Fingerprints or anything?"

Wyatt nodded. "We could, but that would involve getting my department in on this. And if they think we should get the ATF or FBI out here... Well, that's a whole can of worms that I don't want to open." He ran his hands over his face. "Maybe keeping me in the dark on this one wasn't such a bad idea. I can't *not* investigate this, Colter."

"Thanks for finally seeing things from my perspective, man," Colter said with a chuckle. "You need to give us a few days, at least until after the party, before we start getting other people involved. Hopefully by then, this will all have stopped or we will have the person responsible in custody."

"We're going to have to work fast," Wyatt said. "Do you guys have any idea, any clues as to who may be behind this?"

Colter shrugged, but Whitney glanced outside.

"Whitney?" Wyatt asked as he must have noticed her reaction.

She nibbled at her lip. "I… I just have a feeling that Sarah is involved. Whoever is doing this has to know something about how the ranch functions. She has been around a lot lately."

"Why would she do something like that? And threaten everyone?" Wyatt asked.

She looked over at Colter and then down at the floor.

"Let's just say that Sarah has some misplaced feelings when it comes to me," Colter said, trying to take some of the pressure off her.

Wyatt gave him a knowing look. "So she's a jilted lover?"

Colter almost choked and had to cough to clear the distaste from his mouth. "No. We're not lovers. We went out once, but it was nothing like that. But, even so, I don't think she would stoop to hurting or threatening anyone on the ranch. She made a point of telling me that her success depends on the ranch's success. I just don't think she has it in her. She may be imperfect, but she's not evil—not like that."

"You found this all out when you *went out with her*?" Whitney asked, shock infusing her words.

"It was right after her divorce. We were set up, and it didn't go well. Seriously, it was bad. I think that's why she wants another shot to make things better this time."

Wyatt shifted his weight, clearly uncomfortable with what was happening in front of him. "I'm going to step out back," he said, walking over to the side door of the barn. "When you're done…" He clicked the door shut behind him.

Colter tried to ignore the tangle of nerves that had descended on him. The last thing he wanted to do right now was fight with Whitney. He had been hoping that they could just move forward, that everything could just be forgiven and forgotten, yet when emotions got involved, it always seemed to go awry.

He turned to face Whitney, and as he opened his mouth to try to reassure her, she came rushing toward him, flinging her arms around him. She crushed her mouth to his. She ran her tongue over the bottom of his lip, sucking and pulling it between her teeth. It felt so good, soft and warm, yet flecked with the scraping of her teeth against him. It was everything great about a kiss—promises of more, heat and passion, yet the dangerous hints of the kinds of pains that always came with ecstasy. He loved everything about it—and her for it.

He pressed her against the wall of the barn and lifted her hands above her, holding them with one hand as the other searched for her skin beneath her winter coat. He slid his hand up, unquestioning, unwavering in his need to feel her. He pushed his hands under the edges of her bra and cupped her soft skin. She was so warm, but as he ran his finger over her nipples, they pressed against him like perfect little nubs. He wished he could lift her shirt and pull them into his mouth. He wanted to taste her so badly that he moaned.

She sucked in her breath, and the cold air glazed over the place on his lips made warm by her kiss. God, she could do things to him that made him long for her like he had never longed for anyone before. He wanted to take her, here, now, hard.

There was the creak of the side door. "Guys, you have to take a look—" Wyatt stopped and cleared his throat.

Colter slipped his hand out from under her jacket, and taking a moment to collect himself, he turned to face his brother. "What is it?"

"I, uh, think I found something," Wyatt said, but he stared at the ground as Whitney readjusted her shirt and jacket.

Colter tried not to feel sorry for himself as they made their way out of the barn, following his brother. It always seemed that as soon as something started going right, the world had a terrible habit of getting in the way.

He slipped his hand in Whitney's. If nothing else, at least she had seemed to forgive him and maybe had implied that they could really, truly start fresh. He'd take her kiss as a good sign.

"Look," Wyatt said, stopping near the side of the barn and pointing at a set of tire tracks in the fresh snow. "Do you notice anything strange about them?"

Colter shook his head. They looked like regular tire tracks, but then again, he wasn't trained in forensics.

"Look right there," Wyatt said, squatting down and pointing at the pattern. It was deep and made up of a pattern of triangles and ridges. "That right there is a new set of tires. Look at the tread. And based on the pattern, it's not just any set of tires, but BF Goodrich All-Terrains."

"What does that mean?" Whitney asked.

Wyatt smiled. It was the smile of a man who knew

exactly what he was doing. It was the smile of a man who was about to win. "Those tires are expensive truck tires. Tires we don't use on any of the ranch vehicles."

"How do you know that this person was the one going into the barn to make explosives?" Colter asked.

"There was only one set of footprints when I came out here. They were leading to and from the side door of the barn, but nowhere else." He motioned around them. "And whoever parked here must have realized that their truck couldn't be seen by anyone unless they were out in the pasture areas. It's a great place to park if you don't want to be caught."

"That's all circumstantial," Colter said, feeling like he was raining on his brother's attempt to help.

Wyatt's smile widened. "Sure… All except that." He motioned over to the snow where there was a single beer cap lying only slightly sunken into the snow, almost as though it had simply fallen out of someone's hand. On the cap was the distinctive red star of those that had been in the loft.

"Who do you know that drives a truck?" Wyatt continued. "Someone who has the money to drop into high-end tires? If you can figure that out, I think we may have just found our man."

Chapter Fifteen

No matter what Sarah said, she had to be behind it.
Whitney checked all the boxes. Motivation. Opportunity. New truck. Money. Whether or not Colter wanted
to see the woman for who she really was and what she
was capable of was up to him, but Whitney wasn't falling for the woman's games. She knew all too well how
spurned lovers could do things that would surprise a
person—and how little they cared about the truth or the
cost their actions would have on others. All they saw
was the person they loved and nothing else—it was
what made them so dangerous, their lack of empathy
and their disregard for consequences.

The thought made shivers run through her.

Maybe someday the ghosts of her past would leave
her, but hoping for something so unrealistic seemed
like an exercise in futility.

Colter and Wyatt were taking pictures of the tire
tracks. She felt bad for the brothers, who were both in a
terrible predicament. It was hard to be in a place where
you couldn't tell the truth out of fear it would affect the
lives around you. She'd been there too many times. She
thought back to when she had first realized that Frank
was stalking her. It had been at the prom. She'd gone

out with her friends and a boy whom she had known since grade school. The boy was gay but hadn't told anyone except her.

When they were at dinner, Frank had looked in the window of the restaurant. Even without closing her eyes, she could still see him standing there, his warm breath fogging up the glass as he stared daggers at her date's back. When they came out of the restaurant, her date's car's tires had been slashed and they'd had to call her mother and father to take them to the high school for the party. They hadn't done much dancing. Her date had been consumed with trying to find a way to get his tires replaced and all she had been able to think about was whether or not she should tell anyone.

In the end, she hadn't turned Frank in out of fear that he would strike again. She had tried to explain to him that her date was nothing but a friend when he threatened to come after him. Luckily, when she'd told him about his sexual orientation, it made things easier and he'd promised to lay off. Yet nothing about it had made her feel good. She had felt completely bound to the will of a madman. He had seemed unstoppable and capable of anything. And, if anything, her terror of him and what he was willing to do to hurt her had been well-founded.

She had made so many mistakes in her past. She couldn't allow herself to make another in her present. Making her way to the parking lot, she noticed that Sarah's truck was missing. Strange. Maybe the woman had seen them go into the barn, or overheard them and had hightailed it out of there before she could fall under suspicion.

Too late.

Whitney looked down at her watch. If she rushed into town she would still have time to do what needed to be done. For a moment she thought about going back to tell Wyatt and Colter where she was going and what she was thinking, but Colter would just come to Sarah's aid. It was what he always did; he couldn't be objective. As much as it should have annoyed her, that he would still have a soft spot for his former girlfriend— or whatever he would have classified her as—it didn't. His graciousness of spirit was something that she admired about him.

He had been through just as much as she had, yet he wasn't hardened by the world. Instead he always seemed to take it in stride and deal with things as they came to him without looking at all the pain and memories.

If only she could be more like him, and was able to learn to forgive and live for the present instead of being held back by the weight of her past.

It didn't take long to grab the keys and hit the road. She passed by Colter's truck as she made her way carefully down the road and to town. By the time she made it to Sarah's shop, dusk had started to descend on the little town and its late-nineteenth-century-style buildings. The town was quaint and full of charm, a throwback to an era and a lifestyle that was completely different from now. She wondered what it would have been like to live in a time like that, when the West was still wild, lives revolved around mining and stripping away minerals and oil from the lands, a world where danger lurked around every corner.

Thinking about it, she wondered if maybe it wasn't really so different from life now. Only the clothes and manners in which they went about mining had changed.

In Kentucky, coal was their main source of mineral wealth rather than gold, silver and uranium. There, when she'd been growing up, the old-time miners had still been succumbing to black lung, while in Montana the workers were falling to a variety of cancers caused by the chemicals used in mining.

No doubt, in twenty years another generation of miners would succumb to some mysterious disease brought on by their livelihoods and the swords they had chosen to live by.

She got out of the truck. Since she had left the ranch and the sun had gone down, the temperature had fallen at least twenty degrees and the cold had taken on the same dangerous edge as the night before. As she thought about the hike and being stuck out in the cold with Colter, a certain warmth took hold in her belly. Even though it was a terrible situation, she wouldn't have wanted to take it all back. It was one heck of an adventure; and life should be spent in adventures—the kind that made her want to hold her breath, the kind that made her heart hurt from happiness and joy, and the kind that could be shared with those she truly cared about.

Whether or not the time was right, or that it was a good decision, Colter was the man she wanted in her life. She couldn't justify giving her heart away in any logical way, but there was something about him that made her thankful that she had come to this place, where life still spoke to bygone eras and intrigue. She loved this place almost as much as she loved him.

Making her way to the front door of the café, she stopped and stared inside. The place looked warm, and bits of condensation had started to collect at the corners of the front bay windows and frieze. It made the mural look as though it was painted on a layer of ice. Sarah was nowhere to be seen, but there was some metallic banging that sounded like pans coming from inside the kitchen.

She had no idea what she was going to say to the woman, or the kinds of questions she should ask.

A part of her wondered if she was even on the right track, or if she was a bit like Colter and unable to be objective because of the way she felt about the woman. She hated the thought that perhaps she was falsely accusing Sarah—she had been in those shoes, but the one doing the finger-pointing was the same woman in question. There was nothing like a little projection—when the guilty person was caught, he always had a way of pointing the finger away from himself.

Perhaps more than anything, what she feared if she was wrong was the fact that the guilt might fall to someone else whom she knew far better and who scared her far worse—Frank.

Just the thought of his being there made her stomach ache and a wave of nausea pass over her. She hated that the thought of him could still provoke a physical response. She hated that he still held the power of terror over her. It was so wrong. Yet there was no making it right. All she could do was hope that he hadn't found out where she was, and that he wasn't behind this.

Heck, if he was, it would be just like he had been a few years ago when he stuck his face in the window of the restaurant and ruined her night. He'd never been particularly sneaky when it came to her. If anything, he'd only been good at not getting caught—or at least penalized for his crimes.

She looked back over her shoulder thanks to the

thoughts of Frank. He wasn't there; he couldn't be—unless that was who Sarah had been talking to. It would have made sense. He had always accused her of setting that fire—even in court he had told his lawyer that she was responsible for it. He was the king of gaslighting—so good, in fact, that his lawyer had ultimately taken his side and believed his lies and tried hard to prove that his client wasn't guilty. He had nearly gotten him acquitted.

No one was on the sidewalks. Most of the stores were still open, but this was likely out of some desperate hope that people would come in for their Christmas shopping. There were a few cars parked along the road, but none she recognized.

She slipped into the café. The place always smelled so good, like warm bread and butter, but today it had something different in the air—almost musky like some kind of spice used in antiquity. She tried to put her finger on the smoky scent, but try as she might, it wouldn't come to her.

"Sarah?" she called, hoping that she would just think of the right thing to say the moment the woman came out of the kitchen.

There was no answer.

"Hello? Is anyone here?" she asked, walking toward the back and the kitchen, where she had met Sarah's cousins. There was the sound of glass breaking and she rushed toward the noise.

As she dashed into the kitchen, the back door slammed shut. Someone in a dark brown knit cap and heavy work coat sprinted to the left and out of sight.

"Wait!" she screamed. "Stop!"

She moved to go after the person, but was stopped by the heat. On the floor, and running up the wall, was a fire. Terror filled her. All she could do was stare at the blue base and orange curling tips of the flame. There was liquid. Accelerant. She had seen it before. She had felt the heat. The same heat.

She was going to die. This was the end. There was no way she could make it out of a fire again. Her luck was gone. This was the way she was meant to go.

She could be with Rudy.

Black smoke poured up from the flames, filling the kitchen with its spicy, acrid stench—the scent of burning motor oil and gas. Oh, God, she hated that smell.

She had to move. She couldn't just stand here and let it have her.

Fight. She had to fight.

This time, there was no one to save—only herself— she had to make the choice. She couldn't stay here.

Forcing herself to look away from the fire, she broke the spell it had cast upon her.

She ran toward the front door. There, the window that had only minutes before been covered in ice was now shattered on the floor like spent tears. At the center was a steadily growing circle of fire around a green Heineken bottle that thankfully hadn't been broken when it was thrown through the glass.

Someone had tried to trap her.

They *had* trapped her.

She looked through the flames toward the door. She'd have to move quick to get out. The only way out was around the side of the room that was steadily filling with the black smoke.

The smoke. It always got a victim first.

She got down on her knees and started moving toward the wall and around the steadily growing pool of flames. The broken glass on the floor cut at her hands and pierced through her jeans and pressed into her knees, but she didn't care. She simply kept moving forward. Another foot. Just one more foot. One more.

Finally, she found the door and pressed out into the night. As she spilled out on the steps and down to the sidewalk, she saw the reflection of red and blue lights coming from the distance. She closed her eyes and let her body fall into the snow and ice that littered the sidewalk.

She had fought—and once again, she'd won. She'd survived.

Chapter Sixteen

Colter's buddies had called him the moment they saw the ranch truck outside the café, but they hadn't needed to—he and Wyatt had heard the call on his radio while they were pulling his truck out of the snowbank.

He should have known where Whitney had gone. One minute she was with them, talking about the tire tracks, and the next she had disappeared. Just when he thought he knew the girl, she did something like this.

All he could hope was that she was really okay. His friend had said she had gotten out in time, just some smoke inhalation, but she would be fine. Though Colter knew his friend had been telling him the truth, his heart wouldn't let him believe it until he saw her with his own two eyes.

He pulled the truck to a stop and got out. The building was engulfed in flames, and the fire crew was doing its best to stop the fire's advancement into nearby buildings. These old places were built with brick and mortar, but they had enough wood in them that one bad fire could easily jump to the next building if they didn't get on top of it quickly.

Whitney wasn't anywhere to be seen. Where was she? The battalion chief, his friend Turner, was standing next to the crew, giving an order to one of the men on the hose. Colter made his way over to them as the BC turned toward him.

"Why aren't you in your gear?" Turner asked, from his tone only half kidding. "We could use an extra set of hands."

"I was at the ranch, but if you want, I can—"

Turner waved him off. "We're hoping to get another truck in here from rural. We'll see how quick they get here."

They were in dire straits if they were calling in re-inforcements from the volunteer rural sector. Colter should have been working, but he couldn't go get his gear and get back here—at least not until he found Whitney.

He glanced around, but couldn't see her. However, across the street was Sarah's black Chevy pickup.

There was a collection of people who had spilled out from the stores on Main Street and the nearby homes, no doubt all come to see the biggest source of gossip this week. This would at least keep them from talking about his family for a little bit, though... He was sure they would be tied back to this.

He stopped. What if this fire did have something to do with his family and the threat they had received?

"Was there anyone else in the building at the time of the fire besides Whitney?" Colter asked.

"I don't know. Ms. Barstow hasn't spoken to anyone." Turner shrugged. "She's with the EMTs now."

Colter turned to leave, heading in the direction of the lights of the ambulance.

"Wait," Turner said, grabbing him by the arm to stop

him. "How well do you know this girl?" There was a look of deep concern in his eyes.

"Pretty well. Why?" Colter hated the way his friend was looking at him. It was like there was something more, something he was afraid to ask or tell him. "What are you thinking, Turner?"

He let go of his arm. "This fire was no accident." He skidded his bunker boot around in the slushy, wet snow. "Sarah made a point of telling me that there had been some kind of incident between her and your friend. She seems to be of the mind that Whitney had something to do with this thing. And you know, if that's the case…"

He didn't have to say anything more.

"Whitney wouldn't do this. She's innocent," Colter said, meaning it with every ounce of his being. Yet, as he said it, a nagging feeling rose from his gut.

What if he was wrong? What if he'd been wrong about this woman all along?

No. He trusted her. She had revealed her past to him. She had told him about her past, and the pain that came with it. And her opening up like that, trusting him, was a gift. If he listened to the idle gossip and naysayers around him, what kind of person would he be? He needed to respect and appreciate her, and trust her for the person he knew her to be, not the person others were portraying her as. In the long run, the truth would come to light—he would look back on this and either be humbled or be proud of his actions.

Today, he would stand up for what he knew was right and for the love he held in his heart.

Today, he would fight for her.

"Colter, how can you be sure she's not behind this?" Turner continued. "From what Sarah had to say, this girl has only been around for a couple of months. You notice that as soon as she started working here, trouble has been cropping up regularly."

"You know just as well as I do she's not responsible for everything at the ranch."

He tried to stanch the anger that was boiling up inside him. Turner didn't mean anything by it, and he couldn't possibly know how Colter felt about her. If anything, he was just trying to make sure he was doing his job, but it didn't make the contempt Colter was feeling for his friend any easier to bear.

"The last thing this girl would do is have anything to do with another fire. She is terrified of the damn thing. This just isn't something she's capable of. Trust me."

Turner's eyebrows rose and his eyes darkened. "What do you mean *another fire*? Is there something I need to know about? Something that pertains to this case that you aren't telling me, Colter?"

He shook his head, wishing that he hadn't opened his stupid mouth.

"If you don't talk to me, Colter, you will find yourself in need of another job." Whatever friendship they had seemed to fall apart with his words.

"You don't have the power to fire me, Turner."

"If you are withholding information that will tell me who is behind this fire, then you can make damn sure that this will find its way to the powers that be, who will gladly throw you out on your ass."

Colter raised his hands in submission. This was going in a direction he couldn't let it go. He couldn't risk everything just because he was pissed and felt like he needed to protect her. "Look, Turner, you and I are friends," he started. "Let's not blow this all out of proportion."

"Then answer my question, Fitzgerald," Turner said through gritted teeth.

He sighed. "Whitney and her family were victims of an arson a while back. It's why she's here. She's running from her past."

Turner nodded, listening.

"You just have to believe me when I say that I don't think she's behind this," Colter continued. "If she is, I'll…"

"You'll what?" Turner asked, this time some of the anger seeming to seep from his tone.

"I'll throw in my hat. No investigation. No fight. I'll just quit."

Turner nodded, apparently mollified. "Okay. I'll have my guy look elsewhere, but you better hope to all that is holy that you aren't wrong and love ain't blind."

Colter turned around and made his way toward the ambulance in hopes Turner couldn't see the look of complete shock over what he had just agreed to that he was sure was on his face. He had just gambled his entire future on a feeling.

Colter was a lot of things, but he had never thought himself a fool. It wasn't time to start changing his feelings toward himself now. He'd just have to ride it out and pray he had been right.

But he'd been wrong before.

He'd never thought his biological parents would have been the kind to leave him. Sure, he'd been a kid and naive, but he had trusted them—and they had done him wrong. And here he was, back in the same position of blindly trusting someone he loved.

The back doors of the ambulance were closed and he knocked on them before opening. Whitney was sitting on the gurney, alone. An oxygen mask was over her soot-covered face, but even under the ash he could tell she was pale. The look in her eyes told him that she'd been to hell and back.

He stepped up into the back of the ambulance and, careful not to touch her in case she was hurt, sat down next to her. "Are you okay?"

She wrung her hands and looked down at her fingers. They were covered in black ash, and her nail beds were as pale as her face. If he wasn't careful, she could easily slip into shock. He had to get her talking. Anything would be fine as long as it took her mind off what had just happened.

"Lassie wants you to come home," he said, trying his very best to make her laugh.

She blinked a few times but remained silent and staring.

"You should have seen the little rat dog. She's been running in circles trying to tell me something. If I was smart, I would have known that she was trying to warn me. You'd think I'd speak dog by now."

She looked up, and her lips trembled as though she wanted to smile. She pulled the oxygen mask from her face, letting it drop to her neck. "You're certainly fluent in smart-ass."

He laughed, but the boom made her twitch and he shut up.

"We all have gifts. And really, I think my articulateness is really due to my brothers. They trained me so I could bring my very best to the dating table." He leaned closer and brushed back her hair, thankful when she didn't shudder from his fingers grazing against her skin. "I mean, it got you. Didn't it?"

"Colter…"

The way she said his name told him that he wasn't going to like whatever was going to come next.

"Stop," he said, cutting her off before she could go any further. "I'm a real catch. I mean, who wouldn't want all this?" He raised his arms, flexing them like some kind of bodybuilder on display.

"You really are ridiculous," she said with a little giggle.

"Oh, baby, you ain't seen nothin' yet," he said, some of the trepidation he'd been feeling disappearing with the sound of her laugh. "If the goon squad says you can, how about we get out of here?"

"They want my statement," she said, and some of the color that had finally come back to her cheeks disappeared.

"They can wait until tomorrow. I'll just tell them that they can stop by the ranch. Sound good?"

She nodded and her lips turned up into a slight, relieved smile.

"I'll be right back." He slipped out and walked up to Turner.

It didn't take long for him to get the man to agree to let them head back to the ranch, but it had come with another stern reminder of what hung in the balance.

Chapter Seventeen

The ride back to the ranch seemed to take longer than usual, but it could have rested in the fact that he had made sure to drive extra slow in an effort to keep his truck on the road. They couldn't go on a hike through the tundra as they had the night before. Not that he had minded spending more time with her. It was just that he hated the fact that he had put her in needless danger.

Nothing seemed to go right when it came to their time together.

He put his hand in the middle and she slipped her fingers into his, not saying a word. For a thousand reasons, most of which she had been careful to express to him, they couldn't be together and he heard them all—but there was no stopping what the heart wanted.

"Do you want to tell me what happened in there?" He ran his thumb over hers.

She sighed and stared out into the night. "I don't want to talk about it. I never want to talk about it…"

He could understand her response, but part of him had to know what had gone down.

"I covered for you back there," he said. "They seemed to think that the fire was suspicious. They wanted to take you in, but I held them off."

She finally looked over at him and she gave his hand a squeeze. "You did that for me?"

He nodded.

"Why?"

His gut ached as he thought of the risk he had taken. "I know you. I know what a good person you are. If I thought for a second that you actually had anything to do with it, we wouldn't be here right now—we wouldn't have ended up where we were last night, either. Kissing, I mean."

"Do you really think you know me?"

The ache intensified. "I think I do. Do you think you know me?"

She smiled. "Your favorite food is ham, potato casserole and green beans. And you love action movies."

He laughed. "How do you know that?"

"Your mother was talking about it. She said you're an avid *Lethal Weapon* fan."

"You were talking to my mother about me?" He was equally surprised and pleased. "So, how long have you been in love with me?"

"Shut up." She clenched his hand. "You know how I feel."

Right now he wasn't entirely sure. He understood what she was implying and what she had told him she wanted and how she felt, but when they were together there was just something magical between them.

He pulled the truck to a stop as they got to the ranch. It had been his plan to go home tonight and finally get into his own bed instead of staying at his parents', but right now the last thing he wanted was his own pillow.

She wouldn't want to have anything to happen between them. Not after everything.

He got out of the truck and walked over to her side. He was overthinking this. There was no point fretting about any of it. Regardless of how confused he was, she had made her wishes clear—they couldn't be together.

That didn't mean that he couldn't be a gentleman and see her to her door.

She stepped out of the truck and took his hand. She gave it a squeeze but said nothing and led him to the house.

The place was quiet, though it wasn't particularly late—at least not in comparison to last night.

She walked into her bedroom. It was small, maybe a bit cramped.

When he'd been a kid her bedroom was kept as a place for guests to stay. Thinking about it, he wondered why his mother had put her there. Had she not assumed that Whitney would stay?

He pushed the thoughts from his mind. His mother had a method to everything she did, and he wasn't about to start questioning it now.

Colter stopped at the door and let go of Whitney's hand, letting it slip from his fingers like hopes. "Have a good night. If you need anything, I can stay or... I was going to head home." He motioned toward the hall, fully aware of how awkward it was between them.

He wanted to follow her into her room, push her down onto the bed, but he couldn't. Not now and, for all he knew, not ever.

"Do you really want to go home?" she asked, a hint of longing in her voice.

Or maybe it wasn't longing but his need to hear a longing that he heard.

"I… I don't have to. I can sleep out on the couch or something." He looked down the long, empty hallway.

"There was someone in Sarah's café… Tonight," she said, catching him off guard.

"What? Who? You *saw* someone?"

She took his hand and closed the door. She pulled out the chair at her tiny desk and motioned for him to sit down. "I don't know if it was a man or a woman. I just saw someone running out after they threw the bottle."

"They threw a bottle? Why didn't you tell anyone what you saw?"

She shrugged. "I was shaken up. And I didn't know what you had said and to whom. I wanted to make sure I didn't get you into trouble."

He stepped closer to her, taking in the scent of smoke from her skin and the heat of her nearness. Ever so carefully, he reached up and cupped her face in his hands. "You don't need to worry about me. You never have to worry about me. I will handle whatever needs to be handled, but you need to keep yourself safe and out of trouble. If they knew you were hiding something like that… I told you that they thought—"

She touched her finger to his lips, stopping him from going into a full tirade. "I'll talk to them in the morning. Everything will be okay."

She traced her finger around his lips, making his body come to life.

"In the meantime," she whispered as she leaned toward him and pulled away her finger before her lips met his. "I need to forget, and I want to explore."

His lips were slightly chapped, the mark of cold winter weather and the dry air of Montana. She moved to her tiptoes, and his breath caressed her lips as she drew nearer to him. There were still millimeters between them, yet this was the closest emotionally she had been to anyone in a long time—ever since Frank. Not that she wanted to think about Frank. Not now. Not ever. But with the fire…it was no wonder she had gone back to that place and time. No matter how hard she fought against the memories of him, his actions would always leave a mark on the canvas of her life.

She leaned back slightly as thoughts of him moved through her.

Maybe it was a mistake, taking this step with Colter. Anytime she grew close to a man, it was only bound to end in agony. Colter was a good man, an everyday hero, but that didn't guarantee that things between them would end in anything but heartbreak. If truth be told, she wasn't sure her heart would stand being broken again—but she couldn't keep on a path that meant she stopped living. She needed this. She needed him.

She needed a future that brought happiness. And right now the happiness and escape she longed for could only be found in his kiss.

"Are you okay?" he asked, his voice airy and light as his thumbs moved over her cheeks.

She reached up and took his hand in hers. "I'm going to be fine as long as you kiss me."

It was exactly the invitation he needed. He rushed to her lips, the coarse lines of his pressing against hers, a harsh comparison to her softness, but she liked the way they scratched against hers. It was almost as if his lips were pulling her closer, reaching for more.

He ran his tongue over the places where his lips had rubbed, and the sensation made her think of all the

places his tongue could travel on her body. She ached
for more. So much more. She reached up and ran her
fingers through his short hair. It was soft but sharp from
a fresh cut—just like the rest of him, it was the perfect
combination. Perhaps he was made to be the man she
had always been longing for.

His kiss moved from her lips and over her neck.
She let her head fall back, reveling in the touch of him
against the tender lines of her collarbone. As he kissed,
he moved her toward the bed, and as her legs touched it,
he picked her up and wrapped her legs around his waist.
She could feel his responding body rubbing against her,
telling her that he wanted this just as much as she did.

He laid her down on the bed, their bodies flexing
and pushing against each other. In one fluid motion,
he reached down and opened the buttons of her shirt,
revealing her lace bra. As he sat up and pulled the shirt
from her, she caught the scent of smoke and lust. It was
a heady mix, danger and want—the scent of love.

"Dance for me," she said, trying to get back control
over the urgency that she had been feeling. She wanted
to savor their time together—every second of it.

"What?" he asked with a surprised laugh. "Really?"

"Or I could dance for you," she offered with a playful tip of her head.

"You…always surprise me." He stood up and gave
her a sexy, almost shy grin.

He started to hum as he pulled up the edge of his
shirt. It wasn't a song that she recognized, but it sounded
a bit like an old country hit. He swiveled his hips as his
fingers moved down the buttons of his shirt. Slipping
the last button free, he turned around and gave her a
playful wiggle of his behind.

She laughed. "Oh, yeah, baby. Just like that."

He gave his butt a playful slap as he started to get into it, moving and dancing as he unbuckled his pants.

He really did have a nice ass. Unable to control herself, she reached up and gave it a little squeeze. It was just as muscular as the rest of him.

"Hey, now, no touching the merchandise," he said, pulling out of her grasp.

"But what if I want to touch you?" she asked with a little whine.

He gave her a lift of his brow. "How bad do you want it?"

She wiggled her finger, motioning for him. "Come here and I'll show you."

He took a step.

She reached up and took hold of the waist of his jeans and pulled him even closer. His body was pumping off heat. The palm of her hand moved against him as she lowered his zipper, exposing his red-and-black gingham boxers. She let his pants drop to the floor and he stepped out of them.

"Very classy," she said, tugging at the bottom of the leg of his boxers. It wasn't that they were anything remarkable, but sitting there alone in her room with him, she suddenly felt the reality of the entire situation—and what it would mean.

If she went there with him, everything would change. There would be no going back to being simple friends. Even if they did this only once, the air between them would always be flecked with the knowledge that they had spent this night together. He would know her as very few men did, and she would know him.

The act of lovemaking was a gift, and once given,

the memory of those moments spent together would last a lifetime. There was no forgetting the way a man felt in her arms, or the way his kiss moved over her lips. There was no ignoring the little jolt of excitement she would feel whenever he was near.

She wanted it all.

Reaching down, she slipped off her jeans and her panties. He sucked in a breath as he watched her shimmy them off and drop them to the floor atop his pants.

"You are so beautiful."

She moved to cover her nakedness, to make up for her mistake with the convenience store's camera in some way, but she stopped herself. Men wanted a woman who was confident, who took control in the bedroom and wasn't afraid to be who she was. She hadn't been that woman in the past, but she had been through so much. The one thing she could give to herself was love and acceptance, the same things she wanted from him.

Instead of covering her breasts, she ran her fingers over her curves and smiled up at him. She lay down on the edge of the bed, her hair splaying around her. With her feet, she reached up and pulled down his boxers.

He was the perfect man, and as thick and proportionate as the rest of him.

"Come here," she whispered, running her fingers down her belly, teasing him as she brushed against the soft tuft of hair between her legs.

He moaned as he stepped closer. He leaned in and kissed the inside of her knee. Each kiss moved incrementally higher until she met his mouth. It felt so good, his tongue against her, that she could barely breathe.

"I...want...you..." she said, running her fingers through his hair.

He looked up at her.

"Please," she begged.

He smiled and moved until he was pressed against her. He kissed her lips and thrust into her, making her call out his name with ecstasy.

Their bodies did all the talking that was required. It was more than she had expected, or ever could have imagined—feeling him inside her.

There was no doubt—he had been meant for her.

Chapter Eighteen

If Colter could have asked for one thing for Christmas, it was that he would have a lifetime of what he'd had last night. Whitney Barstow was nothing short of amazing. It wasn't just the sex that had him thinking of only her this morning as he puttered around the ranch, cleaning out the stalls and getting the barn ready for tonight's Yule Night festivities.

Sure, the sex had been great, but there was so much more to it and the way he was feeling about her. He couldn't even really remember what his life had been like before her, as she seemed to fill him up. Every time he closed his eyes, all he could see was her smile and the way her hair had haloed around her head on her pillow when he forced himself to get out of bed.

He hadn't wanted to leave, but he had thought it better that way—he didn't want anyone at the ranch to know their private life and about the moments they shared.

Though he knew they wouldn't be able to keep their blooming relationship secret for long, he had to honor her request for utmost privacy—though he wanted to shout her name from the top of the grain silos for the whole world to hear and to know that she was his entire world.

He raked the hay as he was met with the telltale sound of the grinding metal as the barn door opened.

"Hello?" he asked, unintentionally sounding annoyed at the prospect of someone disturbing the thoughts he was having of last night and being in Whitney's arms.

"Colter?" Whitney called. "Are you in here?"

He dumped his rake and poked his head out of the stall. "I'm in here. How'd you sleep?"

She left the door open, looking at it one more time before making her way toward him. "It was just fine until I woke up to find that you were gone. Did I do something wrong?"

It hadn't even occurred to him that she would have thought something like that after everything that had passed between them.

"Absolutely not. Are you crazy?" he said, wiping the thin sheen of sweat from his forehead with the back of his hand. "I just didn't want anyone to find out that... you know." He walked over to her and kissed her on the head. "You could never do anything wrong. At least not in bed. You were incredible."

She looked up at him and smiled. "I think you did the lion's share. Tonight I want to have a chance to take the reins."

He smiled wildly at her open invitation to once again share her bed. "I'm pretty sure you took the reins several times last night, but I'm more than happy to let you do as you wish to my body." He laughed.

There was a light cough from the open door of the barn. His mother was standing in the open doorway, the snow behind her making her look like nothing more than a silhouette.

"Hey, Mom. Good morning," he said, stepping back from Whitney. His face warmed as he realized what his mother might have just heard him say.

"Mornin'," she said, coming in and starting to close the door behind her.

Whitney's eyes opened wide with fear as she watched Eloise.

"Mom, you mind leaving that open?" he asked, motioning for her to stop.

"Oh, yeah," she said, glancing toward Whitney with an apologetic tip of her head. "I forget, my dear. My apologies."

Whitney waved it off. "It's okay… It's getting better. It's just with last night…and the fire…"

"I completely understand. I was just being an old fool for forgetting," his mother said, moving toward them. "And actually, last night's fire was why I was coming to look for you. Wyatt told me everything about what you've found and the note. You shouldn't have kept it a secret."

"I was just trying to protect you."

"That's what Wyatt said, but you should know that I can handle the truth by now."

"I'm sorry. I thought you had enough on your plate."

She reached over and gave his hand a quick squeeze. "Have you talked to Sarah this morning?"

"No. Why?" Whitney did a good job of not letting her distaste for the other woman flicker over her face, though he was sure that she was thinking about her.

"I've been trying to reach her. She called and left a message that all the food for tonight's party was in the café. It's ruined." She sighed, but he could still see the stress and panic in her eyes. "I don't know what we're going to do. Who is going to want to come tonight when we don't have any food to give them? I wouldn't pay good money to come to a party only to be left hungry." She threw her hands up in the air with exasperation.

"Mom, no one is coming to Yule Night for the food. They come here to be with the people of the ranch, to celebrate."

She looked at him and gave him a weak smile. "That fire is going to be another mark against us. Whether we like it or not, people are talking about the fire and are starting to say that they think it had something to do with this ranch." She hugged her arms around herself and looked down at the concrete floor. "Maybe we should just cancel tonight. We can't risk the lives of our family, friends and guests just for some party."

"No," Whitney said, shaking her head as though by doing so she could stop his mother's words from filling her thoughts. "We can't let fear stop us from having the party—it has to go on. The ranch needs this source of income—"

"And we need to show the community that we're not going anywhere—that we're not afraid," Colter added.

"What if something does happen? What if everyone is right and whoever set the café on fire is just waiting for the right time? When everyone is in the barn? The last thing we need is another tragedy on our hands."

His mother was right. There could possibly be hundreds of people filling the barn and pouring out into the ranch's yards tonight. If someone wanted to send a horrendous message—tonight would be the night. They had been warned.

"What if we call in reinforcements?" he asked, smiling at his idea.

"Huh? What do you mean?" his mother asked.

"We could have Wyatt call a few of his department buddies, and I could call some of the guys from the station. I'm sure that they would all be happy to pitch in and help with security if we told them what was going on."

"You don't think they would try and stop tonight from happening? You know, we don't want to put them at risk, too."

"First, we don't know for sure if that fire had anything to do with the ranch or the threats it has received." As he spoke, he knew how ridiculous that sounded. Of course the fire had something to do with the ranch and him—the green beer bottles and the fact that it happened the night before their party had to be more than coincidental. Whoever was after them was amping up their game.

Who knew what else they would be capable of? They were just lucky that no one had gotten hurt so far—though Whitney had come painfully close.

His mother gave him the look that told him that she had heard how ridiculous he had sounded, too.

"Okay, what if we do cancel it?" he asked. "What about the ranch?"

His mother's face pinched. "We've invested quite a bit into the party already, marketing, food, drink, invitations, deejay… The whole shebang, but it'll be okay."

"It won't be if you don't turn a profit from the event," Whitney said. "I saw the letter on your desk. You don't have to hide it."

"What were you doing looking at my private things?" His mother jumped and anger flashed over her features.

"I... I didn't mean to... I just meant..." Whitney stammered.

"Mom, she didn't mean to invade your privacy. Besides, it's not as if we didn't know this place was going through a hard time."

Eloise's face fell and she sighed. "Of course. I'm sorry, Whitney. I didn't mean to get upset. It's just that..."

"You thought you could protect us," he said, reaching over and giving his mother's fingers a light squeeze. "And we love you for it, Mom. But for once, let us help you. Let's work together and do this for the place that we all love. We want this to be a success."

"What about the food?" she asked, not letting it go.

"Don't worry, Mom. I'm sure that we can figure something out. You just focus on getting everything lined up for tonight here."

His mother's eyes brimmed with unshed tears. "You really are a sweet boy. I'm so lucky to have you in my life." She threw her arms around his neck and gave him a quick kiss on the cheek before hurrying out of the barn.

His mother wasn't the kind who displayed much emotion. She was always metered in her approach and he could think of only a handful of times when he had seen her that close to tears. It only made him want to help her that much more.

Whitney turned to him. "What are we going to do?"

He waited until he couldn't see his mother. "I have no idea. Go to the store?"

"It would take hours to get everything we need and

get back and put it all together," Whitney said, glancing down at her phone to check the time. "But I guess if we hurry, we can put something together."

"Are you a good cook?" he asked.

She gave him a guilty smile. "I can make grilled cheese sandwiches like nobody's business."

"And I can make peanut butter and jellies," he added.

Whitney laughed. "Okay, so cooking may not be our strong suit, but if it makes you feel any better, I can order takeout like nobody's business."

"I thought all Southern girls knew how to cook," he teased.

"And I thought all Northern boys knew how to mind their manners and be quiet," she said with a gentle, playful nudge.

"Whenever I'm with you, the last thing I want to do is be quiet." Before she could come up with a rebuttal, he pressed his lips against hers, hoping that it would make her think of last night and all the time they had shared making noise.

She pulled him closer, taking his lips with a hunger that made his thoughts race to the memory of her climbing on top of him. As hard as he tried, he couldn't stop his body from coming back to life and yearning for him to re-create last night.

She rubbed against him, teasing his body with the graze of her touch. "We have sandwiches to make," she said, pulling him back to some semblance of reality.

He groaned. She was right, but the last thing he wanted to do was go back to real life, where chores and danger waited.

Whitney stepped back from him and gave him a

longing smile that told him that she wanted to continue things just as badly as he did.

A thought struck him. "You know who is a fantastic cook? Wyatt. I need to call him. Maybe he can help us out, too." He took out his phone, but before he dialed he took a few breaths and allowed his body to come back to normal.

"Even with him and Gwen, that is still going to be tough to get all the food bought, prepped and ready before the event. I mean, depending on what we end up doing, we may not even have enough oven space," Whitney said.

"I know, but if we don't have him help, we really will be stuck with sandwiches," he said, dialing his brother's number. "My mom and dad have been through enough. I want to make this special for them—something that they will never forget."

"I have a feeling, no matter what the food is—this is one Christmas that will be going down in their record books," she said with a sad smile.

"True, but I want it to be for something positive—not the year everything went to hell." He pressed the phone to his ear as it rang.

"Hey, brother, what's up?" Wyatt sounded tired and drawn.

"Did you guys find anything that could help us nail down the suspect?" Colter asked, hoping beyond all hopes that his brother would tell him that they had found the person responsible and that all his worries were for naught.

Wyatt sighed on the other end of the line. "Just some fragments of the bottles we were able to retrieve from the fire. Unfortunately, they weren't able to get any fingerprints. So I gave them some of the bottles we recovered from the barn. Same deal. It's almost as if whoever is behind this knew what our next play would be. They're brazen, but they're not entirely stupid."

"Did you come up with anything?" Wyatt asked.

Colter glanced over at Whitney and put his phone on mute. "I have to tell him about what you saw, or you do."

She nodded and motioned for the phone. Unmuting it, he handed it over.

"Hey, Wyatt, this is Whit. About last night…" She put it on speakerphone.

"What about it?"

Colter could hear the apprehension in his brother's tone.

"I saw someone as they were leaving. I didn't see their face, but from the body type, I think it was a man. He was wearing a dark brown knit hat and one of those buckskin-colored work jackets. You know, Carhartt or something."

"Why didn't you tell us about this last night?"

"I—"

"You can't be serious. You held back information that could have helped us figure out who this person is. The only real information we've gotten so far," Wyatt said, cutting her off in his rush to anger.

"Don't be upset with her, Wyatt. She thought she was doing the right thing," Colter said, trying to talk his brother down from the ledge.

"You two haven't done a single right thing over the last few days," Wyatt seethed. "I can't believe you. You should know better—and you should know what could be at stake by keeping something like this from me."

The world was pressing in on Colter from all directions. His brother wasn't wrong, but he didn't and couldn't possibly understand the kind of pressure and fear Whitney was feeling. All he seemed to see was the world from an officer's perspective—which was great, but also stopped him from feeling as Colter did.

"Whitney was upset. She's been through a lot. Cut her some slack."

There was a long pause on the other end of the line. Colter doubted his brother would step down; he wasn't the kind. With something like this he was like a dog with a bone—he wasn't going to let it go.

"Fine. I'll let the detective know about it. Is there anything else you guys need to tell me—anything else you've been keeping a secret?" Wyatt pressed.

There were a lot of secrets floating around the place, but none he needed to know.

"We just talked to Mom. She's upset. All the food for tonight's party is gone."

Wyatt sucked in a long breath. "Does she have a plan?"

"She's totally overwhelmed. We managed to convince her not to cancel the party."

"Maybe that would have been for the best," Wyatt said.

"No. If they do, they'd lose thousands—and they needed to draw revenue from the event. Without it... I don't know what they're going to do."

"What do you need from me?" Wyatt said, not pressing the issue.

"First, we need to make sure that everyone here is going to stay safe. Do you think you can call some of your guys and have them come and keep a watch?" A truck rumbled to a stop in front of the barn, and from outside he could hear his mother talking to what sounded like a deliveryman.

"Done. I'll send a few down as soon as I can."

"Yeah," he said, looking out the window to see the florist's truck sitting in the parking lot. "There are going to be a lot of comings and goings today. If we could keep an eye on things, that would be great."

"About the food," Wyatt said. "I have an idea. You guys don't worry about a thing. I have a few favors I think I could call in."

"What favors?"

"Don't worry about it. Just know that I've got it handled," Wyatt said, but some of the dryness had left his voice and he almost sounded excited.

It was in times like these, when the world was nothing more than a spinning ball of stress, that Colter loved being a part of this family. Though they had their problems and their histories, when push came to shove they all had each other's backs. Even more, they had been taught the art of forgiveness, understanding, the power and support that it meant to be a family, and above all—love.

Chapter Nineteen

As she laced a string of garland over the barn's door, Colter and his father set up the Christmas tree, and several of the staffers added lights and decorations to the barn. The place still carried the aroma of horses, but lingering over it was the scent of pine and the fresh cedar chips that they had put on the floor for the party. With each hour that passed, the place was starting to look more and more like something out of a Norman Rockwell painting and less like a place where disturbing events had occurred.

Colter and his family always left Whitney in awe. They weren't all biological family, yet they shared a bond and a love for each other that seemed to transcend any and all differences. She thought back to her own family. Not every Christmas was like this. There were the two years in which the holidays had ended in fights and turmoil between her boyfriend's family and her parents, and both had ended in tears.

She had always thought she'd had a good family, but watching this one made her realize that, while they were in the midst of turmoil, their true strength lay in their apparent ability to love each other—no matter what.

It was almost as if this family was the embodiment of

what the Christmas spirit was meant to be. They were all selfless, protective, loving, caring and generous.

She loved Colter, but now seeing them together, she questioned her place in all of it. There was a part of her that made her wonder if she was good enough to fit into so much greatness. She had so many skeletons in her closet—and if Frank was behind this... As kind and affectionate as the family was, she wouldn't blame them if they didn't have the ability to forgive her for bringing that kind of turmoil into their already problem-ridden world.

Closing her eyes, she tried to remember exactly what she had seen when the man left the café. There was nothing that told her it was Frank, but there was nothing that told her it couldn't have been, either.

If it had been Frank, why hadn't he stopped to face her? When he'd come after her in the barn, he'd made it clear that he hated her—and it was his wish that she died. Yet this person had seen her and run. He hadn't wanted her to be able to identify him.

Maybe Frank had learned his lesson in court last time. Maybe he hadn't wanted her to be able to identify him. Yet the little knot in her gut told her that if Frank ever came after her again, he wouldn't simply just try to kill her with fire. He would stand there and make sure that he watched her burn. He'd never let her live.

She swallowed back the wave of nausea that passed over her.

It couldn't be Frank threatening everyone. It just couldn't be.

But that didn't leave her with any more answers. They needed to figure out who was threatening them before anything else happened or someone else got hurt.

Her thoughts moved to Sarah.

Colter had tried to convince her again and again that Sarah wouldn't want to hurt anyone, and he'd made a good point, but that didn't take her off the list of suspects. The perfect way to have everyone point the fingers away from her was to start a fire in her own store. Maybe she had wanted Whitney to spot her as she left through the back door—maybe she had worn the hat and coat in order to look masculine, all in an effort to throw off the investigation.

She had accused Whitney of starting the fire back in Kentucky in an attempt to get insurance money. Had Sarah gotten that idea because she herself was planning on doing exactly that—defrauding an insurance company?

She wouldn't have to worry about money anymore.

On the other hand, there were plenty of other people out there who hated the ranch and the people who worked on it—none more so than William Poe, the county tax appraiser. Maybe he had a hand in all of this. Lately, every time something bad had happened at the ranch, it could be traced to some kind of string he had pulled—not that any of it could be proved. He was a smart man—and Wyatt had said whoever was the maker of the bombs had been smart.

At least smart enough not to get caught.

She climbed down from the step stool and checked her work. The garland hung in graceful arcs and the red poinsettias the florist had brought were scattered around the barn, adding drops of color in the forest of brown, green and white.

"Do you guys need help with the tree?" she asked, making her way over to Colter and Merle.

Colter had a guilty smile as he looked over at her, and he slipped his dad a look that made her wonder what they were talking about before she had interrupted.

Merle handed her a box of red ornaments. "Here you go. If you want, you can put these up. I need to go check on Mother anyway. She was going to call the bartenders and make sure that everything was in order."

She took the box of ornaments and started to put them one by one on the spruce. The thing had to be at least twenty feet tall, as the angel's wings were almost grazing the ceiling. Something about the tree, maybe it was the mere size of the thing, reminded her of the Capitol Christmas Tree. It certainly would have done the nation proud.

"How's Lassie doing?" Colter asked, motioning toward the little dog that was sitting in the open door of the barn, looking at her.

"She's good. Got her a bath and a brushing. Now she thinks we're besties," she said, walking over and giving the dog a scratch behind the ears.

Now that the animal was clean and not in the arms of its owner, it didn't look like a rat creature. In fact, she had grown to think it almost cute in its awkwardness. If anything, she could relate to the poor creature. It had fallen and required the world to come to its rescue, and even with its fur matted and shivering and quaking, those around it had come to care for it.

She lifted the dog into her arms and carried it back to the tree, setting it down on the tree skirt as though it was a present. Milo came prancing in and, seeing the little dog, made his way over to lie down next to her. The pup they had likened to Lassie was no more than a fourth the size of Milo, and next to him looked like little more than a month-old puppy, but what she lacked in size she made up for in personality as she stood up and made her way between Milo's paws and forced him to move to accommodate her.

"It looks like he found himself a girlfriend," Colter said, motioning to the pups.

"That kind of thing seems to be catching," she teased, moving closer to him and giving him a quick peck on the cheek.

"Are you saying that you're my girlfriend?" He gave her a look of surprise, like he couldn't believe that she had suddenly changed her mind about their having more than just a physical relationship.

"If you play your cards right," she teased, even though the only thing she really wanted was to jump into his arms and relive their night of lovemaking.

His touch had made her come alive again. It had made her want to forget everything about her past and what had happened, and it had even managed to dull the reemerging fears that had come after the fire. Though it had seemed impossible, he made her whole again.

There was the sound of a truck rattling to a stop in front of the barn, pulling her from her thoughts. The dogs lifted their noses, taking in the scent of something she couldn't quite make out.

"Who do you think that is?" she asked.

Colter shrugged. "No idea," he said, putting the last ornament from his box on the tree and dropping the box in the nearly empty crate.

She followed him outside. Backed up to the front of the barn was a large truck pulling a trailer. Strapped to the trailer was an industrial-sized black grill. The driver stepped out of the truck.

"Hey, Mayor Thomas," Colter said, but he had a look of confusion on his face. "What are you doing here?"

"Your brother told me that you were in a bit of a bind thanks to last night's fire. I had a grill sitting around, thought it might come to some good use around here."

"Wyatt called you?" Colter asked.

The mayor nodded. "He's a good man, as are you. It's the least I can do after all the years you and your brother have devoted to the town. Without men like you, and a ranch like this, it would be hard to keep our town afloat."

She couldn't help wondering if the mayor was using this chance to do goodwill in order to make a run for reelection, but his motivations didn't matter. All that mattered was that he was here, doing the right thing when they really could use the help.

"Thank you, Mayor," she said, shaking the man's hand in appreciation.

"Unfortunately, we don't have anything to go on it," Colter said, motioning up toward the grill.

The mayor turned toward the road. A line of cars made their way toward them over the cattle guard and parked in the gravel lot.

She recognized several of the men: the owner of the local bar called the Dog House, the grocery store owner and even the town's main butcher. There were also several people she didn't know. One by one, the men and women made their way to the barn, all carrying boxes full of meats and cheeses, fruits, nuts and premade little quiches. There was even one box full of chocolates.

With all the activity, Merle and Eloise had come outside. Eloise was standing on her front porch, covering her mouth in shock.

"Oh, my goodness…" Eloise said, her eyes brimming with tears as she walked over to them. "What did you all do?"

The boxes of food kept coming until the tack room of the barn was nearly full.

Mayor Thomas smiled. "Mrs. Fitzgerald, your boy told us what you all were facing. We want you to know how much you and this ranch means to this town. Over the years, you and your family have given so much to this community. It's time that we return the favor."

"Oh, my… You all… You all didn't have to go to all this trouble. We…" Eloise said, emotions making her voice crack as she fumbled to find the right words.

"We wanted to," Mayor Thomas said. "More, we are going to make this the best Yule Night celebration that Dunrovin Ranch has ever seen."

A tear slipped down Eloise's cheek and a lump lodged in Whitney's throat as she watched the beautiful scene unfold in front of her. It was moments like these that gave her hope there were people out there who wanted to do the right thing—especially when those who wished them ill were looming just over the horizon.

Even with all the love in the air and the joy that filled her heart, there was something inside her that told her not was all as it seemed. Something didn't fit. Maybe it was her history, maybe it was her somewhat cynical ways, but Whitney couldn't let the little niggle of concern stop from pulling at her.

Maybe it was just that once everything started to go right in her life, the world had a way of crashing around her. This one time, she held the hope the world would wait—and for once people would continue to prove to be mostly good and her dreams of a bright future could continue to persevere.

Chapter Twenty

Fifteen minutes before the party was scheduled to begin, the parking lot of the ranch was full. The officers who had volunteered to help keep an eye out for anything that could compromise the party had been forced outside to direct traffic to park along the roads and anywhere they could safely get a car in and out of the snow. Wyatt and Gwen stood near the doors with a few of the off-duty officers, talking.

His mother and one of the ranch hands were standing by the front door of the barn and taking donations and money as guests started to make their way in. The country Christmas music echoed out of the barn as it mixed with the cacophony of voices coming from within. Everything was perfect, all the way down to the Christmas lights they had strung around the loft door and the peak of the barn. The blanket of snow made the multicolored lights a natural kaleidoscope, and the effect cast the place in a glow that reminded him of a Hallmark card.

The guests were all talking about how beautiful the decorations were as they waited in line to get in the doors.

The scent of cooking meats wafted toward him from near the front doors, making his mouth water.

Everything about tonight would go great. It just had to. Something this perfect couldn't go wrong.

His mother waved him over to the line. "I just got a phone call," she said, excitement filling every syllable. "Your brother Rainier… They granted him parole. He'll be home next week."

He hadn't seen his brother since he had gone to prison. Though his mother was excited, he couldn't decide how he felt—Rainier had sworn up and down he had been unjustly sentenced, but there had been no denying he had assaulted the man. Maybe it was time Colter let bygones be bygones—just so long as when Rainier got home he could prove to them all he really had turned over a new leaf and was going to make choices not only good for him, but good for the family, as well.

Things were finally starting to go right; he would hate it if his brother's return also made his old troubles return.

"That's great, Mom," he said, giving her a hug.

His mother gripped him tight, squeezing him as she had done when he was a child, but she no longer seemed to have the strength she'd been full of back then. It was as if, over the last month or so, she had grown older.

"And he'll be home just in time for Christmas. We'll have the whole family here. Waylon, Wyatt, you…" She fanned her face as though she were trying to hold back tears. "This is proving to be the best year. After everything that has happened, it's a miracle."

He glanced over at Whitney. She was smiling, but he could see a darkness in her eyes. He couldn't blame her for not trusting the world around them. She had been through hell and back. If he got a chance tonight, he would make it his personal goal to make her truly light up again—no matter what it took.

He gave her his best sexy smile, a smile that he hoped would tell her exactly what he had on his mind. As she looked over at him, her cheeks reddened and she looked away to one of the guests standing at their table.

The wind rustled the edge of her dress as she bent over to hand the guest a drink ticket, exposing her black panty hose high on her thigh.

Yes, he'd definitely have to see those later.

COLTER WAS IN rare form tonight and Whitney watched as he made his way into the barn with a man whom he had introduced to her as an old friend from his high school days. It wouldn't have surprised her if he knew almost every one of the hundreds of people who filled the barn and now had started to spill out into the yard and collect under the heat lamps they had set up.

It seemed surreal that just that morning there had been talks about canceling the party. So many people were here, expressing their hopes and good wishes for the ranch and all who worked, lived and played there. One of the guests had even talked to Eloise about running the story on the nightly news.

Hopefully something like this, something that showed the community's true soul, would go viral.

Eloise nodded toward her. "Would you mind going and getting my camera? It's in my office. I would love to get some more pictures for our website. I want to make sure to publicly thank everyone who came tonight."

She made her way across the yard, passing by the

husband and wife who had left her with Lassie. She smiled at them, but they pretended not to notice her, as though she wasn't worthy of being recognized as human just because she was a simple staff member.

The idea of having to give the dog back to them made her want to go get the poor little thing and dognap it until they were gone and the animal was safe. Yet, no matter how much she wanted to keep the animal, it wasn't hers.

Wasn't hers to keep… The thought turned her mind toward Colter. She had teased him about their relationship and what it could be and what she longed for it to be, but just like the pup, some things just couldn't be. Some things just weren't meant to be hers.

She walked through the quiet house, feeling strange that the place could be so full of silence when the barn, not even a few hundred yards away, was so full of noise. It was almost lonely. After grabbing the camera from the shelf in Eloise's office and being careful to avoid looking at anything on her desk, Whitney walked to the kitchen to get a quick drink of water before going back to the party.

It was nice to just be alone for a moment and to let her mind wander as she thought of all the things that had happened over the past few days. It shouldn't have surprised her how much a life could change in a matter of hours, yet it did. Perhaps what surprised her this time was how something so positive could all come from someone's evil deeds. It was almost as if the universe was finally trying to make up for some of what she had been through.

She took a sip of water, setting the glass beside the kitchen sink. There was a ripple of orange and a sparkle of red on the condensation on the kitchen window, catching her eye.

Outside, the toolshed had fingers of flames running up its siding, searing the wood. She grabbed the fire extinguisher from under the kitchen sink and rushed outside. As she looked down to pull the pin, she realized that she was still holding the camera and she dropped it in the snow.

She pulled the pin on the extinguisher as she drew close to the fire. Looking up, she stared at the orange tips of the flames. How did she always find herself near the inferno when all she wanted to do was find peace?

"Stop. Right. There," a man said from somewhere behind her.

She turned. Standing in the shimmering light was a man. His dark hair was greasy and matted against one side of his head and in his hand was a wooden baseball bat.

"Daryl? What are you doing here?" she asked, trying to stop the fear that was curdling the blood in her veins. Though the man looked slightly mad, he couldn't have come here with the intention of doing her any harm. She barely knew him. "Did Merle hire you for the party?" She tried to sound nonchalant.

The man laughed, the sound maniacal and edged with danger. "You stupid woman."

"Daryl…" she said. Edging away from him, she lifted the fire extinguisher and pointed it toward him. "What are you doing?"

He smiled at her and in the fire's light his smoke-stained teeth looked nearly brown. With the reflection of the flames in his eyes, he was almost the picture of what she had always imagined the Devil looked like.

"What are you gonna do with that thing?" he asked, pointing toward the extinguisher in her hands. "You gonna try to spray me to death?"

She raised it higher like a club. "If you take one more step toward me, I'll show you exactly what I'm going to do."

He laughed again, tilting his head back with mirth. "It's too bad that things have to play out this way. But one by one, I'm going to make sure that everyone in this place gets what's coming to them."

"Are you the one who left the note?"

His teeth glittered and a bit of spittle had worked its way out of the corner of his mouth. "If you were smart, you would have listened to my warning. You would have run. So if anyone is really at fault here, it's you. You are so arrogant. Just like the rest of them. It's no wonder you love Colter. He's just like you."

"But Wyatt said you helped him… Everyone here likes you. You're friends with Merle. Why would you want to do any of these people harm?"

He rushed at her, swinging the bat. The wooden bat connected with the metal tank in her hands as she held it up to block his swing. It made a loud twang as it connected. She hoped that someone in the parking lot or in the yard had heard the sound. Maybe they would see the smoke that had started to rise from the toolshed.

"Help!" she screamed.

She thrust the extinguisher at the man, but he simply jumped out of the way with a laugh. Something fell out of his back pocket and landed in the snow at his feet.

"Do you really think you can hurt me?" he asked.

She stared down at the little black object. He swung

again, and as if in slow motion, the toe of her boot stuck in something in the snow, sending her sprawling.

The bat connected with her ribs, and pain shot through her chest so sharp and ragged that she was sure she would lose consciousness.

She rolled over, tearing at the snow as she tried to get out of the man's range. But it was too late. Her luck had run out.

This was it.

He swung. The bat connected with her temple. The love, the pain, the Christmas lights and the orange fingers of the fire—it all disappeared.

Chapter Twenty-One

As the deejay picked a slow song, couples emerged from the crowd and took their places on the dance floor. They moved as if they were all part of a machine, each couple a little cog in the party. Colter smiled as he watched them. It was all going so well even Wyatt and his friends had begun to relax and now a few were drinking beers as they stood guard by the doors.

Thankfully their fears hadn't been realized. Perhaps whoever was behind the fire at Sarah's had gotten spooked and finally come to the point that they were ready to stop—maybe it was just some dumb kid behind it, a kid who thrived on crazy self-righteous ideals that had not yet been tested by the world.

He glanced around the barn, looking for Whitney. Sarah was standing beside his mother. Her blond hair was pulled tight, making the tired lines around her eyes look stretched and harsher in the thin light of the barn. He made his way over to the women.

"Hi, ladies. Sarah," he said, with an acknowledging tip of his head. "I'm surprised you came. How are you feeling today?"

She shrugged. "Still in shock… I just can't believe it."

"Did the fire inspector come by today?"

Sarah nodded. "He was with a detective. They found what they called incendiary devices. From what they said, someone used some kind of accelerant to start the fire."

"Do they have any idea who may have been behind it?" he asked, even though he was more than aware, thanks to Wyatt, of how little information they were going on.

"No, but when they find out who's behind this…" From the look on her face, it was no idle threat.

"Don't worry, Sarah. I know they're working to get to the bottom of this." He left it vague, but his mother gave him a look that told him he shouldn't tell her exactly how far all this went. "We're all doing our best to make sure that the perpetrator gets the justice they deserve and that no one else gets hurt."

A cold wind kicked up and blew through the open door of the barn, making goose bumps rise on his arms even though he had thought himself warm.

Sarah snorted in derision. "Everything I ever worked for is gone. My future. My home. Everything. Unless the person behind this dies, they will hardly get what they deserve."

The way she spoke made her sound nearly as dangerous as the person who had struck the match, and from the look on his mother's face, Sarah had made her just as uncomfortable as she had made him.

"Have you ladies seen Whitney?" he asked in an attempt to help change the subject.

Sarah set her jaw at the mention of Whitney's name.

"I sent her to the house," his mother said, ignoring the displeasure on Sarah's face. "I wanted her to get the camera. It must have been fifteen minutes or so ago."

"You haven't seen her again?"

His mother shook her head. "She's probably around, taking pictures. I was hoping we could use them to market this for next year."

He could tell that she was trying to meter the excitement in her voice, but she was pleased with the turnout.

"We are lucky to have such great support," he said. "You know, Sarah, maybe we could do something here to help raise money to rebuild your café. I'm sure everyone would be interested in helping. There's been all kinds of talk about what we could do."

She gave him a weak smile. "I had insurance. Hopefully it will come through. I don't want to take handouts."

Just when he thought he didn't like her, Sarah surprised him with her resilience.

"Just a thought," he said, patting her on the shoulder.

"Actually," his mother said, taking the lead, "it wouldn't be a bad idea. We could even do it when the café gets up and running again. Like an open house kind of thing."

"You mean *if* I get up and running again."

"Well, we're going to need our caterer for future events," his mother said.

"If you ladies will excuse me," he said, motioning outside, thankful that some of the darkness had seemed to lift from their conversation. "I'm going to go check on Whit."

The women were so wrapped up in their plans that his mother simply waved him off. He almost could have sworn that, from his mother's playful grin, she had done it on purpose to let him off the hook. He couldn't have been more thankful. Though he liked Sarah and felt sorry for all that she was going through, he didn't want to get wrapped up in her business, out of loyalty for Whitney.

Maybe someday the two women could be friends, but he wasn't about to hold his breath in hopes that that day would be soon to arrive.

Outside, people were huddled near the heat lamps, laughing and talking as they drank their warm mulled wine and bottles of beer. Whitney wasn't anywhere to be seen. And though he asked around, no one had seemed to have seen her.

He made his way through the yard. The winter air smelled like wood smoke and cinnamon, sharp and earthy. He glanced around for the campfire, but there was none. The aroma of smoke had to have been coming from the woodstove in the ranch house. He'd always loved that scent, but something about it tonight was off.

He waved as he made his way past the crowds of people and to the ranch house. The front door was open, and as he slipped inside he was met with uncomfortable silence.

"Whit? You in here?"

There was no answer.

The lights were off throughout the house, all except the kitchen, and he made his way to the back. There was a glass of water sitting next to the sink, and a single droplet slipped down the edge from the pink stain of lipstick on its rim. If that was hers, she had to be close. He called her name again, but again there was no answer.

He walked over to the sink and picked up the glass. It was still cold. The doors of the cupboard under the sink were open and he clicked them shut. Odd.

A flicker of red caught his eye and he peered out the

window. In the backyard, the toolshed was completely engulfed in flames.

He rushed outside and toward the fire. Halfway to the shed, lying in the snow, was his mother's camera.

His body went numb.

"Whitney!" he yelled, terror rippling through his voice. He knew she wouldn't answer.

He rushed toward the flames, and as he grew near he was met with the red stain of droplets in the snow. To the left of them was a fire extinguisher. She must have come out here in hopes that she could stop the fire's advance. But what had happened to her? Where was she?

The snow around him had been trampled down, and a few feet from him there was a splotch of blood nearly the size of one's head. He carefully stepped around the mark, but as he came closer he could see a set of footprints in the snow and what looked like drag marks, leading directly to the back of the toolshed.

He ran next to the marks. Around the corner, behind the shed, lay Whitney. Her hair was matted with blood that had started to spill out into the snow around her, making her look as though she lay in a red, otherworldly cloud.

He rushed to her side and pressed his fingers against her neck. There was the faint but reassuring thump of her heartbeat. She was still alive, but just barely.

"Baby, wake up." He brushed her hair back from her face. He needed her to wake up. He needed to know she was okay.

On the side of her head was a large lump and the blood poured from a cut at its center. She didn't open her eyes.

He couldn't leave her here, not this close to the fire.

Not with a killer on the loose. But he couldn't get the help he needed without doing something.

He pulled his phone from his pocket and dialed Wyatt. He answered on the first ring and his voice sounded happy as he answered.

"Wyatt… There's a killer on the loose. They attacked Whitney. Toolshed is on fire. Call it in. We're going to need help."

Chapter Twenty-Two

Hate filled him. For the first time in his life, he wanted to kill.

Colter slipped his fingers between Whitney's as he waited for the ambulance to arrive.

"It's going to be okay," he said, not sure whether or not she could hear him. "Help's on the way. You're going to be okay. You are safe now."

He never should have left her alone. He shouldn't have let the party happen. He shouldn't have put anyone in this kind of danger. He had been so stupid. So naive. So idiotic to trust that for one night the world and the evil within it wouldn't tear away at this place and the people he loved.

They should have listened and taken it more seriously, but no. He had been too wrapped up in the needs and wants of his heart. He had been blinded by love. Love had kept him from being objective and from the one thing he had vowed he would do—protect the people he cared about.

In that moment, it was like he was a scared kid again, sitting outside the fire department, his world destroyed.

Wyatt rushed to the backyard, running toward him with two men at his heels. "What happened?"

Colter shook his head. "We have to find whoever is behind this. They're here. Somewhere."

A few steps from him, Wyatt stopped. There was the crunch of something under his foot. Reaching down, he picked up a black cell phone and wiped the snow clean from its screen. Though the glass was cracked, it came to life.

"Is this hers?" Wyatt asked, holding it up for him to see.

There was a picture of a big rig as the phone's wallpaper screen.

Colter shook his head. "Her phone's pink."

"Is she…alive?" Wyatt said, motioning toward her.

"For now. Did you call 911?"

Wyatt nodded. "They should be here anytime."

The deputies who had followed Wyatt rushed to Whitney's side, and one started to take her vitals. "Her pulse is sixty-eight," the man to his right said, like Colter could take some measure of comfort from the fact that the number was normal.

Yet, no matter how normal the number, it didn't change the fact that she wasn't regaining consciousness—or that she might never come back to him.

The thought made a lump lodge in his throat. How was it that when he finally found the one woman in the world whom he wanted to share his future with, the world stole her from him? Perhaps he was never meant to have anything good in his life. Perhaps he was going to be forever cursed.

Wyatt tapped on the phone, pulling up the most recent calls.

There, at the top of the list, was the name William.

Wyatt hit the redial button, putting the call on speaker.

The phone rang. On the second ring, someone picked up.

"Hey, brother. How's the party going?" William Poe asked, his voice souring the air around them. When Colter didn't answer right away, William said, "Daryl?"

Brother? He'd had no idea. From what Wyatt had told him, Daryl was from Canada and they didn't share the same last name. He and William must have only been half brothers, but he'd never heard mention of them even knowing one another before.

"Daryl? You there? What happened?" William pressed. "Did you do as I asked? No one caught you, did they? It's vital that they don't find out we are connected in any way."

Colter reached over and clicked off the phone.

He and his half brother were going to pay for what they had done.

Wyatt reached over and gripped his shoulder. "It's going to be all right. You need to stay with me."

He jerked out of his brother's grip. "If she dies, I will kill William and his damn brother with my bare hands."

Wyatt motioned toward his friends. "We need to find Daryl Bucket. Put out a BOLO. If he's smart, by now he's left the ranch, but he couldn't have gotten far. And one of you needs to go make sure everyone in the barn is safe. For now, let's try and keep everyone inside, but let's not reveal anything. We don't want to cause panic. Calm. Collected. In control. Go."

The two men took off in the direction of the barn.

Though Colter knew he could trust the men to do what had to be done, he couldn't help the feeling of dread and disdain that crept through him. They wouldn't find Daryl. No one would. If Daryl was anything like his brother, he'd be more slippery than an eel and harder to catch.

"You go clear the house," Colter said, motioning toward Wyatt. "We need to make sure that he hasn't planted anything." He looked toward the house as thoughts of the Molotov cocktails came to mind.

Wyatt nodded. "Are you sure you'll be okay?"

"I've got her. We just need to make sure that, like you said, everyone else stays safe. He's going to be out for the family. For all we know, he came after her first in hopes of creating a diversion so he could go after everyone else. You need to make sure that doesn't happen."

"I have my phone if you need anything." He turned to go.

"Wait."

Wyatt stopped, turning back.

"Leave me a gun," Colter said.

Wyatt frowned at him. "Why do you need a gun?"

"If I find Daryl…"

Wyatt shook his head. "We have to stop him. You're right about that. And he needs to pay for what he's done. But you need to stay true to who you are—they win if you sink to their levels. We're Fitzgeralds. We're better than them."

Right now, though he could hear the logic in his brother's words, he couldn't agree with them. Sometimes the right thing wasn't the easy thing. And what could have been better than stripping the world of Daryl's kind of filth? Anyone who wanted to hurt a woman deserved to die.

Wyatt took off, disappearing around the corner of

the house and out into the road as he made his way toward the barn and stables.

Whitney moaned.

"Whit, baby, it's going to be okay," Colter said, running his hand over her hair. "We're going to find Daryl. He's going to pay for what he's done."

Her eyelashes fluttered as though she was struggling to regain consciousness.

"It's okay, baby. You're going to be okay," he cooed, but as he watched her struggle, rage filled him.

If only he hadn't left her side, this wouldn't have happened. He should have been there to protect her and to stop this from happening. He had known there was danger out there.

"No matter what happens, baby, I love you," he said, rubbing his thumb over the soft skin of her cheek.

Her eyelashes fluttered, but once again she lost the battle for consciousness and her head rolled to the side.

It wasn't how he'd wanted this to go, any of this. All he'd wanted was to build a life, a future with the woman he loved.

Why did the world have to be so cruel?

"Isn't that sweet?" a man said, his voice hoarse and crackling like that of a smoker.

Colter looked up, in the direction of the fire and the man's voice. Standing behind the toolshed was a man dressed all in black. His face was blotched with bits of soot and sweat and his dark hair was matted against the side of his face with streaks of drying blood. In his hand was a bat, the end of it covered in crimson drips.

"Go to hell, Daryl," Colter said, slowly rising to his feet.

The man laughed. "Oh, no, that's where you and

your family will be going. And as soon as you all are there, my brother and I are going to take your ranch and everything you care about and burn it to the ground."

"Like hell you are," Colter said, taking a step toward the man.

"Take one more step and you will look like that girl there." Daryl raised the bat, readying to strike. "You should have seen her go down. It was just like a bag of potatoes."

On the ground at Colter's feet was a dented fire extinguisher. He knelt down and picked it up, not taking his gaze off the maniac standing near the flames.

Daryl laughed. "You're one hell of a firefighter if you think that little thing is going to put out those flames," he said, motioning toward the toolshed. One side of the building was starting to list dangerously toward him.

"I have no intention of putting out the fire." This time he was only going to be a fighter—life or death, he was going to find out and he was going to give everything he had…everything for his family and for Whitney.

He lunged toward Daryl, who swung wildly at him with the bat. Colter used the extinguisher to block the man's shot, and when it connected with the metal it made a twang and vibrated like a bell in his hands. Before Daryl could pull the bat back, Colter reached down and took hold of it. He pulled it, but Daryl wouldn't let go.

In one swift motion, Colter lifted the fire extinguisher and swung it at the man's head. It connected with his temple, sending blood spattering over the steadily melting snow.

Daryl staggered and swung the bat drunkenly. He stumbled over his own feet, listing toward the toolshed.

He moved as though he was trying to avoid the flames, but his body disobeyed and he crashed into the building.

Embers careened into the air around him and the small shed collapsed around the man, engulfing him in its superheated grip.

For a second, Colter stood watching the flames. He could let the man die. There would be no reprisal. Only William Poe would come after him, and he was already undoubtedly a target on that man's list.

The smoke curled into the night air.

Wyatt had been right. If he let the man die, if he stood by and did nothing, he would be no better than the men who tried to do them harm. In fact, he would be just like his own biological father—abandoning the one thing that made him who he was and gave him purpose, in order to fulfill the unjust and dark desires of the wolf inside him.

He pushed back a burning two-by-four, grabbed Daryl's foot and pulled.

Colter was, and would always be, a good man. A man who believed in the goodness and redeemability of people—even those who had wronged the people he loved.

Chapter Twenty-Three

Ten stitches and two days later, Whitney was finally starting to feel better. She wasn't seeing the flames every time she closed her eyes, and the smell of smoke was finally starting to dissipate from the ranch. Colter had been great, and even when they had kept her at the hospital overnight for observation, he hadn't left her side.

He was on the phone with Wyatt, and from what she could make out, Daryl was still under guard at the hospital. He was in critical condition because of his burns, but in his pain-medication-induced honesty he had confessed to starting the fire at Sarah's café. If he recovered, he would head to jail. She should have felt some degree of relief that he was going to pay for what he'd done to her. Yet, as she ran her fingers over the bandage on her temple, the only comfort she could find was that she had Colter. They would protect each other from the world.

The door to the office opened and the hoity-toity husband and wife made their way in. The woman was wearing a different pair of stilettos, equally high and equally as unpractical in the knee-deep snow and ice outside.

"Hello. How was your stay?" Whitney said, welcoming them with as much warmth as she could muster.

The wife wouldn't look at her, but the husband nodded. "It was very nice. We were just hoping to check out and pick up Francesca."

"So that's the dog's name," she said with a sad laugh as she glanced over at Lassie and Milo, who were currently snuggling together on Milo's bed. She'd forgotten it completely.

The woman glanced over at the dog and snapped her fingers. "Come, Francesca."

The dog looked up at her for a moment, then pushed its face under Milo's armpit as though it could hide from the woman.

"I guess she's not wanting to go home," Whitney said, trying not to sound as brokenhearted as she felt.

"That's ridiculous," the woman snapped. "She's just not listening." She clapped her hands, the sound as shrill as the woman in the small space of the office.

The dog only pushed its way farther under Milo's front leg.

"Come. Here. Dog," the woman commanded, pointing at the floor at her feet.

Watching the woman in action, Whitney thought it was really no wonder that the dog wanted nothing to do with her.

The dog started to shake under Milo.

The woman walked over and reached down to pick up the pup. Milo looked up at her, and with a lift of his lip, such as Whitney had never seen, he snarled at her. The woman recoiled.

"Did you see that thing?" she said, pointing to Milo. "Your dog was going to bite me."

And what was more, Whitney couldn't blame him. "I think they have fallen in love. He doesn't want to see her go."

"And neither do we," Colter said, clicking off his phone. "You know, if you'd like, you are more than welcome to leave Francesca here. We promise to give her a good home, one full of care and love."

Whitney smiled at him. "Absolutely. We'd love to have her."

The woman frowned. "But she's mine."

Her husband shrugged. "Don't worry, love. I'll just buy you another. One that is better trained this time."

"Fine," the woman said. "But next time, I want a prettier one." She pushed her way outside as the husband paid their bill.

He didn't leave a tip.

Colter laughed as soon as the couple was safely outside and away. "Wow. Is that what you have to put up with every day?"

"Most are better than them, but hey, at least we got something good from it." She motioned toward the dog. "Come here, Lassie."

The dog untangled itself from Milo and came hopping over, licking her hand as she reached down to give it a scratch behind the ears.

"I'm sure we can't be half as happy as she is," Colter said, looking at the dog. "And hey, we have our first animal together."

She smiled. "You're definitely the kind of guy I want to own a dog with."

Colter chuckled. "I'll take that as a high compliment. And if you're open to dog ownership, I'm taking it you're going to stay?"

"Well, if I am invited, I just may," she teased.

"Hmm. I guess an invitation could be extended. After all, you went out of your way to take down a killer."

"More like I stood in the way, but hey... I'll play the hero." She walked to the door and looked out at the old blue pickup, complete with BF Goodrich All-Terrain tires, which had belonged to Daryl Bucket. "Are they going to come tow that thing away?" she asked, motioning to the truck.

"Wyatt said he'd send someone out later today and they'd take it to the county's impound lot."

She didn't care, as long as she never had to see that thing, or Daryl, again.

"Why don't we get out of here for a little bit? All the other guests are checked out, right?"

"Yeah, that would be great." It would be nice to get out of the office that still smelled of the guest's perfume.

Colter slipped on his coat and she followed suit. They made their way outside and to the barn.

She watched Colter as he lifted the bale of hay and threw it into the wheelbarrow. Breaking off a couple of flakes, he took them to the mare closest to them and dropped them into her stall. There were still the cedar shavings from the party on the floor, and the Christmas tree stood at the end of the barn, not moving now until the holidays were over.

Lassie and Milo made their way into the barn and sat by the door, keeping them company and watching on with approval.

The horse nickered in thanks and started to munch on the hay he'd given her. Whitney walked over to the wheelbarrow and grabbed a couple of flakes and dropped them into the next stall. Clark stuck his head out and she gave him a scratch at the top of his head. He ignored the hay she had thrown in, instead choosing to take in more attention.

"You're a little stinker," she said, smiling at the horse.

"Is that what you think of me now—I'm a stinker?" Colter teased, though from his smile she could tell that he knew she was talking to the gelding.

"I would use much stronger words for you, Colter Fitzgerald."

He got an innocent look on his face. "Who, me? The man who saved your life?"

"How about I just call you God's gift to women?" she said with a derisive snort.

He smirked as he pointed toward himself. "I guess you could call me that or Superman or Firefighter Extraordinaire. Better yet, you could call me your husband."

He said it like it was just another name and he hadn't just made her entire body clench with excitement.

"What?" she whispered. "Why would I call you that?"

His wicked smile grew larger. "Well, you don't have to." He walked over to the wheelbarrow. Tucked into the bale of hay was a small black velvet box. He picked it up and knelt down on his knee in front of her.

She cupped her hands over her mouth.

"Whitney Barstow, I know we hadn't talked about this, and that it's a bit impulsive, but there are some things in life that you just *know*. I know that I love you. I know that I want to spend the rest of our lives together."

"But…what about my past?" she said. "About Daryl and William?"

"What about it? Them?" He looked up at her. "We all have a past, and if anyone ever comes after you again, I promise that I will always be at your side and ready to protect you. I'm never going to let anyone hurt you again. Seeing you there…by the fire…"

She reached down and ran her fingers through his hair. "It's okay, Colter. That wasn't your fault. You couldn't have stopped that. Sometimes bad things just happen."

"Well, let's make a stand. Let's focus on the good. Let's get married and start the great," he said, clicking open the box.

Inside was a cushion-cut diamond ring set in white gold. It was simple and elegant.

"It's one of a kind, just like you," he said, smiling up at her.

"Oh, Colter…" She leaned down and kissed his lips.

"Is that a yes?" he said, his lips brushing against her as he spoke.

She nodded, throwing her arms around his neck. "Always… I love you, Colter Fitzgerald."

He held her, box still in his hand. "I love you, too. I always will."

She let go of him and he slipped the ring onto her finger.

Clark threw his head and whinnied at them from his stall.

"It looks like the little stinker is excited, too," Whitney said, staring at the new ring on her finger. "You know…" She glanced over at the horse. "If we're going to have great new beginnings, you know what I want to do?"

Colter slipped his hand in hers. "What?"

She motioned toward Clark. "How about we go for a ride?"

"I thought you'd never ask." Colter picked her up and she wrapped her legs around him. She cupped his face in her hands and gave him a kiss and, with it, the silent promise that they would be together forever—and that she would love him until the end of time.

Just like his smile, their future looked merry and bright.

* * * * *

Can't get enough of MYSTERY, MONTANA?
*Check out the previous titles in the series
from Danica Winters:*

*MS CALCULATION
MR SERIOUS*

And don't miss the final book:

MS DEMEANOR

*Available December 2017
from Mills & Boon Intrigue!*

Mara froze, watching as the sheriff, completely clothed, stood in front of a very naked her.

Billy had seen her naked on several different occasions while they had been together. What was beneath her clothes wasn't a mystery to the man; however, she expected him to at least give her a once-over. Even if she was caught between utter confusion as to why he was standing in front of her in the first place.

Yet, Billy's gaze never left her own.

He closed the space between them so fast that she didn't have time to question it. He grabbed her face in his hands and crashed his lips into hers without a second thought. Mara, too stunned to react, let alone speak, stood stock-still as he pulled back, breaking the kiss.

"I'm just glad you're okay."

SMALL-TOWN FACE-OFF

BY
TYLER ANNE SNELL

MILLS & BOON

First Published in Great Britain 2017
By Mills & Boon, an imprint of HarperCollins*Publishers*
1 London Bridge Street, London, SE1 9GF

© 2017 Tyler Anne Snell

ISBN: 978-0-263-92932-4

46-1117

Our policy is to use papers that are natural, renewable and recyclable products and made from wood grown in sustainable forests. The logging and manufacturing processes conform to the legal environmental regulations of the country of origin.

Printed and bound in Spain
by CPI, Barcelona

Tyler Anne Snell genuinely loves all genres of the written word. However, she's realized that she loves books filled with sexual tension and mysteries a little more than the rest. Her stories have a good dose of both. Tyler lives in Alabama with her same-named husband and their mini "lions." When she isn't reading or writing, she's playing video games and working on her blog, *Almost There*. To follow her shenanigans, visit www.tylerannesnell.com.

This book is for Liz.

Thank you for reading every book, making every birthday cake and understanding I just don't like lemons. Every book I write is because you never stopped supporting me and for that I love you more than you'll ever know. Thank you for being an anchor to a kid who could have been left drifting.

Prologue

Billy Reed looked down at the body and wished he could punch something. Hard.

"This is ridiculous," Suzy said at his side. "She's not even eighteen."

His partner was right. Courtney Brooks had turned sixteen two weeks ago. The car she had been found in was a birthday present from her father. Billy knew this because he'd known of the girl since she was in middle school. She was a part of one of the many families in the small town of Carpenter, Alabama, who had lived there through at least two generations.

And now she was dead in the back seat of a beat-up Honda.

"Anyone tell her folks yet?" Billy asked. He'd arrived on the scene five minutes after his partner, Suzanne Simmons, had. By the time he'd cut through lunchtime traffic and bumped down the dirt road in his Crown Vic to the spot where poor Courtney had met her end, a set of paramedics, the deputy who had first responded to the call and the boy who had found her were all gathered around, waiting for what was next.

"No, Rockwell wanted to make the call," Suzy answered. Billy raised his eyebrow, questioning why the sheriff would do that when he hadn't even come to the crime scene yet, and she continued. "He's fishing buddies with her dad. He heard Marty call in the name."

Billy could imagine their leader, a man north of sixty with a world of worries to match, breaking the bad news from behind his desk. He'd let his stare get lost in the grain of the oak while he broke a family's heart with news no parents should ever receive.

"There's no signs of foul play, as far as I can tell," Suzy commented. One of the EMTs broke off from the car and headed toward them.

"We both know what this is, Suzy," Billy said. The anger he was nearly getting used to began to flood his system. The deputy could save the EMT time by telling the man he already knew what had killed her. An overdose of a drug called Moxy. The current scourge of Riker County. However, Billy's mother had taught him the importance of being polite. So he listened to the man say that he thought Courtney had been gone a few hours before they'd gotten there, and if the paramedic was a betting man, he'd put his money on an overdose.

"I've already taken pictures, but I'd like to look around again, just in case," Suzy said. Billy was about to follow when a call over the radio drew him to his car instead. He asked dispatch to repeat.

"The sheriff wants you here, Billy," she said. "Now."

That gave him pause but he confirmed he understood. Suzy must have heard, too. She waved him away, saying she could handle it from here. Billy's eye caught the teen who had found Courtney. He was standing with Marty, one of the other deputies from the department, and they were deep in discussion. Every few words he'd glance back at the girl. And each time he looked closer to losing it. He'd likely never seen a dead body before, and judging by his expression, he'd never forget it, either. It made Billy grind his teeth.

No one in Riker County should have that problem. At least, not if Billy had a say about it.

It had been six months since an influx of Moxy hit the county. In that time, Billy had seen four overdoses and an escalation of violence, two of those incidents ending in murder. For all intents and purposes, Moxy brought out the worst tendencies in people and then energized them. While Riker County, its sheriff's department and police departments had had their problems with narcotics in the past, the new drug and its ever-elusive supplier had caught them woefully off guard. It was a fact that kept Billy up at night and one that stayed with him as he drove through the town and then cut his engine in the department's parking lot.

Movement caught his eye, distracting his thoughts, and he realized he was staring at the very man who had called him in. Billy exited the cruiser and leaned against it when the man made no move to go inside the building, arms folded over his chest. Sheriff Rockwell put his cigarette out and stopped in front of him. He looked more world-weary than he had the day before.

"I'm going to cut to the chase, Reed," the sheriff said, leaving no room for greetings. "We need to find the Moxy supplier and we need to find him now. You understand?"

"Yessir," Billy said, nodding.

"Until that happens, I want you to work exclusively on trying to catch the bastard."

"What about Detective Lancaster?" Billy asked. Jamie Lancaster's main focus had been on finding something on the supplier since the second overdose had been reported.

"Lancaster is crap, and we both know it," the sheriff said. "His drive left the second we all had to take a pay cut. No, what we need now is someone whose dedication isn't made by his salary." The sheriff clapped Billy on the shoulder. "In all of my years, I've learned that there's not much that can stand against a person protecting their own. You love not only this town, but the entire county like it's family, Billy."

"I do," Billy confirmed, already feeling his pride swelling.

The sheriff smiled, briefly, and then went stone cold.

"Then go save your family."

Two MONTHS LATER, Billy was sitting in a bar in Carpenter known as the Eagle. In the time since he'd talked to the sheriff in the parking lot, he'd chased every lead known to the department. He'd worked long, hard hours until, finally, he'd found a name.

Bryan Copeland.

A businessman in his upper fifties with thinning gray hair and an affinity for wearing suits despite the Alabama heat, he was running the entire operation from Kipsy. It was the only city within the Riker County Sheriff's Department purview, Carpenter being one of three towns. But where he kept the drugs—whether it was through the city or towns— and when he moved them were mysteries. Which was the reason Billy hadn't had the pleasure of arresting him yet. They couldn't prove anything, not even after two drug dealers admitted who their boss was. Because, according to the judge and Bryan's fancy lawyer, there was no hard evidence. So that was why, late on a Thursday night, Billy Reed was seated at the Eagle finishing off his second beer when a woman sat down next to him and cleared her throat.

"Are you Deputy Reed? Billy Reed?" she asked, voice dropping to a whisper. Billy raised his eyebrow. He didn't recognize the woman. And he would have remembered if he had met her before.

She had long black hair that framed a clear and determined face. Dark eyes that openly searched his expression, trying to figure him out for whatever reason, high cheekbones, pink, pink lips, and an expression that was split between contemplation and caution. All details that created a truly beautiful woman. One who had the deputy's full attention.

"Yes, that's me," he answered. "But I don't think I've had the pleasure."

The woman, who he had placed just under his own age of thirty-two, pasted on a smile and cut her eyes around them before answering.

"I believe you're trying to build a case against my father." Billy immediately went on red alert, ready to field whatever anger or resentment the woman had with him. However, what she said next changed everything. Her dark eyes hardened, resolute. With a voice free of any doubt, she gave Billy exactly what he needed. "And I can help you do just that."

Chapter One

Three years later, Billy Reed was kicking off his shoes, digging into his DVR and turning on a game he'd been meaning to watch for a month. During the season he hadn't had time to keep up with teams or scores but he liked the white noise it produced. And, maybe if it was a close enough game, his focus might leave his work long enough to enjoy it.

He popped off the cap of his beer and smiled at the thought.

He'd been the Riker County sheriff for under two years, although he'd lived his entire life within its lines, just as his father had before him. It was one of the reasons Sheriff Rockwell had personally endorsed Billy to take his place when he'd decided it was time to retire.

"You always want what's best for Riker and I can't think of a better outlook for a sheriff," Rockwell had said. "After what you've helped do for this place already, I can't imagine a better fit."

Billy's eyes traveled to a framed picture of the former sheriff shaking his hand. The picture had been taken during a press conference that had come at one of the most rewarding moments of Billy's career as deputy, when drug supplier Bryan Copeland had been locked behind bars for good.

He didn't know it at the time, but that case would help

him become the man he was today—the sheriff who was trying desperately to pretend there was such a thing as a night off. He took a pull on his beer. But as soon as he tried to move his focus to the game on the TV, his phone came to life.

So much for trying.

The caller ID said Suzy. Not a name he'd wanted to see until the next morning. He sighed and answered.

"I just got home, Suzy," he said.

Suzanne Simmons didn't attempt to verbally walk carefully around him. Never mind the fact that he was the boss now. He didn't expect her to, either. She'd been his friend for years.

"That ain't my problem, Sheriff," she snapped. "What *is* my problem is Bernie Lutz's girlfriend drunk and yelling at my desk."

Billy put his beer down on the coffee table, already resigned to the fact that he wouldn't be able to enjoy the rest of it.

"Say again?"

He'd known Suzy since they were in middle school and knew that the short pause she took before answering was her way of trying to rearrange her thoughts without adding in the emotion. As chief deputy she couldn't be seen flying off the handle when her anger flared. The sheriff's right-hand man, or woman in this case, needed to appear more professional than that. Though that hadn't stopped her from expressing herself within the privacy of his office from time to time.

"Bernie Lutz, you remember him?" she asked. "Short guy with that tattoo of his ex-wife on his right arm?"

Billy nodded to himself, mind already going through old files.

"Yeah, drug dealer until he went the straight and narrow

about a year ago." Billy remembered something else. "He said he found Jesus and started doing community service when he got out of lockup."

"Well, it looks like he just found a whole lot more than Jesus," Suzy said. "Jessica, his girlfriend, just ran into the station yelling about finding him dead in a ditch when she went out to their house. She's asking for our protection now. And, by asking, I mean yelling for it."

Billy ran his hand down his face, trying to get the facts straight.

"So, did you check out if what she said was true?" he asked.

"Working on it. I tried to get her to come with me to show me exactly where she found him but, Billy, she freaked out big-time. Said they could still be watching her."

Billy stood, already looking for the shoes he'd kicked off when he'd thought his night off might stick. His cowboy hat was always easier to find. He scooped it up off the back of the couch and put it on. The act alone helped focus him even more.

"They?" he asked.

"She claims that two men came to the house last week and asked Bernie for drugs, and when he said he didn't deal anymore, they told him they'd come back and get them both." Suzy lowered her voice a little. "To be honest, I think Jessica is under the influence of *something* right now—why didn't she call us from the scene?—but I sent Dante out there to check it out. I just wanted to give you a heads-up if this thing ends up escalating and poor Bernie really is in a ditch somewhere."

Billy spotted his shoes and went to put them on.

"Go ahead and get descriptions of the men she claims paid them a visit," he said. "They could very well be suspects in a murder. And, if not, at the very least, they could be trying to buy or spread narcotics in the community." His thoughts flew back to Bryan Copeland.

"And we don't want any more of that," she finished.

"No," Billy said. "Definitely not."

"Okay, I'll give you a call when this all pans out."

"Don't worry about it," he said, tying the laces to his shoes. "I'm coming in."

"But—"

"The people of Riker County didn't elect me to sit back when potential murderers could be roaming the streets," he reminded her. "Plus, if there *is* a body and a crime scene, we need to act fast so that the rain doesn't destroy any evidence. Call Matt and tell him to go ahead and head out there. Even if it's a false alarm I'd rather be safe than sorry. Don't let Jessica leave the station until I get there."

Suzy agreed and said goodbye. She might have been his closest friend, but she still knew when to not argue with an order. Even if she had been trying to look out for him.

Billy turned the game off, not bothering to look at the score, and mentally checked out. He tried recalling where Bernie had lived when he'd arrested him and the road that Jessica would travel going there. Billy had grown up in Carpenter, which was one of the three small towns located in Riker County, and Billy had driven all of its roads at least twice. It was the epicenter of a community fused together by humidity, gossip and roots so deep that generations of families never left. Billy Reed was a part of one of those families. He lived in the home he and his father had both grown up in, and a part of him hoped that one day his kids would walk the same hallways. Not that he had any kids. However, it was still a thought that drove him to try and keep the only home he'd ever known a safe, enjoyable one. If Bernie and his past drug habits were back at it, then Billy wanted to nip that in the bud.

Billy tried to rein in thoughts from the past as he searched for his keys, the one item he always seemed to lose, when a knock sounded on the front door. Like a dog trying to figure out a foreign noise, he tilted his head to the side and paused.

It was well past dark and had been raining for the last hour. The list of visitors he'd typically receive was relatively short, considering most wouldn't drop by unannounced. Still, as he walked through the living room to the entryway, he considered the possibility of a friend coming by for a drink or two. Just because he'd become sheriff didn't mean his social life had completely stopped. Then again, for all he knew it could be his mother coming into town early. If so, then he was about to be berated for his lack of Christmas lights and tree despite its being a week away from the holiday. While Billy knew he had to maintain a good image within the community, even when he was off, he hadn't found the time or will to get into a festive mood. Though, if he was being honest with himself, the holidays had lost some charm for him in the last few years. Still, he opened the door with a smile that felt inviting, even genuine.

And immediately was lost for words.

It was like looking in a mirror and recognizing your reflection, yet at the same time still being surprised by it. That's what Billy was going through as he looked at Mara Copeland, dark hair wet from the rain that slid down her poncho, standing on his welcome mat.

"Hey, Billy."

Even her voice pushed Billy deeper into his own personal twilight zone. It kept whatever greeting he had reserved for a normal visitor far behind his tongue.

"I know it's late and I have no business being here but, Billy, I think I need your help."

BILLY DIDN'T MAKE her spell out her situation standing there on his doorstep. He'd regained his composure by the tail end of Mara's plea. Though she could tell it was a struggle.

"Come in," he said, standing back and gesturing wide with his long arms. Mara had almost forgotten how tall he was. Even in the mostly dark space outside his door, she could still make out the appearance of a man who looked the same as he had almost two years before—tall, with broad shoulders and a lean body rather than overly muscled. Lithe, like a soccer player, and no doubt strong, an attractive mix that carried up and through to a hard chin and a prominent nose. His eyes, a wild, ever-moving green, just sweetened the entire pot that was Billy Reed. Mara had realized a long time ago that there wasn't a part of the dark-haired man she didn't find appealing.

Which didn't help what had happened back then.

She hesitated at his invitation to come inside, knowing how meticulous he was with keeping the hardwood in his house clean. Which she clearly was not. The poncho might have kept the clothes underneath dry, but it still was shedding water like a dog would its fur in the summer. Not to mention she hadn't had a hood to keep her long tangles of hair dry.

"Don't worry about it," he said, guessing her thoughts. "It's only water."

His smile, which she'd been afraid she'd broken by her arrival, came back. But only a fraction of it. The lack of its former affection stung. Then again, what had she expected?

"Sorry to intrude," she said, once they were both shut inside the house. Its warmth eased some of the nerves that had been dancing since she'd gotten into the car that morning, although not nearly enough to keep her stomach from fluttering. Although she'd known her destination since she'd buckled her seat belt, seeing the sheriff in person had stunned her, in a way. Like finding a memory she'd tried to forget suddenly within reach. She started to wonder if he had tried to forget her. "I would have called but I couldn't find your number," she lied.

Billy stood back, giving her space. The small part of his smile that had surfaced was disintegrating. Mara's stomach began to knot. She had a feeling that Billy's politeness was sheer Southern reflex.

And now he was starting to remember exactly who she was.

She didn't blame him or the mistrust that distorted his handsome face next.

Though, that stung a bit, too.

"You could have called the department," he deadpanned. "You might not remember, what with you up and leaving so quickly, but I'm the sheriff. I'm sure if you asked for me they'd patch you right on through."

Mara kept the urge to flinch at bay. In her road trip across Alabama, back to the last place she'd ever thought she'd return—especially with Christmas only days away— a small part of her had hoped Billy would have somehow forgotten or forgiven what she'd done. That when and if they ever met again, he would smile that dimpled smile that used to make her go weak in the knees and they'd— what?—be friends? Her thoughts had always derailed at that question. They always seemed to when she thought of Billy.

The little girl asleep and hidden beneath the poncho, held up by Mara's arm, didn't help matters.

"I *do* remember that you're the sheriff," she said. "And, you're right, I should have called there, but—" Mara had rehearsed a speech in the car explaining the exact reason she had driven back to Carpenter, back to his house, instead of just calling. Now, however, the words just wouldn't come. All she could find were his eyes, ever searching for an answer. "Well," she started again, trying to find a stronger voice. "It seemed too important to not talk about face-to-face."

Whatever reply Billy had been brewing behind those perfect lips seemed to stall out. His brows pulled together, his nostrils flared and then, just as quickly, his expression began to relax. He took a deep breath.

"Fine," he finally said. "But make it quick. I just got called out."

That was as warm as she'd bet the man was going to be, so she nodded. The simple movement shook water free from the bright yellow poncho covering her. She tried to give him an apologetic look.

"I didn't have an umbrella," she explained.

"You never did," he said, also, she believed, on reflex. Like the nod, it was such a simple statement that Mara wondered if he'd even registered he'd said it at all. "Here, let me help with that." Billy reached out and took the bag from her shoulder. Any mother might recognize it as a diaper bag, though it was designed to look like an oversized purse, but she could tell Billy Reed hadn't caught on to it yet.

Or the bulge beneath the poncho.

She must have really thrown him for a loop.

"Thanks. Do you have a bag or something I could put this poncho in?" She motioned to the very thing keeping their conversation from diving headlong into the foreign topic of kids.

"Yeah, give me a sec." He set her bag on the entryway bench and headed toward the kitchen. It gave Mara a moment to take two deep breaths before letting each out with a good shake.

It had been two years since she'd seen Billy Reed. More than that since she'd met him in a bar, ready to do her best to help him take down the only family she'd had left. Now here she was, standing in his house, dripping on the hardwood.

"This is all I have to put it in," he said, coming back. His smile was still gone but at least he wasn't stone-faced.

"Oh, thanks," Mara said to the Walmart bag he extended. She didn't take it. "Actually, I'm going to need your help with this one. I don't want to drop her."

And, just like that, Billy Reed must have finally looked at her—*really* looked at her—taking in the large bulge beneath the poncho. Wordlessly, he helped her pull it off. He stood there, eyes wide, as the dark-haired little girl came into view. She wiggled at the sudden light but, thankfully, stayed asleep. One little blessing that Mara would more than take.

"This is Alexa," Mara introduced her. She watched as his eyes widened. They swept over the little girl with attention she knew he was proud of. For a moment she forgot why she'd come. So many times over the last two years she'd thought about this meeting. Would it happen? What would he say? What would *she* say? However, Mara reminded herself that she hadn't come back to Carpenter because she'd decided to. No, a man and his threats had made that decision for her. Mara cleared her throat. It was now or never. "Billy, meet your daughter."

Chapter Two

Billy, bless him, didn't say a thing for a good minute. Though his eyes ran the gamut of emotions.

Mara took a tentative step toward him, arm still holding their daughter up, and opened her mouth to speak, but Billy's phone went off in his pocket, ringing too loudly to ignore.

He shook off the spell he'd fallen into, though when he spoke, his voice wasn't as strong as it had been before.

"Please, hold that thought. I have to take this," he said, pulling his phone out. He didn't look at the caller ID as he answered. "Reed."

Mara's mouth closed as a woman's voice filled the space between them. She didn't stop for breath as she relayed whatever she needed to the man. Slowly his attention split and refocused on the new information. His brow furrowed and his eyes took on a look Mara knew all too well.

This was Work Billy and she'd come at a bad time. That much was clear.

"Okay, thanks," he said when the woman had finished. "I'll be there in twenty."

Mara's stomach fell as Billy ended the call. She didn't know what she had expected of the man she'd left with no more than a note on his pillow and no hint whatsoever that she was pregnant with his child. But his taking a work call hadn't been on the list of possibilities. She straightened her back. Alexa squeezed her little arms around Mara's neck in her sleep. The slight movement wasn't missed by Billy. He looked at his daughter before his eyes cut back to her.

"You have a world of explaining to do," he started, voice low. He had finally landed on an emotion. Anger. "First you just up and leave, then you don't talk to me for two years, and now you're saying that—" He stopped his voice from going any louder. Without breaking eye contact he reached for the raincoat on the wall next to them. "A body has just been found and I need to try and get to the crime scene before this rain messes everything up. If it hasn't already." He slid into the coat. "I'm sorry." He ran his finger across the brim of his hat. "It's been a long day and I didn't expect to see you." His eyes trailed down to Alexa before meeting Mara's again. His expression softened, if only a little. "I would ask you along, but I don't think a crime scene in the rain is a good place to have this talk."

"I'll agree to that," Mara said. Before she could add anything the sheriff's expression changed again. It became alert, ready.

"Wait, you said you needed my help?" he asked. The angles of his face seemed to go tight. While Mara had no doubt he was ready to listen to her with all of his attention, he was also still thinking about the crime scene. The sound of pounding rain probably wasn't helping.

"I can wait until you're done," she said. The urgency that had driven her from their home that morning had ebbed considerably, especially now that she was there, standing in Billy's house. Maybe she had been foolish to leave so suddenly and come running back to Carpenter.

And its sheriff.

"Are you sure?" She could see his resolve splitting. She nodded.

"I can go check in to the hotel off Miller Street, if you think it will be a bit."

"Why don't you just wait here? It's not like you don't know your way around." Heat rushed up to Mara's cheeks at the comment. She doubted he'd meant to stir up old memories. He was just stating a fact. She *did* know her way around, having spent countless hours there trying to plan a way to stop her father. A pursuit that had had unexpected outcomes.

"Oh, I wouldn't want to intr—"

"Mara." Billy's voice took on a low edge. "Stay."

An easy command for any smart woman to follow from Billy Reed.

Alexa stirred in her arms.

"Okay," she relented. It would be nice not to have to run Alexa back out into the bad weather. Plus, she doubted after the information she'd just hit him with, Billy would leave his house until he had the whole story. She couldn't blame him. "I'll wait until you get back."

An expression she didn't quite understand flashed across Billy's face, but when he spoke his voice was normal, considering everything.

"Help yourself to any food in the fridge," he said. "I'll be back as soon as I can."

Mara thanked him and moved out of his way as he went out into the storm. The Billy she'd known years before hadn't changed. Justice and protecting those within his jurisdiction still prevailed.

"Well, Alexa," Mara said once she'd heard his Tahoe leave. "This is the Reed family home."

A little uncertainly, Mara slipped off her shoes and padded through the entryway and into the living room. Surprisingly, or maybe not, nothing seemed to have changed since the last time she'd been in the house. The old dark hardwood grounded a room that had been the heart of the Reed family for two generations. Sure, some of the furniture had changed—the black leather couch certainly hadn't been Billy's mother's choice, and neither had the plasma flat-screen—but the cozy feel of a house well loved and well lived-in hadn't diminished one bit.

Mara kept on her tour with a growing smile. From the living room she went to the kitchen, the dining room and the open office. She was looking for clues that might tell her what had happened to Billy since she'd left Carpenter. The family pictures of the Reeds still dotted the walls, including some new additions and marriages, while other pictures specific only to Billy also popped up occasionally. Mara stopped and smiled at one in particular that caught her eye.

Standing in front of a crowd of Riker County residents was the dark-haired man, moments after he'd been officially elected sheriff.

The old affection began to break through an emotional dam she'd spent years building. Then, just as quickly, she was back to that morning, when she'd stood on her front porch across from the stranger who had threatened her life and the life of her child. If anyone could deal with the mystery man it was the Riker County sheriff.

Alexa moved in her arms. This time she woke up.

The cold that had started to spread in the pit of Mara's stomach turned to warmth.

"Well, hello there," she whispered.

Alexa looked up at her mom. Just shy of fifteen months, the toddler might not have known much about the world, but that had never stopped her beautiful green eyes from being curious.

Just like her father's.

IT TOOK FIFTEEN minutes to get to the ditch that held Bernie Lutz's body. Billy could have taken three hours—hell, three days—and still not have been able to completely process what had just happened. A herd of elephants could have stampeded alongside his Tahoe as he navigated the muddy back road and it wouldn't have distracted him. Mara's sudden reappearance alone would have stunned him. But this? Alexa? Mara Copeland on his doorstep with a baby?

His baby.

"Get a hold of yourself, Billy," he said out loud. "You've got a job to do first."

Had Mara been wearing a wedding ring? Billy shook his head. He needed to focus on one thing at a time. He needed to put everything that wasn't Bernie Lutz out of his mind. At least for the moment.

He sighed.

Yet, there Mara had been. Staring up at him through her long dark lashes, asking for help.

And he'd just left.

His phone went off, dancing on the dash before he answered. This time it was Matt Walker, currently Riker County's only detective, thanks to the retirement of his former partner. Like Suzy, Matt was direct when he spoke about work.

"Henry got a tarp up, Billy," he yelled over the weather. "But the road runoff is washing everything away. I went ahead and called in the county coroner."

Billy swore.

"It hasn't rained in weeks, and the one time we need it dry is the one time all hell breaks loose."

"It could be worse," Matt said. "We could be the body in the ditch."

Billy nodded.

"You're right," he said, sobering. "I'm a few minutes out. If the coroner gets there before me, go ahead and load him up. Maybe if we act fast enough we can salvage some evidence."

"Ten-four." Billy started to hang up but Matt cut back in. "And Billy? Just from looking at him, I'm going to say that his girlfriend might have been telling some kind of truth. He's beaten pretty badly. His death wasn't fast, by any means. See you when you get here."

He ended the call.

Thoughts of the past half hour were replaced by the need to solve a murder.

IT WAS JUST before midnight when Billy unlocked his front door. The storm raged on. Every part of him was soaking wet, and his boots and jeans were more mud than anything. He didn't even try to keep the floor clean. Instead, he sloshed inside and stripped in the entryway.

It wasn't until he was starting to pull off his shirt that he spotted the bright yellow poncho sticking out of a Walmart bag. He froze as his brain detached from work life and zipped right back to his personal one.

Mara.

With more attention to the noise he was making, he left his shirt on and, instead, got out of his boots. Only one light was on. He followed it into the living room. For one moment he thought it was empty—that Mara had left again, this time with his daughter in tow—but then he spotted a mass of dark hair cascading over the arm of the couch. Coming around to face it, he was met with a sight that used to be familiar.

Mara was asleep, body pulled up so that her knees were close to her stomach, making her look impossibly small. It wasn't the first time he'd come home after work to find her in that exact spot, lights still on, waiting for him. Even when he'd tell her not to wait up, Billy would come in after a long day to find her there. She'd never once complained. Seeing her lying there, face soft and unguarded, Billy took a small moment for himself to remember what it felt like to come home to her. But it didn't last.

There had been too many nights between then and now. Ones where he'd come home to an empty house, wondering why she'd gone.

I'm sorry, but it's over.

Billy shook his head at the one sentence that had changed everything between them and looked at the one idea he'd never entertained after Mara had gone.

Alexa was tucked within her mother's arms, simultaneously fitting and not fitting in the space between. Her hair was dark, but still lighter than his, and it fell just past her shoulders and, from the looks of it, was as thick as her mother's. Before he could police his thoughts, a smile pulled up the corners of his lips.

He might not have known her the day before, but that didn't stop the affection for the little girl.

And, just like before, the feeling of warmth, however brief, was gone.

Why had she been kept a secret?

Billy took a step back. While he had questions, he didn't want to wake either one, but the creak in the floor that had been there since his father was a child sounded under his weight. Mara's eyes fluttered opened and immediately found him.

"I tried to be quiet," he whispered.

Mara shook her head and slowly sat up while trying to disengage herself from the toddler.

"No, I'm sorry," she whispered back once she managed to get free. "I didn't mean to fall asleep."

She followed him through the entryway and into the dining room, far enough away that they could talk in normal tones.

And, boy, did they have a lot to talk about.

"What time is it?" she asked, taking a seat at the table. She stifled a yawn.

"Close to midnight. I was gone a lot longer than I thought I would be," he admitted. Billy took a seat opposite her. "This storm couldn't have come at a worse time."

Mara nodded, but the movement was sluggish. He was tired, too. It was time to stop delaying and finally ask the current question on his mind.

"Mara, why are you here?"

Chapter Three

"A man came to my house this morning and asked about my father," Mara said, knowing full well that once the words were out there Billy wouldn't forget them. Finding a way to take down her father—to catch him in the act—had been an emotional and physical drain on them both. The collective hope that Billy would save Riker County had pressed down heavily on him, while betraying the only family she'd had had never left Mara's mind.

As if an invisible hand had found the strings to his puppet, Billy's entire body snapped to attention.

"They wanted Bryan?"

But he's in prison, Mara silently finished.

"The man didn't want *him*," she said out loud instead. "The guy wanted something important of my father's and I needed to tell him where it was. I had no idea what he was talking about."

Billy's dark brow rose in question. "Something important," he deadpanned.

"He didn't say what, past that," she admitted, recalling how the man had been careful when choosing his words. "But what really spooked me was when he said he wanted to take over what my father had built, my family's business. And I don't think he was talking about my dad's old accounting job."

Billy's forehead creased in thought. She could almost see the red flags popping up behind his eyes.

"Moxy," he supplied.

She nodded. "I told him I had no part in that slice of my father's life, but he didn't seem to care," she continued. She twisted her hands together, and when she recounted what happened next her stomach was a knot of coldness. "Then he saw Alexa playing in the house behind me. He told me that I might change my mind if I had the right incentive."

Billy's body managed to take on an even greater tension.

"What did he want you to change your mind about?" he asked. "Telling him the location of *something important* or wanting nothing to do with your father's past business?"

Mara sighed.

"I don't know. After he looked Alexa's way, I told him he needed to leave." Mara let her gaze drop. "He didn't argue, but he did say he'd be seeing me again soon."

Billy's chair scraped the hardwood as he pushed back. Mara could feel her eyes widen in surprise as she read-justed her attention to his expression.

Anger. And it definitely wasn't meant for her this time.

"I'm assuming he didn't give you a name," Billy said, walking out of the dining room and disappearing. He was back a second later with a small notepad and a pen in his hands.

"Just a first name. Beck."

"And did you call the cops?"

A burst of heat spread up her neck and pooled in her cheeks. Mara had *thought* about filing a police report, but the mention of her father had thrown her completely off-kilter. What she would *normally* have done went out the window. Instead, her thoughts had flown south to Riker County. And the only man who had ever made her feel safe. Suddenly, that feeling that had burned so strongly hours before when she'd packed the car and taken Alexa on a trip across Alabama seemed rash.

"No," she admitted. "I should have but—well, I thought if someone was trying to start up my father's business again that they would start it here. I thought that I should—I don't know—warn you or something." Again, her words sounded lame compared to what she wanted to say. But at least they were true. In his prime, Bryan Copeland had grown a drug network that nearly swallowed the whole of Riker County. His dealings had cost the lives of several residents, including teenagers. Not to mention a cascade of repercussions that were harder to measure. The fact that all of her father's former connections hadn't been found was one that had always made the man in front of her nervous. Part of her father's business hadn't been accounted for...which meant that if this Beck person *was* trying to start up again, it would only stand to reason he might have found the people law enforcement hadn't. Or maybe that's what Beck was looking for.

For the first time since he'd stepped back through the door, Billy's expression softened a fraction. The lines of tension in his shoulders, however, did not.

"Could you describe to me what this Beck guy looks like?" He flipped open the notebook and clicked his pen. "And did you see his car?"

"Yes and yes."

Mara spent the next few minutes painting a picture of the stranger named Beck until Billy was satisfied it was enough to try and look him up through the department's database.

Mara thought it curious that Billy never asked where she was currently living. It made her wonder if he'd looked her up at all in the last two years. She hadn't gone far, but far enough that Riker County had been firmly in her rearview.

"I want you to come to the station with me tomorrow," Billy said, closing the notepad. "I'm going to see if the sketch artist from the state agency can come in and work with you. Maybe the new guy can draw us a good picture to work with if this Beck person isn't on our list of people with warrants out on them."

"So, you think Beck was serious?"

Mara sat straighter. The possibility of someone revitalizing Moxy, or any drug, within the community using the foundation her father had laid was finally sinking in. Just another reason for the residents of Riker County to despise her and her family. "You think he's really going to try and start up where Dad left off?"

Billy let out a long breath. He ran his hands through his hair. How attractive she still found him was not lost on Mara. Looking at him now, a well-built, fine-tuned man with miles and miles of goodwill and good intentions, she could feel the stirring of feelings she needed to stay still. Not to mention the heat of attraction that always lit within her when Billy was anywhere near. But now wasn't the time or place. If there was a chance he could forgive her for leaving, she doubted he'd forgive her for keeping their daughter a secret—a topic of conversation she was sure would take place once the cop side of him was done flexing his professional muscles.

The sheriff cleared his throat. His eyes hardened. He had something to say and she doubted she'd like it.

"We found Bernie Lutz in a ditch tonight," he started. Mara felt recognition flare but couldn't keep it burning long enough to connect. Billy helped her out. "He was one of the drug dealers your dad used who escaped the serious charges after Bryan went to court." There it was.

"The one with the ex-wife tattoo," she said. He nodded. "This was never confirmed, but the story his girlfriend spun was that two men came to their house looking for something the other day. Whatever it was, Bernie didn't know or didn't tell. This could all be a coincidence, but you know me, I don't believe in those." Billy put his finger on the paper he'd just written on. He jabbed it once. "Not only do I think this mystery man is going to try to start up your dad's old business, but I think he might have already started."

BILLY WAITED FOR Mara to process everything and then excused himself to go to his room. He slipped into his attached bathroom and splashed cold water on his face. The night had thrown him several curveballs and he hadn't hit one of them.

Even if he filtered out Mara's sudden reappearance and the absolute bombshell that was their daughter, Billy still had Bryan Copeland's legacy to worry about. Whoever this Beck person was, Billy would be damned if he was going to let him repeat what had caused Riker County so much pain years ago. Especially not during the holiday. That was no present any family should have to get.

Billy splashed another wave of water on his face. He stayed hunched over, resting his elbows on the edge of the sink, and kept his eyes closed. There. He could feel the weight of Riker County's newest burden settling against him. It pressed down on his shoulders and kept going until it hit his chest. No, he wasn't going to stand by while the residents of his county endured another Bryan Copeland incident.

Billy opened his eyes.

Not while he was sheriff.

He dried his face, and without changing out of his wet clothes, he walked out to find Mara, his mind already made up.

She was standing in the living room, Alexa asleep in her arms. Her bag was thrown over her shoulder and her expression was already telling him goodbye.

"You're leaving."

Mara's cheeks reddened but her answer came out clear, concrete.

"Yes, but not town. To be honest, I don't like Beck knowing where I live so I don't want to go back there just yet," she answered. "Plus, to be even more honest, I'm really tired. The faster we get to the hotel, the happier I'll be."

Billy wasn't a complicated man. At least, he didn't think he was. Yet, standing there a few feet from a woman who had left him in the dust, he knew he shouldn't have felt any joy at her admission that she was staying. Or an ounce of desire from looking at her hardened nipples through her light pink T-shirt—the result, he guessed, from the AC he had turned up despite the cool they were getting from the storm—or how her jeans hugged her legs just right. But he did.

"Stay here instead," Billy said before he realized he'd even thought it. Mara's eyes widened a fraction. Her cheeks darkened slightly. "The guest bedroom is free, the sheets are clean and you don't have to drive in the rain to get there. Plus, Miller's parking lot looked pretty full. Probably lousy with in-laws and extended family members that no one wants in their house."

He grinned, trying to drive his point home. It didn't work.

"I don't think it's a good idea," Mara said, eyes straying from his. He wondered if she knew he was thinking about her naked and against him. It was a fleeting thought, but by God it was there. "I've already upset your life enough by coming here."

Billy cleared his throat and tried to clear the feelings

of attraction he was currently wading through. He needed some space from her, but he wasn't about to let her leave without a fight, either. Something he wished he could have done two years before.

"Then stay in the guesthouse," he offered.

Mara met his gaze.

"I finished it last summer," he explained, remembering she hadn't known he'd thrown all of his spare time into finishing the apartment that used to be the detached garage. It had been less for his mother when she came for long visits and more of a distraction. "Come on, Mara," he continued when she still seemed to be weighing her options. He moved closer but stopped when the floorboard squeaked. It earned a small movement from Alexa. Billy let himself look at the little girl before fixing her mama with a look he hoped didn't show how hard it was to just talk to her. "Please, Mara. Just stay."

Mara shifted Alexa so she was more firmly on her hip. A wisp of a smile pulled up her lips but it blew away before she answered.

"Okay, we'll stay in the guesthouse if it really doesn't bother you."

Billy nodded and moved to grab her bag. His eyes lingered on Alexa but he didn't ask to hold her. He couldn't be a father right now. Not when things in Riker County were starting to heat up. Not when Mara had attracted the attention of a mysterious man who had no problem threatening children. Not when he'd been in contact with Mara for less than an hour and was already having trouble focusing on anything else. He shouldered the bag and led the two down the hall and to the back door, grabbing an umbrella in the process.

It wasn't raining as hard as it had been, but it was enough to warrant pulling Mara close to him to stay dry beneath the umbrella. She didn't move away or argue as she folded into his left arm and against his side. The inner war he was fighting was downright impossible to ignore as they walked in silence along the stone path that led to the guesthouse door. Billy pulled the keys out of his pocket and unlocked it.

"Here you go," he said, voice low, even to his ears.

He watched as she stepped inside and wordlessly looked around the living space. A kitchenette, three-piece bathroom and a small bedroom made up the rest of the apartment. He'd built on to expand it but everything was still small. At least it was private.

And far enough away from him that he'd never know if she left.

"Oh, it's beautiful, Billy," Mara said after a moment. "You did a wonderful job."

Billy would have taken the compliment with pride if anyone else had given it at any other time. But Mara's words flipped a switch within him. He felt his body stiffen, his expression harden. The pain of finding her note on his pillow came back to him in full.

"I'll come get you at seven," he said. He stepped back out into the rain but didn't look away from those dark eyes that made him crazy. "And, Mara, try not to leave this time. Once we get this guy you're going to tell me exactly why you kept my daughter a secret."

Chapter Four

Mara and Alexa were up and ready when Billy knocked on the guesthouse door the next morning.

"You're late," Mara greeted him, a hand on her hip. She nodded to the clock on the wall behind her. It was ten past seven.

"I thought I'd give you some wiggle room," he admitted. He looked down at Alexa, who was, for the first time, wide-awake since they'd shown up on his doorstep. Her attention stayed on the stuffed dog in her hands as she played on the floor.

"There's no such thing as wiggle room when you have a toddler," she said with a smirk. It was meant as a quick comment, but Billy couldn't help but wonder about the foundation it was born from. When had Mara learned that lesson? Whenever it was, all he knew was it was without him.

Mara's smirk sank into a frown. She cleared her throat, humor gone.

"Listen, about Alexa," she started, but Billy was already a step ahead of her. He held his hand up for her to stop.

"Again, I want to have this talk. I really would like to know why you kept my daughter from me," he said, serious. "But not right now." Mara opened and closed her mouth, like a fish out of water, trying to find what words,

Billy didn't know, but he didn't have time to find out. "Right now we need to find Beck and figure out what it is he's done and is trying to do so we can stop him," he continued. "My first priority is to keep you two safe. You can tell me all about your reasoning for not letting me know I was a father later." While he spoke with what he was trying to pass off as authority, he couldn't help but hear the anger at the end of it.

He'd spent most of the night lying awake in bed, coming up with a plan of action for the day. In the plan was a large section related to how he wanted to handle Mara and Alexa. After hours of no sleep, he'd decided the best way to do his job—to keep everyone safe—was to detach himself emotionally from the dark-haired beauties in front of him.

However, maybe that was going to be harder than he'd thought.

"Okay," Mara finally said. "I'll follow you to the station."

She grabbed her bag and scooped up Alexa. The little girl clung to her stuffed animal with laser-like focus. Billy wondered what other toys she liked.

"There's a coffeehouse that opened up across the street that has pretty good breakfast," Billy said as he locked up the guesthouse behind them.

"I actually packed enough cereal to last for weeks for this one," Mara said, motioning to Alexa. "She's a nut about Cheerios as soon as she wakes up in the morning." Alexa swung her head up to face Mara and let out a trill of laughter. It surprised Billy how he instantly loved the sound. "Yeah, you've already scarfed down two helpings, haven't you, you little chowhound?" Mara cooed at the girl. Together they laughed, bonded in their own little world.

One that Billy didn't know.

He cleared his throat and Mara straightened.

"But," she continued, expression turning to the same focus her daughter had worn before. "If they have good coffee, I won't turn that down." She smiled but it didn't last long. "And, Billy, I know it's not my place, but I noticed you didn't have a tree or any Christmas decorations or lights…"

Billy sighed.

No matter what was happening in their lives, leave it to the women of the South to still care about Christmas decorations.

THE RIKER COUNTY Sheriff's Department was located in the very heart of Carpenter but was by no means in an extravagant headquarters. That never stopped Billy from feeling a boost of pride when it swung into view. Placed between the county courthouse and the local television station, the sheriff's department was two stories tall and full of men and women tasked with protecting their Southern home.

Wrapped in faded orange brick and concrete, its entrance opened up to a street almost every Carpenter resident had to drive along to get somewhere, while its parking lot around back butted up against a business park that housed a bistro, a coffeehouse and a clothing boutique called Pepper's. Billy and Mara angled their cars into the assigned and guest parking, respectively, and headed straight to the coffeehouse. Billy had tried to convince Mara to ride with him but she'd pointed out his day could get hectic and she liked having the option of her own transportation. Not to mention the car seat was already in her car. Billy decided not to push the topic since she was a flight risk. Instead, he decided to act like everything was normal when they went into the coffeehouse. There they earned a double take from one half of the owner pair known as the Chambers. Becky, a bigger woman with short hair and an even shorter temper, was surprisingly tactful as she addressed them.

"Well, Sheriff, can't say I was expecting to see you on your day off," she started, then she switched her attention to Mara and Alexa. "And certainly not with two lovely ladies in tow."

Billy ignored the affectionate part of the statement, along with what felt suspiciously like pride, and showed just how happy he was about being in on his off day with a frown.

"A sheriff's job is never done," he said solemnly.

"Not with that attitude." Becky winked at Mara, but the dark-haired beauty's gaze had been drawn to the corner booth.

"I'll take my usual," Billy said. "She'll take one of your mocha iced coffee concoctions I always complain about."

Becky raised her eyebrow.

"Does the lady not get a say?" she asked, voice beginning to thread with disapproval. Her changing tone must have snagged Mara's attention. She turned back to them with a small smile.

"She definitely does, but this one here apparently hasn't forgotten my guilty mocha pleasures," she said. "With whipped cream, too, if you have it, please."

Becky seemed appeased that Billy wasn't rolling over Mara and went about making their drinks while they hung off to the side of the counter. Billy expected Mara to comment about his remembering her favorite caffeinated drink but the woman seemed focused on the corner booth again. So much so that she hardly noticed when he moved close enough to drop his voice so no one else heard him.

"What's going on?"

Alexa looked up from her place on Mara's hip and stared at Billy with an expression caught somewhere between inquisitive and concerned. He couldn't help but stare right back into those green eyes. Like looking into a mirror when it came to the same green.

"That's Donna Ramsey," Mara answered, in an equally low voice. Billy broke his staring contest with Alexa and angled his body to glance at the other side of the room. True to her words, Donna Ramsey was sitting in the corner booth, head bent over the magazine and coffee on the table in front of her. He nodded.

"It is."

Billy watched as Mara's face grew tight. She furrowed her brow.

"Do you know Donna personally?" he asked, his own concern pushing to the forefront. Mara shook her head.

"I've only spoken to her once."

"About?"

He knew Mara well enough to know that her thoughts had turned dark. From anger or sadness or something else, though, he couldn't tell.

"About my father," she answered, voice nearly lost amidst the clatter of the espresso machine. Mara lost her dark look and replaced it with something akin to nonchalance.

"Don't worry," she said. "It was before I left and nothing I didn't already know."

Becky bustled into view before he could question Mara further. She handed them their drinks and looked at Billy.

"Remember, Sheriff, complaining always makes problems ten times worse," she said sagely. "So stop complaining and start drinking some of the best coffee this town has to offer."

Billy couldn't help but smirk.

"You got it, Becky."

Mara waved goodbye while Alexa giggled, and soon the three of them were walking to the back of the station.

"I like her," Mara commented.

"Next time you order from her, tell her that," Billy said. "Suzy did and now she gets a discount."

Mara laughed and Alexa started to babble. Billy craned his neck to look down at her face. Whatever she was saying must have been normal because Mara didn't skip a beat.

"Suzy," she started. "I—I haven't seen her since you were sworn in."

They had made it to the back door used by employees only. Billy pulled out his key and went ahead and addressed the elephant in their shared room.

"She's still one of the few in the department who knows about us working together to bring down your dad. I never told anyone else about the other us. Or what we used to be," he amended. With his key hanging in the lock he looked over his shoulder to the woman he'd been ready to spend forever with and then to their child. "I'll leave it up to you what personal details you want to disclose to my staff. And I'll follow your lead. But whatever you choose to do today, don't think I won't undermine it tomorrow if I need to."

Then Billy opened the door and headed inside, mind already going into work mode. He had a murder to solve and a man named Beck to find.

It was comforting, in a way, to walk into the department alongside Billy. Because, unlike their lives in the last two years, the building hadn't changed. At least, not any way that Mara could tell.

They took the back hallway that ran behind dispatch and the break room and turned the corner to where Mara knew offices lined one of the hallways that led back toward the lobby. Billy's office was smack dab in the middle of the others. His nameplate shone with importance. Mara couldn't help but feel some pride creep in at the sight of it.

"Walden, the sketch artist, said he'd be here by eight thirty," Billy said, walking them past his office. "Until then I'd like you to officially make a statement about this Beck fellow. I'm going to double-check that no one fitting Beck's description is a part of an open case with us or local PD." He stopped two doors over and motioned her inside. It was the conference room and it definitely wasn't empty.

Mara felt her cheeks immediately heat at the sight of mostly familiar faces. Alexa tucked her head into the side of her neck, suddenly shy. Mara didn't blame her. Billy motioned to an open chair, one of many, around the long table in the middle of the room. Mara sat down with tired grace. Alexa's sudden shyness didn't help either one of them adjust from standing to sitting down.

"Most of you already know Mara, and Mara you know them." Billy continued to stand. He motioned to Suzy, Matt Walker and Dane Jones. The last time she'd seen them Suzy had been a deputy along with Billy, Matt had been a deputy, too and Dane had been on his way to being sheriff. Now, sitting across from them, Mara doubted their titles were the same. She wondered what title Dane had now but she wasn't about to ask for clarification.

On the same side of the table was the one face she didn't recognize, a pretty young woman with curly blond hair and a smile that looked genuine. Before Mara could stop the thought, she wondered if Billy found the woman pretty, too.

"Mara, this is Cassie Gates," Billy said, making the introduction. "She's training to be a dispatcher." Mara couldn't stop the confusion that must have crossed her expression as to why a dispatcher, a *trainee* dispatcher, was in the room with them when the woman answered the question herself.

"I'm the youngest of six siblings, most of whom have a kid or two under their belt, so I'm very experienced in the art of keeping little ones entertained when their mamas need to do something important," she said, voice as sweet as her appearance. She flashed a quick smile at Alexa and addressed the toddler directly. "And what's your name? I bet it's something pretty."

The entire room seemed to wait as Alexa peeked out at Cassie. There was nothing like waiting for a toddler's judgment. Seemingly based on some unknown factor, there was no telling how a child would react to something new. That included people. However, instead of hiding away again, Alexa seemed intrigued. She looked back at Mara for a moment, as if asking for permission.

"This is Alexa," Mara introduced them with a smile, showing Alexa her approval of the woman next to them. She might have been a stranger to her but she wasn't to Billy. Mara trusted his judgment. And Alexa trusted Mara's.

"Well, what do you know. That *is* a pretty name," Cassie said, animation in her words. It reeled in Alexa's attention. The blonde reached for a bag next to her. From her seat Mara could see it was filled with books and toys. Billy had prepared for the morning, despite short notice. "If it's okay with your mama, how about we go next door and play in the sheriff's office? You could even help me read this." Cassie held up the children's book *Pat the Pet* and Alexa nearly lost it.

"Dog! Dog," she exclaimed, already trying to get off Mara's lap.

It earned a surprised laugh from Cassie. Mara reached into her own bag and produced the same book.

"Welcome to her favorite book," she said to the trainee. "She likes petting the dog the most."

Mara gave Cassie permission to go next door and play, since Alexa seemed to have lost any doubt about the woman as soon as the book had come into view. Mara didn't miss the way Billy's eyes stuck to the cover of the copy Mara had brought along. With more than a twinge of guilt, she realized that, like the stranger who was Cassie, he hadn't had a clue in the world what his daughter did and didn't like.

But Mara couldn't change what she'd already done and turned to face what was left of the group. The men each gave her a friendly smile. Suzy, on the other hand, gave her a stiff nod. While the other two had known about their working relationship, Suzy alone had known about Mara and Billy's romantic one and her sudden departure. As one of Billy's closest friends, Suzy probably knew better than even her how he'd handled it, too.

"Now, Mara," Billy started, setting a tape recorder in the middle of the table. "If you could start at the beginning, when the man named Beck visited you."

Mara repeated the story she'd told Billy the night before, making sure to give them as clear a picture as she could of Beck. Before she could finish describing his clothes and car, however, a man knocked at the door. Despite his dark complexion, Mara mentally likened his expression to "looks like he's seen a ghost."

"Excuse me, Sheriff, we have a problem," he interrupted. Like fans passing on a wave in a football stadium's stands, Billy and his staff became visibly tense.

"What is it?" The man hesitated and looked at Mara. "It's fine. Tell me," Billy added, showing that Mara's presence didn't bother them with whatever news he had.

Which wasn't good news at all.

"We just got a call about two teens who are being taken to the hospital," he started. "They were both overdoses."

Mara's eyes widened. She asked him what everyone else was thinking.

"Of what?"

Bless him, he didn't hesitate in responding to her, though Mara would have been happier if it had been with a different answer.

"Moxy. They overdosed on Moxy."

Chapter Five

Billy tried to not feel like he was suddenly several years in the past, staring at the deceased Courtney Brooks in her car. But there he was, sitting in a conference room and feeling exactly as he had then.

Sad.

Guilty.

Angry.

If he had been alone, he would probably have thrown something. Instead, the best he could do was toss a few expletives in the direction of Deputy Dante Mills, who, thankfully, didn't seem to take open frustration personally.

"They were at the abandoned drive-in theater out past the town limits," Deputy Mills continued. "The owner of the gas station across the street saw their cars hadn't moved in a while and decided to investigate with her husband. Neither had ID on them. As far as their status, it was unclear how bad the damage was, other than they needed medical attention ASAP."

Billy had heard enough. He turned to Suzy, who rose at the same time.

"We're going to the hospital," he told her. Then to Matt, "And I want you to go to the theater grounds and look around. Talk to the gas station owner, too." Billy turned to Dane Jones and a look of understanding passed between them. For his own personal reasons, Dane had taken himself out of the running for sheriff and, instead, applied for Captain of Investigative Bureau within the department after Rockwell had retired. He preferred fighting the good fight from behind a desk instead of out on the streets. Billy couldn't blame him after what had happened to the man years before. Some cases just went south and there wasn't anything anyone could do about it. That was a lesson Dane hadn't let himself learn yet.

"I'll finish up here and see what we can do to find this Beck person. See if we can't connect some dots to Bernie Lutz, too," Dane said. "I'll even give Chief Hawser a call and see if he's had anything come across his desk."

Billy nodded. It was a good idea to go ahead and touch base with Carpenter's police department. Although Billy was sheriff of Riker County, the town of Carpenter and the city of Kipsy had their own police departments and anything that happened within those municipalities was their jurisdiction. Bernie's body and the overdoses had been found just outside the town limits, which meant Billy was running the show. But he didn't have an ego too big to not have an open dialogue with the local PD. He happened to be a fan of Chief Hawser, too.

Billy finally looked at Mara. Her expression was pinched and worn at the same time. He assumed the news had put her on the line between the present and the past, just as it had him, anger and guilt both squarely on her shoulders. He wanted to go to her, even took a small step forward, but caught himself.

"The sketch artist should be here soon," Billy said. "You can wait in my office if he takes too long."

Mara's jaw tightened.

"As long as you figure out who's doing this," she said.

"Believe me. I will."

Suzy wordlessly followed him to the parking lot and into his Tahoe as the rest of the department went on with their tasks. She kept quiet as he pulled away from the department and got on the main road that would lead them to Carpenter's hospital. However, no sooner had they passed the first intersection when Suzy asked the one question Billy knew she would.

"Is Alexa yours?"

Billy had already resigned himself to following whatever lead Mara wanted to take about telling the department who the father was. But she hadn't expressed herself one way or the other.

"Yes," he answered, surprising himself. "I just found out last night."

He cast a look over at his friend. Suzy, a mother herself, didn't seem to pass any judgment either way on the information. Instead, she kept her gaze focused out the windshield.

"She's a cute kid," she said, as if they were talking about the weather. "I'm glad she didn't get your nose."

Billy laughed. He somehow felt better.

THE SKETCH ARTIST'S name was Walden and he very much looked like what Mara suspected a Walden would look like. Slightly rounded in the gut, thick glasses, a crown of blond hair around a shiny spot of baldness and a patient, even temperament, the man took his time in sketching out Beck.

"Is this close?" he asked when he was finished. He slid his notebook over to her. Alexa, who had taken a snack break next to her mother, peeked over at the drawing.

"That's perfect," Mara said, quickly moving the notebook out of Alexa's line of sight. As if the man could do her harm from it. "You're very good at your job, Walden," she added, thoroughly impressed. He'd even managed to add in the sneer that had pulled up the corner of Beck's lips as he said goodbye.

"I'd always wanted to be an artist, though even I'm surprised that I wound up here." Walden motioned around the conference room but she knew he meant the department as a whole.

"I can understand that," she admitted. "I used to dream of running my own interior design business. Now I work at a flooring company trying to convince people redoing their floors is the first step to a happy home." Mara gave him a wry smile. Walden shrugged.

"Hey, the floors are the foundation of a home. Not a bad place to start at all," he pointed out. Mara laughed.

"You seem to be a very optimistic man. I suppose your glass is always half full?" Walden pushed his glasses back up the bridge of his nose and stood with his notebook.

"It's better to have a half-full glass than an entirely empty bottle." He gave her a nod. "I'm going to take this to the captain now. It was nice to meet you, Mara."

It took her a moment to return the sentiment, as she was slightly stunned by the weight of his previous statement. She wasn't the only one with pain in her life, and compared to most, hers wasn't the worst. Her thoughts went to the teens in the hospital. She looked at Alexa, transfixed by her bag of cereal. At a time when families and loved ones were supposed to be coming together for holidays, Mara couldn't imagine what she'd feel like if she were to get a call like the one the families of the teens were no doubt receiving.

"Knock, knock." Mara shook herself out of such dark thoughts and focused on Cassie standing in the doorway. "Now that you're finished, I've been told to tell you that you don't have to hang around here any longer," she said, all smiles. Her gaze went to Alexa. "I'm sure there are much more exciting places to be than a sheriff's department."

Although Cassie was no doubt being polite, Mara couldn't help but wonder who'd told the woman that Mara should leave when finished. Had it been a polite suggestion to start off with or had the young woman changed the tone to stay nice? Mara mentally let out a long, loud sigh. Feelings of uncertainty, self-consciousness and guilt began to crop up within her again.

And she hadn't even been in Riker County for a full twenty-four hours yet.

Instead of telling the truth—that she'd like to stay until Billy came back—Mara stood with an equally warm, if not entirely true, smile.

"There are a few places I'd like to visit," she tried, attempting to wrangle her child's toys and food back into their appropriate places within her bag. "Plus, it does seem to be a nice day outside."

Cassie nodded, following Mara's glance out of the conference room windows. Every Southerner had a love-hate relationship with winter. South Alabama had an annoying habit of being humid and hot when it should be chilly or cold. Christmastime was no exception. Mara had left her jacket in the car. She doubted she'd need it while in Carpenter, though she wouldn't have minded being proven wrong. At least in North Alabama, where she lived with Alexa, the promise of being cold in time for the holidays was sometimes kept.

"Could you ask the sheriff to call me when he gets a chance?" Mara asked when Alexa and her things were finally ready to go. Cassie nodded and promised she would. Together they walked past the hall that led to the back door and, instead, moved past the offices to the lobby.

It was hard to not smile at the department's attempt

at decorating. Colored lights and garlands covered every available inch. On the lobby desk there was even a small Charlie Brown Christmas tree—twigs and a few colorful glass ornaments. An unexpected wave of guilt pushed against Mara at the sight. Not only had she disrupted the life of the sheriff by showing up, but she'd also left behind her own planned Christmas with Alexa back home. Decorations and toys, even holiday treats she'd already baked and packaged. But now that Billy knew about her, what would the holiday look like?

The deputy who had given the news of the overdoses earlier gave them a quick smile while still talking to the secretary, another person Mara didn't recognize. The only other people in the lobby were two women waiting in the chairs.

As she had with Donna Ramsey in the coffee shop, Mara recognized one of them, a woman named Leigh Cullen. Unlike Donna, Leigh recognized Mara right back. She stood abruptly, pausing in whatever she had been saying.

"Thank you again for everything," Mara said in a rush, cutting off eye contact and disengaging from her spot next to Cassie. "See you later."

"You," Leigh exclaimed, loud enough to catch the entire lobby's attention. Mara had the wild thought that if she could run out of the building fast enough, Leigh would somehow forget about seeing her. That she could literally outrun her past. But then Leigh began to hurry over toward them, her face reddening as she yelled, "How dare you show your face here again!"

Mara angled Alexa behind her and braced for a confrontation. One she hoped wouldn't be physical. It was one she deserved but not one she was ready to let Alexa witness. However, Cassie surprised them all.

In all of her compassionate glory, she stepped between

Leigh and Mara, and held up her hand like she was a traffic guard telling the driver of a vehicle that they'd better halt their horses. It stunned both women into silence.

"No ma'am," Cassie said, voice high but firm. "You do not act that way in a sheriff's department and certainly not in front of a child."

For the first time, Leigh seemed to notice Alexa on Mara's hip. Still, her eyes remained fiery.

"Don't you know who this woman is?" Leigh continued, though her voice had gone from an explosion to a low burn. Probably because the deputy's attention was fully on them now. "Do you know what she let happen?"

Mara's face heated. Her heartbeat sped up. How had she thought coming back to Riker County wouldn't end in disaster? That someone wouldn't recognize her?

"I know exactly who she is and you don't see me hollering at her like this," Cassie said. Though she'd been polite before, Mara could see her sharp edges poking out in defense now.

"Maybe you should take a breather, Leigh," the deputy added with absolute authority. He looked confused by the situation but determined to stop it.

"You shouldn't be here," Leigh said. She turned away, grumbling a few more not-so-becoming words beneath her breath, and stomped back to her companion, who'd remained seated.

"I'm so sorry, Mara." Cassie didn't take her eyes off Leigh's retreating back. "I don't know what came over her."

That clinched it. Cassie didn't know who Mara was.

"Thank you," Mara said, honest. "But it's alright. I don't blame her one bit." Without explaining herself, Mara took Alexa and left the department.

It wasn't until they were locked inside the car, "Jingle

Bells" playing over the radio, that Mara broke down and cried.

Leigh's husband had been gunned down while trying to stop an armed robbery almost three years ago. His killer had been one of Bryan Copeland's drug dealers. If Mara had tried to turn her father in the moment she found out who he was and what he had done, then Leigh's husband wouldn't have bled out in the convenience store on Cherry Street. Mara knew that.

And so did Leigh.

A HALF HOUR LATER, Mara was letting the laughter of her child soothe her wounds as best it could.

They had gone from the department straight to Anthony's Park. Not as green as it was in the summer, the three-mile stretch of trees, walking paths and recreational spots was located near the town's limits, closest to the city of Kipsy. Because of that fact, Mara had often visited the park when she'd first started to meet up with Billy. They'd sit in the parking lot, huddled in Billy's late father's old Bronco, and try to figure out the best way to stop *her* father and his drugs.

Are you sure you want to do this? I can take over from here. You can go home and I won't ever fault you for it, Billy had said one night. Mara still remembered how he'd looked at her then. Concern pulling his brows together, eyes soft, lips set in a thoughtful frown. Compassionate to a fault, Billy had offered her an out.

And would you go home if you were in my place, Billy?

Despite his lower rank back then, in hindsight Mara realized Billy Reed had always been a sheriff at heart. The resolution that had rolled off him in nearly staggering waves as he'd answered had helped Mara come to terms with her own choice to stay.

No. I would see this through to the end.

Mara smiled as Alexa began to giggle uncontrollably at the sand hill she'd just made. Who knew that *seeing it through* then would have resulted in a daughter.

"You're brave."

Mara jumped at the new voice behind her. Afraid it belonged to Beck, she didn't feel much better when she saw it belonged to another man she didn't know. That didn't stop her from assuming he was into some kind of drug, either. Thin, with red, almost-hollow eyes and stringy brown hair, there was a restlessness about him that kept his body constantly moving. He rubbed the thumb of his right hand across his index finger over and over again but, thankfully, the rest of him stayed still on the other side of the bench.

"Excuse me?" Mara said, body tensing so fast that she nearly stood.

"You're brave to let her play in the sand box," he said, motioning to Alexa. The little girl looked up from her spot a few feet away but lost interest immediately after.

"How so?"

Mara slowly moved her hand to the top of her bag. The playground they were at was out in the open, which made it very easy to see how alone the three of them were now. The man could have looked like George Clooney and Mara still would have been trying to get her phone out without being noticed.

"The sand. It's going to get everywhere," he offered. "I'm sure it won't be fun to clean up."

"I've dealt with worse," she replied, politely. "Plus, she loves it."

The man shrugged.

"I guess you're a better parent than most." He never stopped rubbing his finger, like a nervous tick. It made Mara's skin start to crawl. She opened her bag slowly and reached her hand inside. "So, Mara, was Bryan a good parent?"

Her blood ran cold and froze her to the spot. The man's smile was back.

"Who are you?" she managed. "What do you want?"

He answered with a laugh.

"Let's just say I'm a friend of a friend." Mara's fingers brushed against the screen of her phone. All she had to do was unlock it and tap twice and it would connect straight to 911. But apparently the man had different plans. "If you don't take your hand out right now, I'm going to teach you a lesson in manners in front of your daughter," he said, his smile dissolving into a look that promised he'd carry through on his threat.

Mara pulled her hand out to comply, but she wasn't about to submit to him completely. She stood, slowly, never taking her eyes off him.

"What do you want?" she repeated.

All the fake politeness left him. When he answered his tone was harsh and low. It made the hair rise on the back of her neck.

"Bryan Copeland's drugs and blood money. What else?"

Chapter Six

Her father might have been a lot of things, but Mara had learned a few good lessons from him. Once he'd told her a story about when he was a young man working in a big city. He'd decided to walk home instead of taking a cab, wanting to enjoy the night air, and a man tried to mug him at knifepoint.

Bryan refused to let anyone take advantage of him and used the only weapon he had on him. He took his house keys, already in his hand, and slid the keys between his fingers so when he made a fist, his keys were sticking out, ready to teach his attacker a lesson.

Mara had never heard the rest of the story, only that her father had left that alley with all of his belongings still with him. He would use that story throughout her youth to try and teach her to, at the very least, always keep her keys in her pocket instead of her purse. Because no attacker feared a weapon their victim couldn't get to in time. And usually they didn't care about keys, either.

So as soon as her new friend asked about drugs and blood money, Mara's hand went straight into her pocket.

"I don't know what you're talking about," she said, pulling her keys out. "I think it's time for us to leave now."

The man shook his head, which Mara expected. Leaving, she gathered, wouldn't be easy, but at least now she had *something* that would hurt him if he got physical. Which she prayed wouldn't be the case. Alexa could still be heard playing behind her.

"You don't leave until I say you leave," the man bit out.

Mara angled her body slightly to hide the hand with her keys. She threaded one between her index and middle fingers and then another between her middle and ring fingers. If he noticed her making the fist, he didn't comment on it.

"My father doesn't have any blood money or drugs left to find," she answered. "And if he does, I'm the last person who would know where they are."

The man seemed to consider her words for the briefest of moments before a sneer lit his face.

"He said you'd deny it."

That made Mara pause.

"Who?" she asked. "My father?" Billy hadn't been the only man in her life she'd not spoken to since she'd left Riker County. She hadn't communicated with her father in any form or fashion since he'd been sentenced. And even then that had been brief.

In the time in between then and the present, had he been talking about her?

"Your friend Beck."

Mara's stomach iced over. She tightened her grip on her keys until they bit into her skin. Apparently Beck worked fast, whoever he was.

"I haven't talked to my father in years," Mara said, trying to keep her voice even. The man behind the bench looked like he would prey on anyone showing fear. Like a shark waiting for blood. "If he has anything hidden, I'm not the one to ask to find it."

"You know, you keep talkin' but I still don't believe you."

He cut his eyes to the space behind her that Mara knew

contained Alexa. On reflex, Mara stepped to the side to block his view. The ice in her stomach might have been created in fear but that didn't mean she wouldn't use that to fight tooth and nail to keep the creep away from her daughter.

Maybe the man sensed that. He lazily slid his gaze back to hers and put up his hands in defense.

"Now, I don't have any weapons on me, little miss," he started. "But if you don't come with me I can still make some trouble. For all of us." He dropped his gaze to show he was trying to look at Alexa again. The mistake cost Mara her patience.

"I'm leaving," she said. "If you try to stop me I'll call the cops."

"There won't be any need for that," he replied, his sneer dropping again. In its place was an expression filled with intent. Evil or not, Mara wasn't going to stick around and find out. Mara tried to recall everything Billy had ever taught her about protecting herself in the few seconds it took for the man to round the bench. But all she could think about was a football game she'd watched with her father a few weeks before they'd caught him.

Sometimes the best defense is a good offense.

So, with Billy's voice ringing in her ears, Mara lunged out at the man with her fist of protruding keys. However, Mara's lunge turned more into a stumble. No matter how much she wanted to keep the creep away from her and her daughter, her lack of experience in attacking strange men and the surge of adrenaline through her wasn't helping her. Her fist missed his face but snagged his ear before she lost her footing.

The man let out a strangled cry as one of the keys cut into the side of his ear. Mara tried to steady herself enough to throw another punch that would do more damage, but the man was faster. He grabbed her wrist and squeezed hard.

"You little—" he snarled, but Mara refused to give in. She brought her knee up hard into the man's groin. The hit connected and whatever thoughts he was going to convey died on his yell of pain. He let her go and immediately sank to the ground.

It was the opening she needed.

Mara turned tail and went to Alexa. She grabbed her so quickly that the little girl instantly started to fuss. When Mara started to run toward her car, the little girl went from annoyed to scared.

Maybe she sensed her mother's fear.

Or maybe she heard the man get up and start chasing them.

BILLY WASN'T HAVING a good day.

Though he knew he had no room to complain. Not after he'd seen Jeff Briggs's mother in Santa earrings weeping for her son who was lying in the hospital in a coma. Stanley Morgan wasn't much better than his friend. The doctor had told Billy and Suzy they were certain that Stanley would wake up, they just couldn't say when.

Billy had personally given each set of parents the news once a nurse identified the teens from her neighborhood. None of them had any idea that either boy had been using drugs.

Billy let out a long, loud breath.

"I'm going to call the office to see if we have a good sketch of Beck to work with," Suzy said when they were back to driving.

Billy nodded and turned the morning talk show down as Suzy spoke with Dane. He watched as downtown Carpenter flashed by their windows. It was a warm day, but not as humid as it could have been. Still, Billy wouldn't have minded changing out of his blazer to one of his running tees. His sheriff's star shone on his belt, reminding him that just because it was warm didn't mean he could start slacking in his appearance.

"She did what?" Suzy asked, voice laced with surprise and simultaneously coated with disapproval. Billy turned the radio off. He raised his eyebrow in question but Suzy held up her index finger to tell him to hold on. "Yeah. Okay, I'll tell him," she continued into the phone. "Shouldn't be a problem. Thanks, Dane."

"What was that about?" Billy asked once Suzy ended the call. For a brief moment he wondered if Mara had left town again. This time taking a daughter he knew about.

"Leigh Cullen tried to start something with Mara after she was done with the sketch artist. Apparently Leigh's been saving up some anger for her." The knot Billy hadn't realized had formed in his chest loosened. Mara hadn't decided to run off into the night, or day, again.

"What do you mean, she tried to start something?"

"While Mara was leaving the station, Leigh started hollering and came at her." Billy tensed with a flash of anger. Suzy didn't miss it. "Don't worry, she didn't get far. Deputy Mills and Cassie handled it while Mara went off to take Alexa to the park. At least, that's where Jones said he thinks they were going. He wasn't sure. You know how he is when Cassie's trying to talk to him. His attention breaks a hundred which ways."

Billy couldn't help but let out a chuckle. He had, in fact, noticed how Dane couldn't help but lose some of his concentration when the trainee dispatcher was around.

"You give him such a hard time about her, you know?" he pointed out. Instead of continuing straight, taking them in the direction of the office, Billy was already putting on his blinker to turn. Anthony's Park wasn't that far away.

"And he gave me a hard time when I went out with Rodney a few years back, so I'm still getting even." She gave an indifferent shrug. Billy couldn't argue with that. "So, we're heading to the park?"

"I don't know how serious this Beck person is, but I don't want to take any chances until we catch him, or at least know more. And after seeing those kids laid up in hospital beds, and knowing that Beck showed up at Mara's house and threatened Alexa—" Billy's grip momentarily tightened around the steering wheel. "Well, I'd feel a lot more comfortable if Mara and Alexa stayed a little more hidden while in town." Billy didn't slow down as he took another turn, his sense of urgency growing. "Plus, I have a feeling I'm going to need to have a talk with Mara."

"You want to visit her father," Suzy guessed.

Billy nodded.

"If things start escalating, then I want to talk to the source himself before this thing gets out—"

"Billy!"

Suzy pointed out her window into Anthony's Park to their left. Billy had already been focused on driving to the running trail entrance, what used to be Mara's favorite path to walk, and hadn't noticed the playground or the green expanse between it and the parking lot.

But one look at Mara running with Alexa in her arms and a man chasing them, and a meteor could have crashed down next to them and he wouldn't have noticed.

"Hold on!"

The side road that ran to the parking lot was too far away for his comfort, not when the man was so close to Mara and Alexa, so he cut the wheel hard. The Tahoe went up and over the curb with ease.

"Can you see a gun on him?" Billy yelled, blood pumping as he sped up.

"Not that I can tell," Suzy hollered back.

The man heard the approaching vehicle and turned. Billy was close enough to read the shock on his face. Apparently seeing a Tahoe barreling toward him was enough of a threat to make him rethink his current plan of action.

"He's changing direction," Suzy yelled. "Heading for the walking trail!"

Billy floored it toward the concrete trail that ran through the woods, knowing that once the man broke through the first line of trees the Tahoe wouldn't have enough room to follow. The man, however, was fast. Billy slammed on the brakes as the fugitive slipped between the trees.

But that wasn't going to stop Billy.

He flung his door open and only hesitated a moment to look behind them at Mara.

"Are you okay?" he called, adrenaline bombarding his system. The second he saw her nod, Billy turned and was running. "Stay with them," he yelled to Suzy.

And then Billy was in the trees.

Chapter Seven

The man opted to avoid the only paved walkway that Anthony's Park had to offer. Under normal circumstances that would have been just fine. While there wasn't enough space for a vehicle to drive between the trees, there was more than enough for someone to explore or deviate if you were truly bored with the even, smooth path.

However, chasing someone?

That was a different story.

Billy weaved through the trees, attempting to copy the perp's zigzag route while adjusting his pace to the uneven terrain. At least if the man had a gun, Billy would be able to fall back to cover without much issue.

"Riker County Sheriff, stop *now*," Billy yelled out as he swung around another tree and barely avoided the next. The man didn't even hesitate. "Stop now or I'll shoot!"

That did the trick in breaking the man's concentration.

His foot caught on a tree root and down he went. Billy was on him in seconds, gun drawn and ready for a fight if needed.

"Don't move," he commanded. "Put your hands on your back!"

The man obliged, but not without complaint. He wheezed and groaned into the dirt before catching his breath enough to mumble out some heated language. It didn't bother Billy. He'd heard worse.

"I didn't do anything." The man finally had the brass to yell as Billy pulled his cuffs out and slapped them on his captive's wrists. The run seemed to have burned him out. The heat wasn't helping matters.

"It looked to me like you were chasing a woman and her kid," Billy said, tugging on the cuffs to make sure they were secure. "And I don't know about you, but to me, that looked like something."

"You don't know what you're talkin' about," the man hurled back.

"Well, good thing I'm going to explain it to you back at the station." Billy secured his gun and helped the man get to his feet. "You run again, or try anything funny, I'll show you just how much more in shape I am than you," Billy warned. The man, covered in sweat, spat off to the side in anger. "And you spit on me or mine, and that's felony assault against an officer of the law. Got it?"

The man grumbled but didn't kick up too much of a fuss as Billy led him out of the woods. Suzy, ever alert, was standing in front of Mara and Alexa, sandwiching them between the Tahoe and herself. Her hand was hovering over the gun at her hip, ready to defend the civilians at her back. When she saw them, there was nothing but focus in her expression.

"I called for backup," she said, not leaving her spot. "Deputy Mills was in the area. Should be here soon."

On cue, the sound of a distant cruiser's siren began to sing.

"You're making a mistake," the man tried again. "I'm the victim here! Did you see what that bitch did to my ear?" Billy kicked out at the back of the man's leg. "Hey," he cried out, stumbling forward. Billy pulled back on his cuffs to keep the man from falling.

"Watch your step there, buddy," Billy said. "Wouldn't want you to hurt yourself."

Deputy Mills came into view soon after. He drove around to the parking lot that looked out at the playground and stopped. Billy used his free hand to fish out the keys to the Tahoe he'd shoved into his pocket before.

"Will you take the Tahoe back to the office?" he asked Suzy. "Our friend here can ride with Mills." Billy glanced at Mara. She was rubbing Alexa's back while the little girl cried into her neck. "I'll catch a ride back with you."

It wasn't a question, but still Mara nodded. Her face was pinched, concerned.

"Sounds good, boss." Suzy caught Billy's keys. "I'll go ahead and call Chief Hawser and tell him what's happening. I'm sure he won't mind, though. As long as we get men who like to terrorize women and children off the streets." She cut a piercing look at the man.

"Agreed. Call ahead and tell them to make the interrogation room *comfortable* too," he added, in a tone that let his perp know that his humor was sarcasm only.

"Will do," Suzy said. She was already dialing the department's number. Billy passed her but made sure to angle his body between the man and Mara and Alexa as they passed.

Mara didn't comment as they all walked over to Deputy Mills's cruiser, a few spots down from Mara's car, but Billy didn't miss her soft reassurances to their daughter that everything was going to be okay. It sent another flash of anger through him. When Deputy Mills helped get the man into the cruiser Billy might have been a little rougher than usual with him.

"Read him his rights, deputy," Billy said when he was

shut in the back of the car. "And don't let him give you any trouble."

Deputy Mills nodded.

"Yessir."

Billy watched as the cruiser pulled out and away before he went to Mara. She was leaning against the side of her car, still rubbing Alexa's back. The little girl wasn't crying anymore but a few sniffs could be heard. Those little sounds carried a much stronger punch than Billy thought was possible.

"Is she okay?"

"Oh, yeah, she's fine," she assured. "I just scared her a little when I had to grab her and run."

"Tell me what happened, Mara."

"Can we get out of here first?" she asked. Her gaze swiveled past him to the playground in the distance.

"Yeah, we can." Billy tried to search her face for an indication of how she felt. The Mara he knew had been easier to read than the mother standing in front of him. She was guarded. Once again he wondered what her life had been like in the last two years.

"How long have you been here?" he asked. Mara shifted Alexa so they both slid into the back of the car.

"Not long," she said, starting the dance of buckling the toddler into her car seat. Alexa's eyes were red. Tear tracks stained her cheeks. Billy didn't like the sight. Not at all. "Oh, Billy, can you open my bag and grab a wipe or two?" She motioned to the bag she'd put down next to the car. Billy complied, thinking the wipes were for Alexa, but Mara held out her keys to him instead.

"You want me to drive?" he asked, confused.

Mara gave him a small smile.

"There's blood on my keys," she explained. "But if you want to drive, I don't mind that, either."

"You used your keys like Wolverine uses his claws," Billy deadpanned after she'd told him the story of what happened in the park. "I can say that I've never seen that self-defense tactic used in Riker County. Though I guess it was effective."

Mara looked into the rearview mirror and gave him a sly smile.

"Believe me, if I'd had something more useful I would have used it instead."

Billy held up one of his hands to stop her thought. "Hey, it did the trick, didn't it?"

Mara's attention shifted to Alexa strapped into the car seat next to her. She had calmed down in the few minutes they'd been driving, but Mara couldn't help but see the little girl who had cried out as Mara had grabbed her and run. More for her sake than Alexa's, Mara held on to her daughter's little hands.

"It helped us get away, but who knows what would have happened had he caught me." Mara paused. "Actually, I know what would have happened," she said, sure of her thought. Billy kept his eyes on the road but she knew he was listening with all of his attention. "He would have taken me and tried to make me tell him where this fictional stash of my father's is. And when I didn't tell him, he would have used our daughter against me."

Mara had gotten so swept up in her own anger that the words had flown from her mouth without realizing she'd used the word *our*. One little word that had never meant much to her had made Billy react in a very small yet profound way. No sooner had she spoken than his hands tightened around the steering wheel.

"Billy, I—" she started, feeling the immediate need to apologize. Though the car ride wasn't long enough to explain herself or her actions, and certainly not long enough to apologize for them.

"So you think the stash isn't real?" Billy interrupted. There was a tightness to his voice. It caught Mara off guard but she didn't ignore the question.

"I think that guy and this Beck person believe there is," she admitted. "But, really, I can't see how. The investigation into my father's business was exhaustive. Don't you think we—or you and the department—would have come across this cache of money or narcotics? At least have heard a rumor about it?"

In the rearview mirror Mara could see Billy agree with that.

"Still, like you said yesterday, we never were able to fully flush out your father's network," he pointed out. "Maybe that includes this stash."

Mara felt her cheeks heat. She was frustrated and she had a feeling it was only going to get worse. Putting her father in prison should have been the end of this particular brand of headache. And, with some loathing on her part, she realized, heartache. Memories of her childhood filled with a loving father, always watching out for her and taking care of her, tried to break through the mental block she kept up at all times. It was too difficult to remember the good times when she had so thoroughly helped bring in the bad.

"Either way, I don't think it really matters whether or not it's real," she said, hearing the bitterness in her tone just as clearly as she assumed Billy did. "As long as they think *I* know where it is, then Alexa is in danger."

The car slowed as they took the turn into the parking lot of the station. Billy pulled into a staff spot, quiet. Mara wondered what was going on behind those forest green eyes of his. He cut the engine and she didn't have to wait long for him to tell her.

"Well, then, we're going to have to convince them that you don't."

THE MAN'S NAME was Caleb Richards and he'd made a nice little petty criminal career for himself in the past decade. With breaking and entering, convenience store theft, a multitude of speeding tickets and an aggravated assault charge, Caleb's history painted a picture of a man who didn't mind stepping over the line of what was right or wrong. Law be damned.

"That's quite the track record," Billy said to the man after reading his record out loud. They were on opposite sides of a small metal table in the department's lone interrogation room. Behind a two-way mirror sat Suzy and Captain Jones, watching. He'd asked Mara to stay in his office. She might not have admitted it, but her run-in with Caleb had shaken her up more than she was letting on. "And now running from the cops after attempted—what?—kidnapping? That's a bit of an escalation for you, don't you think?"

Caleb's face contorted into an ugly expression of anger.

"Kidnapping? That woman attacked *me*," he yelled. "I was just minding my own business. She should be the one wearing these, not me!" He yanked his hands up as much as his restraints would let him.

"She said you came up to her asking about money and drugs," Billy went on, playing it cool. "In your words, *blood* money. Again, from where I'm sitting that doesn't sound like you were the innocent one in all of this." Caleb shook his head but didn't respond. Which was probably the smartest thing he'd done that morning. Billy pressed on. "Listen, Caleb, Mara doesn't know where the stash is.

Despite what Beck tells you, I assure you, she doesn't. I would know," he said honestly. "And I think it's time I tell him that face-to-face. Caleb, where is Beck?"

The man's anger seemingly transformed. Fear registered clearly when he uttered the four words Billy hated in interrogations.

"I want a lawyer."

"This would all be a lot easier if you'd just cooperate with us," Billy tried. "Make a deal and tell us everything you know about your boss and we might take running from a cop off the table."

Billy already knew Caleb wouldn't bite. He was that special kind of stupid criminal, motivated purely by fear. And right now he wasn't afraid of Billy or being charged. Which was more telling than if he'd just stayed quiet.

"I'm not talking until I have a lawyer," Caleb responded. "Got that?"

Billy rapped his fist against the tabletop and smiled.

"Got it."

He shut the interrogation door behind him just as Captain Jones and Suzy stepped out of the observation room.

"What now?" Suzy asked, following him as he started to go to his office. He paused long enough to catch Dane's eye.

"I have an idea," he said. "But I think it's time the captain takes a coffee break."

Dane respected, and what's more, trusted Billy, so he decided to play along.

"I've been needing a refill anyways," he said. "And anything that happens while I'm getting that refill, I'll have no knowledge or part of, is that understood?"

"I wouldn't steer you wrong," Billy assured him. Dane nodded and left them outside Billy's office.

"Okay," Suzy said, unable to hide her trepidation. "What's this bad plan of yours?"

Chapter Eight

No sooner had Mara slipped into the interrogation room than Caleb tried to tell her to leave. He was more than surprised when she shushed him.

"Be quiet, you idiot," she said in a harsh whisper. She shut the door quietly behind her but paused to listen for anyone who might have heard. At least Caleb was good at following some instructions. He didn't make a peep.

"I suggest you don't raise your voice," she said, taking a seat in the chair opposite the man. He watched her through a shade of confusion and an even darker shade of mistrust, both apparent in his widened eyes and pursed lips. He hadn't expected to see her, she suspected. Certainly not alone. That was just fine by Mara. She didn't need his trust. She just needed to avoid his suspicion. "The sheriff just stepped out on a call and the rest of them are otherwise distracted, but I wouldn't push our luck by wasting any time."

Mara leaned back in the chair, crossed her arms over her chest and lifted her chin enough to show that she was above the business she was about to discuss. And, by proxy, above Caleb. His round eyes took on more of a slit as he, in turn, tried to size her up. Criminal background or not, Mara knew she was smarter than he was.

"I told you all that I'm not talking until I get a lawyer." He said it slowly, testing her.

"Well, good thing I don't care about all of that," Mara said dismissively. "What I *do* care about is this." She dropped her arms from her chest and jabbed one finger on the tabletop. Not dropping her fixed stare into his beady little eyes, Mara kept her voice clear, yet low. "How did Beck find out about my father's stash when we spent so much time trying to keep it a secret?"

Caleb's reaction was almost laughable. His eyebrows floated up so high they nearly disappeared into his hairline.

"You're saying you do know about the stash, then," he said with notable excitement.

Mara shushed him again for his volume.

"Yes. What do you think I am? An idiot like you? Of course I know about the stash. I'm Bryan Copeland's only child. Do you really think he'd build his own drug empire and *not* tell me? We always knew he might get caught, so he came up with a backup plan. Me."

Caleb's look of surprise morphed into a smugness. He leaned toward her.

"I wasn't buying you not knowing anything," he said, matter-of-factly.

"Glad to know you've got some brains in that head of yours," Mara replied with a little too much salt.

"Hey, you better watch that mouth of yours," Caleb warned.

Mara snorted.

"Or what? You going to magically uncuff yourself and beat me while in the middle of the sheriff's department? Honey, you can't honestly think *that's* a good idea."

Whatever smart retort, or at least his version of one, was about to tumble from between Caleb's crooked teeth stalled on his tongue. Like she'd suspected, Caleb was a small fish in a big pond. If he had been prepared to kidnap a woman and her child for Beck then he was either a very loyal lackey or just one who responded to the confidence of the man in charge.

Or, in her case, the woman.

"Now, here's the deal," Mara continued, lowering her voice but not enough to lose its strength. "I want to know how Beck found out about the stash and, for that matter, who this Beck person is. Because I've heard of a lot of people—a lot of big players—and I promise you I haven't heard his name even once."

There it was.

Clear behind his damp straw-colored eyes. An internal struggle while he weighed his options. To help her image Mara tapped her fingers on the tabletop.

"Don't let my mom jeans fool you," she added. "I'm not this soft, compassionate creature you think I am. And more than the same goes for my father. So answer me. *Now*."

"Or what?" Caleb shot back with more bite than Mara had anticipated. If she couldn't sway him to see her, or her father, as more threatening than Beck, then he wouldn't give her any of the information they needed.

"Or what?" she repeated, stalling. "I'll tell you what." And then it was Mara's turn to have a terrible idea.

BILLY WATCHED THROUGH the two-way mirror in absolute awe as the woman he thought he knew completely and intimately grabbed the front of Caleb Richards's shirt and, in one quick, smooth motion, pulled him down hard. The man was so caught off guard that he didn't even try to shield his face. It connected with the top of the table, making a *whack* so loud it was nearly comical.

"If you don't tell me, my father will figure it out soon anyways and then he'll tell everyone it was you who snitched on Beck," Mara said, sitting back in her seat like she wasn't the cause of Caleb's current pain. He put his elbows on the table so he could cradle his nose. There was no blood that Billy could see, but that didn't mean the man wasn't hurting. "Then you'll have not only Bryan Copeland and his associates gunning for your head, you'll also have this Beck fellow and whoever it is he deals with waiting for you to show up. Jail or not, you'll become a target. And I don't have to spell out what will happen when your boss finally catches up to you." Even from Billy's angle he could see the corner of her lips pull up. "Or do I?"

Caleb let out a volley of muttered curse words but he didn't outright try to fight Mara.

"Damn, she's good," Suzy whispered from Billy's side.

He had to agree.

Caleb took a beat to calm his anger.

"I'm screwed either way, then," he finally said.

Mara held up her finger and waved it.

"You tell me what you know and us Copelands will take that as a sign of good faith," she said, diplomatically. "We'll forget your indiscretion of working for a competitor and may even reward you for being helpful. That is, if you *can* be helpful."

A smarter man would have pointed out that Bryan Copeland was no longer competing for anything. That even though some hardened criminals still had a network outside of their prison cells, Bryan's operation had been thoroughly dismantled. Largely thanks to the woman sitting opposite him, promising him a fictional safe haven. However, Caleb Richards didn't appear to be the brightest of men. Mara had found a spot to put pressure on, and after one more long look at her, he cracked.

"I've only heard him go by the name Beck," Caleb started, not looking at all pleased at what he was doing, but doing it all the same. "He found me in a bar, knew my name and asked if I liked money." Caleb shrugged. "I said *hell, yeah, I do*, and he said I could make a lot of it if I came and worked for him."

"Doing what, specifically?" Mara interjected. "Grabbing me?"

Caleb nodded and scrunched up his face in pain. He rubbed the bridge of his nose.

"He said he'd already done the hard part of getting you to town. All I had to do was get you to tell me where the stash was and grab you if you didn't. Then let him get the rest out of you."

"Wait, Beck said *he* got me to come to town?" Mara asked, picking up on Billy's own question.

"Yeah, he said he knew if he let you know he was trying to find the money that you'd probably freak out and want to check on it." A grin split his lips. "He tried to follow you last night but got a flat tire. By the time he changed it he couldn't find where you'd gone so *bam* he tells me to keep checking all of your favorite spots in town to wait you out."

Billy felt his anger start to ooze up through his pores and turn into a second skin. His hands fisted at his sides.

"And how would he know my favorite spots? Is he from Carpenter or Kipsy, or is he just blowing smoke and guessing?" Mara's relaxed facade was starting to harden. She was uncomfortable.

"No, I don't think he's from here. He was complaining about the GPS on his phone the other day."

"Then he just got lucky today with guessing I'd go to the park," Mara offered. Caleb shook his head.

"He told me you used to go running there a lot and probably wanted to show your kid the playground since the sun was shining and all. Though, I guess that was a leap of faith on his part."

"But how did he know that?" Billy asked aloud.

"If he's not from here then how did he know I used to go to the park?" Mara asked a split second later.

"He said his friend knows you. And before you ask, no, I don't know his friend or anyone else he works with, really. I only ever met him at the hotel he's staying at."

"And what hotel is that?"

By God, if Caleb didn't tell her.

A KNOCK ON the door stopped Mara from asking any more questions. Expecting to see Billy or Suzy, she was surprised to find a squat man, sweating in his suit.

The lawyer.

"May I ask what you're doing in here with my client?" the man asked, already bolstering himself up. Mara stood too fast, but recovered with a smile that started with a look at Caleb and ended with the new man.

"Oh, I'm just a friend trying to keep him company until you arrived" was all she said. The lawyer opened his mouth, to protest, most likely, but she was already moving past him into the hallway. It was one thing to pull the wool over Caleb's eyes. It was another to try it with a lawyer.

Mara didn't look back as she walked straight toward Billy's office. The closer she came the more she realized that, while she was happy with the outcome of what she'd just done, something felt off. A lot of Riker County's residents hadn't believed that Mara had been oblivious to her father's dealings. Since it had never been made public that Mara was integral in providing evidence against him, a good number of the general public had assumed she was just clever in how she'd gotten away with avoiding any charge by association. Even though *Mara* knew the truth, she realized now that maybe a part of her didn't.

Maybe there was some side of her that had always known the kind of man her father was. Maybe the person she'd just pretended to be in the interrogation room was the woman she really was, deep down.

Maybe the sweet, compassionate person she portrayed to everyone *was* the cover.

Just like her father.

Mara walked into Billy's office and stopped in the middle. Her heart was galloping and her breathing had gone slightly erratic. She pushed her hands together and twisted them around, trying to physically remove herself from whatever hole she was falling into.

"You did great," Billy exclaimed from behind her. Mara jumped but didn't turn around until she heard the soft click of the door shutting. "I mean, he just opened up and—Mara?"

The warmth and weight of Billy's hand pressed down on her shoulder. Even though she couldn't see his face, she felt his concern through that touch.

When she turned to him, she could feel tears sliding down her cheeks.

"Oh, Billy," she cried.

Billy's expression skirted around deeper concern and hardened. His hands moved to the sides of her shoulders, steadying her. Still, she could feel the warmth of his skin through her shirt. She hadn't realized how much she'd missed it.

"What's wrong?" he asked, lowering his head to meet her gaze straight on. His eyes, a wild green that constantly changed their hue and mesmerized whoever was in their sights, pulled the reluctant truth straight from Mara's heart.

"What if I *am* like my father?"

Mara didn't know if she was looking for an answer from the sheriff or, really, if she even deserved one from him, of all people. But, bless Billy's heart, he gave her one.

Though not the one she expected.

He took a step closer until her breasts were pressed

against his chest. The closeness brought on a new reminder. One of her body naked against his. Sharing his warmth until it became their heat.

"You are *not* like your father," he said. His voice had dropped an octave. Its rich new volume surrounded Mara, trailing across every inch of her body like a silk ribbon. She resisted the urge to let her eyelids flutter closed. It had been too long since she'd heard Billy talk to her like that, and it wasn't helping the images already starting to pop up in her mind. The fear of being like her father started to chip away. But not from his words. It was because the man himself was less than a breath away. If she moved her head up enough she'd be able to meet his lips with hers. Would it be the worst idea she'd had?

No. It wouldn't.

"Mara," Billy whispered, though to her ears, it sounded more like a plea. Mara couldn't find the words to respond, if that's what it really was.

A warm flush started to spread through her body as Billy loosened his hold. Instead of backing away, his fingers trailed down her arms and then made the jump to her hips. The air between them went from fear and concern to something else entirely, charged enough that Mara was left speechless.

That was how it went with the two of them. They only needed an instant for their fire to ignite.

"Mara," Billy repeated. He dropped his head but not his gaze. He angled his lips toward hers and Mara, God help her, finally closed her eyes, ready to feel Billy's lips on hers after two years without him.

But Beck wasn't done with them yet.

The sound of glass shattering ripped away whatever moment they were about to have. But it was the sound of Alexa's high-pitched cry that had them running out the door.

Chapter Nine

The possibility that the sound was something as simple as a cup falling off a table and breaking was quickly dismissed when another crash of glass sounded. This time it was followed by Billy throwing his body into Mara's and pulling her down to the floor. He made a cage around her, his hand flying to the gun at his hip in the process.

"Shooter outside," he yelled. On the end of his words were other shouts from the rest of the department. The empty hallway filled as everyone tried to find the source.

"Shots through the conference room," Billy yelled as a *thunk* split the air.

"Alexa," Mara cried. She nearly broke Billy's hold to go the couple of feet to the conference room door. The room where Alexa had been playing with Cassie. The half wall of glass that made up the interior wall of the room crashed to the hallway floor. Billy's hold was concrete around her. Alexa's continued crying was physically pulling Mara but the sheriff was having none of it.

"Stay here, Mara."

"Alexa—" she tried, but Billy wasn't budging.

"I'll get her."

Mara willed her body to stay still long enough to convince the man she wasn't going to run into the line of fire. The hallway around them was filled with noise as Billy and Suzy barked out orders and relayed information back and forth.

Then Billy was calling out to Cassie, the only person watching Alexa.

She didn't answer.

Billy pulled his gun up high and moved in a crouch until he was in the conference room.

"We need a medic," he yelled as soon as he disappeared from view.

In that moment Mara knew that nothing on earth or in heaven could have kept her from going into that conference room. She mimicked Billy's crouch and was about to rush in when someone grabbed her shoulder.

"Let me go first," Suzy said, brandishing her own firearm.

Mara had enough sense to pause, but no sooner had the chief deputy cleared the door than Mara was in the room.

"Oh, my God!"

The window that looked out onto the street was broken, glass sprinkled on the floor in front of it and on the conference table. However, it was what she saw on the other side of that table that had Mara's stomach dropping to the ground.

Among the scattered LEGOs and books was a blood trail that led to the opposite side of the room, just out of view of the window. There, tucked in the corner, was Cassie, sitting up and bracing herself against the wall with Alexa pushed into the corner behind her.

Even though Billy was at Cassie's side, the injured woman found Mara's gaze and spoke to her.

"She-she-she's o-okay," she gasped.

"Don't talk, Cassie. Save your strength," Billy ordered, tone sharp. He put his hand to the side of Cassie's neck. Blood ran between his fingers.

Mara kept her crouch low as she hurried to their side.

"Get Alexa," Billy ordered. His voice was cold. No doubt helped by the blood he was trying to keep staunched by holding the trainee's neck. Cassie started to move but he stopped her. "Mara can grab her. Don't move."

"Thank you, Cassie," Mara said. She touched the woman's shoulder and focused on her daughter. It was clear Cassie had been shot, yet she still had been trying to protect Alexa. Mara reached over her and grabbed for her daughter. Once the little girl realized who she was, her crying only became more pronounced and large tears slid down her cheeks.

"You're okay," Mara whispered, trying to soothe them both. "You're okay."

"Suzy, take them out of here," Billy ordered as soon as Alexa was pressed against Mara's chest. "Somewhere with no windows. Don't come back until you have a medic with you."

Billy didn't meet Mara's eyes. Instead, he started to talk to Cassie in low, reassuring tones. The whole scene squeezed at her heart.

There was so much blood.

Suzy led them to the dispatcher's small break room, separate from the one law enforcement used, and set down Mara's bag by the door. She hadn't realized Suzy had grabbed it in the first place.

"Stay here until we know everything's alright," Suzy said.

Mara nodded.

Alexa continued to sob into her shirt.

IT WAS SUZY who came to get Mara and Alexa when everything calmed down. The department was filling with people and Suzy had to take them out the back to her car to avoid most of them. She wouldn't explain what was happening until they were driving out of the lot. All Mara knew was that Billy was on the search to find the gunman, along with Chief Hawser and some of his officers. It wasn't every day that someone was brazen enough to attack a law enforcement department. Even more rare was the reality that the shooter had managed to kill, which was the first bit of news Suzy relayed.

"Caleb Richards is dead. The second shot hit him in the head."

"But how?" Mara was shocked. "He was in the interrogation room. There's definitely no windows in there."

"The poor SOB had to use the bathroom. He got his lawyer to let him go as soon as he walked in. He was shot in the hallway, right in front of the door."

A chill ran up Mara's spine and then invaded every inch of her. The one place she'd thought was completely safe hadn't been able to prevent a death.

"We think the first shot was meant for Caleb," Suzy continued, not stopping for Mara's thoughts. She looked out the windshield, directing her car through traffic. They'd decided that leaving Mara's car in the department parking lot was a good idea. They'd only paused to put Alexa's car seat in Suzy's. "He meant to shoot through the conference room windows once at Caleb, I'm assuming, but—" Suzy paused and seemed to rethink what she'd been about to say.

"But Cassie had the bad luck to walk by the window when he shot," Mara guessed. She looked in the rearview mirror to the back seat, where Alexa was nodding off. She'd been able to calm the toddler down during the half hour or so they'd been in the break room. Pure white rage streamed through Mara at the thought that someone could have…

Mara stopped her thoughts before they went to the darkest *what if* she could imagine. Alexa had had a terrifying day, but at the end of it she was safe.

"How is Cassie?" Mara had heard when the first responders had carted the woman out but hadn't stepped out from the break room to see firsthand. She hadn't wanted Alexa to see any more blood than she already had.

"She went into surgery as soon as she got to the hospital. Her sister met her there. Beyond that, I don't know."

Mara felt tears prick behind her eyes. She fisted her hand against her thigh.

"Any idea who the shooter is?"

Suzy's knuckles turned white as she gripped the steering wheel.

"No," she admitted. "But believe you me, the sheriff is sure going to find out."

"Good."

They didn't talk the rest of the way to Billy's and Mara couldn't imagine it another way. When she'd started to work with Billy to help bring down her father they'd kept Mara's involvement a well-guarded secret. Suzy had been the only person in the department who had known from the start. At first, Mara had wondered if Billy's insistence on including the woman was born from a relationship that was more than professional. Now Mara knew Suzy was his best friend.

Suzy is good people, Billy had told her, simply. *I trust her more than anyone. And you should, too. She'll never steer you wrong and will always have your back.*

And that's how Mara knew Suzy knew about Alexa.

"You haven't asked why I left," Mara said when the car rolled to a stop in Billy's driveway. Suzy cut the engine. She'd be staying with the two of them until Billy was back, just in case.

"I assume you had your reasons." Suzy turned to face

her for the first time, keys in the palm of her hand. "And to leave a man that in love with you, they better have been really good reasons."

"I used to think they were," Mara admitted, more honestly than she'd meant. Her cheeks flushed in response.

"And now?" Suzy asked. Her expression softened.

Mara didn't know how to answer that. Luckily, she didn't have to.

"Mama," Alexa fussed. "Mama!"

Suzy smiled. The tension in the air dissipated. Now Mara could see the mother in the woman next to her coming to the helm.

"Now *that's* a sound I have to admit I miss," she said. "There might be some uncertainty you're feeling in your life right now but I can promise you this. Enjoy this time of her life because babies surely don't keep."

For the first time since coming to town, Mara forgot about her troubles. The three of them went into the sheriff's house, talking about the joys of motherhood, and the Alabama heat and humidity, and the rising price of gasoline.

Anything other than the current dangers of Riker County.

SOMETIME LATER THAT NIGHT, Suzy left. Mara woke up from her spot on Billy's bed with a start, heart racing and breath coming out in gasps. She threw her legs over the side of the bed and tried to get her bearings. The sound of glass breaking faded away as full consciousness replaced the nightmare she'd been having. That's when she saw the note on the nightstand.

I have to run. Two deputies are outside and I'm locking you in. I set the alarm so don't try to leave because I don't know the code to disarm it if you trip it. Suzy

Mara put the note back down and looked over at her daughter. The sleeping child with her dark hair framing her face looked like a princess. Tranquil during sleep, unaware of the world around her.

And those in that world who would use her mother's love against her.

Mara leaned over and gave the girl a kiss on the cheek before getting out of bed carefully. Her bare feet touched the same hardwood Billy walked across daily. It made her wonder if any other women had been in his room—his bed—since she'd gone. Surely they had. Billy was a great catch by anyone's standards. Why shouldn't he have taken a lover since? With a sinking feeling in the pit of her stomach, Mara realized Billy could indeed *still* be in a relationship with someone. It wasn't like either one of them had asked about the other's love life. Maybe showing up with his daughter had shocked him enough that he'd forgotten to mention his relationship status.

Mara exhaled until her body sagged. She followed the once-familiar trail that she'd walked during the five months they'd been together from the bed to the bathroom and turned on the hot water in the sink.

Suzy had grabbed her things from the guesthouse, both of them deciding that it would be easier for everyone to be under one roof. No matter the fact that close proximity and Billy Reed were an almost irresistible combination. Suzy had eaten in the kitchen with them before Mara had been able to go through the task of giving Alexa a bath. After that she'd played with her child until both had fallen asleep. That had been welcome yet unintentional. And Mara knew the sleep that had been easy before would now elude her until she heard from Billy.

The water felt great against her skin, warm and soothing. If she wasn't going to go close her eyes again, she might as well use Alexa's being asleep to freshen up. Mara turned off the faucet and went to the shower. Standing under the water she'd still be able to see Alexa, asleep on the bed in the other room. So, more than ready to wash the day off, Mara opened the door as wide as it would go and quickly undressed.

When she stepped into the water stream, she sighed. Then, just to make sure, she moved the shower curtain to the side enough to peek at Alexa. The little girl hadn't moved from her spot. Not even an inch.

Satisfied, Mara stepped directly under the water. It drenched her hair and skimmed down her back while the warmth wrapped around the rest of her. She tried to clear her mind, but all it wanted was to go back to earlier that day.

And to Billy.

Thoughts alone conjured up feelings of pleasure and desire she'd thought would never come again. They weren't complicated feelings, but when they had to do with their past, how could those feelings be anything *but* complicated?

Then, as if just thinking about the man gave her the power to conjure him up, Mara heard the sheriff call out her name. Guilt flooded through her as she tried to erase where her mind had just taken her. She stepped back and quickly wiped at her eyes.

"In here," she answered, reflexively taking a step back so she couldn't be seen through the gap between the shower curtain and the tub. Billy's heavy shoes sounded outside the door.

"Can I come in?" he asked. Something in his voice snagged on a branch of her concern but she answered all the same.

"Yeah. Just please leave the door open for Alexa." Mara

reached out, ready to move the curtain to look at the man, but hesitated. "Is she still asleep?"

There was a pause as he checked.

"Yeah, she's snoring a little."

"Good," she said, glad Billy's entrance hadn't woken the little girl.

They both grew silent, only the sound of water hitting Mara's chest filling the small room.

"I'm sorry for being in your space. I would have asked but you were busy and, well, the guesthouse didn't feel as safe," Mara finally said, unable to keep the quiet going any longer. Every part of her body was on alert. Even more so when Billy didn't answer. "You there?" she ventured.

"Can we talk?" He asked it overlapping her question. Something definitely was wrong. Billy's voice was low and ragged.

Raw.

"Of course."

The sound of plastic running along metal made Mara turn to face the other end of the shower. Billy pushed the shower curtain open enough for him to step over the lip and into the tub.

Mara froze, watching as the sheriff, completely clothed, stood in front of a very naked her.

Billy had seen her naked on several different occasions while they had been together. What was beneath her clothes wasn't a mystery to the man. However, she expected him to at least give her a once-over. Even if she was utterly confused as to why he was standing in front of her in the first place.

Yet Billy's gaze never left her own.

He closed the space between them so fast that she didn't have time to question it. He grabbed her face in his hands and crashed his lips into hers. Heat and pressure and an almost dream-like softness all pulsed between their lips. Mara, too stunned to react, let alone speak, stood stock-still as he pulled back, breaking the kiss. He pressed his forehead against hers and spoke with such a strong sound of relief, Mara felt her heart skip a beat.

"I'm just glad you're okay."

Chapter Ten

The first time Billy ever kissed Mara they'd been in the dining room of his house. It had been a long night of trying to track down a dealer who would decide to flip on Bryan, and Billy could tell the world was weighing heavy on Mara. As he had been bringing in their reheated coffee, he'd caught the woman in a moment she'd been trying to hide.

Elbows on the table, head in her hands, shoulders hunched, and with what must have been a myriad of emotions running up her spine and filling her shoulders, Mara had looked beyond the definition of exhausted. And not just physically.

Billy hadn't known he had romantic feelings for the woman until that moment, though he supposed he'd suspected they were there all along. Seeing her so obviously hurting, he had wanted nothing more than to comfort her. To soothe her wounds. To assure her that, even though things were grim, it didn't mean they always would be. And so Billy had pulled her up to him, kissed her full on the mouth and then, while resting his forehead against hers, told Mara that everything would be okay.

How funny that over two years later, and two rooms over, he'd be doing almost the same thing. Yet this time he was the one who needed strength. Though, admittedly, he hadn't planned on seeking it out fully clothed in the shower.

He'd come into the house without any thoughts in his head of kissing Mara Copeland. But then she'd spoken to him through the shower curtain, just like old times, and everything in him had shifted. What if Caleb had taken her in the park? What if she'd been the one shot trying to protect Alexa? Then he'd looked at Alexa on the bed, snoring soundly, wrapped in a pink blanket with some Disney character or another on it.

When Mara had asked if he was there, Billy hadn't cared about the question. Just the voice asking it. In that moment, he'd only been certain of one thing.

He needed to touch Mara, to feel her. To know that without a doubt she was real and alive and simply *there*.

Now, though, Billy wasn't so certain of himself.

True, moments before he'd all but forgotten the world around them. But now?

He raised his forehead off hers and let his arms fall down to his sides.

"I'm sorry," he said, more aware than ever that he was standing fully clothed in front of a naked Mara. "I shouldn't have just—"

Mara threw her arms around his neck, pushing her mouth back over his. Any hesitation on his part went down the drain with the hot water. Billy pulled her body against him while deepening the kiss and letting his tongue roam a familiar path. Their lips burned against each other, suddenly alive with a mutual attention that always flamed red hot.

The rest of him began to wake as his hands pushed against her soft, wet skin. Unable to stay still, he turned and pushed her against the wall. Water cascaded down his sides as he deepened the kiss, pulling a moan from her.

He suddenly wished he had taken his clothes off *before* entering the tub.

And maybe Mara had the same thought.

She broke the kiss long enough to grab the bottom of his shirt and pull up. It stuck halfway off. Billy moved away from her to do the deed himself. He yanked it off and shucked it somewhere over his shoulder. Mara openly looked over his chest before moving her lips right back to his. She let her hands linger at the buckle of his belt. Soon it, along with everything else Billy had been wearing, was kicked out of the tub until there was nothing but skin between them. Billy hoisted Mara up and against the wall. She wrapped her legs around his waist.

They might have lived separate lives in the last two years, but in that moment, it felt like nothing had changed.

THE HOUSE HAD sounded the same for two years.

Occasionally, it creaked, thanks to the wind, despite having long since settled. Sometimes the branches of the tree outside the guest bedroom scraped against the outside wall. An owl that lived somewhere in the trees away from the house would hoot every so often, while the frogs and insects had a constant rhythm that carried from dark until light. The refrigerator's ice maker and the air conditioner both fussed a little when they came on, too. These were the noises Billy was used to, the ones he heard but never really thought too much about.

However, lying awake in his bed, two new sounds began to mingle with the house.

He turned his head to the right and looked at Mara.

Dimly illuminated from the bathroom light that filtered under the door, Billy could see the woman's face, relaxed in sleep. Her hair was splayed across her pillow like something wild and her lips were downturned. His gaze stayed on those lips for a moment.

He hadn't meant for anything to happen between them. But once Mara had kissed him, he'd known that he couldn't resist her. They might have a complicated past but there was no denying the two of them were connected by something stronger than simple attraction. They'd started a relationship during an intense investigation because being together without *being together* had been too much for either one of them to resist. They needed skin against skin, mind to mind. They needed each other, even when it wasn't what they needed separately. And it was that need that had given him something unexpected.

His attention moved to the little girl between them. Mara had curved her body toward Alexa, protecting her even when sleeping, while Billy had taken up guard on the other side.

After he and Mara had gotten dressed, Billy had been ready to sleep in the guest room or even on the couch. They both knew that their time together hadn't fixed their time apart. Especially when it came down to the fact that Mara had kept Alexa a secret. However, Mara had been quick to ask him to stay.

If only to make sure Alexa doesn't roll off the bed, she had said with a little laugh. Billy didn't know if she was joking or not, but he took the job seriously.

It *was* the first one he'd been given, after all.

For the umpteenth time since their shower together, Billy couldn't stop the blanket of questions that was being woven around him. Holding in every question he had for the mother of his child. The child she'd kept a secret. Why?

And why hadn't he asked her. Why hadn't he gotten an answer before they'd kissed or before they'd gone further?

Billy knew why.

His body hadn't cared that he didn't have answers to why she kept Alexa a secret or why she'd left at all. All it had needed was to know that Mara was safe and then all it had needed was her.

Still, lying there now, Billy knew he should have asked. Because, even if he didn't like the answer—how could he?—he needed one. Just as badly as he needed to stop Beck.

To protect Mara and his daughter.

Billy's cell phone started to vibrate just as thoughts of being a father picked back up in his mind. Both dark-haired ladies stirred. As quickly and quietly as he could, Billy got out of bed and took his phone into the hallway.

"Reed," he answered.

"We found Bernie Lutz's girlfriend," Detective Walker said, not wasting time. "After we let her go the other night she apparently jackrabbited to the next county over and got stopped going forty over the speed limit. One of the officers knew we were looking for her so they called up and we got them the sketch of Beck and Caleb. She confirmed Beck was one of the two men who threatened Bernie before he died, but had never seen Caleb."

"At least that's one mystery put to bed," Billy admitted.

"They are going to hold her for reckless driving until they can get the sketch artist back in tomorrow so we can try to figure out who this mystery friend of Beck's is. She didn't recognize any of the men she saw from the database. They warned me it probably wouldn't be until the afternoon that they could get it going, though. Apparently Walden's visit to help us was his last stop before his vacation kicked in."

"Figures," Billy muttered.

He told Matt he'd done a good job and they talked a bit more about everything that needed doing the next day before Billy ordered the man to go get some sleep. He ended the call and figured he should take the advice himself. Being exhausted wouldn't help anyone, especially when he needed to focus.

"Everything alright?" Mara whispered, surprising him when he'd lowered himself back into bed. He stayed on his back but turned to face her. Her eyes were closed and he suspected she wasn't even fully awake. Still, he answered.

"Just found another connection to Beck," he whispered.

"That's nice," she responded, the corners of her lips turning up.

Billy mimicked the smile. It had been a long time since he'd had a conversation with half-asleep Mara.

"We also caught the mayor hooking up with Will Dunlap," he whispered. "It was a pretty big scandal but I got to tase them both, so that was fun."

Will Dunlap was Mara's ex-boyfriend and he'd lived in Kipsy most of his life. They'd stopped dating a year before she'd approached Billy in the bar. Mara had said that she'd broken up with Will because her father didn't like him. In hindsight, Billy wondered if that had meant Will was a really good guy or a really, really bad one. Either way, Will left for Georgia after the breakup and Billy had checked into him in secret over the last two years. Trying to see if he had been working with Bryan, he told himself. But, if he was being honest, Billy had thought maybe Mara had gone to be with him.

Because, again, he still didn't know why she'd left. Pregnant at that.

"Good," Mara answered automatically. "I'm glad."

Billy smirked, satisfied the woman wasn't really coherent, and decided to try and get some sleep instead of continuing to mess with her. The last thing he needed to do was accidentally wake up Alexa, too.

"I missed you, Billy."

Billy froze, waiting for Mara to continue.

But she didn't.

Instead, she reached out her hand and found his, her arm going across Alexa's chest. Neither one of them woke up from the movement. Billy stayed still, eyes wide, looking into the darkness, Mara's hand in his.

Her skin was warm and soft.

Only when Mara's breathing turned even again did he finally answer.

"Once you two aren't in danger anymore you're going to tell me everything, Mara," he whispered. However, he couldn't deny one poignant fact any longer. He dropped his voice even lower. "I missed you, too."

SUNLIGHT CUT THROUGH the curtains with annoying persistence. Mara could only guess that the pervading light was what had woken her. She tried to ignore it and fall back to sleep—because if Alexa was still asleep it couldn't have been past seven—but no sooner had she shut her eyes than she realized it wouldn't happen, for two reasons.

First, the moment she had woken and stared up at the wooden beams that ran across the ceiling, she'd remembered exactly where she was. And what had happened the night before. Even as she shifted slightly in bed, Mara felt the familiar soreness of a night well spent with Billy. Just thinking about him taking her in the shower, both of them riding a wave of raw emotion, made heat crawl from below her waist and straight up her neck.

Second, when Mara turned to look at him, a different kind of pleasure started to spread within her. The sheriff was lying on his back, eyes closed and face relaxed, a sight Mara had seen many times during the time they'd been together. However, what she'd never seen before was

Alexa tucked into Billy's side, also sound asleep. His arm was looped around her back, protectively, while Alexa had her face against his shoulder, her wild hair splayed around them both.

Together, the three of them made a family.

Or would have, had Mara not left.

You had a good reason, she thought to herself angrily. *You wanted to keep him safe, happy.* Mara balled her fists in the sheets. Tears pricked at the corners of her eyes. *You made a choice.*

Alexa stretched her arm out across Billy's chest and then gave him a knee to the side, as she usually did when she slept with Mara, but the sheriff took it without issue. In sleep he readjusted the arm around the little girl until both settled back to comfortable positions.

You made a choice, Mara thought again. *But now it's not just you anymore.*

Mara felt her chest swell as the idea of the three of them together flashed through her mind. Was that even possible after everything? Did Billy even want that? Sure, they'd had quite the experience in the shower the night before, but that could be chalked up to the heat of the moment. But one night didn't erase her abandonment.

Two *thuds* from somewhere in the house shattered Mara's thought process.

"Billy," she immediately whispered. She grabbed his arm but didn't wait for him to stir. Trying to be quiet, she threw her legs over the side of the bed and ran to the bedroom door. It was already shut, but she threw the lock. When she turned, Billy was not only awake, but untangling himself from Alexa, trying to get out of bed.

"I think someone is in the house," she whispered, coming to his side. Alexa rolled over to the middle of the bed and blinked up at the two of them as Billy stood. "Wait, is someone *supposed* to be in the house?" Mara asked, realizing with a drop of her stomach that maybe the night before *had* been just their heightened emotions and that Billy could have a lady friend who frequented his place.

"*No one* is supposed to be here but the two of you." It was a relief that didn't last long. Another noise sounded from the front of the house. "Take Alexa and get in the bathroom. Call Suzy." He grabbed his cell phone from the nightstand and handed it to her. Then he opened the drawer and took out his gun. Mara grabbed Alexa, trying not to seem too alarmed. Thankfully, when the little girl first woke up in the morning, she was the calmest she ever was. She yawned and let herself be picked up.

"Mama," she cooed.

Billy was about to say something else when a floorboard creaked in the hallway near the bedroom door. The handle started to turn. Mara remembered the lock was busted. Billy pushed Mara with Alexa behind him and raised his gun.

Mara's heart hammered in her chest. Was Beck brazen enough to break into the sheriff's house or send someone else to do it? Was the intruder there to take Mara? Or maybe find out what Caleb had told them at the station? What if the shooter was just there to clean house?

"I have a gun trained on the door and I won't hesitate to use it," Billy barked out.

Another creak sounded.

"Billy Marlow Reed, if you shoot me and ruin my favorite blouse, so help me I will come back and haunt you!"

Billy instantly lowered his gun but Mara didn't loosen her stance. She didn't recognize the voice. Another creak sounded and soon a woman was opening the door, a hand firmly on her hip.

"Sorry," Billy said, sounding like it. "But next time, Mom, you've got to call before you show up."

Chapter Eleven

What a sight they must have been for Claire Ann Reed.

Billy had a pair of flannel sleep pants on and a white T-shirt, and he had a crazy case of bed hair not to mention a gun in his hands. Alexa was in Mara's arms and sporting equally wild hair and a Little Mermaid nightgown that went to her shins. And Mara? Well, she wished she could have met Billy's mom wearing more than one of his old sports shirts, two sizes too big, and a pair of his boxers. Why she hadn't declined the clothes he'd handed her after their shower and simply grabbed her own out of her bags, no more than two steps from the bathroom, she didn't know.

"To be fair, I *did* call," Claire said with a pointed glare at her only son. "Twice. And when you didn't answer I decided to let myself in. And, to be fair *again*, I'm your mother, it's Christmastime and you should have known I'd come in early!" For the first time she looked at Mara and Alexa. Her demeanor changed from scolding to polite. She smiled. "Now, I have fresh coffee in the kitchen, if you'd like some."

"Fresh coffee? How long have you been here?" Billy asked.

Claire laughed.

"Long enough to slice up some apples and oranges for

a healthier breakfast than I'm sure you usually eat." Claire looked at Mara. "Maybe the girl might like some?"

"Alexa," Mara offered. "Her name is Alexa. And she does love oranges."

Claire's smile grew until she looked back at her son.

"Now get dressed and come explain to me why you almost shot me." Her eyes turned to slits. "And why there's no big green tree with ornaments and lights all over it in the living room."

And then she was gone.

Mara and Billy stood still for a moment. Mara's cheeks started to cool. She hadn't realized she'd been blushing. While she knew the woman's name and had heard stories, she'd never met Claire in person. Now the chance at a normal first impression was gone.

"Well, this was unexpected," Billy finally said, moving to shut the bedroom door. He managed to look sheepish. "That was my mom."

"I gathered that," Mara said, putting Alexa down on the bed. Mara dragged her hands down her face and let out a long sigh. "Of all of the times I wanted to meet your mother, it wasn't while I'm wearing her son's boxers."

That got the sheriff to crack a smile.

"At least we had Alexa with us," he pointed out. "We could have been in a much more…compromising situation."

He was trying to lighten the mood but the comment reminded Mara to ask an uncomfortable question.

"Does she know about us? Or did she?"

The humor drained from Billy's face. He shook his head.

"She knew we were spending a lot of time together but I said you were a friend. I wanted to keep things under wraps during the investigation and trial. She doesn't know you're Bryan's daughter, though."

"Mama," Alexa said again, drawing the word out. She knew what was next but kept her eyes on Billy. They had less than five minutes before Alexa started yelling for num-nums, her favorite phrase for food.

"And how do we explain us?" Mara asked.

Billy put a hand to his chin, thoughtful.

"We don't," he finally said. "Not yet. Not until we figure out what *us* is. And not until we get this Beck situation straightened out."

It was a sobering statement but one Mara took with her chin up.

"Okay," she agreed. "Then I guess I should change."

Billy went to the closet next to the bathroom. Without looking back he said, "You look pretty good to me."

Mara put Alexa in her favorite blue shorts, a flowery shirt with the words The Boss across the front and tried to manage the girl's thick hair into a braid. It was sloppy, at best, but the toddler was hungry and let her mama know quickly she wasn't going to sit still any longer.

"I can take her out there while you get ready, if you want," Billy said after surveying the process in silence. Though he had laughed when he saw what Alexa's shirt said. Mara didn't want the man and his mother to feel burdened by attempting to negotiate with an early-morning Alexa but she also wanted to look decent before she had to sit down across from Claire Reed.

"Good luck, then," Mara said to the man. He smirked. The image sent a jolt through her. Billy Reed looked good no matter the time of day or situation. He was just one hell of an attractive man.

"Alexa, want to come eat with a crazy lady who likes to

barge into houses unannounced?" he asked the girl with a slightly high-pitched voice.

"Yeah," Alexa shot back with her own high octaves.

"Then let's get out there, partner!"

Alexa was so excited by having someone seemingly on the same wavelength that she reached for Billy's hand. He grabbed hers without skipping a beat. But Mara saw him stiffen, if only for a moment. She realized that it was the first time he'd held his daughter's hand. As they disappeared from view, Mara couldn't help but feel the weight of guilt crushing her heart.

The sheriff was too good for her.

BILLY WAS HELPING Alexa with her orange slices and Cheerios when Mara came into the kitchen frowning. She'd put her hair into a ponytail and was wearing a white blouse and a pair of jeans that hugged her legs.

Those same legs had been wrapped around his waist last night while hot water ran across nothing but naked skin. Maybe when he'd gone into the bathroom to talk to her he hadn't expected or planned for them to end up having sex.

But that didn't mean he hadn't enjoyed it.

He cleared his throat. Sitting in between his daughter and mother was not the place to be thinking such thoughts. Instead, he focused on Mara's downturned lips.

"What's wrong?"

"I hope you don't mind, but Suzy called and I answered," she said, holding out his cell phone. His mom showing up was enough of a surprise to make him forget he'd left it with Mara. He wiped orange juice off his hand and took the phone.

"Suzy?"

"Billy, we've got another problem," the chief deputy said without missing a beat. "I suggest you go into a room

Alexa and your mother are not in so I can use profane language."

Billy stood and held his index finger up to Mara.

"How did you know my mom was here?" he asked. He walked to the bedroom and pushed the door almost closed behind him.

"When you didn't answer, she called me. I told her you should be at home."

"Thanks for that," he said, sarcastic.

"No problem, boss." There was no hint of humor in her tone. Whatever news she had, Billy was sure he wouldn't like it.

"Okay, I'm alone now. Go ahead and get your frustration out and then tell me what's going on."

Suzy took a moment to spew some very colorful words before circling back to the reason she'd called.

"Bernie Lutz's girlfriend is dead."

Billy paused in his pacing.

"Wait, what? How? Wasn't the local PD holding her on reckless driving until the sketch artist could get there? Did they let her go?"

"No."

"But then, how was she killed?" Billy put his hand to his face and closed his eyes. "Tell me she wasn't shot while she was *in* the police station."

"She wasn't."

Billy opened his eyes again and looked at the wall of his bedroom as if it would make sense of everything. It couldn't, but Suzy could.

"Okay, tell me everything and I'll hold my questions until the end."

"I HAVE TO go visit our neighbors in law enforcement," Billy said when he came back into the dining room. He was already wearing his gun in his hip holster, badge on his belt and a button-up shirt beneath his dark blazer. His cowboy hat was even in its position of honor atop his head.

"What happened?"

"Bernie Lutz's girlfriend was supposed to talk to a sketch artist today about the man who was with Beck when he threatened Bernie." Billy went into the kitchen and came back with one of his to-go coffee mugs. "She was in the county over, being held at their police station last night, when a fire behind their building made them evacuate. By the time everything calmed down they realized she was gone."

"She escaped?" Mara asked, surprised.

"That's what they thought. Until a jogger found her a few miles away in a ditch."

"What?" A coldness started to seep into Mara's skin. "So, as far as we know, two of only three people who have had direct contact with Beck have been killed."

Billy shared a look with Mara that she couldn't define. He nodded.

"It looks that way," he said. "I'm going to head out there with Detective Walker to see if we can find anything to help us nail down Beck or his friend."

"Is Beck the man who shot poor Cassie?" Claire asked. She had set down her food to listen when Billy had come in.

"How the heck did you know about Cassie?" Billy asked. "We've been stonewalling the media until we figure out who's doing what."

If Claire was offended by her son's bluntness, she didn't voice it.

"Betty Mills, you know, that nosy old coot who lives in the house behind the Red Hot Nail Salon off Cherry, called me after she talked to her daughter who has a son who works with you—"

"Dante," Billy guessed.

"I suppose so. Anyways, *he* had the decency to call his mama to let her know he was okay because word got around that two people had been shot, including Cassie, at the department. I figured I'd have better luck communicating with you if I came to town a day earlier instead of waiting by the phone." Claire didn't give her son any room to apologize for not calling her. She turned to Mara. "I was here when Cassie first got accepted as a trainee. She was so nice and bubbly."

Guilt dropped in Mara's stomach. She realized she hadn't asked about the woman's condition when Billy had come home the night before.

"How *is* Cassie doing?" she asked, hoping the answer would ease some of her worry.

"The surgery was a success yesterday, but she hadn't woken up yet by the time I got in last night." Billy's shoulders stiffened. No doubt thinking about one of his own being shot in his domain. "Her sister said she'd keep us updated, though."

"I guess you don't have time to tell me what all is going on?" Claire jumped in. "And why this Beck person seems to be killing everyone he meets?"

This time it was Mara who stiffened. Billy didn't miss it. His frown deepened.

"I don't want you to leave this house," he ordered. "Two deputies are already on the way, including Dante Mills. They'll be watching the front and back of the house and will check up on you every half hour." He looked to his mother. "Mom, I can't make you do anything, but I would really appreciate it if you stayed here. If Mara wouldn't mind, she can go over what's happening with you, as long as you don't tell anyone else. Not even Betty Mills, okay?"

Claire sat up straighter, if that was possible, but she nodded, her short bob of hair bouncing at the movement.

Billy walked over and kissed the top of Alexa's head. He hesitated before leaving the room. Mara knew then that Billy Reed was already 100 percent in love with his daughter. Leaving now would be impossible. Even if Billy didn't want Mara to stay.

She sighed. There were bigger issues to contend with.

For instance, Claire was staring daggers at her.

"He's scared someone will hurt you two," Claire guessed. "Why?"

Mara looked at Alexa and felt fear clamp around her heart.

"Because now I'm the only person we know of to have direct contact with Beck, who is still alive."

CLAIRE WAS A LOT like her son. Or perhaps it was the other way around. The older woman listened patiently as Mara told her everything that had happened, starting with Beck visiting her house. One detail Mara didn't include, however, was her past relationship with Billy. And that Alexa was his daughter.

"So, this Beck man wants you alive because he needs you," Claire said when Mara finished. "At least that's a silver lining, considering he seems to have a friend keen on killing."

Mara couldn't help but agree.

"As sad as it is to admit, yes, there's that."

Claire drained the rest of her coffee from the cup and looked at the toddler across the table from her. Alexa crunched on her Cheerios and became transfixed by a cartoon about pigs Mara had playing on her smartphone.

While watching television wasn't exactly a tradition at their house, sometimes it was the only way for Mara to distract the girl.

"So, you came back to town to tell Billy, since he was in charge of the case against your father and is now the sheriff," Claire spelled out. Mara nodded. "And I'm guessing you also told him that Alexa is his daughter."

Mara froze, coffee cup hanging in midair.

"Excuse me?" she said, trying to recover.

Claire actually smirked.

"Any mother worth her salt is going to figure out when she's looking at her grandchild, especially when the little girl has the exact same eyes as her son," she started. "Not to mention, you don't strike me as the type of woman to let your daughter—and you for that matter—sleep in a bed with a stranger. Am I right?"

Mara didn't know what to say, so she answered in a roundabout way.

"I was the one who helped Billy build the case against my father when he first took it over. During that time we… became close," Mara admitted. She paused, trying to figure out what she wanted to say next but found the words weren't coming.

Claire's smirk softened into a small smile. She held up a hand in a stopping motion.

"Listen, my husband was a very private man and I know Billy has picked up that trait," she began. "I've learned a thing or two about respecting his decisions. Because, in the end, he usually has a good reason for everything he does. I'm going to extend that courtesy to you, too, because my son doesn't pick his company lightly. So, I'm going to assume you are a good woman. And a strong one at that, considering what you must have gone through with your father," Claire continued. "But, you coming back here lets me know that at one point you left. And while my son can keep a secret, I know he wouldn't keep one about having a daughter from me for too long." Claire reached over and took one of Mara's hands in hers. "I won't ask you why you didn't tell him about her until now, but I don't want you to sit here and deny that Alexa's my granddaughter, okay?"

Mara, despite the decision she and Billy had made to wait to tell Claire, gave a small nod, unable to look away from the woman. As if she was caught in a trance. Claire squeezed her hand before dropping it. She leaned back in her chair. She still wore a pleasant, warm smile.

"Now, if I wasn't sure you loved my son, I wouldn't be this nice," Claire tacked on. It was a startling statement that instantly got a reaction.

"Love your son? But I—" Mara started, heat rushing up her neck. This time she was interrupted by Claire's laughter.

"Don't you try to deny it," she said, wagging her finger good-naturedly. "The girl's name is proof enough you loved my son—once, anyway. And, if I had to guess, proof that you always intended to tell him about her." She shrugged. "At least, that's my feelings on it."

Mara felt the heat in her cheeks intensify. But this time she too smiled.

"Her name?" Mara asked, though she knew it was pointless. Claire Reed seemed to pick up on things quickly. Much more so than her son. She would have been a phenomenal sheriff.

"Alexa, after Alexander. Which is my late husband's name and one of Billy's favorite people in the entire world." Claire's smile widened. "You named her after her grandfather, didn't you?"

Mara couldn't help it. She laughed out loud.

"Do you know that Billy hasn't even mentioned that

yet?" Mara knew it was no use denying the connection between them all. "I thought it would be one of the first things he asked me about but, no, he hasn't said a word!"

"Well, my Billy might be a lot of good things," Claire said. "But, bless him, that boy can sometimes be just plain oblivious to what's right in front of him, too."

Chapter Twelve

"How in the world did she slip away without anyone noticing?"

Billy looked over at Detective Matt Walker in the driver's seat. They'd spent the morning talking to officers and witnesses to the fire, trying to figure out what had really happened. So far, no one knew anything other than that Jessica had been there one moment and then, the next, she was gone.

"Incompetence on the officers' behalf?" the detective asked. "The fire wasn't bad enough to require all of their attention, especially since the fire department was a few doors down, and yet they still managed to lose someone in their custody."

Billy wanted to say no, because everyone he had met that morning had seemed, well, competent.

"A suspect was killed, not only in custody at our department but *inside* of it," Billy pointed out. "Whoever is behind this, whether it's Beck or his friend, they seem to have a skill for avoiding detection."

"The hotel being a good example of that," Matt said.

Billy nodded. He hadn't gotten the chance to tell Mara yet, but the hotel room where Caleb had said he'd met Beck had been searched.

Thoroughly.

They'd found nothing. Just a cash payment for six days, starting the week before, under John Smith, of all names. The hotel manager and staff had been told to call if there were any more check-ins or sightings of Beck. Discreetly.

"I should have brought more coffee," Billy finally said, massaging the bridge of his nose. "This case is giving me one of those headaches that feels like it will never go away. I've lived in Riker County my entire life and you've been here for years. How is it that two people who've never been here are navigating our home turf so well?"

"Beck's friend could be a local."

It was a thought that Billy had already discussed with Suzy. And one he hated to entertain. Though just because his love for his town and the area surrounding it was great, that didn't mean everyone else saw Riker County with the same fondness.

"If Bryan's so-called stash is in fact real then knowing where it is would help clear everything up, or at least give us a better chance at stopping this guy," Matt continued. "We could use it to bait Beck and end this mess."

Billy sat up straighter. But then he thought about Mara and her body against his, and how much he would hate it if something happened to her or to Alexa.

They'd have to use Mara for any baiting plan to work. That's why Billy hadn't put much stock in that plan yet. He didn't want her to be in any more danger. They'd just have to figure out a way to pull it off with Mara and Alexa out of harm's way.

Finally, Billy balled his fist.

"I need to talk to Bryan Copeland," he admitted. "*That's* what I need to do. Get him to tell me where the hell this stash is if it's real."

"You think he'd tell you anything, though?" Matt asked. "Considering you're one of the reasons he's in prison?"

Billy shrugged.

"I'll just have to be persuasive."

"You think he'd tell Mara?" Matt ventured with notable caution in his tone. While Billy hadn't told the man about his relationship with Mara, he knew Matt was a good detective. Billy hoped no one else suspected a personal connection between him and Mara. Because, if they did, that meant Beck could possibly know, too. If it hadn't been for the storm the night Mara had shown up, he could have followed her straight to his house.

Just the thought made Billy even more anxious. His phone ringing with the caller ID for Mara didn't help.

"Reed," he answered.

"Billy, it's Mara."

"Everything okay?"

"Yeah, we're fine," she said quickly. Then her voice dropped to a whisper. "Billy, do you think you could come pick me up?"

Her tone made him hesitate. He cast a quick look at Matt, wondering if he should also be quiet.

"Why? What's going on?"

There was movement on the other side of phone. A door shut.

"I think I know where Dad's stash is."

"A MAN NAMED Calvin Jackson was a very unhappy man in the state of Washington who, almost a decade ago, decided to use a local high school's basement as his own personal meth lab," Mara said from her spot at the table. Billy stood at its head while Matt and Suzy were across from her. All eyes were focused as she spoke. "No one would have probably caught him had the lab not exploded—taking Calvin with it—because no one expects a meth lab to be underneath Honors English.

"That's what my father said after we saw it on the news," she continued. "He said if you ever want to hide, you do it not in the last place someone would look, but the last place someone would even associate whatever you are doing with. He said Calvin Jackson had the right idea, just not the right approach." Mara let out a quick breath. "I should have realized then and there that something was off about him, but you know. I just didn't."

Billy fought the urge to put his hand over hers. They might have shared a lot in the last twenty-four hours, but since Mara had called they had fallen into a more professional rhythm. Plus, Mara had left right when Billy had thought things between them were going great two years ago. Maybe chalking up their night together as a one-time nod to their past—and their lack of control when the other was around—would give them a chance at sharing a civil future. One where they could be friends.

One where she wouldn't leave and take their daughter with her.

The thought of never seeing Mara or Alexa again made Billy almost physically uncomfortable.

"So when Mom got out my high school yearbook from the attic, it reminded you of that," Billy guessed. He didn't miss the smile in her voice or the fact that she didn't deny his mother had done just that.

"Yes, it did."

Hiding a stash of money and drugs in a high school had seemed a far-fetched notion until Billy had remembered the school had been completely renovated almost three years ago after a series of storms that had taken their toll.

And that Bryan Copeland had been at the ribbon cutting when the addition had been unveiled.

Mara had remembered that detail because she said she'd been tickled to see her dad on the news, even if he had been in the background. It was the best lead they'd had so far. Even if that didn't automatically mean the stash was hidden somewhere on the grounds.

"But where could he have hidden it without anyone noticing?" Matt asked after Mara was done.

"Well, as far as I know, there's no basement," Billy said, trying to recall the layout. "Then again, I've been told it doesn't look like it did during my high school days. I haven't been there in years. If Bryan *was* going to try to sincerely hide it where no one but him could reach it, he could have used the construction as a way to do just that. And it meets the timeline of when the investigation started to get going. He could have used the storm as an opportunity to make his own personal fallback plan."

Suzy nodded in agreement and then cringed.

"So I guess this means we're going back to high school?"

Billy cracked a quick grin.

"I guess it does."

After several calls made by all three members of his team, Billy went back to standing at the head of the table. This time with a plan.

"Here's the deal," Billy said to the group. "Matt, I want you to keep your attention on finding Beck and his helper or helpers. Because at the end of the day, even if we do find the stash, that doesn't mean our problems with them are over. Work the local angle. If someone we know is feeding this Beck information, we need to plug that hole quick. Talk to the local PD again. See if they have anything to help us."

"Got it," Matt said. "I think I might already have a good spot to start looking."

"Good." Billy looked at Suzy. "Suzy, I want you to come with us, because three sets of eyes are better than two."

Suzy crossed her hands over her chest.

"And?" she asked.

Billy let out a long breath.

"And I hate dealing with Robert by myself," he admitted.

"Robert?" Mara asked.

Suzy was quick to answer.

"The principal. He's something of a chatterbox."

"Which wouldn't be bad if he wasn't always talking about nonsense," Matt added.

"But we need him unless we want to wait for a warrant, which might leak to the public what exactly it is we're looking for," Billy pointed out. "Plus, if we're going to search the high school for a cache of drugs and blood money it only feels right that the principal is at least on the premises."

CARPENTER HIGH DIDN'T look like the school Billy remembered.

Its once-stained, shabby and seen-better-days structure was cleaner, brighter and nearly pristine.

One of the last places anyone would look for a stash of drugs and blood money.

Billy followed Suzy into the staff parking lot, where a man was standing next to an old Mazda.

"Is that Robert?" Mara asked from the passenger's seat.

Billy nodded.

"And we're going to let Suzy distract him while we conduct our own search," he said. "Because I can stand a lot of things, but there are some people on this earth I believe were put here just to test our patience."

Mara laughed and soon they were standing across from Robert. He was a short man with a crown of dark hair that had a shiny bald spot in the middle. His gut used to extend past the belt and dress khakis that he habitually wore, but he was much slimmer than he had been the last time Billy saw him.

"New diet," he said, looking straight at Billy. He patted his stomach. "Mama said I wasn't getting any younger and told me it was now or never to take control of my life. Health included." He sent a wayward wink to Mara at Billy's side. "She really just wants me to settle down and give her some grandbabies. I said one thing at a time, Ma!"

Mara gave a polite little laugh.

Suzy cleared her throat. "We're kind of in a hurry, Robert," she said, taking a step forward so that his attention stuck to her. "You understand what we're here to do? And why only you can help us, right?"

Robert, feeling the weight of importance on his shoulders, puffed out his chest and straightened his back. His playful smile turned into a determined crease.

"Yes, ma'am." He made a grand gesture and swept his arm toward the front entrance. "I'm ready when you are."

Billy could tell Suzy was holding back an eye roll, just as he could tell Mara was trying not to laugh, but soon the four of them were heading up the walkway.

"Did you really tell him what we were looking for?" Mara whispered when Robert got out his keys. Since it was a Saturday, he'd promised no one else would be inside during the day.

"That we had reason to believe that harmful substances could have been hidden on the premises and we'd like to take a cursory look on the down low before causing a panic."

"And he just agreed to that?"

Billy shrugged. "He'd rather be sure before he subjects his school to good ole small-town scrutiny."

"I can't blame him there," Mara conceded.

Robert opened the door and they all stepped into the lobby. Like the outside, the inside looked much nicer than the school Billy had attended. Still, he inhaled and couldn't help but feel a twinge of nostalgia. The urge to tell the story about a fifteen-year-old Suzy giving Kasey Donaldson a black eye for saying she shouldn't be allowed to play capture the flag because she was a girl was almost too great to resist. Especially when Billy realized the principal's office was still straight ahead, next to the stairs that led to the second floor. He'd watched Suzy do several marches into that office with her chin held high.

Hell, he'd done a few himself.

"Okay, why don't we split up to make this faster," Billy said, shaking himself out of his reverie. "Suzy, you and Robert take the gym and detached buildings, and we'll search the first and second floors of the main building."

Suzy didn't even bat an eye at being paired up with Robert. By the hard set of her jaw, Billy saw that she was in work mode. They had a problem that needed to be solved.

Finding Bryan Copeland's stash would solve it.

Robert followed Suzy, already babbling about something, while Mara turned her attention to him.

"You know, in movies, it's usually a bad idea to split up," she mused.

"Stick with me and you'll be alright, kiddo."

Mara was quick to respond with a wicked grin. It made Billy feel a lot of things he shouldn't be feeling. Maybe they should be splitting up, after all.

It wasn't until they made it to a second-floor classroom that the idea of *them* pairing up showed itself to be a bad one.

Mara noticed a panel of ceiling tiles that were painted a different color than the many others they'd already seen.

Since their motto was to leave no stone unturned, she pulled a table over and stood on top of it. She wasn't short, but she wasn't the tallest woman, either. She pushed one tile up but she couldn't see inside the ceiling. She needed just a little more height.

"Billy, get up here and look."

"I don't think so," he said seriously. "I'd snap that table in two."

"Then—"

"It's probably not the best idea for me to get on those chairs, either. Donnie Mathers tried to jump from one to the other in tenth grade and one broke from under him. Broke his arm, bone sticking out and everything." Billy shook his head. "But what I can do without breaking anything is hoist you up."

"Then how about we nix the table and chairs. You're certainly tall enough to be better than a table."

Mara didn't wait to be invited to him. She jumped down and stood in front of him expectantly.

"Just like the time I helped you get that branch that was hanging off of your roof," she said. When he hesitated, Mara feigned offense. "Unless you think I'm too heavy to pick up."

"Don't even pull that," he said, but it got the job done. He wrapped his hands around her and hoisted her up until she was able to move a tile.

"A little more," she said, trying to keep her mind on the task at hand and not *Billy's* hands. He was quiet but adjusted to give her a little more height. It always amazed her how strong Billy Reed was. Mara brought her phone up and shone the light around inside the ceiling.

"Nothing," she reported, not surprised. "At least we looked."

Mara braced for Billy to let her down fast but, instead,

he lowered her slowly. Like molasses crawling down a tree, her body slid against his until her shirt caught on him. It had dragged the fabric up to expose her bra by the time her feet were back on the floor. She moved to pull it down, but Billy caught her hand.

She felt her eyes widen and her breath catch. The heat of his hand burned into her skin, but it was his stare that almost set her ablaze. It pierced through the few inches of space between them, and frightened and excited her more than she wanted to admit. Mara couldn't read what the man was thinking.

She sure found out.

He dipped his head down until his mouth found her own. But it was his hand that surprised Mara. While his tongue parted her lips, his hand let go of hers and traveled down to the cup of her bra. She let out a gasp as he thumbed her nipple until it hardened. It wasn't the only thing. She could feel Billy's arousal as he used his free hand to pull her flush against him.

It was fuel to their already burning fire.

Mara grabbed his belt and pulled the man closer, trying to show him she wanted him just as much as he wanted her. Right then. Right there. However, Billy surprised her by breaking their kiss. His hand dropped away, leaving her exposed skin cold.

Billy met her gaze.

Those green eyes spelled out one word to her.

Regret.

"I-I'll check the rooms at the other end of the hallway," she said, tugging her shirt down quickly. Before Billy could stop her, Mara rushed from the room.

But, with a heavy heart, she realized he didn't even try.

Chapter Thirteen

Mara opened her eyes and tried to make sense of what she was seeing.

Her head pounded and her side lit up in pain. She sucked in a breath and regretted how much it hurt. She tried to move, if only to distance herself from the physical discomfort on reflex, but realized with panic that she couldn't. Her eyes swiveled down to the object pinning her to the ground.

It was a set of metal lockers.

But why were they on top of her? And where—

Then it came back to her.

Mara moved her head from side to side to try and see the rest of the storage room behind her. Except for more lockers and cleaning supplies, she was alone.

She turned her attention back to the weight keeping her against the floor. Tentatively, she pushed her shoulder up to try and free one of her arms. Pain shot fast and hard through her side again but she managed to get her left arm free.

Mara hesitated as footsteps pounded the tile outside the closed door. Someone was coming toward it.

Fast.

Mara put her left hand under the top part of the locker across her chest. She started to push up just as the door swung open.

"Billy," she exclaimed in profound relief.

The sheriff's eyes widened in surprise and then almost immediately narrowed. He came around to her head.

"What happened? I heard you scream," he said, already putting his hands under the top of the locker.

"I'll tell you if you get this off me," she promised, readying herself for the weight to be lifted. A part of her was afraid to see the extent of the damage done to her. She just hoped nothing was broken.

"Alright, get ready."

Billy pulled up and soon the locker was hovering over her. Mara didn't waste any time. She rolled over onto her stomach and dragged herself across the tile between Billy's legs. The pain she'd felt before nearly bowled her over at the movement.

"I'm out!"

Mara turned back to watch the lockers crash to the ground. The noise rang loudly through the room and into the hallway outside. She'd been gone from Billy's side for less than ten minutes. It had been more than enough time for trouble to find her.

"Get your gun out, Billy," she said, a bit breathless. Bless the man, he didn't hesitate. He unholstered his gun, kept his back to the wall and crouched down next to her.

"Someone pushed those over on you?" He motioned to the lockers.

Mara nodded.

"I was looking in them and heard someone walk up. I thought it was you but the next thing I knew I was waking up on the floor under them."

Billy said a slew of curses that would make his mama angrier than a bull seeing red and pulled his cell phone from his pocket. He must have dialed Suzy, because she answered with an update already going, loud enough for

Mara to hear. They hadn't found anything yet in their search.

"Suzy, someone's here with us. Tell Robert to lock himself in a room and you come up to the main building pronto. We're on the second floor."

"Want me to call in some—"

The unmistakable sound of gunshots rang through the air. Mara heard it through and outside of the phone. Billy stood so fast she couldn't hear whatever it was that Suzy yelled.

But she knew it wasn't good.

"Suzy?" he called. "What's happening?"

She didn't answer but another gunshot sounded.

Billy cursed again and pulled the radio from his belt. He called for backup using a tone that absolutely rang with authority. It inspired Mara to get to her feet, though it was a struggle.

Acute pain that made her inhale lit up her side—or, more accurately, her ribs. If she hadn't broken any, she'd at least bruised them something mighty. No other part of her seemed worse for wear. Not even the knot on the back of her head where she'd hit the floor.

The moment Billy had finished his call, he turned to Mara. Surprise was clear on his face.

"I'm fine, let's go," she yelled, waving him toward the door.

He didn't wait to argue with her. Instead, he tossed her his cell phone and then whirled back around, gun drawn.

"Stay behind me," he barked.

Mara had no intention of doing anything else.

They left the supply closet and, when Billy was convinced the coast was clear, moved down the hall, heading for the set of stairs at the end.

The second floor of the school was two wide hallways

in an L-shape with classrooms lining both sides. The stairs were where the hallways converged and Mara had marched by them when she was fleeing from Billy minutes before. She'd been so embarrassed, and filled with shame and loathing and a hundred other emotions, that she'd gone to the farthest room she could find. She should have been more careful, or at least cautious, but no one should have known about their search other than Matt, Suzy, Robert and a few deputies who'd been ordered on standby.

They should have been alone in the school.

Another shot rang through the air. This time, Mara didn't hear the echo come through the phone. This time, the call ended. A cold knot of worry tightened in Mara's stomach for the chief deputy and the principal.

Billy quickened his steps, moving with his gun high and ready. Mara sucked in a breath and started to follow when the sheriff stopped so quickly she nearly ran into his back.

"What—" she started, but Billy cut her off.

"Listen," he whispered.

Mara froze.

The unmistakable sound of footsteps echoed up the stairs from the first floor. Someone was coming. And by the set of Billy's shoulders, Mara knew it probably wasn't a friendly. Without turning his back to the stairs the sheriff began to backtrack. Mara gasped as the quick reversal made the constant thrum of pain in her side triple.

The footsteps stopped but Billy didn't.

He kept moving until they were off the stairs.

"Go hide," he ordered, voice low. He nodded in the direction of the part of the second floor she hadn't explored. But she wasn't about to question him.

"Be careful," Mara whispered. She tried to be quiet as she moved as quickly as she could toward the classrooms at the end of the hallway. She chose the middle of three and turned in the doorway so she could still see Billy.

He was looking at her. With a quick jerk of his head he motioned for her to get inside the room. So she went, leaving the sheriff alone.

THE BULLET GRAZED Billy's arm, but it was the man lunging at him that made him lose his gun. It hit the tile and skidded away while his back connected with a wall. Billy took a punch to his face as the infamous Beck snarled, "Where is it?"

Billy pulled his head back up and slung the man off him. If Beck hadn't shot half a magazine at him as soon as he'd seen Billy on the stairs, forcing the man to take cover long enough so Beck could run up, he wouldn't have had the chance to question Billy. Let alone lunge at him.

Blond hair cropped short against his scalp, blue eyes that held nothing but hatred for Billy, and the thin, drawn face of a man who looked to be in his late thirties, all wrapped in a pair of khaki slacks and a collared shirt, Beck didn't look nearly as threatening as Billy had imagined. Certainly not a man trying to create another boom in the drug industry of Riker County.

But neither had Bryan Copeland.

Billy knew that bad men didn't have just one look. Bad men were just men who did bad things. Whether one wore a suit or a wifebeater, it didn't matter.

While Beck tried to regain his balance, Billy threw his own myriad punches. One connected with Beck's jaw, another with his ribcage. The latter blow pushed his breath out in a wheeze but he didn't go down. Instead, he used Billy's attack against him. Bending low, Beck rammed his shoulder into Billy's stomach, throwing him back against the wall.

"Where is it?" he roared again. Beck's anger was getting the better of him. The man took the time to rear his fist back, like he was winding up for the big pitch.

It gave Billy time to bring up his own fist. Hard. It connected with Beck's chin with considerable force. The man made a strangled noise and staggered backward. He held his jaw with both hands. Billy didn't waste time watching what he did next. He turned to look around for his gun.

It lay beneath a water fountain a few feet away.

Billy was running for it, already mentally picking it up and swinging it around on Beck, when he registered a new noise. Footsteps, coming fast.

Could Mara have tried running up to help?

But it wasn't Mara.

He turned in time for something to slam against his head.

Then everything went dark.

"WHERE'S BILLY?"

Matt Walker stood in the doorway, a frown pulling down his lips. Sirens sounded in the distance.

"He's okay, but—"

"But what?" Mara walked past him, pain be damned.

"Mara, I need you to stay, just in case," Matt tried, but she was already looking for the sheriff.

"Billy!"

Billy was on the ground. Sitting up, but still, on the ground. He had a hand to the back of his head. His face was pinched. He was obviously in pain.

"I'm okay. Got caught by surprise. Apparently Beck's friend is here." His gaze shot to her side. Mara realized she'd been clutching it. The pain kept intensifying the more she moved.

"Bruising, that's all," Mara said. "What happened out here?"

"I turned my back on the stairs and I shouldn't have." Billy looked to Matt. "One minute I was fighting him and then the next I got slammed with something. Then I could hear the sirens. Beck and his buddy must have run."

"Did you pass out?" Mara asked, worry clotting in her chest. She put her hand to the spot Billy was holding to inspect it closer. There was blood.

"For a second," he said dismissively. The detective must have cleared the other rooms down the hallway she'd been hiding off and jogged back to them. "Matt, Suzy should be outside at one of the buildings. She had Robert with her. Someone was shooting at them."

Matt nodded and grabbed his radio. He told everyone who was listening to keep their eyes out for two suspects and to find Suzy. Apparently he had no intention of leaving Mara and Billy. She was glad for the detective's company. Billy wasn't looking too hot.

"Don't move," Mara chided when he tried to stand.

Billy, of course, tried anyway.

Mara rose with him, hands out to steady the sheriff if needed.

"I'm fine, I promise," he said, swatting at her. As soon as his hand cut through the air, though, he started to sway.

"Billy," Mara exclaimed. She grabbed his arm and gasped at the pain from her ribs.

"You *both* need seeing about," Matt said.

"I'm *fine*," Billy tried again. He steadied himself. The hand he'd had against the back of his head was red with blood. Mara pointed to it.

"That isn't fine, Billy."

He shook his head a little, trying to be dismissive again.

"I just need to take a seat—" he started. But then the man tipped backward.

"Matt," Mara squealed, trying to keep Billy from hitting the tile floor. Matt was fast. Between the two of them they managed to stop the sheriff's fall. They eased him back down to the tile as gently as they could.

"He's unconscious," Matt said, reaching for his radio again. However, before he could call anything in, a voice was already yelling into the airwaves.

"We need a paramedic!"

Chapter Fourteen

The ER nurse was brisk when she told Billy he had a concussion and needed to take it easy. At the very least, for the rest of the day.

"I have a job to do," he objected, already slipping his badge back on. His cowboy hat soon followed.

"So do I," she retorted, her brows drawing together. The effect made her look severely disapproving. "And it's to tell you that you need to rest. Sheriff or not, you're just as human as the rest of us."

Billy was getting ready to harp on the fact that he was a human *who happened to be* a sheriff when Matt walked around the privacy curtain. He gave a polite nod to the nurse who, in turn, smiled.

"I'll go check on my other, less stubborn patients now," she said before throwing Billy a parting look of annoyance. Then she turned to Matt. "I'm going to tell you what I told him. He needs rest."

"Yes, ma'am," Matt responded, dutiful. Billy rolled his eyes.

She pulled the curtain back again so they were out of sight of the rest of the nooks that lined the emergency room. Thankfully, it wasn't crowded.

"I thought everyone was supposed to love the sheriff," Matt said with a smirk the moment she was gone.

Billy shrugged.

"Apparently not everyone got that memo." The nurse had been more kind to Mara when he'd insisted she get checked out first. Then, when the tables had turned, Mara wouldn't stop fussing. It wasn't until she went upstairs that Billy realized the nurse wasn't going to cut him any slack. "So, what's going on?"

"Like I told you on the way over here, it's been confirmed that Bryan's stash isn't at the school," Matt started, taking a seat on the doctor's stool. He pulled out his pad to look at the notes he'd written. "After hearing what happened, Chief Hawser offered up a few of his off-duty officers to comb the school again, just in case. He said if that's stepping on your toes to let him know, but he didn't sound like he cared either way."

"I reckon he probably doesn't mind about stepping on anyone's toes," Billy said. "But that's not a bad idea."

"He also said his communications head suggests you hold a press conference to try and let the public know to look out for Beck, his associate and any suspicious activity." Matt cut him a grin. "I told him you already contacted the news station, right after you yelled at the EMTs to turn off the damn sirens because you couldn't hear yourself think."

Billy knew there was humor in what he'd done, but when he'd woken in the ambulance on a stretcher, Mara peering down at him through her long, dark lashes, he'd been feeling anything but humorous. Part of him knew he needed to take it easy but the other part, the sheriff side of him, knew that time was wasting. Beck and his friend weren't going to take a break just because he needed one.

"Was Hawser the only chief in the county that called in so far?" Matt nodded. Billy bet Chief Calloway, from the city of Kipsy, would be on him soon. They were usually

a bit busier than the rest of Riker, but Alexandria Calloway was not the kind of chief to sit back and twiddle her
thumbs about any case.

Billy figured he might as well beat her to the punch.
"I'll get Dane to talk to Chief Calloway and see if she can
make sure all of her officers stay in the loop." His head
thrummed with a dull ache. Like putting a shell up to his
ear and hearing the ocean but, in Billy's case, he couldn't
seem to put the shell down. The doctor had given him
something for the pain and nausea but he'd refused to get
the really good stuff. He had a job to do. He needed to
stay sharp.

"While all of this posturing is going on, I need you
to keep on trying to figure out who this Beck person is
and who's helping him," Billy said. "Use Caleb as a start
since he's the only person we actually know the identity
of. Once I get out of here I'm going to call in a few reserve
deputies to see if we can't narrow down a possibility as
to where our friends are at least staying since we burned
their hotel bridge."

Matt nodded. He wrote something down and closed the
pad. He looked a bit alarmed when Billy swung his legs
over the bed and stood. Billy pointed at him.

"If you tell me to rest, I'll fire you on the spot," he
threatened.

Matt's grin was back.

"Wouldn't dream of it."

"Good, now get to work. I'm going to go upstairs and
then head back to the office."

It hadn't been until a little after he'd come to in the
ambulance that Billy had learned Suzy had been shot.
Luckily she'd been wearing her bulletproof vest beneath
her uniform. The impact, however, had caused her to fall,
shattering her radio and pushing her away from her cell

phone. Robert, in terror, had started to run, and she'd had her hands full wrangling him back inside the gym. He had been so frenzied that he'd hyperventilated and passed out. Which no one blamed him for. He'd expected to simply show them around the school, maybe find something interesting in the process. Not almost get killed by an unknown shooter.

Suzy was standing in the hallway on the second floor in the east wing. She had a scowl on her face and her vest in her hand. Instead of her Riker County Sheriff's Department shirt, she was wearing a plain white T-shirt. When she saw Billy, her scowl deepened.

"He ruined my shirt," she greeted. "The bullet tore right through it."

"I'm sure we could order you a new one."

"Good."

Billy was next to her now and could tell she was holding back. But that's who Suzy was. She held her emotions close to her chest. Sometimes she didn't even let Billy in, and he was her closest friend.

"Besides the shirt, how's everything else?" he asked. Suzy brought her eyes up quick, her mouth stretching into a thin line. Defensive. Billy amended his question. "I mean with the vest. How's the vest doing?"

Suzy started to say something but paused. She let out a breath and played along.

"Okay," she admitted, face softening for a moment. "Glad it wasn't shot more than once, though. It's going to bruise something wicked."

Billy smiled.

"Won't we all."

Suzy nodded, gave her own little smirk and motioned to the room behind her. The door was shut but Billy knew who was behind it.

"How's Cassie doing?" He nodded to the room.

Suzy glanced over her shoulder.

"To be honest, I don't know. All I got is that she hasn't woken up since the surgery, but she's on some pretty intense meds so that's normal."

Billy tensed. For several reasons. One was that he hadn't seen Mara since she'd left him to go with Suzy to check on the trainee. Surely Suzy wouldn't just let her wander off.

"So, Mara's not in there?" he had to ask. It made Suzy's lip quirk up for a second. She pointed down to the other end of the hall.

"Don't worry, Sheriff. Your gal's right there."

Billy ignored the comment but was glad to see the dark-haired woman a few yards away. She stood talking to an older couple he recognized as Mr. and Mrs. Gates, Cassie's parents. He hadn't realized they had already flown in, probably relieving her sister who had a few kids at home. He'd meant to meet with them, but that intention had fallen through the cracks as their case had gone nowhere but south since Cassie had been hurt. Billy scrubbed his hand down his face and sighed. It sat heavy on his chest.

"Buck up, partner," Suzy whispered. "They're coming over."

"Mr. and Mrs. Gates, it's good to see you," Billy greeted them when they stopped. He had no doubt in that moment that neither would leave the hospital until their daughter did. "I'm just sorry it had to be under these circumstances."

Mrs. Gates, a woman who probably exercised her laugh lines during happier times, gave him a weak smile. She looked exhausted and withdrawn. A shadow of the woman Billy had met at Cassie's informal birthday gathering a handful of months before. Mr. Gates, who held the strain of his daughter's near-death experience clearly on his shoulders, was faster with a verbal greeting and a handshake.

"I'd have to agree with you there," he said, pumping Billy's hand once and letting it drop. His eyes dropped with it and focused on Suzy's vest. The chief deputy had tried to angle it behind her as they'd walked up, but Mr. Gates had a sharp eye. Or maybe he was just suspicious of anything and everything. Billy didn't blame him, considering. "The man who did that to Cassie shot you?" he asked Suzy.

"We can't say for certain," she responded. "But it's a possibility."

"Either way, both incidents are being investigated thoroughly by our entire department and other departments in the county," Billy assured him. "And we're about to go back out there and join them." The words didn't seem to offer Mrs. Gates any relief the way they did her husband. Mara must have sensed it. She lightly touched the woman's arm.

"These are good, smart people," she said. "Everyone responsible will be caught and dealt with. Don't you worry about that."

Mrs. Gates turned to look at Mara. She patted her hand and nodded.

"How's she doing, by the way?" Suzy asked. "We couldn't find the doctor, and the nurse just said she was sleeping."

This was a question Mrs. Gates was quicker to answer. There was a noticeable tremble in her voice as she did.

"She's good. The surgery was quick and they say everything will heal." She touched her neck. Her voice broke as she added, "She'll, uh—she'll have a scar, though."

"But a scar we'll take," Mr. Gates jumped in. He put his hands on his wife's arms and squeezed. The pressure seemed to jog her out of the worry she'd been falling back into.

She turned to him and smiled.

"You're right." She took one of his hands and they seemed to get lost in their own silent conversation. They loved each other. That much was apparent. It made Billy want to look at Mara.

He shouldn't have done what he'd done earlier. But being that close to Mara—touching her—he'd just wanted more. His body had taken hold over his mind and reached out for her again.

And she'd reached back.

"Well, you let us know if there's anything we can do for you, but it's time for us to get back out there," Billy said, eyes firm on the couple. He didn't need to look at Mara.

What had happened between them couldn't happen again. Not now.

"THEY GAVE ME something for the pain and wrapped me up," Mara said when she was riding shotgun in Billy's car. "Like I said, it's only a little bruising. No broken ribs. So I'm fine."

"I believe you."

His eyes flickered over to her but didn't settle. It made the guilt of everything that had happened rise again within her.

"Billy, I'm sorry," she said. "I thought the money and drugs would be at the school. I was wrong and you got hurt and Suzy got shot. I just—I'm so sorry."

"It's not your fault," he said with force. "It was a good lead. One we had to chase down, one way or the other." He slapped his hand on the steering wheel. It made Mara jump. "A lead *I* should have chased down. Not you. I shouldn't have dropped my guard." There appeared to be something else he wanted to say, but his original thought must have won out. "You got hurt, too."

Mara wanted to wave off his concern, but she realized

he was right. In part. Her presence might have been the reason Beck and his lackey had shown up in the first place, thinking she knew where the stash was and following her to the school. If she'd stayed at Billy's, then the sheriff and his chief deputy wouldn't have had their lives put in danger. At least, no more than usual.

That line of thinking was a straight shot to Alexa. She was still at the Reed family home with Claire, unaware that she'd come close to losing her father.

"I'm sorry, Billy," Mara whispered before she even realized what she was saying. The haze of medication wasn't as thick as she wished it was. The kind of pain that couldn't be seen was coming to the forefront. The present danger they were in was just salt in her past choices' wounds. She wasn't talking about what had happened at the school anymore. "I know you must hate me."

Billy was silent a moment, probably piecing together a polite way to agree with her, when something she hadn't expected interrupted them.

A truck slammed into the side of their car, right behind Billy. It happened so fast that Mara didn't even have time to scream. The impact rocketed them off the road, past the shoulder and right into the ditch.

Wham-bam-bam!

It wasn't until they settled that Mara realized with relief that they hadn't flipped. She turned to look at Billy, ready to voice the thought, when she saw the sheriff's eyes were closed.

"Billy?" she heard herself screech.

When he opened his eyes, she would have jumped for joy if it wasn't for the seat belt that held her tight. He shook his head a little, dazed, and then seemed to snap out of it.

"You okay?" he asked, already moving.

"Yeah, I think so. What about who hit us?"

Billy whipped his head around and looked back out at the road. The Tahoe was turned at an angle that blocked whoever had hit them from Mara's view. So when Billy started cussing, she didn't understand. But then he said one name that put everything into terrifying perspective.

"Beck."

Chapter Fifteen

Mara's heartbeat was in her ears, thumping with unforgiving relentlessness. The spike in adrenaline wasn't helping. Nor Billy's warning for her to stay down.

And it sure didn't help matters that he'd pulled his gun out.

"Call Suzy" was all Billy said before he opened his door and took aim past the back end of the vehicle.

Mara undid her seat belt and tried to get as low as possible while fumbling for Billy's phone. She found it in a cup holder and dialed Suzy, trying to get her panic under control.

"Beck just hit us off the road," Mara rushed to explain as soon as the call connected. She followed with their location before Billy yelled.

"Come out with your hands up or I'll shoot," he warned. Mara couldn't hear if Beck answered.

"I'm a minute away," Suzy said. "Keep me on the line." Mara nodded to no one in particular and put the phone on speaker. She relayed the information to Billy.

"Having a shoot-out with the sheriff isn't a good idea," Billy hollered.

Mara wished she could see what was going on. Billy had half his body hanging out the open door and gun held high, but Mara couldn't believe it was good cover.

Would Beck really try to shoot him?

She didn't have to wonder for long.

A shot rang out. Mara gasped as the vehicle rocked.

"What happened?" Suzy yelled, but Billy had his own answer ready. He fired his gun once. It wasn't long before Beck returned fire, causing Billy to retaliate. Soon all Mara could hear was gunfire slamming into metal and glass. She couldn't tell who was hitting what. She kept her head covered and her body as low against the floorboards as she could, praying that Billy wasn't getting hit. When she saw the driver's side window spiderweb from a bullet, mere inches from Billy, Mara nearly cried.

However, when the back windshield shattered, covering the interior in a hail of glass, Mara couldn't help but scream. She closed her eyes tight and covered her head. Around the pounding of her own heart, she expected to hear the shots even more clearly without the back window, but then everything went silent.

"What's going on?" she whispered to Billy.

The sheriff's posture was rigid—a stance that said there was no way in hell he was moving until this was over—but he answered her after a moment.

"Beck got back into the car," he said. "The windows are tinted. I can't see either one of them now."

So Beck had his friend with him.

Maybe because that left him more vulnerable than he liked, Billy got back into the driver's seat and shut his door. His head stayed turned, keeping an eye on the truck. It was still on the road, level with them, but at an angle that gave neither Billy nor Beck a good, clean shot.

"They're leaving," Billy yelled, angry.

"Let's go after them!" Mara might not have liked the danger but, with a surge of anger herself, she knew then that the men weren't going to stop.

So *they* needed to be stopped.

"They shot out a tire. I tried to do the same but my angle was off," he growled. "Suzy, they're moving down Meadows, southbound. Driving the same truck Mara described when she came to town. They're missing some windows."

Suzy confirmed she heard while Billy got his radio. He gave an order for the deputies in the area to help Suzy. He also told dispatch to send a tow truck. She asked if they needed medical attention. It seemed to snap Billy out of sheriff mode. His eyes softened with concern. So much of it that Mara felt the sudden urge to wrap herself around him. To comfort him. To feel comfort from him. To feel him.

"I'm okay," she assured him instead. "Are you?"

Billy nodded, but Mara still traced every inch of him she could with her eyes. He told dispatch to hold off on the medic. When he was done with his orders, Billy scrubbed a hand down his face. A sigh as heavy as a boulder seemed to crush him.

"I agree with that sigh," Mara said, moving slowly, gingerly, back to a sitting position. She couldn't help but wince, pain meds or not. Billy's hand covered hers.

Expecting his eyes to be as soft as they had been moments before, Mara was surprised again by the man. He looked like he was ready to kill.

"We have to end this," he said, voice hard as stone. Mara was about to agree, but then the sheriff said something that stopped her cold. "Mara, we have to talk to your father."

THE DRIVE OUT to Walter Correctional Facility took them an hour out of Riker County. In that hour, Mara had barely spoken a word. As he sat across from her father now, Billy didn't blame her one bit for needing the silence to collect her thoughts. She might have to face a man not even Billy wanted to deal with. But the fact of the matter was that Beck was escalating. Ambushing them at the school and then less than a few hours later attacking them again, this time on a well-traveled public road?

It all reeked of desperation.

Billy believed that if Mara hadn't screamed, probably making Beck and his associate remember they needed her alive, that the outcome would have been different. But she had and they'd sped off, disappearing before Suzy or any deputies could catch up to them.

Now here Billy was. In an interview room within the prison looking at a man he'd wished to never see again.

Bryan Copeland had been balding for years but he had never let a thing like losing his hair conflict with his image. He was a confident man. Always had been. He'd always worn suits and expensive cologne, and had a quick wit about him that made people laugh. He was a people person, a schmoozer, a go-get-them type filled with determination and steeped in self-esteem.

Bryan Copeland had been kind and cunning in his dealings with the general public and one hell of a dancer at parties. To his underlings, however, he had been cutthroat. Like night and day, when Bryan needed to get down to business he stripped off his disguise and showed his true face. His wit became a weapon, his charm a tool. Whatever compassion he exuded in his home life and within the community was replaced with menace and greed.

That was the man Billy sat in front of now.

Dressed in prison orange, Bryan Copeland looked across the table at him with the eyes of a snake ready to strike.

"Well merry Christmas to me," he greeted Billy. "Couldn't

stay away from the man who made your career possible, *Sheriff*?"

Billy had nothing to prove to the man. Nothing to defend, either. At the time, Billy hadn't known stopping Bryan would help him become sheriff. He'd just wanted to stop the man and his business before both destroyed his home.

A choice he didn't regret and never would.

"I have some questions for you."

Bryan scoffed.

"If you can't do your job, *Sheriff*, then I'm certainly not going to do it for you."

Billy ignored his comment and put the sketch of Beck on the table between them. He kept it turned over. Bryan's eyes never strayed to it.

"Where's your secret stash?"

Bryan didn't flinch.

"First of all, that's a ridiculous question that makes you sound like you're some preteen on a treasure hunt," Bryan said. "Secondly, I don't have a secret stash."

"And third?" Billy asked with a low sigh. Bryan's nostrils flared. He didn't like it when the person he was talking to showed disinterest or contempt. It rubbed against his ego, something he'd been fluffing for decades.

"If I did have a secret stash, of whatever it is you think I have, why in hell would I ever tell you about it?" Bryan was nearly seething. His dislike for Billy was pure. The moment he'd found out that Mara had betrayed him and helped Billy was the moment Bryan Copeland began to hate him more than anyone in the world.

That's how Billy knew that just asking would get him nowhere.

So, he was going to gun for the man's precious pride instead.

"Because, if you don't tell me where it is, this man will eventually find it." Billy flipped over the picture and pushed it toward him. "And he'll use it to pick up where you left off. But this time he'll do it better, smarter and with your help whether you want to give it or not. He'll take your legacy and make it his own. In fact, he's already started."

Bryan's lips had thinned but his expression remained blank. His eyes, however, trailed down to the picture. If he recognized Beck, it didn't register in his face or posture. When he answered, he seemed as uptight as he had been when he'd been escorted into the room.

"I don't know what you came here to try and accomplish, but I can tell you now that you should have saved the gas." Bryan fingered the picture. "I don't know this man and I don't know his business. What I *do* know is that if I had a *secret stash* it would have been found during the investigation. Unless you're admitting to me now that you're not that great at your job. Which, again, to be honest, I already knew." Bryan's eyes turned to slits. His nostrils flared. "Why else would you need my daughter's help to catch me?"

Billy knew in that moment that the only way he'd get an answer was to use Mara. Because Bryan Copeland might appear to be a man who wasn't affected by the world, but the truth was he had one weakness.

His daughter.

He'd loved her so much that he hadn't ever entertained the idea that she could turn on him. That she *would* turn on him. That's why he was handcuffed to a table, sitting in an interrogation room with an armed guard behind him.

But Billy wanted to keep her out of the room for as long as he could. So he leveled with her father.

"This man goes by the name Beck," Billy started. "As far as we know, he has one associate who isn't afraid of killing. One or both of them were involved in the murders of three people, two of whom were in police custody when they were killed. They are also responsible for putting three people in the hospital, but that wasn't because of mercy. It's because the people they hurt got lucky." Billy purposely didn't name anyone who had been killed or attacked. He knew Bryan wouldn't care. His response confirmed that belief.

"So? I've had nothing to do with this Beck person or his friend. And if you don't believe me then I'm sure the warden won't mind giving me an alibi." He motioned to the room around them, as if Billy needed the fact that he was in prison emphasized.

"I'm telling you because the only reason we know about Beck is because he showed up at your daughter's house and threatened her." An almost imperceptible shift occurred in the man across from him. Billy didn't know if Bryan did or did not know Beck but the fact that the man had been to see his daughter was news to him. "Since then he's had people try to kidnap her, put her in the hospital and they've even shot at her. All because they think she knows where this stash of yours is located."

Bryan laughed out loud. This time Billy was the one who was surprised.

"They think she might be in cahoots with her old man, huh?" he said around another bite of laughter. It wasn't the kind filled with mirth or humor. It was dark. Menacing. "You and I both know how wrong the assumption that my daughter and I work together is, don't we, *Sheriff*?" He lowered his voice. Despite the decrease in volume, his words thundered. "The one who would rather be in your bed than a part of my life."

Billy was trying not to let Bryan get to him, but that one comment created an almost feral reaction within him. One where he felt the need to protect Mara's name and, to some degree, protect himself.

It bothered Billy the way Mara's only family talked about her with such distaste—such hate—while he also had never liked the fact that Bryan suspected he and Mara had been together. It wasn't that Billy had been ashamed of her—he hadn't ever been—but they'd told only a few people about their relationship. Bryan had not only guessed but been certain that Billy and Mara were together. Which meant Bryan Copeland was either really good at reading his daughter or Billy…or someone had told him.

Regardless of which it was, Billy was still bothered by it. He stood and went to the guard next to the door.

"Bring her in," he said, low enough that Bryan couldn't hear.

The guard nodded and left.

Billy returned to the table but didn't sit down. Instead, he moved to the corner of the room.

"And what tactic is this?" Bryan asked, amused. "Trying to intimidate me by sending the guard away? There are much more intimidating men in this place, Sheriff. With some tricks that end in death. This isn't going to—"

The door started to open.

"This isn't a trick," Billy interrupted. He nodded in the direction of the guard. Mara was behind him. Her back was straight, her shoulders straight, and her eyes sharp and cautious. She rounded the table and took a seat across from her father.

The amusement Bryan had shown Billy disappeared in an instant. If it was possible, he seemed to sit up straighter, as if a board had been attached to his back. With the two of them mirroring each other, Billy realized how much the father and daughter looked alike.

Mara was the first to speak.

"Hey, Dad."

Chapter Sixteen

"You've got more nerve coming here than he does."

Mara wasn't surprised by her father's response, but that didn't mean it didn't still hurt a little. She kept her face as expressionless as she could and tried to remember why they were there. Why she was subjecting herself to the emotional torture she'd tried to avoid for two years.

For Alexa, she thought. *To stop this madness once and for all.*

"I'm tired of being hunted, Dad," she said. "Beck—"

Bryan slammed his fist against the tabletop. Mara jumped.

"You wouldn't be hunted if you hadn't betrayed me," he snarled. "You made your bed when you turned on the only family you had and *both* of you are just going to have to lie in it!"

Billy started to move forward, already trying to defend her, Mara was sure, but she hadn't had her say yet.

"You tried to create a drug empire out of an entire county, Dad. That's three towns and a city worth of people," she responded. "What was I supposed to do when I found out? Sit back and watch?"

"You should have come to me," he seethed. "Not him. I'm your *father*, your flesh and blood. I raised you, kept food on the table and a roof over your head. I bent over backwards to make sure you never wanted for anything. And now, what do I get in return? A prison cell, Mara! A damn prison cell!"

This time Mara heard Billy begin to speak but she'd had enough.

"Do you remember what you told me when you decided to move to Kipsy? You said you moved because you needed a slower pace. That you wanted to relax. Those were *your* words. And then you asked me to move there, too. Do you remember what I told you?" Mara was yelling now. Whatever dam was holding her emotions back had broken the moment her father spoke. When he didn't answer, it was Mara's turn to slam her hand against the table. It hurt but she ignored the pain.

"I said I didn't want to," she continued. "I had a good life that I didn't want to leave. I had a good job, friends and a home. But no. When I came down to visit, you talked about missing me and being lonely and how Kipsy was a good city filled with good people. You painted this picture of a life you knew I'd always wanted. One where we'd be happy, where I'd meet a good man, raise a family, and you'd sit on your front porch swinging with your grandkids and sipping sweet tea. I could even start a business and have the dream job I'd always wished for. You tried so hard to convince me to love the idea of Kipsy that it worked. I fell in love with it. So, what did you expect would happen when you started to destroy it all?"

"You could have still had all of those things," he responded, more quietly than he had been before. "I always protected you. You were never in any danger. You could have had everything, but, instead, you sided with *him*."

Her father's eyes cut to Billy with such a look of disgust in them that the dam within her disintegrated further until there was nothing left. Mara fisted her hands and, for the first time in years, yelled at her father so loudly she felt her face heat.

"Don't you *dare* blame Billy or me or *anyone* else for your mistakes. You made them and now you're the one who has to take responsibility for them!" Mara took out the picture she'd tucked into her back pocket. She hadn't planned on using it, but she'd recognized the possibility that she might have to. She slammed the picture down and slid it over to him, next to the picture of Beck.

"You may hate me, Dad. You may not care what Beck and his friends will do to me. You may even want something bad to happen to me. But what about her?" Just seeing the smiling face of Alexa looking up from the picture calmed Mara. Her voice lowered to an even level but she didn't drop any of the hostility. Her father's eyes stayed on the picture as she continued. "This is your granddaughter, Alexa. She didn't investigate you and she certainly didn't have a hand in putting you in here. So, *please*, *Dad*, don't make her pay for our mistakes."

Mara was done. There was nothing left for her to say— to add—to try and sway her father to tell them if he really had a stash and, if so, where it was. She was exhausted. Drained. Yet relieved in a way, too. Not only was she facing her father but she had said exactly what she'd always wanted to.

His eyes stayed on the picture but he didn't say anything right away. Billy took advantage of the silence, perhaps sensing Mara was out of ideas.

"These men believe without a doubt that you have a stash and Mara knows exactly where it is. They've also made it clear that they don't care what happens to Alexa in the process of trying to find it or use Mara. They'll kill her, and then eventually they'll kill your daughter." Even as he said it, she knew he hated the words. Mara knew the feeling. Just the mention of harm to Alexa had a knot forming in her stomach.

"There's no wedding ring on your finger," her father said after a moment. "But she's his, isn't she?" His eyes were slits of rage as he looked at Billy, but she knew what he said next was aimed at her. "Don't you dare lie to me about this."

"We're not together, but yes, she's mine," Billy answered.

The simple admission that Billy was, indeed, Alexa's father should have made Mara happy, and it did—but the first part of the sentence hurt more than she expected. She strained to keep her expression as blank as possible. Maybe the last few days had just been two people caught up in madness, trying to comfort each other for different reasons. Maybe, when everything was said and done, they'd go back to their lives with the only link between them being Alexa. Maybe it had been lust and not love that had tangled them together.

Her father was watching her intently. She didn't need to think about the future when the present was being threatened.

"You two come up here like I owe you something I don't," Bryan Copeland said, standing. "Using a granddaughter I didn't even know existed isn't the way to get me to tell you anything. I can't help you." He turned and looked to the guard. "I'm done talking with them."

"Bryan," Billy tried, but the man wasn't having any of it. Before he was escorted from the room, he looked at Billy. There was nothing but sincerity when he spoke.

"Watch out for daughters, Sheriff. They'll stab you in the back every time."

"Reed, hold up a second."

Billy paused in his walk to the car. Mara, however, didn't. She hadn't said a word since Bryan left. Her eyes, dark and deep, had stayed dead ahead as they went through the process of leaving the prison.

The guard who'd been in the room with the three of them, a man named Ned, jogged up to Billy, mouth already open and ready to talk. Billy wondered if he'd forgotten some procedure for signing out. If so, he hoped it wouldn't take too long. The day had turned into a scorcher.

"I know it was none of my business to listen but sometimes you can't help it when you're in the room." Ned shrugged. "But I didn't know if you caught on to what Mr. Copeland was talking about when he said he wouldn't tell you anything."

Billy felt his eyebrow rise.

"And you do?"

"I guess I can't speak with complete certainty in Mr. Copeland's case, but you see, there's a different kind of world here," he said, thrusting his thumb over his shoulder to the prison. "There are men serving time in there who have done a hell of a lot worse than run drugs. Men who take to killing like it was nothing. Heck, some of them don't even break a sweat trying to do the same thing even when they're living in a cell."

"Yeah, I'd imagine that's true. But what's that have to do with anything?" Billy was frustrated. Not at the man in front of him, but in general. He didn't want to stand out in the heat and talk about prison politics if he could help it.

"What I'm saying is that a man like Bryan Copeland may look intimidating to the general public with his tidiness and fancy talk, but in there—" again he thrust his thumb back over his shoulder "—in there he doesn't have anything going for him. But he's never had any problems as far as we know."

Billy was about to tell the man to go back inside if

he wasn't going to be helpful, but then he heard Bryan's words again.

"He said, *I can't help you* not *I won't*," Billy realized. Ned nodded.

"My guess, if that money or whatever exists, he's using it as insurance to keep him safe in here." Ned shrugged. "I could be way off, but it's happened before."

"So keeping the stash hidden might be the only thing keeping him alive in there."

Ned nodded. "He could use it to buy protection from certain inmates or use it as leverage," Ned confirmed.

"Any idea who he might be targeted by if someone was trying to kill him?"

Ned's expression hardened. The new tension in his shoulders let Billy know he'd not be getting an answer from the guard.

"I don't know," he supplied. "Sorry."

"No problem," Billy said. "At least we have an idea of why he won't tell us." Billy cast a look at Mara. She was leaning against the car, looking out at the road in the distance. Even from where he stood, Billy knew she wasn't there with them. Her thoughts had carried her miles and miles away. "But knowing that might not be a good thing."

"Why's that?" the guard asked.

"Because it still means that Bryan would rather protect himself than protect his daughter and granddaughter."

MARA DIDN'T SAY anything for the majority of their drive back, much like the drive there. But this time, she wasn't sure if it was for the same reasons.

She kept her gaze out the windshield, watching as the road disappeared beneath them. Billy had told her what Ned the guard had said, but that was only the cherry on top of a trip she shouldn't have taken. Any relief she'd felt at finally confronting her dad, telling him about his granddaughter and admitting Billy was the father was no longer warming the cold that had been sitting like a rock in her stomach.

Not only was her father not going to help them, he'd made it very clear that she was no longer wanted in his life. Which, to be honest, she had expected—yet there she was, feeling the sting of it still.

Mara leaned her head back against the headrest and closed her eyes.

The emotional strain of seeing her father—and the past that she'd never be able to change, even if she wanted to—had wiped Mara out physically.

However, no sooner had her eyes closed than Mara was back in that room with Billy saying they weren't together. It shouldn't have bothered her, considering it was a fact she already knew, but still… The finality of the words, said in the strong, clear voice she'd come to enjoy more than she should have, had broken something within her. In a way that she hadn't expected.

Mara let out what she thought was a quiet sigh. One that let the outside world know she was having an internal battle.

"We need to talk about everything that happened."

She opened one eye and looked over at the sheriff. He was frowning something fierce. Mara closed her eye again.

"I don't want to," she admitted. "Not right now, at least."

"But, Mara—"

"Billy, please, don't," she interrupted. "There's only so much a person can deal with all at once. I just want to get back and see my daughter. Okay?"

The Bronco lurched to the side. Mara's eyes flashed open to see Billy cutting the wheel. They'd made it into Riker County according to a sign they'd passed a few miles back, but that didn't mean Mara recognized the Presbyterian church or the parking lot they now were turning into.

"What are you doing?" Mara asked, anger coming to the forefront of her question. It was misplaced, she knew, but that didn't stop it from turning her cheeks hot or spiking her adrenaline enough to make her sit up straight.

"We're going to talk," Billy said, parking in a row of cars already in the lot. A few people were meandering near the entrance to the church but didn't seem interested in them.

"What do you mean we're going to talk? Isn't that what we've been doing?"

Billy put the car in Park, took off his seat belt and turned his body enough that he was facing her straight on. His mouth was set in a frown and yet, somehow, it still begged to be touched.

To be kissed.

Mara shook her head, trying to clear the thought, as Billy confronted her.

"You're shutting down," he said, serious. His eyes had changed their shade of green from forest to that of tall ferns bowing in a breeze.

"I don't even know what that means," she said, keeping her eyes firmly on his gaze.

Billy's expression didn't soften. He wasn't interested in playing nice anymore. Before he said a word, Mara knew where the conversation would eventually lead.

"What you just went through can't have been easy and now you don't want to talk about it? Even with me?"

"Even with you?" The last shred of emotional sanity Mara had started to fray. "You know everything I do about this case. You heard everything my father said in there. Beyond that, there's nothing you have to do to help me. It isn't your job to make sure I talk about my feelings. We aren't together, Billy. Not anymore."

For whatever reason, using Billy's words from earlier against him made Mara break further. She unbuckled her seat belt and fumbled for the door handle. Tears began to blur her vision.

"I-I need a moment," she said before Billy could get a word in edgewise. Mara opened the door and walked out into the heat.

And swiftly away from the Riker County sheriff.

Chapter Seventeen

Mara had to think. She had to walk. She had to move so the pain of everything wouldn't settle. Her father's words, Billy's words, Beck's words all rattled around in her mind. Taunting her, comforting her, threatening her. Why couldn't life have stayed simple? Why had her father turned out the way he had? Why had she fallen in love with the one man Riker County had needed to protect it?

Mara made it out of the parking lot and to a small park beside the church before she heard footsteps behind her. She'd spent the short walk trying desperately not to cry. The strain already was pushing in a headache.

Sure, it made sense to be upset about everything. Her father *had* just chosen himself over her and her child. But what bothered her the most was that, at the moment, all she could do was think about Billy.

"Mara, stop."

A hand closed around her arm and gently held her still. Mara blinked several times to try and dissuade any tears from falling. Instead of turning her around, Billy stepped into view.

Mara felt the sudden urge to take his hat off and put her hand through his hair.

It all hurt even more, knowing with absolute certainty that she'd never stop wanting Billy Reed.

"Talk to me," he prodded. He lowered his head to look into her eyes more easily.

"Why haven't you asked me?" Mara blurted before she could police her thoughts. "Why haven't you asked one single question about why I left or why I didn't tell you about Alexa?" Billy dropped his hand from her arm. A piece of her heart fell with it. "Just ask me, Billy. At least one question. Please."

Tears threatened to spill again, but Mara stilled herself, waiting for an answer. This time, they weren't interrupted and Billy asked a question Mara hadn't expected.

"Would you have ever told me about her?"

Mara realized then that there would never have been a good time to talk about the choices she'd made. That, at the end of the day, she'd kept one heck of a secret. One that would hurt someone, no matter what. Billy's expression was open and clear as a bell, but she knew his tone well enough to realize it was a man waiting for bad news.

She had already hurt him with her silence. It was time to tell him the truth.

All of it.

"You may not believe me now, and I don't blame you for that, but I never meant to keep her a secret in the first place," Mara started. A breeze swept through the park. She wrapped her arms around herself, even though she wasn't cold. "I found out I was pregnant with her two days before you became sheriff. You remember how quiet I was then? You kept asking me if I was okay."

She watched as Billy slipped back into his own memories.

"I thought it was because of your dad," he admitted. "He'd just gotten sentenced." Mara gave him a sympathetic smile. His eyes widened. "Why didn't you tell me then?"

"I planned to, at dinner that night," she said. "I wanted

everything to be nice... But I forgot to get eggs for the cake."

Billy's eyebrow rose in question. Why did that matter? he was most likely wondering.

"Do you remember Donna Ramsey? The woman we saw at the coffee shop?" Billy nodded. "Well, I went back out to buy eggs and ran into her. She wasn't happy at seeing me." Mara remembered the look of absolute hatred burning in the woman's eyes. It wasn't a look she'd ever forget. "Do you know that her husband died overseas? And that her daughter was all the family she had left in the world?" Mara didn't wait for Billy to answer. "Kennedy Ramsey killed herself when her girlfriend overdosed on Moxy. Donna was the one who found her." Mara felt her face harden. Her vision started to blur with the tears she couldn't stop. Caught between anger and sadness, she couldn't tell which emotion had its claws in her heart at the moment.

"I didn't know that," Billy admitted. "But around then it was hard to see all of the repercussions."

"Well, Donna's hatred for me is one that I saw up close."

"It wasn't your fault what happened," Billy asserted.

"If I had come to you earlier about my father—" she started.

"It could have taken us just as long to figure out how to trap him," he jumped in. "Despite our intentions, your father was a very clever man. Two weeks might not have made any difference at all."

Mara shrugged.

"Either way, Donna let me know I was just as much to blame as my father was," Mara continued. "She told me that she would never accept me in Carpenter or Kipsy and neither would anyone else. To prove her point, the cashier who had overheard the exchange refused to check me out." Mara tried a small smile. "That's why there was no cake at dinner."

"But—"

"I didn't want to tell you that night because all I could think about was Donna, all alone, cursing my family's name," Mara explained, cutting him off. "And so I decided I'd tell you the next day, but then you spent it with Sheriff Rockwell and were so excited that, once again, I decided to wait. I wanted you to celebrate to your heart's content. You'd waited so long for the opportunity to be sheriff."

Mara was getting to the part that she'd once thought she'd never tell Billy. But, standing together now, Mara finally felt like she could tell him everything. She didn't want anything left unsaid. She wanted a clean slate again.

She *needed* it.

"I was going to tell you after the ceremony because I couldn't keep it in anymore. I was scared but excited," she continued. The dull throb in her side started to gnaw at her, as if opening up emotional wounds was somehow affecting her physical ones. "I was at the ceremony, standing in the crowd, off to the side, where I hoped no one would notice me. But then someone did. He asked me if I was proud of you—and I was, Billy. I was so proud of you. And he used that against me. He told me that as long as we were together, everything you had worked for would fall apart when people found out about us. The daughter of a man who nearly destroyed the county with the new sheriff sworn to protect it. Billy, I looked up at you and you were so happy, and I couldn't get Donna out of my head and—" Mara couldn't help it. A sob tore from her lips and she began to cry. Overcome with emotions long since buried, she finally got to the heart of the matter. "And, Billy, I believed him. If I stayed, I was sure people would hate you because of me, and I just couldn't take that. I'd rather live with the guilt of being Bryan Copeland's daughter than knowing I was the reason you lost your home."

Billy remained quiet for a moment. His expression was unreadable. Even to her. Every part of Mara felt exposed, raw. Leaving Billy Reed had been the hardest thing she'd ever done.

She waited, trying to rein in her tears. Then, like a switch had been flipped, Billy smiled.

"But Mara, you're forgetting something," he said, closing the space between them. He put his hands on either side of her face, holding every ounce of her attention within his gaze. Every hope she had of the future, every regret she had from the past. All at the mercy of the dark-haired sheriff.

"What?" she whispered, tears sliding down her cheeks. Billy brushed one away with his thumb, his skin leaving a trail of warmth across her cheek.

"*You* are my home."

Then Billy kissed her full on the lips.

Finally, Mara Copeland felt peace.

Unlike their shared moment earlier in the day, this kiss was slower. Deeper. It seemed to extend past her lips and dip into her very core. If he hadn't been holding her, Mara was sure she would have fallen. The kiss was affecting every part of her body, not excluding her knees. They trembled with relief and pleasure and promise as the kiss kept going.

If they had been anywhere other than a public park, it might have gone even further, but reality broke through the fantasy quickly. Billy pulled away, lips red, eyes hooded and with a question already poised.

"Wait, who talked to you at the ceremony?" Billy asked.

"I respected your wishes for us to be a secret until things settled down. I only told the people who needed to know and I trusted all of them. They wouldn't have told," he added, sure in his words.

Mara let out a small sigh. She didn't want to create any bad blood between the sheriff and one of his deputies. Marsden had only told her his opinion. She had been the one who had listened to it.

"Deputy Marsden," she confessed. Billy's body instantly tensed. Mara rushed to defuse his anger. "He seemed really concerned. I think he was just looking out for you. You can't get mad at someone for loyalty."

Billy didn't appear to be listening to her. His eyes were locked with hers, but he wasn't seeing her.

"What is it?" Mara grabbed his hand. She squeezed it. "Billy?" The contact shook him out of his head. He didn't look like he'd be smiling any time soon.

"Marsden held no loyalty or fondness for me," he growled. "The last order of business Sheriff Rockwell attended to before I stepped in was letting Marsden go. That was one of the reasons Rockwell wanted to talk before the ceremony. If he found out about us, it was by accident. I never would have told him. Gene Marsden is not a good man, and the last I talked to him, he cursed my name."

"What?" Mara asked, surprised. She didn't remember hearing about Marsden being fired. Then again, it wasn't like she had stuck around to get the news, either.

"I'd completely forgotten about him. He was with us when we arrested Bryan. He must have heard your father when *he* was cursing my name about being with you. He—"

They both heard the noise too late, both wrapped up in their conversation.

"Sorry to interrupt."

All Mara had time to do was watch Billy tense.

Beck had the element of surprise and he used it swiftly. He pointed the shotgun right at Billy's chest.

"We'll just call this take three for the day."

BILLY WAS LOOKING at the wrong end of the barrel of a shotgun. Holding it was Beck, smiling ear to ear. Billy noticed a cut across the man's cheek, and he took some small satisfaction that he'd probably caused it not more than four hours ago.

"Hey there, Sheriff," Beck said, voice calm. "How you doing this fine day?"

When Billy had turned, he'd put Mara behind him. Even though she was out of the line of fire, that didn't mean he felt good about their situation. Especially since Beck was holding a shotgun. It would be hard to shield Mara from a shell blast from only a few feet away.

"Hadn't figured I'd see you again any time soon. I thought after shooting up your truck you'd be long gone," Billy admitted. "Where is your friend? I'd like to repay him for the knock on the head he gave me." He glanced over Beck's shoulder to see if anyone at the church had noticed that there was a man holding a gun on them. But no one seemed to be any the wiser.

"Oh, look at you, always the dutiful sheriff. In a bad situation and still trying to fish for information." Even though there was humor in his tone, Beck's hold on the gun was serious. Billy's own gun was burning in its holster. They never should have left the car. He never should have pulled over. Not when none of the deputies had found even a trace of the truck. But, when Mara was involved, Billy's actions didn't always make sense. He cursed himself. He'd let his guard down again. There was no excuse for that. "Well, I'm sorry to disappoint you. I'm not here to answer your questions or theories or even suspicions. I have work to do."

"You're not as clever as you think," Mara said at Billy's shoulder. He was proud that her voice was even.

That's my girl.

Beck's smile turned to a smirk, a transformation that gave away the pleasure he must be feeling holding a gun on them. So far he'd shown he didn't believe in an even playing field. Why should now be any different? He was just going to have to find out the hard way that Billy was the kind of man who would go down fighting, especially when there was someone to fight for.

"You don't think I'm clever enough?" Beck asked. "Because I've been so bad at following you, hurting you and pulling guns on you? Or am I not that clever because I haven't killed you two yet?"

Billy's muscles tingled in anticipation.

If he could close the gap between him and the end of the shotgun, he might be able to grab it and move it enough that Mara could run for the car. If he was faster than the shot, that was. If he could disarm Beck or manage to get his own gun out, he could end this. Once and for all.

"Sheriff, calm down," Beck chided. "I'm not going to kill you or Miss Copeland right now. Maybe down the line, if it becomes an issue, but not right now."

"Then put down the gun," Billy ground out. It made Beck laugh.

"Don't mistake mercy for being an idiot. I still have a job to do right now. I didn't just follow you to have a little chat, now, did I?"

"What do you want, then?" Mara asked.

"Funny you should ask, Miss Copeland. Considering it's you."

"I don't think so," Billy cut in. "You're not taking her."

"Oh, but Sheriff, I am. And, what's more, you're going to let me."

Chapter Eighteen

Billy didn't like the confidence the man in front of him was exuding. There was no shaking of his hands as he held the gun, no quiver or tremble or even a fluctuation in his voice. Standing outside, in a public place, holding a gun on a sheriff and a civilian, Beck should have been showing some signs of anxiety or nervousness.

When, in reality, he was showing none.

Which meant one of two things. He was either stupid or he had one hell of an ace up his sleeve.

"And how do you figure that?" Billy asked. "Because I'm here to tell you, that's a tall order you're placing."

"It's because I know your secret," Beck said, simply. "And I intend to use that to make you two do exactly as I please."

Billy didn't need to see Mara to know she reacted in some way to Beck's threat. He himself had tensed, despite trying to appear impassive.

"Secret?" He didn't want to play into Beck's game but, at the same time, he didn't really have a choice.

"If I hadn't already known you two were an item, I would have guessed by that kiss just now," Beck pointed out. "You two really are terrible at hiding this *thing*." He nodded to them when he said *thing*.

"So?" Mara said. "We kissed. How are you going to make me leave willingly with that?"

"I can't." Beck shrugged. "But luckily that's not the only secret you two share. In fact, right now my associate is looking at that other secret of yours. She's pretty cute, you know."

Beck shifted his gaze to Billy with a level of nonchalance he didn't like. Pure rage and fear exploded within Billy's chest. It must have extended to Mara. He felt her hand on his back. A light touch, but with a heaviness only a worrying parent could carry. Beck tilted his head a little, as if waiting for them to fall over themselves responding. His impatience got the better of him. He exhaled, all dramatic.

"Do I need to spell it out for you, Sheriff?" he added.

Billy wasn't ready to believe the man had any kind of connection to his daughter. He could be bluffing for all Billy knew.

"Yes, you do," Billy answered. "We don't want to play any more games with you."

Beck's smile twitched, his nostrils flared and then he was all smirk again. His eyes went over Billy's shoulder to the park behind them. It remained focused on something—or someone—but Billy wasn't going to turn his back to the man.

"I guess you're right," Beck agreed. "Who has time for stupid little games. Here's the deal—the bottom line. I'm short staffed, thanks to the two of you, I'm impatient and I'm over being out in this damn heat. Mara's going to tell me where that stash is and then I'm going to keep her until I've moved it. Then I'll let her go. You may be asking why should you trust me on that? Well." Beck's sneer fell into the most serious expression Billy had ever seen on the man. "Considering you two seem to be an item, how smart would I be if I killed the lover of the beloved sheriff? You'd never stop hunting me until it consumed you or you caught me. Those are odds I don't like playing. Am I wrong?"

Billy shook his head. "No. You aren't."

Mara moved her thumb on his back, a few strokes to show affection or appreciation. Either way, it eased a part of Billy. If only a little.

"Only a fool, or someone out of options, would make that mistake. I don't fall into either category," Beck assured them. "Also only a fool would directly kill the sheriff if it could be avoided, because then that's just painting a target on my head." Beck shook the shotgun a little, not taking it off them but reminding them he still had it. And that they were still in its sights. "But don't misunderstand that as me saying I won't shoot you. I will. But how could you help Alexa and Mara then, Billy?"

The hand on Billy's back dropped. Mara stepped from behind him and stopped at his side. Her expression was blank, but he knew she was filled with a cocktail of emotions, ready to spill out if she was pushed too hard.

"The bottom line," Billy said, words dripping with absolute disgust.

"Mara is going to come with me now and you're going to let her, or you'll never see your daughter again."

"You son of a—" Billy started, but Mara cut him off.

"What have you done?" she asked. Her voice was so calm, so even, it made Billy pause in his rant. It was the steady ice of a mother calculating a situation.

"Nothing. Yet. And it'll stay that way if you come with me." This time Beck's attention was on Mara.

"Alexa is safe," Billy cut in. "You're bluffing."

"And what if she isn't? What if I'm not bluffing?" Beck asked. "Are you going to take that chance, Sheriff?" He returned his attention to Mara. "And are you going to let him take that chance?"

"Mara—" Billy started.

"I want proof," she interrupted. "Or I won't go."

Beck let out a small exhale, frustrated. But he at least was accommodating. Even if it wasn't at all what Billy wanted to hear.

"Billy's mother, Claire, put up more of a fight than Deputy Mills did," Beck started. Every part of Billy contracted. A cold fire spread through him. Anger and fear warred with each other inside him. If that shotgun hadn't been between them, Billy could have ripped the man apart with his bare hands. "In his defense, he never saw my guy coming. But Claire was looking out the kitchen window, so by the time my associate went inside she'd already grabbed a gun and tried to hide the girl. Luckily for both of us, Claire's a bad shot and my guy has a code about killing the elderly, something to do with being raised by his grandmother, I suppose." Mara's hand went to her mouth. Billy fisted his hand so hard he'd bet he was drawing blood. Beck went on as though he was recapping a soap opera episode and not sharing one of the most terrifying situations a parent could hear. "Alexa was in the corner of a closet, a blanket thrown over her head. She was crying so hard that my associate grabbed her bag of toys. I haven't heard yet if they've worked on calming her down."

"You bastard," Billy snarled. His heartbeat was racing now, adrenaline mixing up everything he was already feeling.

"She's just a baby," Mara added. Her voice shook.

"And I'm just a businessman," Beck added. "An impatient one. If you don't come with me now, so help me, I will throw out what little morals I have left and make you two regret ever trying to get in my way."

Billy's stomach bottomed out. He glanced at Mara. She was looking at him. Her dark eyes were glassed over and wide, searching for some way to save Alexa. To save him. Because he knew she'd do anything to keep everyone safe. Just like Billy knew right then that Beck had won. Mara would go with him. And Billy would let her.

Beck's attention swiveled over his shoulder again. This time it was followed by a woman gasping.

"Hey, come here slowly or I'll shoot you," Beck yelled. Billy turned to see an older woman standing a few feet behind them. She must not have noticed there had been a shotgun in their discussion until she was closer. Her terrified eyes took the three of them in. "Come here now," Beck demanded. It was a few shades darker than any tone he'd used with Billy and Mara. It was made to intimidate quickly.

And it worked.

The woman walked over to them. Billy hoped she didn't have a heart attack.

"Now, what's your name?"

"Sa-Sally."

"Hey, Sally. My friend here needs his gun taken away," Beck said with a nod to Billy. "And I need you to do it for me."

Sally looked at Billy, probably trying to understand what was going on. He nodded to her.

"It's okay," he said, afraid she might try to disobey and incur the wrath of Beck. While Billy thought Beck would keep his promise not to kill the lover or child of the sheriff, they all knew Sally had no connection to them whatsoever. "Do as he says," Billy said gently.

Sally, who looked to be in her late sixties, finally moved toward them. She stopped at Billy's other side and looked at Beck.

"Billy, take your gun out and give the clip to Mara," Beck ordered. For the first time, he moved the shotgun. Now it was pointing squarely at Mara. "If you so much as try to take aim at me, I will end this now and you'll lose everyone you love in one fell swoop. So do it now."

Billy did as he was told. He unholstered his gun and ejected the clip. He handed it to Mara. She took it with a slightly shaking hand. He wished he could hold her. Let her know everything was going to be okay.

"Empty the chamber and then give it to our new friend, Sally."

Billy ejected the bullet in the chamber and then handed his service weapon to Sally. She, too, was shaking.

"Now, Sally, I want you to run."

"R-run?" Her face paled considerably.

Beck nodded in the direction from which she'd come.

"I want you to run as fast as you can in that direction and don't stop or come back, or I'll kill these good people. You wouldn't want that on your conscience, now, would you, Sally?"

The woman shook her head. Her eyes began to water.

"Then go!"

Sally began to walk away before picking up the pace, gun in her hand. Billy hoped she didn't hurt herself. He also hoped she had the sense to get help.

"Okay, say *see you soon, Billy,* and let's go," Beck said to Mara.

"I—" Billy started, but Mara interrupted him again.

"I'm going," she said.

Billy took her face back into his hands and brushed his lips across hers. He hoped the kiss told her everything he couldn't say.

He would save Alexa.

He would save Mara.

He would destroy Beck.

In that order.

"Now, Billy, you know the drill. You move, I end this today. Both of their deaths will be because you tried to be a hero. And ended up protecting no one but yourself. Understood?"

Billy gave a curt nod. Anger flowed through his veins like blood. He'd never wanted another man to come to as much harm as he did the man in front of him.

"I'll get you in the end," Billy promised.

Beck grinned. "I expect you'll try."

Beck walked Mara, shotgun to the back of her neck, away from him. He kept looking back to make sure Billy was still there. Billy made sure not to move an inch. He didn't want to push the already crazed man.

A few people outside the church had finally spotted the procession and, Billy hoped, had called 911. No one moved to help Mara. It angered and also relieved Billy. Instead, they all watched in muted terror, some fleeing back into the church, as Beck angled Mara into a car he'd never seen before, parked right next to Billy's Bronco.

He ground his teeth hard, watching, helpless, as the mother of his child was taken away.

BILLY ROCKETED THROUGH the streets of Carpenter toward his house. He had absolutely no way to contact the world outside of his car. When he'd run back to the Bronco, the driver's side door had been open. His cellphone and radio were gone. Thank God he'd had enough sense to at least keep the car keys in his pocket when he'd followed Mara.

He'd tried, in vain, to keep his eyes on Beck's new car as they left the parking lot, but by the time he'd run to the

Bronco, they were gone. It had left Billy with too many options. Too many routes to follow.

Though, if he was being honest with himself, there was really only one place he needed to go.

Chapter Nineteen

Deputy Mills's cruiser was still parked on the street outside the Reed family home. Just like it had been when Billy and Mara had left that morning. However, where Billy had expected chaos on his lawn, shattered house windows and a front door broken off its hinges, all Billy could see was what they'd left behind that morning. Everything looked orderly, calm.

Normal.

But that didn't ease Billy's mind.

He hit his brakes at the end of the driveway and jumped out, already running to the front door.

"Sheriff," someone yelled from behind him. He turned so fast he nearly fell. It was Deputy Mills, standing in the now-open door of his cruiser. Again, Billy expected him to look one way—angry, wounded from the attack—but he looked another—confused, alert. "What's going on?"

"What happened?" Billy asked. He could tell it put the man further on edge.

"What are you talking about?"

Billy heard the squeal from inside the house. He didn't wait on the porch to question the deputy. He flung open the front door and ran inside, attention sticking to a sound he hadn't thought he'd hear in the house.

"Don't move," came a growl of a voice. Billy turned in the entry to see a startled Suzy, gun raised.

"Billy? What are you doing?" she asked, surprised. She lowered her gun but didn't put it away.

"Is Alexa here?" he asked, knowing he must have looked crazy. He didn't care.

"Of course she's here." Suzy pointed into the living room. Billy hurried past her, hearing another squeal of laughter.

Sitting on the floor was his mother, alarmed but seemingly unhurt. Plastic containers of Christmas decorations littered the space in front of her. At her side, amid an explosion of toys that nearly rivaled the decorations, was the most beautiful sight Billy had ever seen.

"Alexa!"

The little girl looked up at him, green eyes wide and curious. She had a stuffed dog in her hand. She held it out to him, unaware of the sheer amount of love flooding through Billy from just seeing her.

"Dog," she yelled. It was enough to get him moving.

In two long strides Billy scooped Alexa up and hugged her tight. He might not have been in her life up until this point, but Billy had never been more certain of any one thing in all his life.

He loved his daughter.

He held on to the moment, closing his eyes and burying his face in her hair. Alexa giggled.

That sound of perfect innocence split Billy's heart in two.

Yes, Alexa was safe.

But what about Mara?

Billy kissed Alexa's forehead before putting her back down, a plan already forming in his head. He turned to his mother.

"Pack your bag and one for her, too."

He turned to Suzy and the deputy as Dante hustled through the front door. He didn't talk to them until all three were back in the entryway. Where he promptly punched the wall.

"Billy," he heard his mom exclaim, but Suzy was closer. She holstered her gun.

"What happened?" she asked. "Where's Mara?"

"Beck lied. He took Mara." Billy heard his mother gasp, but he didn't have time to deal with the emotions behind what had happened. "And I let him."

BECK HAD BLINDFOLDED and handcuffed Mara so quickly she hadn't been able to see the person who ended up driving them away from the church and its neighboring park. All Mara knew was that it wasn't Beck. He'd stayed in the back with her, rambling on about how proud he was to finally have her in his possession. And not only that, but he'd also managed to take her from the sheriff himself.

It wasn't surprising to Mara to find out the man liked to gloat, but that didn't mean that listening wasn't disconcerting.

She tried to keep her nerves as calm as possible by thinking of Alexa. Even if she had no idea what was going on with her little girl, the love Mara felt strengthened her resolve to survive this.

Mara remained quiet for the length of the drive. There were too many questions and she had no way of answering half of them. She couldn't control what Billy was doing, what her daughter was feeling and the fact that she was handcuffed next to someone who was obviously insane. What she *could* do, however, was try and pay attention to how many times the car turned and how long they drove. She might not know the town of Carpenter as thoroughly as Billy, but it couldn't hurt to try and remember as much of the route as possible.

After almost fifteen minutes the smooth road became bumpy, pocked. A few minutes later, they left asphalt altogether. The change in terrain was rough. A dirt road.

Which meant one of two things.

They were either on some back road in Riker County that she didn't know about, or they had left a road altogether and were out in the country.

Mara didn't know which option was better.

"Pull around to the side," Beck said to the driver, giving rise to another question Mara didn't have the answer to. Was the driver the "associate" who had taken her daughter? Was that the same person who'd killed Caleb and Jessica, and wounded Cassie?

Mara tensed as the car slowed and then stopped. The engine remained on.

"Time to go," Beck said, opening his door. Mara sat up, fighting the urge to try and, well, fight—she didn't want to jeopardize Alexa's safety, wherever she might be—and waited until the door next to her was opened. "Stay smart," Beck cooed beside her ear. Mara flinched as he grabbed the handcuff's chain and pulled her out. Once her feet hit the ground, she knew she was standing on grass.

"Stay in the car," Beck ordered his partner. Whoever that was didn't answer. Beck moved his grip from the handcuffs to Mara's upper arm and directed her forward a few feet before turning. In that time, Mara tried to keep her adrenaline in check so she could pay attention once again to her surroundings.

It was colder now, finally starting to feel like Christmas. Though that didn't help Mara narrow down the possibilities of where she might be. But after straining her ears to try to listen around the running car and their footsteps, there was one thing she didn't hear that made her feel even more uneasy.

She didn't hear any other cars.

Which meant they probably *were* in the country, cut off from any normal traffic. Cut off from any easy help. Just plain cut off.

"We're going to go inside and I'm going to take your blindfold off," Beck said at her ear. "If you try to fight me or do anything stupid, I won't kill you, but I'll hurt you really badly. Okay?"

Mara didn't answer. He must have taken her silence as agreement. The sound of a door scrubbing against the floor preceded her being pushed inside a building. She smelled something that was between a wet dog and freshly mowed grass but couldn't pinpoint it any more accurately than that. She didn't have the time, either, before Beck was giving her yet another order.

"Don't move."

The pressure of his hand on her arm went away and soon she could hear him moving something. It scraped against whatever was beneath it, sounding much heavier than a table or chair.

Terror started to seize her chest. Questions and fears shot off in succession in her mind. What was going on? Where were they? What was going to happen to her? Was Beck really not going to kill her? Where was Alexa? Was she scared? Hurt?

Mara jumped as hands moved to the sides of her head. Quick fingers undid the blindfold. She blinked several times, trying to get her bearings. Wherever they were, it was darker than she'd like. Her eyes weren't adjusting quickly enough to make out the location.

"There's a set of stairs behind you," Beck said, motioning for her to turn. "I want you to go down them." Mara looked over her shoulder. The sound she'd heard of something heavy being moved was a large, rectangular canister. It stood next to a hole in the floor.

Not a hole. A trap door.

There was a faint light radiating out of it, but she couldn't tell where it led. She took a second to let her eyes adjust, but still couldn't make out what exactly was down those stairs.

Seeing the trap door and the hidden stairwell might have made some people feel adventurous, but right now, the image only heightened Mara's acute fear of having to walk down them.

Good thing she still had a few questions to ask before she would.

"Where's Alexa?"

Beck cracked a smile. It sent a shiver down her spine. The shotgun he held against his side didn't help.

"She's safe with her dad," he answered. She searched his face, looking for the lie. She was surprised to realize she believed he was being sincere. Besides, if he *had* done something to Alexa, Mara bet he would have been gloating about it.

And she would have already killed him with her bare hands.

Plus, there wasn't much more to do than believe him and hope Billy was doing everything he could to ensure Alexa stayed safe. She had little doubt he would do anything else.

Just thinking about the two of them, without her in the picture, warmed and broke Mara's heart. Despair at potentially never seeing them again inspired her backbone to stiffen. Suddenly, the danger of the man across from her lessened. Mara had much bigger things to fear than a man who had to threaten a toddler to get what he wanted.

"You do know I have no idea where the drugs and

money are, right?" Mara asked, pleased at the steadiness of her voice. She raised her chin a fraction to show the man she was above lying to him. Why waste her time doing it?

For one moment, Mara felt like she had the upper hand. Like she had stumped the man who had been nothing but cocky. But then the moment was shattered.

All it took was one smirk to let Mara know she hadn't won.

"I believe you," he said, seeming amused.

"What?"

Beck gave a little chuckle.

"I know you don't have any idea where the stash is," he continued. "In fact, I've known for a bit."

Mara was dumbfounded.

"Then why come after me?" she asked. "Why go through all of this trouble to get me if I can't even help?"

Beck's smirk stayed sharp when he answered, as if he'd been waiting for those questions for a while and it was finally time for him to deliver.

"Because now I have the only leverage in all the world that would make your father finally tell me where it is."

Mara couldn't help it. She laughed. It wasn't in the least kind.

"Good luck with that. My father wouldn't help me when I asked for it. What makes you think he'll help you now, just because you have me?"

"Because I'm not bartering for your release. I'm bartering for your life," Beck said simply. "You aren't leaving this place alive unless your father does everything I need him to, what I told the sheriff earlier be damned. He's a handsome fella, though, so don't worry. I'm sure he can find another woman to get into his bed and raise your kid if you're gone."

The shiver that had run down Mara's spine before was

back with a vengeance. It crippled any confidence she'd been wielding as a shield against her current situation. And the madman across from her. The strength that had kept her voice steady was gone when she answered.

"My father won't help you," she said.

"You'd be surprised what a father will do for his daughter." He brought the shotgun up and pointed it at her. "Now, get down there, Miss Copeland," he ordered. "I've got things to do."

The last thing Mara wanted to do was go down those steps. To find out where that dim light was and what the destination might mean for her future. But Mara couldn't deny that she felt deflated. She'd done what she could and now she might have to let whatever was going to happen play out.

Without another look at her captor, Mara started the descent down the stairs. She was less than four steps in when the door above her was dragged closed. She waited as the sound of the metal scraping filled the air. Something heavy went on top of the trap door. Mara backtracked until she could put her shoulders and back against it. She tried to push up, but the door didn't budge.

Letting out an exhale of defeat, she started her descent again.

The stairs weren't as long as she'd expected, and soon she was standing in a surprisingly large room lit by two hanging bulbs. They cast enough light to reach the corners.

Which was good and bad for Mara.

It was good because she could tell with certainty that she was standing in a basement, maybe used as a storage room at some point, judging by the lumps of furniture covered by dust cloths and pushed against the walls. And knowing *where* she was felt a lot better than sitting in the dark, wondering.

However, for every silver lining there was something bad that had to be coped with, and tied in a chair against the wall was a woman who looked like she'd seen a heck of a lot better days.

"Leigh?" Mara started, beyond confused.

Leigh Cullen had her mouth taped over and blood on her face. She looked just as surprised to see Mara as Mara was to see her.

That, in itself, would have been enough to make a terrifying situation even more dark, but then Mara noticed the boy in the corner, tied to an old oak rocking chair. His mouth was duct taped, his eyes wide. He didn't look much older than ten.

What the hell was going on?

Chapter Twenty

Mara rocked backward on the floor so that her knees were in the air. Before she'd had Alexa she could have gotten the handcuffs from behind her back to in front of herself without much fuss, but since she'd given birth and become a single parent, her exercise habits had disappeared. That included the yoga routine that had kept her flexible. As it was, it took several tries before she was able to get her hands in front of her. They were still bound, but at least now she could use them.

Her maternal instincts had gone from zero to a hundred the moment she'd seen the boy. She didn't recognize him. Still, she hurried over to him with the most soothing voice she could muster.

"Hey, there, my name's Mara," she started, honey coating every syllable. "I'm going to take the tape off your mouth. Is that okay?" The boy, short brown hair, freckles galore and wide blue eyes already filling up with tears, cut his gaze to Leigh. The woman, in turn, slit her eyes at Mara. "I'm not with them, Leigh. A man named Beck took me and brought me here."

It was the vaguest of answers but seemed enough to satisfy the woman. She nodded to the boy. He looked back at Mara and nodded.

"This might hurt a little, but I'll try to be extra gentle," she warned him.

The boy gave another curt nod. He closed his eyes tight as Mara got a grip on the edge of the tape and did her best to ease it off without causing the boy pain. No sooner had it passed over his lips did he give a cry of relief. It made Mara's heart squeeze.

"You did so good," Mara said, knowing the tears in his eyes were a thin dam away from being an all-out waterfall. "I'm going to try and untie you now, and then you can help me untie her." The boy nodded, sniffling. Mara went to the side of the chair and then to the back trying to find the main knot. Thankfully, it wasn't too complicated, resting at the base of the chair. Then again, the boy was small enough that he probably didn't need much help keeping him tied down. "So, what's your name?"

"Eric," he said, tears behind his words. "Er-Eric Cullen."

"Leigh's your mama," she guessed.

"Yes, ma'am."

She'd known that Leigh had a kid, but what had happened with her husband had always taken priority in Mara's mind. A swell of guilt rose at the realization that she'd never even asked after the boy, but Mara batted it down. She needed to focus. And she needed to try and calm Eric down. Even from her crouched position behind him, she could see he was trembling.

"So, Eric, what grade are you in?" she asked, working on undoing the first part of the knot.

"Fo-fourth."

"Oh, nice! That's a fun grade. So you have any favorite classes you're looking forward to after Christmas break?"

The first part of the knot gave way. There were two more to go.

"I like practicing football," he said flatly. "But Mama says I can't play on the team if I don't bring up my grades."

The second part fell away. Mara found herself smiling at his answer.

"I'd have to agree with her there," she said.

He nodded but didn't say anything else. Mara wanted to know how they'd gotten down here and what had happened to them, but she didn't want to push the little guy to relive whatever they'd gone through. She'd just have to ask his mama instead.

"Okay, there we go."

Mara stood, wincing as the pain in her side reminded her she should have been resting, and helped take the rope from around him.

"You okay?" Mara asked.

He nodded but she helped him stand all the same. Another part of her heart squeezed when she noticed a bruise on the side of his face. Like he'd been hit.

"Now, you think you can help me untie her?"

Leigh's eyes were shining but she didn't cry when Mara took the tape off her mouth.

"Oh, Eric, are you okay?" were the first words out of her mouth. The boy's chin started to tremble but he nodded.

Mara let him stand in front of his mom while she checked him over, uttering assurances that they'd all be alright, while she jumped into untying Leigh. The ropes had more knots, including at her ankles and wrists. Judging by the blood and marks all over the woman, Mara'd bet she'd put up one heck of a fight before they'd been able to get her tied down.

"This might take a little bit," Mara said, fingers fumbling with the knot at the back of her chair. "So let's not waste any time. What the heck is going on? And where are we?"

"We're at the house," Eric said, matter-of-factly.

"The house?"

"We're in a barn," Leigh clarified. "It's on my family's farm. Our house is a mile in that direction."

She nodded to the right wall.

"And this charming little room?" Mara asked, fingers tugging at another knot.

"My great-grandfather put it in to serve as a storm shelter of sorts. It's always creeped me out, so we never come out here. Until today." Leigh said a string of curses before apologizing to her son for doing just that. A heavy sigh followed. "I wanted an old picture of the main house my daddy took when he was a boy that's in one of these boxes. I was going to reframe it as a present for him. Lucky for us, it just happened to be the same day two thugs decided to camp out in the barn. They surprised us after I opened the trap door."

There it was again.

The swelling of guilt. This time Mara didn't let it sit and stew.

This time she let it out.

"It's my fault they're here," she admitted. "They're trying to use me to get something that's hidden somewhere in Riker County."

Mara didn't need to be looking at the woman to know she wasn't happy.

"Eric, why don't you go look for that picture?" Leigh said quietly. "It should be in one of those boxes."

Eric must have known his mom's tones. He obeyed without hesitation, walking across the room from them and pulling off a dust cloth. Mara undid the back knot and was in front of Leigh when the woman had collected herself enough to respond.

"It's about that no-good father of yours, isn't it?" she whispered, low and angry.

Mara nodded. She tried to get into a better position to work on the ropes holding Leigh's ankles to the legs of the chair. Pain flashed up her side again.

"What's wrong?" Leigh asked. Her eyes trailed to the bruise on Mara's head.

"Let's just say I've had a long day," she hedged.

Leigh kept quiet as Mara finished untying her. Such a seemingly simple task had left her exhausted. Instead of jumping up, as the now-free woman did, she pushed her back up against the wall and sat down. All the adrenaline spikes she'd had that day were long past gone. Now Mara felt pain and weariness.

She watched in silence as Leigh ran to her son and nearly crushed him in a hug.

Mara smiled. Pain aside, she'd give Alexa the same greeting.

If she ever saw her again.

BILLY HUGGED HIS mother and kissed his daughter's cheek.

"Are you sure there's no other way? We could just keep all the doors locked and maybe—"

"Mom."

Billy's mother let her arguments go and nodded to her son. She had Alexa on her hip, the diaper bag on her arm and pure concern on her face. But she wasn't going to argue anymore. Time was a luxury they had little of.

"You be careful," she said instead. "And bring her back."

"I will."

She touched the side of his face before giving him and Suzy some privacy. Alexa waved at him, although her eyes trailed between all the adults in the house. She'd been surprisingly quiet since he'd arrived. It made Billy wonder if she was looking for Mara among everyone. It was a good thing she'd taken such a shine to his mother, or else the next step in his plan wouldn't go over as well as they wanted.

"I don't like this," Suzy said, coming to stand in front of him. She met and held his eyes.

"I know, but it needs to be done."

"And you're not asking me just because I'm a woman, right?"

Billy returned the serious question with an equal answer.

"You know damn well it's not that," he said. Still, he saw some doubt there. He tried to diminish it as quickly as he could. "Beck played me like a fiddle just by talking about Alexa. I can't afford to let him do that again, so I need to *know* that she'll be okay. Which means I need someone I trust. Not only with my life, but with my mother's and child's lives, too. Like it or not, that's you, Suze. None of this will work if you're not the one to take them out of town and hide them." He gave her a small smile. "I'm asking as the little boy you once called dumb as nails for tanking the spelling bee in fourth grade. Not as your sheriff."

That seemed to soften the woman. She let out a sigh before her shoulders pushed back. She raised her chin. Not out of pride. It was determination.

"Who misspells elephant?" She smirked and then was deadly serious. "Go get your gal, Sheriff."

And then Suzy was gone, her own bag slung across her shoulder. No one knew how long it would take to find Mara and stop Beck, but Suzy wasn't bringing Alexa or his mother back until both happened.

Billy just hoped that was sooner rather than later.

Dane met Billy in the lobby the moment he walked in. He looked impeccable, letting Billy know he'd already done the press conference. Which he confirmed with his greeting.

"The public should be on the lookout for Beck and his associate, and both the car they drove away in and the truck they had earlier, too. Mara's picture is also out there. Dante is briefing the reserve deputies who just came in, while we have some of our deputies manning the tip lines and social media. The rest, including the local PD, are out on the streets and in the country."

"And no bites yet?" Billy asked, already knowing the answer.

Dane shook his head.

"Nothing we didn't already know. But I think Matt's ready to talk to us about what he's found on Beck's friend."

Billy nodded and they headed deeper into the building.

"Let's hope we finally have a lead."

BILLY STOOD AT the front of the squad room and looked out at his deputies. Those who were close by had been asked to come in. Those on patrol were being filled in on the new situation in person by Mills and one of the reserve deputies. Because the radios were now a problem.

A bigger one than they already had.

"Gene Marsden worked at Riker County Sheriff's Department for twelve years before he was fired by the last sheriff," Billy started. "There was a list a mile long of reasons why he should have been let go sooner but Sheriff Rockwell liked giving second—and sometimes third—chances to his deputies because he knew that this job can be a hard one. But then, when we were working the Bryan Copeland case, Rockwell noticed that crime scenes and evidence were being tampered with on Marsden's watch.

He never found concrete proof that it was Marsden. but after a late night of drinking at a local bar, Marsden started to brag about having his own personal collection of Moxy. Courtesy of the department. He was fired as Rockwell's last act as sheriff, and when he came to me to rehire him, I flat out said no." Billy crossed his arms over his chest. "To put it bluntly, he lost his damn mind."

Two deputies sitting in the back agreed, using more colorful language. Billy pointed to them. Along with Dane and Matt, they'd been present for the scene. "He had to be escorted out. After that, he moved to Georgia, where his sister lives, and didn't make so much as a peep." Billy gave Matt a nod.

The detective cleared his throat to address the room.

"Until two months ago, when he apparently came back." Matt pinned the picture of Marsden they'd been able to get from the security camera at the local bar, the Eagle. "The owner of the Eagle said Marsden has been paying in cash only. One night he got so drunk they called him a cab, which took him to the same hotel where the recently deceased Caleb Richards had been meeting Beck. Around the same time Beck fled, Marsden disappeared."

"We think he might have a police radio, which is why they've always been right there with us every step of the investigation," Billy added. "Even though it was checked in when he was fired, we can't find it." Just saying the words made Billy angrier than he already was.

"Is that the only evidence we have on him? Coming back to town, staying in the same hotel and hating you?" one of the reserve deputies asked. The question might have seemed like the man was unimpressed but Billy knew he was just a straight shooter. He wanted all the information they had before trying to bring down a former cop.

Which brought Billy to a crossroads.

He could tell his deputies to trust him right then and there without any more information and they would. Maybe.

Or Billy could follow Mara's earlier example in the park.

He could finally tell the truth.

"Mara Copeland and I became involved during the case against her father." He didn't wait for any reactions. "After he was convicted, we were going to go public with the relationship but Mara was approached by Marsden, who had found out about us. He threatened Mara with the idea that I would lose my career because of her. So she left." The words tasted bitter in his mouth but Billy continued. "Only a handful of people knew about Mara and I, and none of them have since told. When I talked to Beck, he already knew about the relationship, making me believe Marsden had found out by overhearing Bryan Copeland talking to me about it the day we arrested him." Billy readjusted his stance. When he spoke again he could hear the hardness in his voice. The bottom line. "While it might not be professional, I love Mara Copeland a whole hell of a lot. That goes double for our daughter."

A few surprised looks swept over the deputies' faces but no one stopped him. "That might not be reason enough to warrant us going after a former cop considering, you're right, we don't have anything concrete to tie him to Beck, but Marsden is the best lead we have. We track Marsden, there's a good chance we find Beck. We find Beck, we find Mara. And if any of you have any reservations about this, well…" Billy paused a second to work up a smirk. "Too bad for you. Because I'm the sheriff and this is an order."

He'd been waiting for some opposition, so Billy was

surprised when none came. The men and women sitting in front of him all seemed to agree with gusto.

In fact, some even cheered.

"Alright, let's get to work!"

Chapter Twenty-One

"Why were you at the sheriff's department the other day?" Mara finally thought to ask Leigh.

She let her gaze linger on the picture of Alexa she'd had in her pocket before putting it back. According to Leigh's watch they'd been in the basement for more than three hours. In that time Mara had told the woman everything that had happened, including her part in taking her father down. Something that might not have softened the woman toward her but did seem to surprise her.

The fact of the matter was that Leigh's husband was still dead because of the Copelands. Something she was reminded of every time she looked at Eric, who had finally fallen asleep in the corner. While Mara had been there for a few hours, Leigh and Eric had been there since that morning. The stress of it had been exhausting for the boy.

Mara couldn't blame him. If the need to escape hadn't been so great, she might have tried to get a few minutes of shut-eye herself.

Leigh stopped looking in the box in front of her and turned, already scowling. She motioned to Eric.

"While I was at the grocery store, some man showed up at the house asking all sorts of weird questions," she said. "When Eric asked what his name was, the man refused to tell him. After he left, Eric called me. I was already near the department so I thought I'd drop in."

Mara was about to dismiss Leigh's story when a cold thought slid into her head.

"What did the man look like?"

Leigh pursed her lips, still not happy being stuck in the basement with Mara, but she answered.

"Eric said he was really tall, had brown hair cut really close, almost like what the army fellows wear, looked around his Uncle Daniel's age—midforties—and, not so much like his uncle, he was skinny. Why?"

Mara let out a sigh of relief. Definitely not Beck. She was about to say as much when another terrible thought pushed in. The knot that had sunk to the bottom of her stomach began to spawn other knots.

"What questions did he ask?"

The man might not have been Beck but that didn't mean she didn't recognize the description.

Leigh must have read the fear in her expression. She dropped the contempt she'd been treating Mara with and answered.

"He asked if we'd had any construction done two or three years ago and, if so, where." The knots in Mara's stomach turned cold. Her heart rate started to pick up. "But, of course, all Eric could think about was his dad being killed two years ago, so he said he didn't know. Then he asked if Eric was home alone and, thank God, he lied. That's when he asked what the man's name was and he left."

Mara nearly missed the end of Leigh's sentence. Her thoughts were racing alongside her heart now.

"Leigh, *did* you have any construction done in the last three years? Anyone coming in and out of the property with trucks or trailers?"

Leigh's eyebrow rose but she nodded.

"Right after my husband passed. We had a bad storm blow through. It flung a tree over and messed up the roof." She pointed up, meaning the barn's roof. "Had a company come in to replace it. They were really nice, too. Cut me a deal on account of being a recent widow. Even planted a new tree near the barn and left a note saying I could watch it and Eric grow up together. I thought it was really sweet. Okay, Mara, what is it? You look like you've seen a ghost."

Mara felt like it, too.

"My father hid a stash of drugs and money right before he went to court, as a fail-safe. We thought that there was a possibility that he used construction as a way to help him hide it, but we've only looked one place. The high school." Mara was struck with such a strong realization that a laugh escaped between her lips. "I never would have *ever* thought to look here. The guilt of what happened to you—to your family—would have made me, and maybe Billy, too, never even think to come here. And my father knew that. It's the perfect place."

Mara shook her head again, but she felt like she was right.

"Leigh, I think my dad's stash is here."

"But you said Beck was still looking for it," Leigh pointed out.

"That's just it. I don't think Beck even knows. I think he picked this place because it's remote and he knows only you and Eric live here. You probably would have never noticed them had you not wanted that picture."

Leigh's face contorted into an emotion that Mara was sure was laced with more than a few colorful words, when a scraping sound cut through the air. Someone was moving the canister off the trap door. It made Mara remember the original thought she'd had.

"I think that man who talked to Eric was Gene Marsden," Mara hurried while she and Leigh retreated to Eric. Mara paused and then switched directions. She grabbed an old lamp she'd pulled from a box earlier and pointed to the vintage baseball bat Leigh had found. "And if he's found out the stash is here, I think he'll kill us."

When it rained, it poured.

That was Billy's first thought when his office received a call from an unknown number. He didn't know what to expect, but he thought it wouldn't be good. So when the caller turned out to be Bryan Copeland, Billy was more than a little thrown.

"I told Beck where the stash was," he started.

"You what?" Billy rocked out of his chair, already spitting mad.

Bryan didn't seem bothered by his anger. In fact, he seemed to be harboring his own.

"The deal was Mara's life for the location." Bryan went on. "Apparently, I still love my daughter. Now, you got a pen?"

Billy wrote down the address Bryan rattled off and couldn't help but be surprised by it but didn't have the time to say so. He also didn't have the time to ask what number the man was calling from or how Beck had gotten hold of him. Those were issues he'd tackle later.

"Now hurry, Sheriff, and go save the girl. I don't believe for a second this Beck will let her go alive," Bryan said, already cutting the conversation short. Billy almost didn't hear it when he tacked on a last question. "And, Billy, is Alexa safe?"

While he had no reason in the world to answer the man, Billy did.

"Yeah, she's safe."

"Good."

Bryan ended the call. Seconds later, Billy was out the door.

No sooner had Beck walked off the last step than Mara smashed the lamp against his head. He made a wild noise as the glass shattered against him, but the wrath of the women he'd imprisoned wasn't finished. Mara slid to the side as Leigh swung her bat for all she was worth into his crotch.

Beck never had a chance.

He hit the ground hard and didn't move. The shotgun he'd been holding thunked next to him. It was closer to Leigh, so she scurried to grab it while Mara readied for the next bad guy, hoping she could still do damage even though her grip was off thanks to the handcuffs.

But no one came.

The two of them froze and listened.

"I don't hear anything," Mara whispered.

"Maybe Marsden isn't here?"

"Let's not just stand here and wait to find out."

Leigh nodded, but hesitated.

"Have you ever shot a gun?" she asked, motioning to the shotgun in her hands.

"Not one of those."

Leigh gritted her teeth.

"I'll hold on to it, then," she said. "Follow me up. Eric, get behind Mara."

Eric crawled out from his hiding spot in the corner and listened to his mom. He stood behind Mara and kept his eyes off Beck.

"Wait, he's got a phone on him!"

Mara saw the light from his pocket as his cell phone vibrated. Leigh trained the shotgun on him as Mara fished the phone out. The caller ID was *M*.

"Marsden," Leigh guessed.

"Which means he's probably not up there?"

The thought got them moving. Mara held the phone,

careful not to answer it, and followed Leigh up the stairs while Eric held on to the back of her shirt. If Marsden wasn't in the barn, then there was a good chance they'd be able to get to the house. She could even use Beck's cell phone to call for help once Marsden stopped calling. If he didn't know they had escaped, Mara definitely wasn't going to let him know by answering the phone.

Leigh moved slowly when she ascended, shotgun swiveling side to side, until she was out of view. Mara held her breath, waiting for the go-ahead. Her heart was hammering in her ears.

"We're alone," Leigh whispered down to them after what felt like hours.

Mara, relieved for the dose of good news, led Eric up the stairs. The air smelled musty and damp. The sun that had barely lit the space earlier in the day was gone. Like the basement, there were sets of hanging bulbs. They hung from the rafters, looking tired and weak. The light they emitted wasn't anything to write home about, but Mara welcomed it all the same. At least she could see. A silver lining to the nightmare the day had turned into.

"The house is a mile that way," Leigh whispered, pointing to the wall on their right. "Call your sheriff and tell him we're headed there. I have a lot more guns in that house than I bet Marsden brought to town." Despite their strained, nearly nonexistent relationship, Mara found herself grateful that out of all the women she could have been held captive with, Beck had been stupid enough to pick Leigh Cullen.

Mara fumbled with the phone and dialed 911 with her cuffed hand, ready to tell the dispatcher as quickly as possible everything that was happening and get Billy sent their way. Because they were out of Carpenter's town limits, the call should go straight to the Riker County Sheriff's

Department instead of the local police. Which meant Billy would get to them faster.

Get to *her* faster.

That thought alone put some pep in her step. The idea of seeing Billy after everything that had happened was more than a desire to Mara. Now it was a need. As real and essential as breathing. She needed Billy Reed.

Sitting in the basement for hours had given her more than enough time to think about the sheriff. While she'd known that he would keep Alexa in his life now that he knew about her, Mara didn't know where that left the two of them.

Would they coparent from two different homes? Two different towns?

The mere idea of being away from Billy tore through Mara with surprising ferocity. For two years it had been only her and Alexa. But now that Mara remembered what having Billy around again was like, could she go back to living a life without him by her side?

Going through boxes of Leigh's family's antiques, Mara had realized that, no, she couldn't. She didn't want to go back to a house that didn't have the sheriff between its walls. She didn't want to take Alexa away from her father anymore, not even for the briefest of moments. For the first time in years, Mara had come to a realization so poignant that she'd nearly cried right there in the basement.

Two years ago, she should have fought for Billy—for *them*—instead of running.

She wasn't going to make the same mistake again.

However, Mara never found out how fast her 911 call would have reached the sheriff. Before she could hit the send button, the door in the corner of the barn was flung open.

Mara recognized the former cop, Gene Marsden, as easily as she'd heard his words at the ceremony years ago. He hadn't changed in the time since, matching Eric's description to a T, but the gun he was carrying definitely wasn't police issue. He pointed it at Leigh so quickly that it didn't seem humanly possible.

"I'll kill you first," he warned. His voice was steady, calm. It made his threat all the more believable. So much so that Leigh didn't shoot. Which probably was for the best, since there were several feet between them. If she'd missed...

"Kick the gun over here," he ordered before looking at Mara. "And toss the phone this way, too. You call anyone and I'll shoot the boy in the head."

Eric pulled on her shirt a little and she immediately did as she was told. The same went for Leigh. Even if it meant giving up the only upper hand they had. There were just some chances you didn't take. Especially when you believed the threat if you failed.

One look at Marsden's grin and Mara believed his every word.

"Now, back into the basement," he said, using his gun to make a shooing motion at them. Mara shared a look with Leigh. He didn't miss it. "I'll kill the boy, remember?"

"We're going," Mara said quickly. She put the trembling boy in front of her and followed him back into what was becoming Mara's least favorite place in the entire world.

Beck was still lying on the floor and, for a moment, she wondered if he was dead. It wasn't until they had all stepped over him and were in the middle of the room that he let out a low groan.

"You let two women and some little kid get the better of you," Marsden said, showing nothing but disgust for his partner. "How can you live with yourself?" If Beck tried to answer, Mara couldn't tell. The lamp had cut his face up something awful. Blood ran down it like a fountain. It was almost too much to look at, but Marsden seemed to have no trouble sneering at him. "You know, some men would take their lives rather than lose their dignity," Marsden drawled. "But I already know you'd never have the jewels to do that." Marsden took a step back and pointed his gun down. "So I'll do it for you."

And then he shot Beck in the head.

Chapter Twenty-Two

Eric was crying.

Mara wanted to join him.

Killing someone in cold blood was enough to terrify any witness. Killing your partner in cold blood was downright bone-chilling.

"Don't worry, I was going to do that anyways," Marsden said. "Beck liked to talk a lot, but words aren't street smarts. I don't know how he planned to make this business idea of his work." He looked at Mara expectantly.

"You—you mean bringing Moxy back to Riker County," she guessed when he didn't look away.

Marsden laughed.

"I don't think as small as Beck here does." He paused, then corrected himself. "Or did." Mara kept her eyes on Marsden and not the growing puddle of blood around the man he was so casually dismissing. She wondered if he could hear her heart trying to ram itself clear out of her body.

Marsden took a moment to give each of them an appraising look. It made Leigh move so that Eric was hidden behind her completely. If he was offended, he didn't comment on it.

"Now, here's the deal," he said when no one made a peep. What were they supposed to say? Mara had no idea what he knew or what he planned to do with them. "Unlike Beck here, I'm not going to bore you with nonstop chatter and I expect the same from you." He pointed to Mara then thrust his thumb back to the stairs. Panic jolted through her, rooting her to the spot. "You're coming with me."

"Why?" she couldn't help but ask. As much as she disliked the basement, going anywhere alone with Marsden was worse.

"We've got treasure to dig up, that's why." He pointed his gun at Leigh's head. Eric's crying intensified. "They're only alive because of you right now. If you fight me, I'll kill them."

"Why are you doing this?" Mara cried out. The question seemed to amuse him. He actually laughed.

"For money, what else?" That one little laugh sounded twisted. Marsden had lost his patience. "Now, move it or I kill the boy first."

Mara didn't hesitate this time. She never wanted to be the cause of pain for the Cullens again. She didn't want to be the reason Leigh lost her son or Eric lost his mother.

Mara straightened her back, held up her chin and started to walk. It wasn't until she was outside and looking at the flat, open area between the barn and the woods that her confidence faded.

Her thoughts flew to her daughter, who she prayed was safe, and then to the man who had given her Alexa.

Mara's heart squeezed.

She should have told Billy she still loved him.

And always would.

BILLY RACED ACROSS Leigh Cullen's property in the Bronco cussing. He led a stream of deputies while the local SWAT team was fifteen minutes behind.

He didn't have time to wait for them. While Billy

thought Beck might hold off on killing Mara after Bryan had finally given up the location of the stash, he knew that Marsden wouldn't. He was a greedy man with a power complex. And a former cop. He knew firsthand how witnesses and loose ends could undo even the smartest man's plans.

"Marsden won't go down easily," Matt said from the passenger's seat. He had his gun in hand, ready. "I can't say the same for Beck. I don't know what kind of man he is."

"He likes to talk," Billy said. "If you need to stall, ask him a question about humanity or the line between right or wrong or if he's an Auburn or Alabama fan. I'm sure that'll get him rattling on for a while." Matt snorted. "But you're right about Marsden. If he doesn't have an escape plan set up, he'll make one. And if he can't escape…" Billy didn't finish the thought out loud but they both knew Marsden would kill Mara and Leigh and her kid. As soon as Bryan had told them the stash was next to the barn, marked by a tree that had been planted when he'd brought the cache in, the department had tried to track the Cullens down. Turned out they were missing. Billy only hoped they were still alive, held captive with Mara.

Who also needed to still be alive.

Just the thought of the alternative made Billy cuss some more. It didn't help that in the distance they could just make out a faint light on what must have been the barn. Billy knew Riker County and he'd been out to the Cullens once before, but he didn't know this part of their property. He didn't like the added disadvantage.

"Picked one hell of a night for a showdown," Matt said, leaning forward to look up at the sky. Clouds blanketed the moon and stars. Being out in the country, with no light from above, put them at a further disadvantage. But it at least helped with the next part of Billy's plan.

He slowed and pulled into the grass. Matt radioed the men behind them to do the same. While taking Beck and Marsden by force would be easier, Billy had a feeling it ran the best chance of ending in blood. It was time to rely on stealth.

"Ready?" Matt asked after he checked his gun again. Billy did the same. There was no room to make mistakes.

"Let's finally put an end to this."

There was half a football field's length of flat grass and dirt between them and the barn. An outdoor light hung over one of the doors but it didn't worry Billy. He could make out the outline of a vehicle tucked against the side of the barn they were sneaking toward. Billy'd bet dollars to donuts it was the car Mara had been taken in earlier that day. He knew Beck and Marsden were there. He just didn't know if they were in the barn or on the other side of it.

And he didn't know where Mara was, either.

Billy let his questions shut off as he made it close enough to confirm it was the car he'd seen before. He and Matt stepped quietly while looking in the front and back seats. Then, together, they remained quiet and listened.

The Southern lullaby of cicadas and frogs held steady around them, as normal as the humidity and as loyal to the South as football fans to the game. Billy wouldn't have even noticed the song if he hadn't been trying to hear through it. So when an odd noise went against the natural grain of sound, he tilted his head in confusion.

Matt heard it, too.

"Other side of the barn," he whispered, so quietly Billy barely heard him. But he agreed.

Billy led them along the outer wall, away from the side with the light. He held his breath and kept his body loose as he took a look around the corner. Nothing but more grass, open space and a small amount of clutter lining the back wall of the barn. Even before Leigh had lost her husband, the barn hadn't been used for several years. That fact was merely highlighted when Billy and Matt crept past a door that was heavily chained shut.

They weren't going to be getting anyone in or out that way.

The weird noise Billy couldn't place stopped as soon as they cleared the door. In tandem both men froze at the corner of the barn, guns high and ready.

"I took your cuffs off. You shouldn't be stalling anymore," a man said, loud and clearly frustrated. Billy knew instantly the voice belonged to Gene Marsden. Like nails on a chalkboard, his one sentence was enough to grate on Billy's nerves.

"My ribs are bruised, no thanks to you. If I'm going slow you can thank yourself for that."

Billy could have sung right then and there. Mara was alive.

"You've got a lot of mouth for someone standing in a hole that could be their grave." Billy's joy at hearing Mara's voice plummeted straight down into the fiery depths of pure anger.

No one talked like that to his woman.

"Cover me," he whispered to Matt. He didn't need to see the detective to know he nodded.

Billy crouched, kept his gun straight and swung around the corner of the barn. When bullets didn't fly, he took in several details at once.

There was an old tractor with a flat tire sitting a few feet from the barn's side. Two battery-powered lanterns sat on the ground on the other side of the tractor, casting wide circles of light over two figures. One was Marsden, tall and holding something—a gun, most likely—while Mara was farther away. She was holding a shovel and standing in a hole up to her knees. Next to Marsden was Beck's truck, looking the worse for wear. Neither Marsden nor Mara was directly facing Billy, so he took a beat to look for Beck, Leigh or Eric. When he didn't see anyone else, he started to move toward the back of the tractor.

He could have shot Marsden right then and there—and been happy about it, too—but Mara was too close to the ex-deputy. Billy needed a cleaner shot or a better angle to force the man to disarm himself. Then any chance of that went out the window. Without the lantern's light going past the skeleton of metal, Billy didn't see the beer bottles on the ground until it was too late. His foot connected with one and sent it flying into the other. They sounded off like church bells on a Sunday.

And Marsden didn't waste any time second-guessing the noise. He turned and started shooting.

"Drop your gun, Marsden," Billy yelled after lunging behind the wheel of the tractor. Bullets hit the metal and wood around him, but Marsden didn't answer. He kept Billy pinned down for a few shots until Matt responded to the man in kind. The sounds of gunfire shifted as Marsden must have taken cover behind the truck to take aim at Matt.

"Mara," Billy yelled out, worried she'd be hit in the process. There wasn't any cover she could take easily.

"Billy!"

Like magic Mara appeared around the front of the tractor, seemingly unharmed. There were so many things he wanted to do to her right then and there—appropriate and not so much—but it wasn't the time or place. So he swallowed his desires and got down to business.

"Where's Beck?"

Mara shook her head.

"Dead," she said. "Marsden shot him in the basement." Her eyes widened. "Eric and Leigh are down there still. I need to get them."

The exchange of bullets ceased. Billy bet everyone was reloading.

"You get down there and stay with them," Billy said hurriedly. "Backup is down the road. We'll call them in if you'll stay there."

Mara nodded and turned her body, ready to run, but hesitated. She found his gaze again.

"I never stopped loving you, Billy Reed," she said, voice completely calm. "I promise I'll never leave you again."

Billy, caught more off guard than when the gunfire started up again, didn't have time to respond. Mara didn't wait but kept low, using the tractor as a shield, and soon disappeared around the front of the barn. He heard what must have been the door they'd been using to get in and out of the structure.

The sound shook him from the moment. Billy took a beat to call in their backup and then yelled out to Marsden.

"You're outnumbered," he yelled out. "Put the gun down, Marsden! It's over!"

The shooting stopped again. Billy waited a moment before sticking his head out around the tractor's tire, gun ready. Had Marsden listened to him? Would it be that easy?

"Grenade!"

The two syllables Matt yelled were enough to spike Billy's adrenaline and get him moving, but it wasn't enough time to clear it. He saw the flash-bang arc through the air in the space between him and Matt. Billy dove as far away from it as he could before a deafening blast went off behind him.

The flash blinded him; the sound stunned him.

For several seconds Billy tried to regain some control

of his body, his balance, his senses. But before he could, Marsden went for the only option he had left to possibly get out of this mess alive.

Mara.

IT TOOK MARA longer than she would have liked to push the metal canister off the trap door, but she eventually managed.

"It's me," Mara yelled, hands going up to cover her face seconds before Leigh could pummel her with the bat she'd beaten Beck with. His body was still at the bottom of the stairs, in a puddle of blood. Mara jumped over it as Leigh backed away to the side again. Eric popped up from his hiding spot against the wall.

"What's going on up there?" Leigh asked, not dropping the bat to her side.

"Billy showed up." Mara couldn't help but smile. "He told us to stay here. Backup is down the road."

Mara saw the relief in Leigh's shoulders. She leaned the bat against the wall.

"I guess our friend isn't surrendering," she said as more *thunks* could be heard from above.

Mara wrung her hands and shook her head.

"He's definitely not su—"

"Grenade!"

Mara flinched backward and put her hand to her mouth. She gasped as a loud *bang* shook the barn above them. Leigh shared a look with her, eyes wide, as silence filled the world above the basement stairs.

"No," Mara said, shaking her head and still backpedaling. Surely it was Billy who had thrown it, right? He'd had enough of Marsden and thrown a grenade to end it?

Even as Mara thought it, she knew that wasn't the case.

"Is it over?" Eric asked, bringing her attention to the

fact she was at the back wall. Her hand still over her mouth, she didn't have the will to pretend to look like everything was okay.

She wouldn't do that until Billy came down those stairs.

"Should we—" Leigh started. She was cut off by the sound of footsteps coming down into the basement. Mara dropped her hand, a smile coming to her lips thinking of Billy. It was because of that smile that Leigh dropped her guard.

And that's why she didn't beat Marsden to a pulp as soon as his feet hit the floor.

Instead, when she belatedly tried to do some damage, Marsden hauled off and pistol-whipped her. Eric yelled as the force of the hit made Leigh sink to the floor. All she had time to do was look up as Marsden brought up his gun and pointed it at her son.

"For that, I'll kill him before I kill you," he sneered. He looked at Mara. "And then we're leaving."

Mara didn't have time to tell the man that she had no intention of leaving with him.

So, instead, she showed him.

With nothing but the image of Alexa firmly planted in her mind, Mara jumped in front of Eric just as Marsden fired.

BILLY RAN DOWN into the basement and shot Gene Marsden in the head.

His ears rang something awful, his movements were still sluggish and he was having trouble seeing, but none of that could hide one horrifying fact.

Marsden had created Billy's worst nightmare.

He'd shot Mara and he'd done it seconds before Billy could stop him.

"Mara's been shot," he yelled back to Matt.

She was on the ground with Eric standing behind her, crying.

"Are you okay?" Billy yelled at him even though he knew the boy was. Where Mara was lying on her side, it was obvious she'd taken the bullet for the boy. Eric nodded just as Leigh swooped in and grabbed him. They gave Billy space while he dropped down to his knees.

"Mara," he said, still yelling. As gently as he could, he rolled her onto her back. Immediately he cursed. The shot had been to the chest. "It's okay," he said, surprised when her eyes opened. "You're going to be okay. Matt's called in some help."

Mara smiled up at him, but it was as soft as a whisper. Her eyelids fluttered closed.

Billy couldn't help the fear that tore from his mouth.

"No, stay with me!" Billy pulled her into his lap. Matt appeared at his side and, without words, put pressure on the wound. "Come on, Mara," he said, trying to keep her conscious. Despite Matt's attempt, blood poured out around the detective's hand.

The sight alone tore at Billy worse than any pain he'd ever known.

"You promised you'd never leave me again," he said to her. "You can't leave me again. You promised!"

But Mara kept quiet.

Chapter Twenty-Three

Alexa's hair was a mess. Billy was man enough to admit that that was his fault. He'd finally gotten her used to him brushing out her hair after bath time and right after she woke up, so he'd gotten cocky and tried to do something a bit more adventurous that morning. He'd searched hairstyles for little girls and found a video that showed him how to do a fishtail braid.

Now, looking down at her sleeping against his chest, Billy accepted that the braid looked more like a rat's tail than a fishtail anything. He sighed. Maybe one day he'd get it right. But, for now, no one who'd visited had given him grief about his fathering. That included his mother, surprisingly enough.

He turned to look at the chair next to his. It was empty. She must have stepped out to get coffee or another book while he and Alexa dozed off in his own chair. There was just something about hospital machines and their beeping that created a noise that carried him off to sleep.

Then again, he hadn't gotten much sleep in the last few days.

Billy's eyes traveled to the hospital bed in front of him.

He'd positioned his chair next to Mara's feet so he was facing her. He wanted to know the second she woke up.

He wanted to be there for her. If it hadn't been for Alexa, he wouldn't have left her side during the last few days.

Billy closed his eyes again and rested his chin on top of his daughter's head. It was nice to feel her against him after everything that had happened.

Beck's and Marsden's bodies had been collected and buried outside Riker County with their families. Beck turned out to be Kevin Rickman, a college dropout who had tried to desperately follow his father's long criminal career. But, like his father, he'd been killed over power, money and drugs. Beck had only focused on Bryan Copeland's legacy because his father had helped Bryan at the beginning of his drug running, right before he'd been killed. Bryan hadn't ever met Beck, but was able to pick the man's father out of an old picture. Kevin had used an old friend of his father's to get a message to Bryan in prison. Then Bryan had used his connections to relay the stash's location and then call Billy and warn him.

Billy felt the letter folded in his wallet like it was on fire. It was from Bryan to Mara and had been sent to Billy's office. As guilty as he'd felt about reading it, Billy was glad he had. Bryan hadn't given Mara any grief and he hadn't apologized for his past. He'd only said he was glad she was okay and asked if she would send him pictures of both herself and Alexa.

Billy would never like Bryan, but he was glad he'd finally put his daughter's life above his own. So much so that Billy called in a lot of favors, including some of Sheriff Rockwell's, and gotten the news that Bryan Copeland's stash had been found, or even ever existed, kept secret. Just until Bryan could be moved to a prison out of state. Then Billy would personally let everyone know, including anyone with bad intentions, that there was no reason to ever dig on Leigh Cullen's property again. Otherwise there would always be someone who would look for it. The stash had been right where Bryan had told him. A handful of deputies had spent the night digging out a metal container that held more money than Billy would probably make in a lifetime. Plus enough Moxy and other assorted drugs to help any budding drug runner start out strong.

Billy had just started to think about all the paperwork he'd have to fill out when a sound made his eyes flash open.

"Mara," he said, surprised.

Mara, propped up on a pillow, was looking right at him. There was a smile across her lips.

"Don't—" she started but coughed. Billy was already getting up, trying not to jostle Alexa too much. She squirmed once before he laid her down on the love seat on the other side of the room.

"Here," Billy said, voice low, as he grabbed his cup of water and popped a straw into it. He held it up to Mara and she drank a few sips.

"Thanks," she said. "My mouth was really dry."

Billy put the water down on the table and sat on the edge of the bed to face her. He couldn't help but smile. She was the most beautiful woman he'd ever seen.

"I didn't want you to move," Mara said, giving her own smile. "You two were so cute."

Billy glanced back at Alexa and felt a bit sheepish.

"I tried to braid her hair," he explained. "It looked better yesterday."

Mara's brow furrowed. She looked around the room and then down at herself.

"How bad is it?" she whispered.

Billy felt his smile falter.

"You're expected to fully recover. But…" Billy let his hand hover over her chest. The doctor said there'd be a scar there but she'd been damned lucky. The second woman to get the same diagnosis in a week on his watch. "There were a few close calls to get you there."

Billy felt the pain and fear and anguish he'd experienced when Mara had flatlined twice in the ambulance. He'd nearly lost his mind with worry as he'd paced outside surgery afterward.

"I'm okay now, then," Mara said softly. She reached out and patted the top of his hand. Billy realized that, even though she was the one in the hospital bed, she was trying to comfort him.

It made his smile come back and he finally did something he should have done two years before. Reaching into his pocket, he pulled out a small box. He held it up to Mara. Her eyes widened.

"I always thought I'd do something elaborate and romantic when I proposed to you but dammit, Mara, I can't wait anymore." Billy opened the box. He'd tell her later that he'd bought her the ring two years before, but for now he had to tell her what he wanted in the future. "You don't have to marry me now, tomorrow or even next year, but Mara Copeland, I sure do need you to be my wife." He took the ring out and held it up. "Marry me and let's grow old together?"

Mara's expression softened. Those beautiful lips turned up into the smallest of smiles. When she answered, Billy couldn't help but laugh.

"Sounds good to me, Sheriff."

THE CHRISTMAS TREE was going to fall over. Its branches hung down with the weight of too many ornaments, half from Billy's childhood and the others they'd bought together for Alexa. At the time, Mara had been more than happy to fill their cart with bits and bobbles, but now she was worried the sheer weight of them all was going to kill their tree. Even if it was fake.

"Personally, I think it looks amazing."

Mara turned and smiled. Billy was grinning ear to ear. "I'm sure everyone at the party is going to be jealous that their trees aren't as great as this one." He opened his arms wide, motioning to the tree. Mara caught sight of the wedding band on his finger. It made her glance at hers before answering him. The sight made her feel a warmth spread through her. Every single time.

"That their trees *weren't* as good," she corrected him. "You know, considering it's the end of February and no one has decorations up anymore. Or are celebrating Christmas."

Billy waved his hand dismissively.

"I wasn't about to let my first Christmas with my girls go by without a proper celebration," he said, defiance in his voice. Billy sidled up beside her and placed his arm around her waist. "Plus, I think we deserve a pass to do that, don't you?"

Mara's smile grew.

It had been almost three months since Mara had woken up in the hospital. In that time, several things had happened. The first was that she'd learned Christmas had come and gone while she'd been unconscious. Claire had still taken the day to shower her in gifts and love, but Billy had told everyone that he'd wait until the three of them could celebrate together. As a family.

The idea of their first Christmas together had made her cry, which had, in turn, alarmed the sheriff, but she'd promised they were tears of happiness. Something she realized she'd always feel after Suzy, of all people, had been ordained and married them on the back porch of Billy's house. It had been a short and sweet ceremony. Claire had cried while holding Alexa, while Detective Walker and Captain Jones had been the official witnesses.

Since then, life had moved quickly. Mara quit her job, broke her lease and together with off-duty sheriff's department employees, Billy and she had moved all of her belongings into the Reed family home.

While she felt the love from the department, a part of Mara had been more than worried that the residents of Carpenter wouldn't ever accept her because of who she was. Especially after the news that she and Billy had a child had traveled through the town like wildfire. However, so far no one had said a rude thing to her. And if they even looked like they were thinking about it, Leigh Cullen would puff up, ready to point out that Mara had died—twice if you counted her heart stopping—to save her son, and if they didn't like her they'd have to deal with Leigh. She'd only used that speech once on a man who hadn't meant any disrespect, but Mara couldn't deny it made her feel good that Leigh didn't seem to hold any more animosity toward her. In fact, while Mara had been in the hospital, Leigh had visited her almost every day.

They'd talked about the serious things first—the sorrys and thank yous for anything and everything that had happened—and then moved on to the personal sides of who they were. It turned out Leigh had been wanting to start her own business—something creative and hands-on— but hadn't found a worthwhile fit. When she found out that Mara had wanted to start up an interior design shop, Leigh had decided that not only could they be friends but they could be business partners, too.

Once Mara was out of the hospital, Leigh proved to have meant every word she'd said. They were already working up the design for an office space downtown. It wasn't large, but it was a start. One Mara was looking forward to. One that her father also praised in a letter. Mara didn't know what their particular future held, especially concerning Alexa, but she couldn't deny she missed her father. They'd agreed to start writing to each other. It, too, was a new start.

Which left one last, life-altering decision that had surprised them. Tough-as-nails, sweet-as-honey Claire Reed. Instead of going back home, she'd pulled a Mara and sold her house, instead.

"I've been bored in retirement anyways," she'd told them one night at supper. "Plus, now that I have a grandbaby, you won't be able to keep me away." She was currently living in the guesthouse but promised she was looking for a place of her own. Though Mara had to admit, it was nice having someone to help with Alexa when she and Billy wanted some alone time.

Which was just as much fun as she'd remembered.

Mara sighed, the warmth of the man next to her seeping into her heart. It made his gaze shift downward.

"Who would have thought that we'd really end up together?" Mara mused.

"I knew we would," he said, matter-of-factly.

"You have to admit, it was quite the journey," she said. "Ups and downs and bad men with guns. Not to mention your mother."

Billy let out a hoot of laughter.

"I hadn't seen *that* one coming," he admitted. "But…"

Mara let out a small yelp of excitement as Billy spun her around. His lips covered hers in a kiss that she'd never forget. When it ended, he stayed close.

"But, as for us, I always knew we'd be here eventually," he whispered, lips pulling up into his famous smirk. It was a sight she was ready to see every day for the rest of her life. "Merry Christmas, Mrs. Reed."

Mara didn't miss a beat.

"Merry Christmas, Sheriff."

* * * * *

Look for THE DEPUTY'S WITNESS,
the next book in Tyler Anne Snell's series
THE PROTECTORS OF RIKER COUNTY,
in December, wherever
Mills & Boon Intrigue books are sold!

And don't miss the books in her most
recent series, **ORION SECURITY:**

PRIVATE BODYGUARD
FULL FORCE FATHERHOOD
BE ON THE LOOKOUT: BODYGUARD
SUSPICIOUS ACTIVITIES

Available now from Mills & Boon Intrigue!

MILLS & BOON®

INTRIGUE
Romantic Suspense

A SEDUCTIVE COMBINATION OF DANGER AND DESIRE

Join Britain's BIGGEST Romance Book Club

50% OFF your first parcel

- **EXCLUSIVE offers every month**
- **FREE delivery direct to your door**
- **NEVER MISS a title**

Call Customer Services

0844 844 1358*

or visit

millsandboon.co.uk/bookclub

MILLS & BOON®

Why shop at millsandboon.co.uk?

Each year, thousands of romance readers find their perfect read at millsandboon.co.uk. That's because we're passionate about bringing you the very best romantic fiction. Here are some of the advantages of shopping at www.millsandboon.co.uk:

* **Get new books first**—you'll be able to buy your favourite books one month before they hit the shops

* **Get exclusive discounts**—you'll also be able to buy our specially created monthly collections, with up to 50% off the RRP

* **Find your favourite authors**—latest news, interviews and new releases for all your favourite authors and series on our website, plus ideas for what to try next

* **Join in**—once you've bought your favourite books, don't forget to register with us to rate, review and join in the discussions

Visit **www.millsandboon.co.uk**
for all this and more today!